12/93   **DATE DUE**   ⊗

JAN 0 4 1994	FEB 1 1 1999
JAN 1 8 1994	
JAN 2 6 1994	JAN 3 0 2000
FEB 1 5 1994	JUL 0 2 2005
MAR 1 5 1994	
APR 0 1 1994	
APR 1 8 1994	
MAY 2 7 1994	
JUN 1 5 1994	
AUG 1 8 1994	
AUG 3 1 1994	
SEP 1 2 1994	
OCT 1 0 1994	
SEP 0 9 1995	
OCT 1 0 1995	
NOV 0 1 1995	
AUG 2 6 1996	Printed in USA

REED'S
BEACH

Also by Bret Lott

Jewel
A Dream of Old Leaves
A Stranger's House
The Man Who Owned Vermont

REED'S
BEACH

BRET
LOTT

POCKET BOOKS
New York   London   Toronto   Sydney   Tokyo   Singapore

Pattiann Rogers, "The Next Story" reprinted from *Splitting and Binding*, © 1989 by Pattiann Rogers, Wesleyan University Press. Reprinted by permission of University Press of New England.

POCKET BOOKS, a division of Simon & Schuster Inc.
1230 Avenue of the Americas, New York, NY 10020

Copyright © 1993 by Bret Lott

Library of Congress Cataloging-in-Publication Data

Lott, Bret.
   Reed's Beach / Bret Lott.
      p.   cm.
   ISBN: 0-671-79238-5
      1. Marriage—New Jersey—Cape May—Fiction.   2. Parent and child—Fiction.   3. Children—Death—Fiction.   I. Title.
PS3562.0784R43   1993
813'.54—dc20   93-24894
                                                                              CIP

First Pocket Books hardcover printing October 1993

10   9   8   7   6   5   4   3   2   1

POCKET and colophon are registered trademarks of Simon & Schuster Inc.

Printed in the U.S.A.

For Gary and Judy Swank

*and with thanks to
Ed and Gail Bly*

Mothers, fathers, our kind, tell me again
that death doesn't matter. Tell me
it's just a limitation of vision, a fold
of landscape, a deep flax-and-poppy-filled
gully hidden on the hill, a pleat
in our perception, a somersault of existence,
natural, even beneficent, even a gift,
the only key to the red-lacquered door
at the end of the hall, "water
within water," those old stories.

Pattiann Rogers, "The Next Story"

Where now is my hope?
And who regards my hope?

Job 17

One

He LOOKED THROUGH the eyepiece, tried hard not to squint for fear the moon might disappear. The sextant was heavy in his hands, and he watched as the moon above him fell to the horizon, brought there by his own hand as he moved the index arm down.

The moon touched the black line of the bay. Across the water lay Delaware; due west of him, he knew from the nautical chart in the house, the St. Jones River on Murderkill Neck. Each time he thought of that name, of the thin piece of land he'd seen yesterday afternoon from the dock he stood on now, he wondered how it had come about: Murderkill. Each time he imagined old Dutch fishing boats hundreds of years ago, a nameless body pulled in from just off shore, and the place-name that had followed.

He brought the sextant down, held it with both hands. Its weight somehow comforted him here in the dark, and in the cold. He looked out across the water, blinked at the wind in his eyes, felt them tear. He breathed in, the air cutting into him, and he felt comforted in that as well.

His son's own name rose in him now. He felt the warmth of it in his throat, the tender feel of it ready to be uttered. He formed the word in his mouth, held it there a moment.

Then from behind him came the sound of the front door closing. He turned, saw he'd left open the sliding glass door onto the porch. He could see through the inside of the house to where his wife stood leaning against the front door, her straw handbag hiked up to her shoulder, a white plastic grocery bag in each hand. Light from the kitchen fell out onto the porch, cast sharp shadows on the boards.

"Hugh!" she called out, and he knew she couldn't see him for the dark out here. The taste and feel of his son's name was suddenly gone. He said, "I'm out here."

"It's freezing in here," she said, and pushed herself away from the door, made her way toward him through the house to the kitchen. The table sat just inside the sliding glass door, and she set the bags there, hooked her handbag over the back of a chair.

"Sorry," he said, and turned back to the bay, the sextant still in both hands. "Forgot again."

He heard the soft pull of the door through its tracks, then her footsteps moving on the boards of the dock. A moment later she stood next to him.

He looked at her. Her arms were crossed against the cold, and she was staring out at the water. For a moment he believed she might say their son's name for him.

But she said, "There's four more bags out in the car. Everything's rolling around in the trunk. The kid at the Acme just tossed whatever he felt like into the bags. No rhyme or reason."

He nodded, took in another breath.

She moved close to him. They stood side by side, and she leaned against him, her head on his shoulder, her arms still crossed. She whispered, "If I've told you once,

I've told you three times, don't leave the door open. It's February, remember?"

He said, "How could I forget." He was silent, the only sound the silver push of the waves beneath them. He said, "Won't happen again."

"Right," she said.

She uncrossed her arms, put one around him. She hadn't looked at him. She said, "Let's go on inside."

But they only stood there.

Then he brought the sextant up again, found the moon, made it touch the line of the bay again.

He had been out here at the end of the dock each night since they had come down from Englishtown—three nights now—and stood with the sextant and made the moon do his will. The dock was more a small pier that jutted thirty feet out from the porch of the house. At low tide the water stopped just beneath the end of the dock, the pylons the dock and porch and house were built on all exposed; at high tide the water lapped beneath the house.

Tonight the moon was almost full, the right edge sanded away and soft, and through the eyepiece he could see the barest edge of the dark side, black against the blue night sky.

Neither the sextant nor the house were his, but belonged to his boss.

"A cottage, really," Mr. Halford had said when he'd first told Hugh of the place. "We're down there every weekend rain or shine April through October." He stood at Hugh's desk, his yellow bow tie as tight to his neck as every morning. Hugh was turned to the monitor, hands to the keyboard, so that he was looking up at Mr. Halford over the top of the screen. He hadn't heard him come in, hadn't seen him, his thick white hair, tan face. He had no idea how old Mr. Halford was, his skin taut yet aged somehow, smooth but worn. And now here he was speaking to him of a cottage, and Hugh had had to blink, swallow, afraid he'd missed part of the conversation with his boss.

He'd been at Hess for seven years already, had graduated from Middlesex Community with an Associate's, gotten on at Hess as a programmer, and now it was seven years later, and he was still here. There'd been promotions: first to a program supervisor, then into payroll. Now he was on the seventh floor, his office one of the glass-walled cubicles he'd only caught glimpses of those years ago.

"Nothing more than that," Mr. Halford was saying. Hugh nodded, eased back in his chair the way he'd seen others do when he was first brought up here two years ago. He put his hands behind his head, smiled, still with no idea what his boss was saying.

Hugh nodded again. "Sounds like a nice way to spend the weekends."

Mr. Halford was quiet a moment, his smile still. He cleared his throat, folded the piece of paper in his hands in half. He lost the smile. He said, "It's yours, you want it."

Hugh blinked. "Sir?" he said. He brought his hands from behind his head, sat up at the keyboard again.

"Walker," Mr. Halford said, and he cleared his throat again, moved to the front of the desk. He stopped, folded the paper in half again. "Hugh," he said.

"Sir?"

Mr. Halford put his hands in his pockets, the square of white paper in the left hand disappearing with the move, and for a moment Hugh wondered if the piece of paper were only a prop to get him in here, to speak to him using his first name. This was the seventh floor, but there

was the ninth floor, too, a place where the walls were
oak paneled, pictures on the walls, carpet. Mr. Halford's
floor.

"There's no walking around this. There's no getting
away from it." He wouldn't look him in the eye, Hugh
saw. Mr. Halford, vice president of finance, could say his
first name, but couldn't look him in the eye.

"Simply put, the wife and I want to offer you the place
for a while. You and Laura." He turned from the desk to
find the single chair pushed against the glass wall behind
him, sat down.

Hugh turned from the monitor, laced his fingers in
front of him on the desktop. Printouts lay in neat piles
on either side of the blotter, piles suddenly thicker than
they'd been before.

Mr. Halford's eyes finally met his, and Hugh felt his
own smile disappear, though he tried hard to hold on to
some shard of it.

"Leave of absence," Mr. Halford said. "With pay. Mr.
Hess himself approved it." He paused. He leaned forward
then, his elbows on his knees, hands out of his pockets
and clasped before him. Hugh wondered at how tight the
bow tie was, how choked his boss must feel leaning forward like that. "Not that Mr. Hess's approval means anything in this matter. I would have offered you this myself
even if he'd said no." He paused. "All we ask is you come
back up here a couple days a week, help hold things
together."

Mr. Halford smiled, unclasped his hands. "So, the
place is down at Reed's Beach, on the Delaware. Almost
to Cape May. Just a strip of houses, really, all summer
cottages. But a couple years back the wife and I weather-
stripped the place, insulated it, put in those windows,
you know, the double-pane jobbers. Forced heat."

He stopped, sat up in the chair. He put his hands on his knees. Hugh still tried to smile.

"What do you think?" Mr. Halford said.

Hugh swallowed. He lay his hands flat on the desktop. He said, "I'm okay, Mr. Halford."

"Son," Mr. Halford said, and now his eyes were on Hugh's, cut into his in a way he'd not known before.

"I have three boys," Mr. Halford said. "I have three of them, grown up and gone. And believe you me, son, you are not okay."

Hugh felt his palms suddenly go wet. He said, "It's not the work, I hope. It's not how my work is going," and now the piles of printouts were no thicker than they had ever been. His own words were only some sort of shield set to deflect what Mr. Halford was really saying to him: *You are not all right.*

Mr. Halford smiled, shook his head. "Hugh," he said, "I'm giving you the key right now," and he stood, reached into his left pocket. He pulled out that square of paper and a key ring with a single key.

"We spruced up the place last weekend. The inside at least." He laid the keyring on the blotter, unfolded the paper. "Brought you a map, too."

Hugh watched as Mr. Halford's hands spread the paper flat on the blotter, heard words from him, his finger tracing the course of a road that intersected another road and another and another, finally stopping at a small box marked with an X.

But Hugh saw only lines there on the paper, numbers, a few words. Not a map at all, but some configuration of symbols drawn by a man who had three sons, grown and gone.

Hugh nodded and nodded, acted as though the words being delivered to him by this man were the most important he had received since the death of his only child.

He took the paper, folded it into the same square Mr. Halford had, as if in following those creases his boss had made he might know something of the touch of those three children, of a father who had seen them through. Then he stood, picked up the keyring, and put both the ring and paper in his left pocket.

Mr. Halford's hand was out to him, and Hugh took it, shook hard.

He said, "Thank you, Mr. Halford," and tried the smile again, felt a piece of it play across his face. "I'll give Laura a call right now, see what she thinks."

"Dennis," Mr. Halford said.

"Sir?" Hugh said, and stopped shaking his hand.

"First name's Dennis," he said. "Me. You shacking up in my place means you have to call me by my first name." He smiled, put those hands back into his pockets again. "At least when it comes to matters involving our cottage."

Mr. Halford turned, moved for the doorway. There were no doors into the cubicles, the glass walls lending no privacy to anyone's desk, and for a moment Hugh wondered how many of the other seventh-floor junior executives had witnessed this exchange, the handing over of a key and fingers moving across a hand-drawn map. He wondered, too, what they would make of it over lunch in the cafeteria.

Then the truth of what they would make of it came to him: His son had died three months and five days before, and now the vice president of finance was loaning him his cottage. Nothing more than that: only the truth.

Mr. Halford stopped, turned. He said, "It's the view down there will help you out. Seeing a different place. Being somewhere else. Not parking your car in the same damn driveway every night." He took a hand from a

9

pocket and gave a short wave. He said, "Get down there soon as you can."

Hugh waved back. "Thank you," he called, and started to say that first name, *Dennis*. But Mr. Halford was already headed toward the elevators.

He felt the square of paper in his other hand, the hand still in his pocket. The key was still warm.

"The groceries," Laura said. This time she turned from him, took two or three steps back toward the house, her steps dark and hollow on the boards of the dock.

He still had the sextant up.

She stopped, said, "You know how to use that thing yet?"

He was quiet, then said, "I've got those books." He said, "Give me time."

She said nothing.

He brought the sextant down again, the moon returned to its place high above the two of them, above this cottage and Reed's Beach and all the earth. And above their car not parked in the same damn driveway as every night of their lives, but on the dirt road in front of this place, a car inside of which rolled loose food items some kid from the Acme had thrown into bags. No rhyme or reason.

That was when the word rose again in him. But this time he did not lose it in the voice of his wife calling out his own name.

He looked at the dark line of the water, scattered across it the small broken pieces of light a near-full moon gave out.

He said, "Michael."

He heard no sound after his son's name, not even the waves beneath him, moving closer to shore, the tide on its way in. He heard nothing.

Then, from behind him, he heard the word whispered, like an echo, but not: *Michael.*

He turned, saw his wife there, her arms still crossed against the cold. Behind her fell the light from the kitchen, so that she was a silhouette to him, a shadow.

But he could see her head was bowed, then saw how her shoulders quivered, and then all trace of the name was gone on the wind out here, and in the dark.

🌸 LAURA'S ONLY WORDS to him on the matter when he'd phoned her: "When can we go?" She'd had no responsibilities to fulfill, no job to leave. She'd quit at the hospital the day after they'd buried their son.

They left at six-thirty the Saturday morning after Mr. Halford had given him the key. Hugh had pulled closed the door of their home, tried the knob to make certain the place was locked tight. This leave of absence was designed, he knew, to try and heal what had happened to them, the open wound. But he knew he wasn't through with it. He tried the knob one last time, and hoped he would never be through with it.

Laura was already in the car. She had her own keys, had the engine going, the heater on high, though he knew only cold air poured out. It was an argument they had carried on all ten years they had been married: whether the heater worked faster turning it on first thing or leaving it off until the engine had warmed up enough.

This morning he said nothing, only climbed in. Cold air shot out onto his legs, cut through his ankles. But he only looked at the house before them lit with their headlights. The rough gray clapboards soaked up the light so that the house and its dark windows, even the

12

door he had just tried, seemed swallowed up by the gray morning. Snow lay along the foundation of the house, this, too, gray even in the headlights.

He turned, glanced at his wife, then behind him. Her hands were in her lap, gloves on. He said, "We're off," and laid his arm along the top of the seat, backed out.

She said, "We're off."

They took the Parkway down, stopped at Toms River and had breakfast at Friendly's, then got back on the Parkway, the trees and grass and growth all brown and yellow and gray, the snow gone. Just past the Barnegat exit, they saw five deer grazing on the matted grass that lay along the highway, all of them bent to the food before them without looking up as their car passed by. They were fearless, he saw, made so by how thin they seemed: He thought he could see the outline of ribs, the bones in their legs.

"Look," was all Laura said, and Hugh had nodded.

They made it to the Cape May Court House exit by nine, found their way along the streets and past the old court house itself, the map Mr. Halford had drawn spread now across his wife's lap. "Turn right here," she said at the end of the exit ramp. Then, "Left on Route 9." Then, "Turn right up here, onto 658."

He looked at the town as they moved through it: convenience stores, gas stations, a supermarket. There was traffic, too, and people on the streets, all of them bundled against the cold. The sky was cloudless yet filled with a haze that made the air look even colder, and it seemed to him there was too much going on here, too many people out and places to buy food and liquor.

Then they were out of the town, moving west on 658, a two-lane road suddenly lined with bare trees and pale scrub pine, and he breathed out.

13

Only then did he hear the giant silence inside the car with them.

Their son had been dead for three months and eight days. Since then, they had never ridden in the car together for longer than it took to get to Laura's parents in Matawan, a good twenty minutes; now they had been together inside the car for almost three hours, and there had come from the back seat no child's voice reading aloud books and showing the pictures to him in the rear-view mirror, no whine asking how long it would be before they would get there, no thin snore as their child slept away the trip.

"Turn right on 47," Laura said, and he searched her voice, those few words, for some trace of his child's voice. But he found nothing.

This was how each day thus far had played itself out for him: a million small and sharp revelations, pieces of the world he walked through cutting into him each moment. Nothing he saw was what it seemed, but held inside it a piece of his son.

Already that day there had been the silence from behind him, that absence that made his son's presence even larger. And there had been the people on the street, so many of them walking and moving, driving cars, as though there had been no death anywhere on the face of the earth, no one lost to any of them. And there had been the gray house they had left behind them, their home, and an upstairs bedroom in which had lived their child.

They had not touched the room since their son died, left the bed just as he had made it, the spread merely thrown over bunched and wrinkled sheets, the pillow crooked at the head. The small blue desk was littered with colored pencils, scraps of construction paper, a bottle of white glue. His blue canvas bookbag hung on the back of the chair.

Each morning he entered the room, looked things over. He did not know what the project his son had been working on was, and each morning he knew the construction paper and pencils would never find their intended order, never find which pencils would be applied to which pieces of paper, what would be glued to what.

So that each of his days began with its own self-inflicted wound, the small cut into him made by his own presence in the room. He could do as his wife did, he knew, and not go into the room, never mention the colorful materials across the table, the lay of the sheets and bedspread. But he went into the room regardless, finding in his moments there, before coffee and the forty-five-minute drive into Woodbridge and the Hess building and his glass cubicle, a sort of orientation for the day, a reconnaissance of the loss he hadn't yet endured.

He felt his foot ease off the gas, felt the car slow down, the trees and scrub pine fall away. *Turn right on 47* was all she had said, but before this moment, before this alien road and whatever cottage lay before them, he knew he would have been able to find evidence of his son in her voice, somewhere inside her the hidden pitch and timbre of their son.

Across the highway stood a yellow road sign, black arrows pointing left and right. This was where 658 ended, 47 their only choice, and neither right nor left seemed to him any choice at all. Around him were houses he did not recognize, landmarks for someone else, not himself.

Laura said, "Looks clear." She turned to him. "No cars," she said.

He looked at her.

She reached a hand across the seat, touched his arm.

15

He could not feel her touch through the coat he wore, only knew she was touching him by what he saw: her gloved hand, his sleeve.

He said, "I don't know if this is a good idea."

He felt her hand then, the small squeeze she gave. Then her hand was gone, and she turned to her window.

She said, "This is the best idea."

From behind them came the dull blast of a horn. Hugh looked in the rearview mirror, saw the grill of a pickup truck, two men with billed caps.

This was no place he knew.

They passed a few farmhouses, white clapboard with screened porches, pickups and Camaros out front, cars up on blocks behind them. They passed the Mosquito Control Center on the left, and the campground.

Then came the small green street sign, Reed's Beach Road. He signaled left, and turned onto a dirt road.

Pine trees lined the road that snaked off before them, no beach to be seen at all. Then the trees stopped, and the road ran through marsh, on either side of them the flat plain of high grass for what seemed miles. Before them, maybe a half mile away, lay a strip of cottages, rooflines cutting up into the horizon.

They reached the piece of land the cottages were built on, and he eased the car to a stop, the road splitting off to the left and right. At the fork sat a square building, clapboards painted yellow what looked maybe a hundred years ago, a rusted tin roof, one window. Double doors and a porch were at the left end of the building, above the doors a hand-painted sign, letters in red on a white background: *Dorsett's Marlinspike General Store*. At either end of the words were rope anchors nailed and shellacked to the sign. Inside the window hung an old plastic 7-Up sign, a light inside it blinking on and off.

16

REED'S BEACH

Their headlights were still on, pale light shining on the yellow clapboards. He wondered if he had left them on through breakfast in Toms River, and thought then of his own home those many miles behind him, and of the light from the same headlights cast on a house in what seemed now a different country.

Laura said, "Marlinspike."

He said, "Which way?"

She was quiet, and he saw from the corner of his eye her gloved hands lace together in her lap, covering the map. She let out a deep breath, a signal, he knew, but one he did not care to pick up.

She said, "Left."

He reached down and turned off the headlights. He turned left and away from the store, inched the car along a dirt road that seemed to have been scraped into place only a week ago: On either side of them lay a row of heaped dirt three or four feet high. On the other side of the heaps were the houses, nothing like what he'd imagined. They were ramshackle things, buildings made of rooms piled one on top of another and beside each other.

There were no cars on the road, and he could hear beneath them the crack of ice as they moved through frozen puddles. One house, the first on his left, butted up to the mounds of dirt before it; on a clothesline beside the house hung a single beach towel, *I Discovered the Eighth Wonder of the World* printed across it in a faded purple. The towel whipped in the wind, and he wondered how long it had been hanging there. Another house, this on the beachfront—he could see pylons now, caught glimpses of the gray sheet of the bay between these houses—appeared to have been nailed together overnight, the wooden walkway to the front door sagging, the doorway itself out of line, leaning to the right. A piece of plywood covered the bottom half of the front door, a blue

17

happy face spray-painted on it. Another place, this one to his left, was only a trailer with a screened porch around it.

Laura said, "Mr. Halford's vice president of finance, right?"

He still took in the cottages, saw one with green asphalt shingles for siding. He said, "Yep."

"Wonder if he had to take out a loan for one of these things," she said. He turned and saw her smile.

Then she pointed ahead, said, "There it is. Last one on the right."

He looked, saw up ahead where the road ended in piles of dirt even higher than those beside them now. And he saw the house, the last one on the right. Beachfront.

"Now this is more like it," Laura said.

It was a cottage: a porch with railing, pylons, a walkway over the mounded dirt to the door. Gray clapboards no different from their own.

He pulled up alongside the house, left the engine running, and leaned forward to take the place in through the windshield: three windows and the front door faced the road, the window frames and door painted a forest green, and the shingles on the roof were green, too. The roof shot up at a high angle, the roofline parallel to the water. There were two downstairs windows on the side of the house, an octagonal window at the very peak.

Laura opened her door before he could shut off the engine, was up the steps of the walkway and on the porch before he could climb out. Then she disappeared around the side of the house, her footsteps quick across the wood.

He followed her, walked along the porch to the back of the house. She was already at the end of the dock, her hands on the railing before her, eyes out to sea.

She looked over her shoulder at him and smiled, her

hands still holding tight to the railing. Water lapped beneath them, and already he was logging in the items around him on the porch and dock, those things that belonged to Mr. and Mrs. Dennis Halford: a forest green Adirondack chair, a conch shell the size of a football, three crab traps in front of the sliding glass door. A single duck boot, no laces, was jammed between two railing banisters. A hibachi, rusted through where the charcoal was supposed to go, sat next to a blue and white lattice lawn chair.

Somebody else's history, he saw. All of this was somebody else's history, and now here they were, dumped in the midst of it in order to figure out their own history. He wondered why he hadn't refused his boss's offer, simply shrugged and never stood to shake Mr. Halford's hand. *No,* he could have said. He could have said, *I know I am not all right, but I will be,* and he could have smiled at Mr. Halford, smiled right on through the lie he could have given.

He stopped at the sliding glass door, leaned over the crab traps, and peered through the glass into the house: a table, kitchen appliances, cupboards. Anybody's guess what each of these meant to their owners.

Then the five deer came to him, their rib cages, the fact they had not looked up at them as they had driven past. He searched that image in his head, pored over it for some shred of the death of his son, and for a moment, he believed he had found something, had drawn some line between the two, the starving deer and the loss of Michael. He could make anything become something to do with his child.

But then he lost it, felt it break up like thin sheets of ice beneath him: The deer had been fearless, he saw, had given up the cover of February sunlight through trees to

19

square off beside cars on the Parkway. They'd chosen to eat, instead of starve.

His breath fogged over the glass so that the appliances and table and chairs and all else in this house seemed to disappear, given over to the gray mist.

"Come look at the water," Laura said from behind him, her voice closer than ever to no one he knew.

✿ His history:

At three-fifteen each day their son's school bus stopped at the corner of Bryant Court and Milk Farm Road, let off ten children. From there those children dispersed to their respective homes, Michael Walker and Gerry Rothberg and Melinda D'Abo the three to head on down Milk Farm a quarter mile to their street, Canterbury Court.

The bus driver's story was that even before she'd pulled to a stop, four children rushed up the aisle to the front of the bus in some contest to see who would be off first. Michael Walker had ended up in the lead, and the bus driver said Michael had been looking back at the losers of the race, Gerry Rothberg and Carl Hagerty and Henry Joiner, as he'd stepped off into the street, when the car struck him. The car was either brown or blue, she couldn't remember which, it had all happened so fast.

Hugh had been in meeting just then with the other two seventh-floor payroll program heads.

At ten minutes to four he was still in that same meeting, Ed Blankenship at the schematic board and diagramming away, when a secretary had leaned into the

21

glass-walled room, looked at Hugh, said, "Telephone."
She shrugged, said, "A doctor."

He'd parked in front of the emergency room doors, the
glass doors sliding open and staying open in the presence
of the car.

Then he saw her. She stood outside a door just past
the reception desk. She was sobbing, hands to her face.
She had on her maroon sweatpants and heavy white
socks, no shoes, and her Rutgers sweatshirt: her uniform
every afternoon once she was home. A heavy nurse with
red hair had a hand to her shoulder and was speaking
quietly, her words lost in the sound of his wife's sobbing.

He himself was crying, too, he realized, the doctor's words
still the same shards pressed into him as when he'd first
heard them over the phone at the secretary's desk: The
word *accident* burned in the skin across the palms of both
hands as he moved toward his wife and the nurse and
burned in his eyes and in his ears and tongue. There had
come the word *Michael* and *son* and *accident* again, all
of them burning in and through him, and the world and
how slowly it moved—the elevator down from the seventh
floor had taken an hour, the drive over had taken days—
shimmered before him as he cried, walking to her, walking to her, his wife and the nurse electrified, quivering,
so that when Laura lifted her head, saw him, and started
toward him with her arms outstretched, it seemed to him
none of it was happening at all, that this was some old
movie, the moves people made forced and too large.

She fell into him, her arms around his neck and holding
on tight. Already he felt her tears through his shirt, then
buried his own eyes in her hair. The nurse was speaking to
them both, a hand to a shoulder of each. But he turned
from her, pulling his wife toward a white and sparkling
wall, where he leaned them both, and they wept.

A few moments later he felt a hand at his shoulder,

but didn't turn to it. Then he heard a woman's voice say, "Mr. Walker, Mrs. Walker."

He turned at the voice. This was the same voice that had delivered each of those burning words to him, and for a moment he wondered how those words could have ever been uttered, how the heat of them and the way they had cut could be given away without the speaker herself succumbing to them.

She was a short woman with blond hair pulled back in a ponytail. She had a stethoscope draped around her neck and wore a short lab coat. She had her hands together in front of her. She was still alive.

She said, "I am truly sorry."

He looked at her, measured her, and saw in her eyes that, yes, she was in fact sorry for them. She'd given him the truth. But she'd given him the words, too, and slowly the fact of what had happened—the truth of the words he'd heard over the phone—began to cut into him even deeper.

He said, "Where is he?" his voice quivering as much as the image of his wife had. He didn't recognize his own voice, and thought yet again that none of this was happening.

"I'm Dr. Ford," she said. "I'm the admitting doctor." She paused, looked down, then up at him again. She said, "I'm sorry."

Laura leaned slightly away from him, and he turned to her.

She was looking up at him. Her mouth was open, her face wet. Tears fell freely from her eyes, though she was no longer sobbing. Beside her eyes he could see minuscule broken blood vessels, there from the force of her crying, and she took in quick breaths, her lower lip trembling.

She looked at him, looked at him, her eyes searching him, he knew. She searched him, quick breaths going in

23

and in, tears falling. Then she shimmered again, and he felt his own breath giving way.

He knew she wanted words from him, wanted him to speak to her. But nothing came to him, the sudden truth that all of this had indeed happened an occurrence that denied spoken words even existed.

So he turned to the doctor, again said, "Where is he?"

She looked at the floor again, hesitated, then turned, and started off to the door his wife and the nurse had stood outside.

He looked at Laura again, but she'd already buried her face in him, and he held her tighter, pulled her close to him. They started after the doctor.

His son lay inside the room, and the world he'd known collapsed around him. There was no other room than this one on the face of the earth, no other doctor, no other woman than his wife. There was no other bed or sheet, no other walls. And there had never existed any other pair of beaten and scuffed tennis shoes than those that lay on the foot of the bed, nor had there ever been another pair of jeans, nor another blue and green plaid flannel shirt, another yellow canvas belt, all of these folded neatly and stacked next to the only pair of tennis shoes on earth.

Just as he believed all this were happening in a way larger than life had ever seen, he burst open, his sobs filling the room.

Still no words came, the cry he gave still not huge enough to consume what he saw: There lay his child, a sheet up to his naked chest, his mouth open, eyes closed.

Laura sobbed yet again, her sounds and his mixed to make no sound at all, nothing he could hear.

He felt his own arm move away from around his wife then, his hand given some mind of its own, and he watched as his hand moved toward his son's face, watched as he touched a brow with a thumb, the touch so gentle and small that he was convinced he had not really touched his son at all: His finger was still cool, and he felt nothing. Then he watched as his hand touched his son's cheek, felt again nothing, then watched yet again as he held his son's jaw in his hand, gently touched his neck, his chest, touched his shoulder and rubbed it, as if to encourage the boy, or to soothe him.

He watched all this from miles above, years away. He watched all this from a different life, one he hadn't known existed.

Then he felt himself and his wife lean toward the boy, the two of them falling to earth at a speed so slow they were not moving at all, until all at once his lips were touching his own son's cool forehead, and he kissed him.

There'd been no external injuries, the doctor said. Massive internal trauma was how she had put it. They were seated in plastic chairs outside the room. They still hadn't spoken to each other, and he only watched the doctor as she spoke, left the ugly work of words to her and her alone.

He was thinking of the cool feel of his son's skin on his lips, and of the look in Laura's eyes when she'd leaned away from him, waiting for words from him. He'd realized even then, even before the proof of his own lips on his son's forehead, the inadequacy of words, the outrageous nonsense of them in the face of what had happened, what could not be encompassed by anything anyone could say. The doctor's words were only information, nothing more. Any words Hugh were to give to Laura would be words that meant nothing other than an inability to let the silence of Michael's disappearance stand on its own.

So that when at the end of the hall Laura's parents

appeared, first her mother, then, a few steps behind, her father, the two of them dazed and bewildered, he could see already that the world was moving itself right back in, reasserting itself, when all he had wanted was to exist before any of this had ever happened or, at worst, to be left inside the room behind him, the one that acknowledged no other earthly existence than the evidence before him: neatly folded clothes, clean white sheets, the cold flower of their dead son.

But as soon as Laura saw her mother and father, she stood, ran to them, and he watched as she fell into her mother's arms, and watched as her father reached to her shoulder, rubbed there just as he had his own son's minutes or hours or days before, he could not say.

Then he heard his wife's howl, heard her pitiful and empty first word: *No*

There would have to come words now, his kiss and the look in his wife's eyes while he had no words for her exploding outward, these moments soon to be diluted with so many words to so many people, when all he wanted was to hold it, keep it as strong as the feel of his son's skin against his lips, as the feel of his wife's arms around his neck.

Laura's father came to him then, and Hugh felt himself stand, his legs weak beneath him. He'd had to hold the edge of the chair as he looked past his father-in-law, a well-meaning man who smiled at him for no reason he could fathom. He put his arms around Hugh then, hugged him, and Hugh felt his arms go up of their own, pat his father-in-law's back, as though he were the one to comfort.

But his eyes were on his wife, and he had listened to her repeated word echo down the depths of the corridor: *No no no*

☦ HE LAY THE sextant on the red velvet cloth on the desktop, then placed the corners over it one at a time in the exact order he had found them: lower right, upper right, upper left, lower left.

He was in the upstairs room, the room with octagonal windows at either end. The stairs came up at the far end of the room, the side where no houses were. At the top of them he could look out that window, see a mile or so up the beach. Two parallel rows of broken black pylons trailed up a couple hundred yards, the pylons each two or three feet high, all of them swallowed up when the tide came in. The ceiling was the roof itself, Sheetrocked and sprayed. He had to lean his head one way or another if he weren't standing in the middle of the room.

The desk filled the only dormer, above the desktop a large window—a double-pane jobber—so that he could sit at the desk and look out to the bay and the end of the dock. In daylight he could see neither the beach to his left nor the house next door, only the water out there, and the dock.

In the dormer ceiling was a recessed light that shone down on the charts and books and the sextant and the other instruments—a protractor, a compass, a stopwatch, pencils, a yellow legal tablet—in a clean and even manner, a light so perfect he could imagine only a man with a yellow bow tie and clean tanned skin as having been the one to install it, right along with the weather stripping and insulation and the Sheetrock.

He finished with the velvet, wrapped the bundle with the soft brown cord he had found around it that first day. He stood from the desk, ducked his head, and moved across the narrow room to the wall behind him and the row of low bookshelves there. This was where he had found the sextant, third shelf up, second set from the right, that empty space at the end of the row of *Nautical Quarterlys*. He knelt to the shelf, eased the sextant into its place as he had all three nights before. He wondered how long it would take Mr. Halford—minutes, hours, days—before he would know how thoroughly Hugh had been through his things.

Then he saw Laura looking at him through the banisters. She was only a couple of steps up the stairs, her head even with the floor, and he felt his face go hot, as though he had been caught at something.

She said, "The groceries, believe it or not, are still out there." She smiled at him.

He pushed himself to standing, careful not to bump his head on the ceiling, his head swinging to one side and away, the move already rote in him.

She said, "If I have to do the shopping, then you have to do the putting away. Fair and square." She paused, smiling up at him. "Quite marlinspike," she said, nodded at the sextant. "The way you take care of that thing."

He made himself smile, said, "Just let me put the rest of this stuff away. Nothing's going to sour out there." He went to the desk, assembled the ruler and compass and protractor in a neat row along the upper right corner of the desktop, this, too, just as he had found it.

28

"True," she said, "true," and then she was gone. But he had seen her face, and how she'd looked away from him, letting her head drop, her eyes on the steps before her for a moment. She had sent him another signal, her coming up here quietly, watching him for who knew how long as he put away the sextant, then smiling innocently, calling for his help.

He made it to the bottom of the stairs, reached to the switchplate, and turned off the upstairs light, this for some reason the switch for the second floor. For all its taste and clean design—its clapboards and green shingles and glistening cupboards—there were touches that revealed Mr. and Mrs. Halford as tacky in their nautical way: The switchplate at the bottom of the stairs was a gold-painted angelfish, as were all the switchplates in the place; on the walls were framed needlepoint scenes of waves crashing on rocks, sailboats out to sea. On one wall of the bedroom were seven needlepoint pictures, each one of a different lighthouse on the East Coast, *Owl's Head* or *Barnegat Light* or *Solomon's Lump* stitched in black beneath the appropriate light. A lampshade in the reading room, the room the stairs led up from, was painted with tropical fish, bubbles up from their mouths; on the sill of the window above the kitchen sink sat a frog and monkey and giraffe all made of shells glued together, black dots of paint for eyes, red lines for smiles.

He moved through the living room. The walls were paneled with unfinished pine slats, a TV in one corner, a sofa and love seat settled in another. Rows of bookshelves went up the wall with the doorway into the kitchen, the shelves filled with *Reader's Digest* condensed books and cased *National Geographics* set in proper chronological order.

He reached the doorway, put a hand to the fish

switchplate, and looked around the room once more. Above the love seat was a large wooden plaque, mounted on it shellacked bits of rope tied off into intricate knots he had no clue how to tie. Beneath each knot was a name in flowing white script: Sheep's Head, Bowline, Fisherman's Bend.

He hesitated a moment, looked at it all as though he had never been in here before, as though he had been upstairs or out on the dock all this time, and nowhere else.

Then he cut off the light, turned quickly from what was behind him, because he had seen the truth in what he thought: Except for meals and sleep and chores like taking out the trash or, now, bringing in the groceries, he had in fact spent every waking moment in just those two places: either upstairs or out on the dock.

Laura sat at the kitchen table, spread out before her the maps and brochures that had been there since she'd come home from her first drive the first day. Each day she was out of the house, either driving somewhere on errands, she told him, or out on the beach and walking. Her evenings were spent going through visitor materials and AAA road maps.

She looked up at him. In her hands was a glossy pamphlet with photographs of people wearing three-cornered hats and shoes with huge buckles.

She said, "It descends from the mountaintop," her voice a caricatured deejay's, all solid and strong and, he knew, meant to be funny. But he said nothing, only reached to the tabletop and got the keys. Then he was out the door.

He hadn't put on his parka, the wind cold off the water, the keys ice in his hands as he tried in the darkness for the right one. He found it, his fingers already numb as he twisted it, lifted the trunk lid.

The moon hadn't yet cleared the house, the road and car dark out here; there were no streetlamps, their own porchlight was burned out. He peered down into the trunk, the only light the dull yellow of the bulb in the trunk lid, and made out vague gray shapes, like clouds at night. But they were only plastic bags of groceries, and he reached in, groping for the handles on the bags. He found all four of them, held two in each hand, the cold and the weight of the bags cutting through his fingers.

With an elbow he managed to pull down the trunk, push it closed. Even though he'd already lost feeling in his fingers, he still got the front door open, and moved into the house, kicking the door closed behind him.

There stood Laura, hands on her hips. Her chin was up, and he could see her jaw was clenched.

He said, "Here they are," and moved past her to the table, set the bags there.

She said from behind him, "Self-pity. That's all."

"Nope," he said, ready. He was looking at the sliding glass door, somewhere out past his reflection the dock, and the water.

He said, "Mourning. That's what it's called."

"Its called self-pity. God-damned self-pity is all it is. Calling it anything else is a lie. Plain and simple."

She hadn't moved, he could hear, and now the sound of the water rising beneath them came to him, the soft sound of the moon doing its own will without him. He had no control over it, its image through the sextant, its play along the horizon only a trick done with mirrors.

He looked down at the table, at the array of brochures about places he knew had no bearing whatsoever in the world he and his wife now inhabited: Batsto Village,

31

Cape May Bird Observatory, Historic Points of Interest on the Jersey Cape. *What did this woman believe was important?* he wondered, and he saw that he could not know her, never knew her.

"It's called mourning," he said. He reached down, picked up the Historic Points of Interest flyer, a blue rectangular piece of paper, printed on it a list and description of things to see and do in Cape May. "I don't know what you think is important, but I think remembering him is. You call it what you want, but I know what it is." He held up the paper to her, said, "Museums, buildings, shipwrecks. If that's what you think is important, then you're free to have it."

She'd already moved to the table, her eyes down. She rubbed her nose, sniffed, then picked open one of the bags. She pulled out a box of Cheerios and a yogurt. She said, "Remembering him," her voice ready to break. "Remembering him," she said again. She put the cereal in a cupboard, then opened the refrigerator, set in the yogurt. She left it open, went back to the bag, and took out celery and two more yogurts. "It's not remembering," she said. She'd put her voice back together; her moving back and forth in the kitchen, it seemed to him, was all she needed to dismiss the idea of their son.

"You're not remembering," she said, "but dying yourself. You can't even see it, you're dying so quick." She placed a bag of Oreos in another cupboard and started in on the second sack of groceries.

Her words continued, but he did not hear them. They were the same words she had used on him time and again. He himself was dying, she would say, and she could see it, and so could everyone they knew, from the Rothbergs next door to the man at the Wawa on Route 9, where he stopped for beer Friday afternoons on his way home from Hess. Everyone could see him wasting away.

About this time, too, she would ask if he were listening. He would nod his head, just as he was doing right then, the blue piece of paper still in his hand. He was looking at the paper, though, reading it. He had heard her words of his own death enough times to know her voice would soon rise in pitch, and shatter. She would no longer be able to say those same words, and he would have to go to her, place his arms around her, hold her and comfort her, because, he knew, she was not through with it either. Mourning, self-pity, whatever she chose to call it, was as much a part of her as it was of him.

He listened not to her words, then, but to her pitch, looked for the quiver in it as he read the piece of paper in his hands about Guard Towers in Cape May Point and Wildwood: "The threat of German U-boat attacks in World War II prompted the construction of submarine lookout towers. Abandoned after the war, three remain today as reminders of the beachfront blackout of the '40s."

Now she had worked Mr. Halford's name into the words, pointing out, he knew without listening, that this state of decay was apparent even to his boss, hence, their trip down here, a trip that, by every indication thus far, he knew she would say, had proven to be useless. Still she kept on, emptied the second bag and then the third, and still her voice did not rise, her words still the string he knew by heart. He read the next paragraph on the piece of paper, this under the heading Shipwrecks: "Three of the thousands of ships lost on the Jersey Cape beaches have been memorialized, one in Ocean City and two at Cape May Point. The newest but most unusual is *The Atlantus* just off Sunset Blvd. in Delaware Bay. An experimental World War I concrete ship, she was decom-

missioned as a failure. Salvaged from the Navy's grave-
yard at Baltimore and towed here in 1926, she was to
have been sunk as part of a ferry slip but was beached
by a storm and could not be raised."

Then he realized her voice had quit altogether. He
looked up from the flyer. She stood in the middle of the
kitchen, in her upheld hands empty plastic grocery bags.

She said, "The rest of the groceries?" and gave a quick
shake of the bags, the sound like dead leaves in the room.

He put the flyer down on the table and tried to picture
a beached concrete ship.

He said, "Yes?" and tilted his head, tried to seem
attentive.

Slowly she let her hands fall to her sides, the bags soft
and full of air, white clouds now instead of the gray in
the trunk. She said, "There's more stuff out in the car. I
told you stuff was rolling around all over the place." She
paused, let out a breath. She turned from him, slowly
shook her head as she went to the cupboards, opened one
and another and another, worked her way around the
room toward the refrigerator. She still held the bags as
she opened and closed each cupboard, moved to the next:
"A big can of V-8," she called out; "two cans of chili, a
bag of bagels," then, "instant oatmeal." She opened the
refrigerator, peered at shelves and into the crisper:
"Three oranges, a block of cheddar, cream cheese."

She stood, finally looked at him. She held out a bag to
him. She said, "Who knows what else is out there."

He stepped toward her and took the bag. He'd listened
for her words, that pitch, to break, but it had not, the
surprise of what hadn't happened a dull weight on his
chest. She was in control of her words; he'd heard nowhere on them the thin quiver he'd waited for, the tum-
ble and scrape of words caught in her throat. Before him
stood his wife, this Laura Walker, formerly Pulaski, a

34

woman who, it suddenly seemed, might already be over the death of their son: Here was her brown hair worn just below her shoulders, and her thin white wrists, the pulsepoints places he'd kissed in the dark, that smooth skin and the nameless trace of her smell more fragrant than any perfume she ever wore.

And there were her brown eyes, eyes that, before this new history of theirs, had pierced him in a way he had held close. They'd demanded only the truth from him, the truth of his love for her and for their marriage and for their child. But now he feared her eyes, feared them in the same way he feared the taste of her skin, the feel of her hair in his hands.

Her eyes knew the truth of him, and how he'd had no words for her. Now, in this kitchen, he saw that she was waiting for him yet again, waiting for all the things of their life—all the pieces of the two of them—to be collected, knit up finally, into a self that could be counted on to operate in this world. This, he could see in her eyes, was what she was waiting for.

He'd not had to comfort her as he had planned, had not been needed to take her in his arms and hold her while she cried. She hadn't cried.

He wadded the bag into a ball, cleared his throat, the moves his own signals to her of his intent: He would not give up.

He said, "Back in a minute," and left.

Still the moon had not cleared the roof, and the wind ripped at the bag in his hand. He'd found two of the oranges, the V-8 and cheddar and cream cheese, and leaned farther into the trunk for something he could barely make out far back inside.

Then the black of the trunk changed to a deep gray, the trunk itself taking on depth as it filled with light until finally he could see just past his fingertips the bright blue and white and green label on a jar of peanut butter.

He turned, saw behind him a pair of headlights pull up at the house next door. He'd not heard the engine for the wind, and now the headlights went out, the car not fifty feet away.

He heard two car doors slam shut, saw two people moving toward him, a man and a woman. He knew he must do or say something, if only give a small wave, a short Hi out here in the dark.

"Hello," came the man's voice, a dark shock of sound out here. "You must be Hugh."

"Now slow down, Roland," came the woman's voice. "You just blinded the man. Ease up."

Hugh gave the small wave, said, "Hi," and felt already his face going hot for the knowledge whoever these two had of him. This Roland had already tossed his own first name at him.

"Roland Dorsett," the man said. In the darkness Hugh could make out the large shadow of the man, saw him put out his hand. He had on a billed cap, Hugh could see, just as those men had in the pickup that first morning, and what looked like nothing more than a windbreaker against the cold.

Hugh took the man's hand. It was calloused and big and warm. They shook, and Hugh let go the hand as quickly as he could, in his other hand the half-filled grocery sack bumping against his leg with the wind.

"Denny Halford told us you'd be down here." The man put his hands in his pockets. Hugh heard the sound of coins and keys.

"Roland," the woman said.

"Oh," he said, and nodded at her, then at Hugh. "This is Mrs. Dorsett," he said. "Winnie." Then Roland Dorsett leaned a little toward Hugh. He couldn't see his face, thought only that perhaps he saw the barest outline of a pair of glasses. He said, "You are Hugh Walker, right?"

"Yep," Hugh said. "Pleased to meet you both."

Winnie had on a windbreaker, too, her arms crossed. She had a scarf over her hair, that hair high and full on her head. She gave a quick nod, and Hugh was glad she hadn't put out her hand for him to shake.

She said, "Denny and Sal told us you'd be down here. We'll be right next door, you need anything," and she nodded again, turning from him.

The man cleared his throat. Hugh heard the coins and keys stop, saw him take his hands from his pockets and cross his arms just as his wife had done. Winnie was already back at what Hugh could see now was a van. He heard the side door slide open.

"Yeah," Roland Dorsett began, his voice low and quiet. He turned, faced the slip of bay that could be seen between their two houses. Hugh made out the man's profile and saw he did wear glasses. He had a small nose, his neck thick beneath his chin. The billed cap sat low on his head, almost touched the glasses. "This wind's bringing in some good air from down south," he said. "Should warm up by tomorrow."

"Great," Hugh heard himself say. He moved the grocery bag from one hand to the other.

"Yeah," Roland Dorsett said again, almost whispering this time. He turned from the water, faced Hugh. "Old Denny said you'd be down here. Told us what you been through, too."

Hugh's face felt as though it were suddenly on fire, the wind some hot blast of flame: His history was not his own now, had been given out even to his boss's next door neighbor.

Hugh said, "I have to head back in now," and turned, took the first two steps up toward the porch.

"Okay," Roland Dorsett called out, his voice full and expansive, like some friend Hugh hadn't seen in years. "You two take care now, and just like Winnie said, you need anything, we're right next door."

Hugh nodded without looking at him, was at the top of the steps, his free hand at the knob.

"Hey, Hugh," Roland Dorsett said, and he'd had to turn, the door already open a crack, light from inside cutting out into the dark.

He stood at their car, one hand on the open trunk lid. He said, "You want this thing left open all night? Kill your battery quick." He was peering down into the trunk and said, "Looks like you left a couple things in here, too." He reached down, brought something up. He looked at Hugh, held out his hand. "Orange," he said. He gave a small laugh, tossed the orange up, caught it. Hugh thought he could see the smallest reflection of light from the open door in this man's glasses.

Hugh held the door open a moment, then pulled it closed. He didn't want the light out here, didn't want it shining on anything.

He said, "I'll take care of that," and moved down the steps.

🌸 THE BEDROOM WAS off the dining area and had a window that looked out to the house next door.

Hugh had come back into the house, placed the last of the groceries on the table, Laura there and looking at another brochure as though they hadn't discussed anything a few minutes before. Then he had headed to the bedroom, pulled back one corner of the sheer curtains.

Now Laura stood beside him, and they watched, wordless, as lights went on from one end of the house to the other: first the yellow porch light at the front, then one and the other of the two downstairs windows, then the upstairs window, a square one at the peak. Last to go on were the floodlights on the end of their dock, lights turned back to illuminate the dock and house. Then the Dorsetts were in and out of the front door, passed each other as they brought in things from the van: an ice chest, clothes on hangers, groceries.

From the Halfords' bedroom window, Hugh and Laura could see into the kitchen window, the second of the two downstairs windows; there were no curtains. Then the Dorsetts began to put things away. They moved back and forth across the window, arms full of food items, then empty, then full again. He could see a table from where he stood, some cupboards, the top right corner of the refrigerator as it opened and closed, opened and closed.

Laura said, "Who—"

"The Dorsetts," Hugh said, his answer too quick, too loud for the dark of the room. He whispered, "Roland and Winnie."

"Dorsetts," Laura whispered. "Do they own the store?"

Hugh kept his eyes on the two moving inside the house. He hadn't paid much attention to the house until now, had only taken note that it seemed some sort of renovation was taking place there: The front of the house, the side that faced the dirt road, was covered with old tin siding, pale blue and rusted through in places, while the side that faced the Halfords' was finished with new, clean white siding. Vinyl, he figured. Now, looking inside the window, he could see, too, that the walls of the kitchen hadn't been painted, were the gray of bare Sheetrock. Intersecting white lines and spots in rows ran up and down where joints and nailholes had been spackled over.

He whispered, "What store?"

She was silent a moment, then sighed. "Dorsett's Marlinspike General Store."

He shrugged, said, "Didn't ask."

"I will," she said. "Tomorrow morning." She turned from him and headed back to the kitchen. She said, "You'll be gone tomorrow and Wednesday. I could use the company." A moment later he heard the dry static of the grocery sack, heard their own cupboards open and close.

"Tomorrow," he whispered. He took in a breath. He'd forgotten about tomorrow, about going back to work.

Later, after he'd finished straightening things in the upstairs room, and after Laura finished with her bro-

40

chures and maps, they went to bed. On the wall past the foot of the bed were those lighthouse needlepoint pictures, things that showed up as only pale square shapes when Hugh lay in bed awake at night. But now he could make them out clearly, thought he could even read the stitched names from where he lay. Every light was still on in the house next door.

Laura finished in the bathroom and opened the door, the bedroom flooded with light for only a moment before she turned off the bathroom light. Then the room went black until his eyes readjusted, and here came the needlepoint lighthouses.

She slipped into bed next to him, and he could feel her warmth there under the sheet and blanket. The only sound was the thick rush of air from the baseboards, that forced heat Mr. Halford had put in himself.

Denny, Hugh thought. He couldn't picture anyone ever addressing his boss that way, not even this Roland Dorsett next door, the man with the thick neck and too many lights on. *Denny*, he thought.

He stared at the lighthouses. *Michael*, he thought, allowing himself the word.

This was when he moved onto his side and faced Laura. He could see her profile, white against the dark of that side of the room. He thought her eyes were open.

He reached a hand to her, moved a lock of hair from her neck, placed his lips against her white skin.

She moved almost imperceptibly, her face turning from him but in a way that gave to him even more of her neck, and he kissed her there again, slowly, and again, until she moved onto her side, faced the wall. Then she reached to her hair, with one hand pulled all of it away from the back of her neck. Gently she pushed herself into him, and he kissed her neck and the top of her back above the long-sleeved T-shirt she wore to bed each night.

Their making love always followed this same chain of moves and countermoves, a sequence of small events between them that had established itself the fourth night after their son had died, when the two of them had spent their first night together and alone.

He had awakened in the middle of that night, his eyes shooting open to the dark of their bedroom in Englishtown, a room that seemed to him no place he had ever been. Even in the dark he would have known his room, the shapes and outlines of furniture, pictures on the walls, the valet next to his dresser hung with the clothes he had worn the day before.

But that night he recognized none of it, and he knew that, even if the lights had been on, he was surrounded by a room, a house, a life he would have to learn all over again. Innumerable words had already passed from him, words on it all: The funeral had been only that morning, and he'd had to say things to co-workers and neighbors and relatives he either hadn't seen in years or did not know existed.

He'd sat up in the dark, looked around him at all the useless things he could not know, and then saw his wife lying next to him. She was on her side, facing away from him, and he had leaned to her, kissed her neck. He was unprepared for the warmth of her skin and quickly drew away, the feel of his lips against his son's forehead still the closest memory he could hold. But on that first night alone, Laura's parents back in Matawan, the hospital far away, their son buried just that day, the feel of his lips there and the smell of her were the only things he believed he knew, and he kissed her again.

She had moved her face away from him, just as she did this night, and pushed herself into him, lifted her hair, and then they had made love, all with the same moves they carried through here in the near-dark of the Halfords' bedroom.

And, just as each time since their child had died, they made love in the same position, Laura beneath him and on her knees, before him as he moved into her the smooth white length of her back, his hands tracing slowly across her and up and beneath to her breasts and back to her hips, him holding on and moving into her as she moved against him, all the moves together a seamless design of joy and sorrow, Hugh believed: This was the way they had conceived their first and only child on a late summer evening in Maine, the last night of a vacation that had led them to the birth of their son almost eight years ago.

There was no way to tell, of course, that that had been the night, the two of them exhausted after a day of driving from Schoodic Point to the top of Cadillac Mountain and on down to the bed and breakfast in Clark Isle. The inn was a converted quarrymen's dormitory, and from their window on the third floor, they could see the entire small bay, lobster boats at anchor out there at high tide when they had arrived, those same boats dead and useless at low tide that night, when the water disappeared completely to reveal nothing more than rock for a mile or so out. It was on that last night, the boats silhouetted against the light of the same moon he watched each night now, that they had made love that way, cool September air in the open window sweeping the curtains toward them. He could remember looking away from her just as he had climaxed, Laura shuddering beneath him, and out that window to the black shadows of hulls on the empty bay and to the moon perched above it all, framed and caressed by the window frame and the curtains. Later, once they had found she was pregnant, he would claim that moment as the one in which they had conceived.

So that now, making love this night in a room filled with artificial light and not the light of the moon, their bodies together were the only thing he knew in a world filled with items and people he would never understand now. Though he feared her eyes, that nameless perfume of his wife, feared the taste of her when he kissed her, feared the feel of her hair, it was this sequence of wordless events in the dark that seemed the only piece of the old world he could keep and have mean what it had always meant: This was the way they had found their child.

When they had finished that first time after their son had died, he had suddenly whispered out loud to the room words that stunned him with their presence, surprised him even more than the warmth of her neck against his lips, words that, even to this night in Reed's Beach in a room he couldn't have imagined a week ago, still seemed huge and coarse and intractable once they had been uttered: "We need to have another," he whispered, that last word, *another*, the ugliest word he had ever spoken, as though the one they had just lost were only a boy in a row of children, the pick of which they might be allowed. These were the words he let himself utter to his wife, the first words, it seemed, that could have mattered since their son had died.

Laura had wept then, the sound sharp and cold in the dark, but she whispered through that sound the word *Yes*. Then he had held her, and she cried until she fell asleep.

The next morning he had watched from the bathroom doorway as Laura, her hair not yet brushed out, eyes heavy from too much crying and too little sleep, pulled from the medicine chest the beige plastic box of pills, and dropped them into the empty blue trashbasket beside the toilet, the sound as it hit the bottom as intractable as his words the night before.

She had turned to him, given him a broken smile, and then wept again.

They made love in the Halfords' bed, the bare skin of her back before him luminous in the light from next door. She hadn't yet gotten pregnant, though it seemed they made love more often now than they had since their first year of marriage. Still, a hidden part of him took shelter in the fact she had not conceived. He wanted the new child, but wanted the room with the bedspread askew, the construction paper scraps spread across a table. He knew he could not have both.

They finished. Laura pulled away from him and moved onto her side. He lay down next to her, careful not to touch her. She hadn't cried afterward since that first time, and now in the Halfords' bedroom there appeared the same silence that always arrived, some familiar ghost visiting the room to remind them of the importance of this endeavor. He looked at the ceiling, at the lighthouses. He looked at the sheer curtains, and believed, finally, their making love might be all he would ever know from his old life.

A few moments later she sat up in bed, made her way to the bathroom, and left off the light. Then the toilet flushed, and she stood next to the bed, found her underwear and T-shirt in the sheets, slipped them on. He saw all of this as clearly as if there had been only an overcast sky outside, and then she was next to him again, turned away from him, her breath in and out moving slowly toward sleep.

He was still awake when she finally fell asleep, but he wanted it this way. Even though he would be up early for the drive to work—he'd forgotten about tomorrow and Wednesday, his two days this week of having to "help hold things together" for Mr. Halford at Hess; had forgotten, too, about having to spend tomorrow night at home in Englishtown, his unrecognizable room even more remote because Laura would not be there—he wanted to stay up, wait out the light from next door, as though this were some sort of triumph of grief over ice chests, clothes on hangers.

He sat up, found his own underwear and T-shirt, and put them on. He slipped his feet into the house shoes on the floor beside the bed, then went to the dresser beneath the lighthouses, gently pulled a drawer open. He took out a pair of sweatpants, put them on, made his way in the dark to the kitchen.

The moon was directly above the house now, the kitchen, dining area, and living room shadowless as he moved, hands out, waiting to touch on something. But he touched nothing until he felt the staircase railing in his hand, and he mounted the stairs, taking each step slow and deliberate, listening for how little noise he might make.

He reached the top of the staircase, and remembered the switch at the bottom, the gold-painted angelfish, the lights up here operated from down there. He stood at the top of the stairs, thought a moment on going back down to turn them on.

But then he looked out the window to his left, the octagon of gray light that looked down upon empty beach and those broken pylons trailing up the shore. The tide was up, touched at the pylons, and he watched each lap of water carry itself up and around the pylons down there, surround them, let them go, surround them again.

There was no need for light up here. He could see all he needed to see.

He turned from the window and looked at the darkened room. He'd planned to come up here and read through more books, gather more information about sun and moon sightings, tide tables, anything else that might acquaint him with what Mr. Halford did up here.

Because that was what he'd intended by spending all his time up here or out on the dock: He wanted to find out how Mr. Halford—Dennis, Denny—spent his own time. He had spent all three days down here trying to find what Mr. Halford knew in the belief that somehow the landmarks surrounding him in this room—the desk in the dormer, Coast Guard chart 12304 thumbtacked just below the octagonal window on the opposite wall, a sextant swathed in velvet—might become his own, and he would be the one returned to his old life, the one he'd inhabited before their son had died.

But even here, the only safe haven he thought he could find, and even now, in the middle of the night, a near-full moon outside lending light enough for him to see all of the world he believed he needed to see, there came through the octagonal window at the other end of the room light from next door.

Light made its way through the window at an angle up, so that another octagon, this one collapsed and tilted, shone on the slanted ceiling. Slowly he went to the window, looked down to see the Dorsetts from a different angle now, the kitchen window below him and to his right.

They were seated at the table, near the corner of the room a kerosene heater, on the floor a few feet away from it the empty ice chest, lid open.

They sat across from each other, Roland Dorsett's back to Hugh, so that he could see just over his shoulder. *USS Yorktown* was printed in large yellow letters across the back of his blue windbreaker. Hugh could see, too, that he still had on his billed cap, the little hair above his neck silver. Winnie still had on her windbreaker, buttoned up to the neck, small yellow letters above the right breast pocket. She had the scarf off, her hair done up as high and wide as he'd imagined it would be, but black, a black so black he knew she'd had to dye it to get it that dark. Her face was white, her lips a bright red he could see even from here, and there was that hair.

They were playing some sort of card game. He could see the cards in Roland Dorsett's hands, bright green and red and blue and yellow in the light from whatever fixture was above them. He couldn't make out any numbers or letters, only the colors, and watched as they took turns laying a card on a pile on the table. If one of them couldn't lay a card down, he saw, he or she had to draw from a second pile in the middle of the table, these cards face down. The back sides of the cards were black, had something printed in red and white in the center.

He'd seen the game before, he knew, recognized it from somewhere: the bright colors of the cards, the discard pile, the pickup pile.

Roland Dorsett put down a card, then another. Winnie did nothing this time, only held onto hers. He put one more card down, and Hugh watched as Winnie drew four cards from the pickup pile. Then Roland Dorsett put down his last card.

Winnie smiled, her red lips parting. Then her mouth closed, her smile gone coy, and he watched as she gently shook her head, tilted it to one side. She placed her own cards—there must have been eight or ten of them—on the table before her, her own bright colors suddenly revealed. Then she reached to her husband's hand there on the table, palm up and empty after having surrendered his last card, and she softly slapped at his wrist.

Roland Dorsett tried to grab hold of her hand, but she quickly brought it back, still shook her head, still smiled.

Then he eased back in his chair and shrugged, his hands out to either side as if to say he had no choice in the matter.

Winnie shrugged herself and, still smiling, pulled a pencil and pad from a corner of the table he hadn't been able to see, started writing on it. He watched her mouth move, her eyes to the paper.

Roland Dorsett's shoulders shot up and down, his head tossed back: He was laughing. He gathered up the cards and started shuffling them.

Uno was the name of the card game they played, he remembered, and quickly he turned from the window, from the series of small and intimate moves this couple he did not know and never wanted to know made on their own, moves as private, he knew, as his own love-making with his wife: There'd been her touch to his wrist, his try at holding onto her, the smooth tilt of her head as she let, perhaps, her husband win at this game.

But it had been the game, he believed, that made him turn from them, made his eyes go from the bright light down there to the pitch black of this room.

He waited for his eyes to readjust to the dark, but they wouldn't, and the game, the colorful cards, the discarding and picking up, and the delivery of that last single card that made the bearer the winner came to him: Here were his wife and their son sitting at the breakfast table in Englishtown, empty cereal bowls pushed to one side, two piles of those same cards on the table before them. Behind them was the bank of windows that looked out on the backyard and the line of green, full trees out there. Here, too, was himself hurrying to put on his coat, making certain all was right with his briefcase, then heading toward the door, coffee in hand for the drive into Hess; then came the single word ringing out from behind

him: his son's voice—Michael's voice—shouting out to
Laura, "Uno!"

He'd turned to that word, he remembered just then.
Laura had on her white nurse's uniform; Michael, a day-
glo orange and gray-striped crewneck shirt, black shorts,
white socks. And his tennis shoes. His legs kicked beneath
him, his blue bookbag slung over the back of his chair.

Mr. Halford's room still as black as if his eyes had been
shut tight, Hugh saw Laura draw one last card from a
pile on the table, then saw Michael lay down his last
card. "I beat you!" he hollered.

Hugh saw himself turn back to the front door as
though it were a target, point of entry for a day he would
spend hunched at a gray monitor, printouts surrounding
him. Hugh saw himself leave, just as he did every day,
Laura Michael's company until it was time for him to
leave for the bus stop.

It was an anonymous morning, a morning like any
other. Not the morning of the day he died, his recollec-
tion of that day something gone past memory. The day
of his son's death had taken up residence with him, the
hours he moved through of every day after that paralleled by the hours of a day three months and ten days
before.

But this anonymous morning, the one he could see
plainly before him, had been forgotten somehow, and he
wondered how he could claim to remember his child if
even the smallest of moments—a card game, legs kicking
beneath a chair—could be lost.

He turned back to the window, let his eyes fall to the
kitchen window next door. Roland and Winnie Dorsett
were both holding new cards, Winnie the first to lay hers
down.

The books behind him, the maps, the chart thumbtacked just beneath the window he stood at right now,

even the sextant would all be there when the Dorsetts chose to turn in, he knew. Once they were gone, those cards put away, he would make his way back down the steps, turn on the light, then get to the business of knowing what Mr. Halford knew about the world.

But for now he watched, saw Roland take his turn, then Winnie, who took her time placing her card down, her hand swirling over the pile in slow and gentle circles, finally settling the card on the pile.

She sat back. For a moment neither of them moved, until Roland shook his head, reached to the pick up pile, and drew off four cards.

He knew then, in the gentleness of her move, in the touch of the card on the pile, in the reach of this man's hand to new cards stacked neatly at the center of the table, that he must get his wife, rouse her from whatever dream of road maps and historic points she wandered through right then herself, and bring her to this room, and to this window. He imagined them standing together at the window, holding tight to each other in the dark of someone else's house, their faces illuminated in the light from the house next door.

But he only stayed there at the window, watching them, an old couple he did not know at a game of cards his son used to play.

Two

🐚 HUGH WAS ALREADY gone when Laura woke up.

The air and light in the room were different, she knew, as though a storm had come through, washed clean the gray and cold, though Laura could remember nothing other than wind the night before, the way it had pushed and twisted the trees and bushes in the light of her headlights as she'd driven home from the Acme.

She sat up quickly, as she did each morning, turned and found on the floor the heavy wool socks. They were ragwool socks, scratchy and soft at the same time. She liked the feel of them on her feet, the difference in the textures, and when she had them on, she stood, suddenly amazed at how comfortable the room was. Each morning here so far she'd awakened to a room too cold, even with the forced heat Hugh's boss had put in. Her skin covered in gooseflesh, she'd hold herself and make for the bathroom, turn on the water, and climb into the shower as soon as it was warm enough, Hugh still asleep, as sluggish about getting up as every morning since it had happened.

She paused, took in a breath.

Today there was the County Museum at Cape May

55

Court House; that was the first place she'd put on her list last night. Next, she remembered, was the library in Cape May, and the wildlife area. Higbee's Beach was the name she remembered. There were other stops, she knew, but those were the only ones that came to her.

She smelled coffee from the kitchen; Hugh must have left on the coffee maker for her. But for now there was this new air in the room, and the new light, and she moved around the bed to the window, pulled back the sheer curtain, looked outside.

Sun shone crisp and clean across the white siding of the Dorsett's house, a white it seemed she hadn't known before. The sun was new somehow, as was the air and the blue of the sky above the peak of the white house. Everything was new, and she leaned a little closer to the window, tried to see between their houses to the water.

It was only a slip of the bay she saw, but of course it was different, too, as she knew it would be: blue now, not gray or black, but blue, and she smiled.

There were places to go today; she'd made that list, remembered tucking it inside the *Victorian Cape May* magazine she'd gotten at the bird sanctuary day before yesterday. The magazine was only an amalgamation of advertisements, everything from Century 21 to Klothes Kove to Stumpo's Italian Restaurant. There were racks of these books and brochures and flyers everywhere: at the Dunkin Donuts, at the Chinese restaurant in the strip mall on Route 9, even at the Acme last night: row upon row upon row of things to do and places to see, so many pieces of paper for her to gather, peruse, decide upon, and prioritize.

She thought then of the boy at the Acme, his white shirt and red apron, and thought of his face, the pimples at his chin and forehead, his red hair cut long on top and shaved at the sides. She thought of how he hadn't said a word as he'd thrown things into the bags, hadn't even met her eyes.

He was just a kid, and though the groceries rolling around in the trunk had annoyed the hell out of her, she'd thought for a moment she might have understood him. It was only a moment, an instant, but for that moment she believed she had seen in that boy's eyes, in the distance, everything she knew of this place, this end of the state she'd been raised in and of which she'd known nothing until three days ago.

As she'd driven down the dirt road through the marsh, the headlights only a pitiful flicker in all this darkness before her, a darkness that included miles of seagrass and the entire Delaware Bay, she believed she'd seen in his eyes the blank cold of winter in a place where winter didn't count, wasn't an acknowledged part of the way things worked: Summer was the time down here, when the streets, even this far from Cape May, would be flooded with tourists, people who'd set up housekeeping in the deserted cottages up and down Reed's Beach and all along the other beaches she'd found driving these past three days: Kimble's Beach, Pierce's Point, High Beach, Norbury's Landing. And she thought she'd seen in his empty eyes the news she'd read in the *Lower Township Lantern*: "Crime Up 10 Percent" was the headline on the lead article; "Son Is Murder Suspect" read another, "Cops Bust Four" read yet another.

These were the items she was drawn to in reading the newspaper here. Certainly there were other stories, plenty of happy news that filled the local paper: "Friends Share Christening Day" and "Sale to Fund Trips for Kids" and "Patriots List Essay Winners."

But it seemed to her these were not the true stories of this place, the real things. The real thing, it seemed to her, had been a boy with a haircut she could not under-

stand, empty eyes, grocery items placed into bags with
no rhyme or reason.

She'd been seeking out the true stories of this place on
her drives. Rather than do as her husband did, who
seemed somehow content with sitting upstairs or holding
an odd nautical instrument up to the moon, as though
any of that might spell out to him what he was to do
next with his life, she decided to move through this place
and try to see whatever truth it was people down here
lived. She simply wanted to know. Just that: pure knowledge of place, a place she'd never been before.

This pursuit, of course, made it easier for her to prioritize all the flyers. If she were after the truth of the place,
she knew, there was no call for visiting fudge factories
or candle shops or even what seemed the biggest at-
traction of all, a guided tour of the Physick Estate. Instead, she'd made a list each day of places she believed
were real.

She'd had no list Saturday, had only driven, letting
whatever road she was on unravel before her. She'd
driven through towns and clusters of homes and along
farmland and by grocery stores and restaurants, eventu-
ally ending in Cape May, with its gingerbread trimmings
and bed and breakfasts and boutiques. She finally
stopped when she reached a dead end, before her a red
and white barrier fence past which lay the beach. Beyond
that, across a small bay, stood a lighthouse.

This was when she decided to map out her routes, and
when she knew driving with no purpose would mean her
own death.

She'd used lists all her life, had written down on whatever slips of paper might present themselves—gas receipts, fast-food napkins—important information and
news and vague or precise plans she might have. So why,

she'd wondered, looking out past the water to a lighthouse that suddenly meant more than any lighthouse ought to mean, had she embarked on this day without an itinerary?

She'd looked out at the lighthouse a moment more, had taken in the white of it, a white not much different than the late afternoon February sky around it. Then she'd turned the car around, headed back along the street until she found a street sign: *Beach Ave.* it had read, and she memorized it, as she did the next street she turned onto, *Broadway*, a street that became *Seashore Road*, a road that bridged the Cape May Canal; then she turned left onto *Ferry Road*, followed that until she saw a bright and shining new strip mall, complete with a Chinese restaurant, a Jamesway, dry cleaners, and the Acme. There, too, was the Book Shoppe, and she parked, went inside, and purchased the Cape May County Street and Road Map so that she'd not have to memorize any more names, and so that she could plan where to go.

And there, beside the cashier's counter, she'd found her first rack of flyers, picked through them in order to know where she was going, which locations would give to her the knowledge of this place she'd suddenly known she needed.

Sunday's list had read:

> Lighthouse
> Cape May Point State Park
> Bird Sanctuary
> Lunch
> Cape May County Park

Monday's list had read:

> Cape May Court House Complex
> Highlands Beach

BRET LOTT

Lunch
Villas
Miami Beach

Last night, once she'd gotten Hugh to bring in all the groceries, a task it'd seemed had taken him hours, and once they'd spied on the couple next door, she'd sat at the kitchen table like the other nights and made another list. She'd been sitting at the table and writing away when Hugh'd moved through the kitchen to the reading room, then on up the stairs and into his haunted attic, where he'd savor all the Marlinspike business Mr. Halford surrounded himself with for the rest of the evening. Her husband had no idea what she was up to, and she savored that secret herself, as much, she knew, as he did the secrets he thought he was uncovering and keeping to himself whenever he was upstairs or out on the dock.

But nothing he did was a secret. She knew all that went on in him, knew how his head worked and the way he wore on his sleeve what had happened to them.

Even last night, when she'd gotten home from the Acme, she knew he thought she couldn't see him out on the dock. But the truth was that she'd opened the front door, the wind from outside pushing its way in to the freezing house, and she'd stood there, watched him through the open sliding glass door for a good five minutes. She'd stood there, a grocery bag in each hand, her straw handbag at her shoulder, and watched him.

She saw the boy who'd fought another boy at Matt Hahn's party after the Madison football game their junior year, a game that, like every game his entire football career, Hugh'd endured from on the bench. She'd shown up with Bud Morrow, first string tailback, and had on her halter top and ultrasuede skirt, the outfit she'd worn on her first date with Hugh. She'd only gone out with

60

him a couple of times, thought he was cute but too shy, too quiet. Then, a little after midnight, there'd come a rush of people out of Matt's basement rec room and on up to the kitchen. She'd had to push through people herself, had had to ask what was going on, only to have Matt's thick beer breath shout out to her above the roar of the crowd, "It's you. They're fighting over you."

Hugh'd had an eyebrow ripped up, a rib bruised. But she'd gone home with him, not for any pity she had for him, but for the fact he'd had a go at Bud Morrow because of something Bud'd said about her. "Nothing you need to know," Hugh'd said to her, finally, when they were in the driveway at her house, his eyes and how they only now met hers in the dark telling her he would have no more talk of it. She'd tried since they had started home to get him to tell her what Bud'd said, but he refused. It was for this initial reason—his refusal to divulge what he thought would only hurt her, that innocent integrity—that she chose to stay with him through the rest of high school, then on into college. And it was to his eyes, how they'd finally touched on her to try and keep her safe, that she could trace the trail of her love for him.

Yet even that far back there'd been no secret about him she didn't know: Mindy Shankley'd been up in the kitchen when the whole thing had taken place, had followed Laura to Matt's upstairs bathroom for Band-aids, so that Laura knew Bud's words even before she'd applied first aid to her future husband's eyebrow: "Bud Morrow said you had tits like tennis balls," Mindy Shankley'd giggled. "Small and firm and fun to play with. That's when Hugh took a swing." She giggled again.

Laura'd felt her face turn hot as she pushed through someone else's toiletries beneath a sink, felt her breasts shrink into themselves beneath the halter top. She'd found the Band-aids, then closed the cupboard, stood.

For a moment Mindy and Laura looked at each other in the mirror, Laura afraid to take herself in, to see her red face and small breasts pretending beneath a halter top.

"That's when Hugh took a swing," Mindy'd giggled again, as though Laura hadn't heard her. Mindy shrugged, put a finger to her mouth. She grinned, said, "He missed."

She'd seen that boy when she'd stood with the front door open, a grocery bag in each hand. She'd watched that boy, the one with the innocent integrity, lift the sextant to the moon.

There he'd stood, looking out at nothing, a dead planet too far away to touch. Her husband, still swinging and missing, still swinging and missing.

Then she'd pushed the door closed behind her, making certain the sound was loud enough to startle him from whatever dream of their son he was wandering in just then.

She'd leaned against the door and hollered out, "Hugh!"

A few moments later came his quiet answer, as if she didn't know precisely where he was: "I'm out here."

Still she stood at the window, taking in this new light, when she saw Mrs. Dorsett—What was her name? Winnie? Wilma?—walk along the side porch. Their house was encircled, just as the Halfords' was, by a porch with a railing, and here came Mrs. Dorsett from the van parked out front. She carried in her arms a power saw, black and scarred and heavy, the cord for it hanging down and bouncing about the woman's knees.

Then Laura took in what the woman had on here in South Jersey in February: fire-engine red polyester shorts, the kind with the stitched crease down the top of the thigh, thin cuffs just above the knees. She wore a pink-flowered sleeveless blouse; the flowers, Laura thought she could make out, were small rosebuds. She had on white sandals with thick two-inch heels.

And there was her hair, stiff and coiffed and dyed black. *Ebony* was the word that came to Laura, then *Black Azure* and *Black Velvet*, colors she read on boxes of dye she'd picked up in the CVS once when she was in high school. But she hadn't had the nerve, the names of the colors intimidating in and of themselves, not to mention the reactions she would have gotten from her mother and father. She hadn't been able to gauge what reaction Hugh might have had, and it seemed to her this inability, her not knowing what he would say or do, was reason enough not to do it. At the time, a few weeks before graduation, when her only plans were to go to Wildwood and Asbury Park as often as she could with her girlfriends or with Hugh, changing her hair color had seemed daring and grown-up: Jackie Stein had done it, changed her strawberry blond hair to Topaz; and there'd been Melanie Franklin, too, who'd gotten a Dorothy Hamill cut and changed the color to boot, her brunette gone to sable brown.

But she'd stood in the drug store, held the boxes in her hand, and had decided that if she could not guess what her boyfriend would do, then she shouldn't do it. This was the boy, after all, with whom she had made love for the first time only a couple of months before. How could she pull this huge of a surprise—Black Velvet, Ebony, Black Azure—on him, risk losing him for the dare of a shade of black?

But those reasonings were archaic now, as dead and gone as a Dorothy Hamill cut; she should have done it, she saw in this Mrs. Dorsett—It was Winnie, wasn't it?— and her black hair. All those considerations when she was a girl were sheer folly.

Even from here, probably thirty feet or so, Laura could see, too, the varicose veins through the white flesh of her legs, the sagging skin on her upper arms. But the woman carried the power saw with no strain, as far as Laura could tell. She only walked along the porch, her strides strong and easy.

Laura envied the woman. She wanted that hair color, wanted the way she walked and carried the tool in her arms, wanted the feel of the electric cord bouncing against her knees. She wanted to be over there, walking on the next door neighbor's deck beneath a sky she hadn't thought possible, and not here, inside looking out.

Before she could figure what to say, she had a hand to the window handle and pulled it back to pop open the window.

She leaned to the opening, shouted, "Hello!"

Mrs. Dorsett stopped, turned. She squinted, searched for where the word had come from.

Laura waved, and suddenly remembered she had on only the T-shirt and her underwear. The sill was waist high, and she crouched only an inch or so, again called, "Hello!"

Then Mrs. Dorsett saw her, gave a quick smile, and said, "Good morning." She half-turned toward Laura, the power saw, Laura could see, bigger than what she'd thought. "Must be seventy degrees out here already," she said.

"Are you Winnie Dorsett?" Laura said through the screen, and smiled, though she wasn't certain the woman could see her for the light outside.

"That's me," Winnie said, nodding once. "You must be Laura."

"That's me," she said.

Then came a man's voice from the window behind Winnie Dorsett: "You had breakfast yet?"

64

REED'S BEACH

Laura paused a moment, tried to see into the window. Last night they'd been witness to everything that'd gone on inside their house; now she could see nothing.

"Not yet," Laura called and carefully lowered herself even more, not certain what could be seen of her from across the way.

"Come on over," the voice said. Roland Dorsett's, of course.

"We got waffles and sausage and grapefruit juice," Winnie said. "Too much for a couple old farts like us." Then she turned, headed for the dock without waiting for answer. A moment later she disappeared with the power saw around the back of the house.

Laura loved this woman.

"Plenty of food," Roland Dorsett's voice said.

She leaned to the screen and said, "Let me take a quick shower. Over in a minute."

She went into the bathroom, twisted on the water in the shower stall, let her hand trail in the water a moment. She smiled and shook her head at whatever might come of her time with these people next door.

Hot water wouldn't show up for another minute or so, and she went into the kitchen for coffee.

She went to the cupboard next to the sink, pulled down a mug painted with a sailboat, *The America* in script beneath it. She poured the coffee—Hugh'd left only enough for one more cup, and she hoped the Dorsetts had more— then went to the table, found last night's list just where she'd left it inside the book of advertisements:

> County Museum
> Library in Cape May
> Higbee's Beach Wildlife Area
> Lunch

BRET LOTT

Cape May Diamonds
Atlantus

She slipped it back in the book, sipped at the coffee, and looked out the sliding door to the water.

The blue of the water seemed even deeper now, the blue of the sky even sharper. She could see a strip of land across the bay, too, a ragged line just at the horizon. Delaware, she knew, but she hadn't known you could see it from here.

Then she went back into the bathroom, where steam had started up from behind the glass door of the stall.

She set the cup on the counter, then brought down her underwear, sat on the toilet.

There in her underwear was the residue from last night. She swallowed, looked at the ugly surprise of it, and its immediate truth of her own place and not the truth of this place to which they'd retreated: They'd made love last night, her face buried in her pillow, her husband rising and falling into her, intent on making their next child. They'd made love that way, him above and behind her, because her husband believed, she knew, that that was how they conceived their only child.

She kicked off the socks, then shook the underwear from around her feet and pulled off the T-shirt. She finished, flushed the toilet.

Then she stood at the counter. Before her in the steamed mirror she saw the vague image of a naked woman whose breasts had grown since a night in her junior year in high school, and whose waist had been lost to the birth of a son, and whose eyes were lost to the steam.

She reached to the makeup kit she'd emptied the first night they were here; she'd made room in the Halfords' medicine chest for her own things right away, nestled

her shower gel, Eucerin, and dental floss right next to
the assorted toiletries of the owners. But her husband
had kept his own in his shaving kit, testament to the
distance she knew he'd keep for as long as he believed
was right and just in this world.

But her makeup kit wasn't empty altogether, and she
opened it, revealing her own truth yet again, one that
distanced herself even farther from her husband than a
sextant held to the moon, or his speaking their son's
name in the dark as though he were the only person on
the face of the earth to know it.

There beneath two panty shields lay her beige plastic
box of pills.

She opened it, popped through the thin plastic the last
one for this cycle, and placed it on her tongue.

She turned back to the counter, saw herself in the mirror. Then she dropped the empty box into her straw
handbag hung on the bathroom doorknob. She would get
to a pharmacy today or tomorrow, sometime this week.

She looked at herself, looked, then brought up the coffee cup, sipped, and swallowed the pill, all without taking her eyes from the mirror, as though daring herself to
look away.

County Museum, she thought. Then the Library.

🐚 ONE DECEMBER DAY the year before Michael went into kindergarten, back before the Rothbergs had built their home next door, when Canterbury Court had only been paved a few months and the houses on the street— there had only been five or six back then—were only visible in winter, trees hiding them until the leaves had been stripped, a snowstorm had blown down from nowhere.

The first flakes had fallen as Laura'd left the hospital, walked out the emergency room door to her car in the staff lot: first one flake, then another, and another, small pinpricks of ice, fine and dry and minuscule flakes that fell like ash, flakes that signaled this snow would be heavy and long, though Laura remembered having driven to work that morning with the sun through her rear window. She'd had to flick the rearview mirror to night vision, the sun right there in her eyes when she'd glanced up and into the glass.

But then had come the front, the sky by noon slate gray and low, then the snow.

By the time she made it to Kinder Kare three blocks away, she'd had to put the headlights on, the snow a thin veil before her. Still none of it stayed on her windshield, only blew away with the movement of the car.

Michael, already bundled when she walked in, his hands in mittens clipped to his jacket sleeves, his Day-Glo orange wool cap pulled down below his eyebrows, smiled up at her and said, "First snow! First snow!" and ran past her and outside. Laura'd had only time enough to smile at Miss Lynn, his teacher, and thank her.

"Be careful!" Miss Lynn called after her once she was outside. Michael was already turning circles next to the car, hands out to either side, palms up, face to the sky. "Helicopter!" he yelled.

"We will," Laura said, and glanced back at the woman, saw her standing in the light of the doorway, arms crossed against the cold.

Laura picked up her son then, smiled, held him close, snow falling down harder now, still just as even and fine. She saw flakes on his nose, saw them land there and disappear in a moment, melted by the warmth of his skin.

"Say good-bye to Miss Lynn," she'd said to Michael.

"So long!" he'd hollered, waving. Then he lifted one arm, put his mittened hand to his forehead. He snapped his arm out and away: a salute, Laura only then realized, and both Miss Lynn and Laura laughed.

Snow lay thick on their street when she pulled off Milk Farm, the wipers on now, sweeping the snow in long arcs from the glass. The headlights seemed useless now, only gestures: The heavy white of the snow swallowed up all light until the world seemed a huge and indifferent white, here and there only glimpses of what might be trees, the idea of a driveway. She'd made it this far through sheer habit, knew where street signs would be, knew when reflectors and guard rails would rise up before twisting curves.

This is only December, she thought.

Then she saw the entrance to her own driveway, the hint of two pines that sat at either end of the mouth. She slowed, turned left into the space between the trees, and saw the looming hulk of their house a few yards ahead. The driveway was a gravel one and made huge and dark sounds whenever she pulled in, pops and cracks that shot up from beneath them.

But this time there was no sound, only the quiet hum of the engine, and the lack of sound startled her, brought to her the fact of what was happening so early in the season, Christmas still three weeks away: This was a blizzard.

Michael unbuckled his safety seat—he'd mastered this trick a year or so before, while Hugh still had problems figuring out the contraption—and climbed down, tried to open his door even before Laura turned off the engine. She'd had to turn in her seat to look back at him, there with the handle in his hand, his eyes out to the snow.

"You know we don't unbuckle until I've turned off the car, Michael," she said and tried to give her voice the edge of a scolding.

Michael looked at her, gave her the smile he'd already found would get him off the hook: His lips never parted, making his dimples even deeper, his eyes crinkling up into a grinning squint.

"You kid," she said, then shook her head and climbed out of the car.

She came around to his side, popped open his door, and he was gone, disappeared into the trees beside the drive. She turned to the woods filling with snow, watched that Day-Glo hat, the dark figure of her son, drift and dart between the trunks of trees. She heard words she could not make out, heard singing, her son's muffled movement and hidden sounds like a harmless ghost meant to claim the woods for its own.

70

Still the snow came down, no longer the thin veil it had been but now a heavy cloak, thick and opaque; the orange cap and the dark jacket gave way to white while she watched.

"Michael!" she called. She thought she saw the hat, a small shard of color, slip between trees. "Michael!" she called.

"He's not here," came her son's voice. She saw nothing, only the shapes of bare trees through the snow.

She paused, waited a moment, felt herself smile. She felt, too, snowflakes on her eyebrows, her nose, her cheeks. She touched at her cheeks, the leather glove soft but cold on her skin. She said, "Well then, who are you?"

"I'm the troll of the forest," he said, his voice loud, carried on the cold air and snow.

"The troll of the forest," she said and waited. He said nothing, and she heard then the sound of the snow itself falling, gathering on the ground. The sound seemed louder than the engine as she'd driven the roads to this place, seemed louder than any snow she had ever heard before: a harsh and secretive sound, a scattering of sand across glass. Nothing she had ever heard before, but beautiful all the same.

"Troll of the forest," she called out, her voice loud and square and heavy. "Troll of the forest," she said again, this time quieter, afraid somehow there might be something she would break with the pitch of her voice. "What has happened to my beautiful son?" she said.

"I ate him up," came Michael's voice. "Like the billy goats," he said. He paused, the air filled with the sound of snow. "Yummy yummy," he said, and giggled.

She saw the orange of the cap then, saw her son was deep into the woods, knew by the movement of the cap, the way it stayed close to the trunk of a tree, no dark

71

figure beneath it, that he was hiding, only poking his head around to see her, to know if she could see him.

"Oh no you don't!" she called out, and she ran for him, for where she had seen the cap, the trees closer now, beside her, still vague for the snow down around her. "You can't eat my beautiful son," she said.

He ran then, too, flushed from his hiding place. The snow was already a few inches deep, her shoes—she hadn't brought boots to work, had seen the sun in her rearview mirror—filling with snow, her toes going cold. Still she ran, her son giggling, laughing, turning and looking up at her every few steps, darting before her, until finally she reached out to him, had an arm around his waist, and the two of them fell to the ground, laughing.

Michael took a handful of snow, threw it at her, and she felt the sudden crush of cold in her face. For an instant she'd wanted to yell at him, pull him up straight and scold him for such a thing.

But then she felt the joy and spark of the snow, the surprise of the cold, and she took a handful, held it up above him, on his back and writhing beneath her arm. "Now," she said, and brought the snow to his face, started sprinkling it over him, "let's see how you like it."

"Yummy!" he said, laughing. His eyes were closed, his legs still moving. "First snow!" he said, and opened his mouth, his tongue taking in the snow, his teeth then working, chewing at snow she knew had already melted inside her child's warm mouth.

But in his laughing, in his face wrinkled up, his mouth open with his words, eyes creased closed at the joy of all this play outside on a snowy day, she had seen a remarkable thing: She saw who he looked like, saw both herself and her husband. He had Hugh's eyes, her own mouth, her eyebrows, Hugh's chin. And Michael's hair, the same color as hers, held the same thick waves as Hugh's.

All of this swirled up and into her in a moment, though none of it was new to her. She'd seen elements of them both from the day the child was born, Hugh holding a slightly blue and bloody baby in his arms, smiling, she could tell by the movement of his eyes above the surgical mask, with the miraculous gift she'd bore, had seen even then somehow herself and Hugh, though in those first days what she saw of the two of them seemed more intuition than fact, more belief than truth. Michael was only a newborn, his face red and wrinkled, fists tight beside him as he wailed or slept or nursed.

But this early afternoon he had become someone else, she saw. This was their son, part of both of them, but in the snowflakes melting across his forehead and cheeks, in the perfect white teeth, the wrinkled closed eyes laughing, he was nothing of them: himself, and only and always that.

She sat up then, Michael rolling free of her. She looked at him as he rolled away from her, then stopped, flat on his back.

He pushed himself up on his elbows, his laughter slowing, his breathing heavy. He said, "I ate him up," and quickly rolled away again, a dare for her to try and get him. He ended up a few feet farther away on his back again. This time, though, he did not push himself up, only lay flat on the ground.

She said nothing, only sat there in snow, the cold pushing up into her legs and feet and bottom. Still she only looked at him.

His eyes were closed, the Day-Glo hat and his jacket and mittens and jeans and shoes caked with snow. His name was Michael, and she believed she knew him.

"Michael," she said, and feared he might not answer to it.

"Yep," he said, eyes still closed.

She took a breath, her fear kept back somehow with his single word. "I want to show you something," she said.

He opened his eyes, rolled onto his side. "Okay," he said. He took a handful of snow, put it to his mouth, ate some.

"Watch," she said and stood, brushing the snow from her as best she could, though she knew there was no reason to. She would be back in it soon enough.

She took a few steps even deeper into the woods, found a place where they had not yet set foot, the snow a white and perfect sheet.

She turned, faced Michael, who was now on his knees, watching her. Then she sat, leaned back in the snow until she lay flat. She put out her arms to either side, let them lay in the snow.

She closed her eyes, then began moving her arms up and down, scraping them across the sheet of snow. She moved her legs, too, out and in, scraping snow there as well.

"Mommy, you're a nut," Michael said, and she opened her eyes, saw him standing over her, looking at her. Above him was the stone gray sky, the rough outline of bare branches.

She stopped moving and sat up. "Scoot back," she said and waved him toward her feet, away from her.

He stepped back, said, "What?"

Then she stood. She reached to him, took his hand, his glove still snow-covered, and they turned to look at the snow.

There lay her outline, and the arms and legs. "A snow angel," Laura said and pointed. "See the wings?" She

74

outlined them in the air before them. "And the legs are like a dress," she said. "See?"

He said nothing, only let go her hand, dropped to his knees in the snow beside her angel, then turned and lay back just as she had. He moved his arms then, his eyes closed, lips tight with concentration.

"Your legs," she said. "Move your legs."

But he didn't, only swept his arms across the snow.

He stopped, shot open his eyes. He sat up, put out a hand to Laura.

"Help me," he said.

She took his hand, pulled him up, amazed at how light he was, this new person suddenly with her, a boy no longer her own, she saw, but someone else.

And suddenly she was kneeling next to him, suddenly taking hold of him and pulling him close to her, because it seemed there might not be another moment like this one, when the entire world had become only snow through trees, a house, snow angels on the ground.

"Mommy," he said and tried to wriggle free of her. "Look," he said, and pointed.

There were two angels now, the first huge and overbearing compared to the one next to it, so small and careful.

"No dress on mine," Michael said. "Boy angels don't have dresses," he said, and she could only nod in agreement, nod at the perfect truth and logic of a four-year-old's observation.

"They're flying together," he said, and brought his arm down, tried to push her arms away from around him, his eyes all the while on the snow. "Look. Their wings are touching, so they're flying together."

She saw it, too, saw how their own hands across the snow had overlapped in the smallest way, the bottom edge of her left wing just touching the top edge of his right wing. They were touching, flying together.

"You're right," she said, his words, the angels in the snow, the snow falling down around them all holding back the fear she held, fear of the knowledge ancient and new in her that this was someone else.

She held him, wouldn't let go as he pushed at her arms, pushed at them, because she knew he would only run deeper into those woods, farther from her, and on this afternoon it seemed he had already started away from her toward a place that could only end with a child grown up and moved out, an empty house and snow all that would be left to her.

So she picked him up and carried her son on her hip, though he had long outgrown this position.

"Let me go!" he shouted, and twisted in her arms, smiling all the while. "I want to play!" he shouted, his words swallowed by the snow, any echo that might have come through the empty woods gone with the white falling all around them.

Inside, after she'd taken off their jackets and gloves and wet shoes and socks, and after she'd dressed Michael in dry pants and shirt and socks, and after she herself had changed out of her uniform and into her sweatpants and Rutgers sweatshirt, she served warm milk and graham crackers. He told her of his day only when she asked, his eyes to the light, the bare trees and white out the kitchen windows. "Fun," he said when she asked how the day had gone. "Colored," he said when she asked what he'd done before snack. "Chicken Charms and peas," he said when she asked what he'd had for lunch.

She hadn't turned on the kitchen light above them, so that the shape of his face, the outline of cheek and nose and eyes as he looked out the window, his face turned from hers, was bathed in soft and giving and cold light, the smooth skin of his face washed in a light that bore no falsehood, gave her only her son, his hair just touching the tops of his ears, the muscles in his jaw moving slowly as he chewed, his hand finding the red plastic mug of milk without looking. His eyes did not turn from the window.

Then she looked away from him and out the window herself, saw what she knew held him, filled him: the joy of snow this early. A new world. She said nothing more, only let him finish his crackers and milk. Only then, with his last sip, his placing the mug back on the table without looking away from the snow, did she speak: "Time for nap," she said.

Quickly he turned to her, his face already in the pout, lower lip out, eyebrows knotted. "Mommy," he said and leaned his head to the right, his eyes hard on her, "I'm not tired not at all."

She smiled, looked down at her own mug. She said, "You want to have plenty of rest before we go out and play." She reached for his plate then, placed it on hers, and stood. "You bring the mugs to the sink," she said.

"You promise," he said.

"Promise what?" She looked at him. He was turned to the windows again.

"Promise me we go out and play when nap is over." He held his empty mug with both hands, looked into it, then out the window again.

He turned in his seat, looked at her. He said, "Promise me."

"I promise," she said, then put a finger to her chest, made an X. "Cross my heart and hope to die," she said.

"Okay," he said, and now he was climbing down from the chair, reached for her mug, brought them toward her at the sink. She moved back from the sink, hands on her hips, and watched this person carry two red plastic mugs to the sink, his chin just above the counter edge, and drop them in, the sound loud and harsh in the room.

He turned to her, dusted off his hands in the exaggerated way she knew he must have seen someone do on television, and looked up at her. "Ready for nap," he said.

She smiled, put out her hand for him to take, but he was already turned away from her, headed out the kitchen.

She opened her eyes, not knowing they had been closed.

The telephone was ringing somewhere, she believed. Or at least what she thought might have been the telephone. It sounded like the telephone.

The telephone rang again and again, and only then did she recognize where she was: Michael's room, a room that had grown dark since she had tucked him in, then sat on the floor across the room from him and watched him fall asleep, as though her watching him slip away to sleep might allow her a longer hold on his life, on the new person in their house this snow day in December.

She sat up, blinked, her face and hands and neck warm with sleep. She touched a hand to her eyes, swallowed, tasted in her mouth a thick metallic and sour taste, and remembered graham crackers and milk just before she'd put Michael down for his nap.

The room was nearly dark, and she stood, still disoriented from sleep in the afternoon, herself, she remembered then, deciding finally to give in to sleep, and she remembered lying on her side, curling up, her hands between her thighs, and gently closing her eyes; remembered the surrender to graham crackers and warm milk and snow outside, a beautiful child not ten feet away from her; remembered how his breaths in and out had been soft and quiet and regular, silver and small in the quiet of the room as she herself took up her own rhythm, and the room, the carpet against her cheek, the gray afternoon light all had folded up and disappeared, and she had fallen asleep.

Still the telephone rang, and she moved toward the doorway, then out into a dark hall, moved slowly toward their own room at the end of the hall, where she knew there must be a phone. She shook her head, walked with one hand touching the wall as though she might be blind, and she wondered for a moment at the vertigo she felt, the roll of her legs beneath her, the shiver she gave into as she entered their room and aimed for the ringing telephone in the dark.

She made it to the nightstand beside the bed, and picked up the receiver. She put it to her ear, said, "Yes?" Her voice failed her, and the word came out no louder than a whisper. She cleared her throat, said louder, "Hello?"

"Laura? You okay?"

It was Hugh, her husband. She recognized his voice through the blanket of sleep she still carried with her, and she tried to picture him. But all she saw was her son, his eyes and chin and hair and nose, the wash of light in a kitchen with no lights on.

"Laura?" he said again.

"Here," she said. "I'm here." She swallowed, still felt the taste in her mouth. She needed water. She needed coffee. "You woke me. We were just taking a nap." She paused. "Sorry it took so long."

"Lush life," Hugh said and gave a small laugh. "Wish I could take a nap here in the afternoon." She heard the shift of the phone, heard a chair squeak, and believed him to be leaning back there at his desk in the office with glass walls.

"I didn't mean to fall asleep," she said. "Just did." She thought to tell him of their son's face, of snow angels and light through windows, but she could think of no words to give him, none that could convey the feel she'd had, the revelation and hue of the afternoon.

"Well," he said, and she heard him take a deep breath. "Just thought I'd call, tell you I'll be late getting home."

"The snow," she said and felt herself sit up straighter on the edge of the bed.

"Yep," he said.

She touched the back of her neck, closed her eyes, and felt the heat of broken sleep still in her. "I love you," she said.

"Hey," he said, "what's wrong?"

"I can't say I love you?" she said, and now she stood, her eyes on the bright green numbers on the clock beside the phone: *4:14.*

"Sure," he said. "I love you, too," he said. "It's just you don't sound okay. You don't sound like you're okay."

She smiled at his voice, finally saw her husband's face: Hugh. She would tell him what she'd seen in their son when he got home, try to find in words what would match up with how she felt, what she knew. But for now she was still too groggy, too close to sleep, the room too dark for the work she knew it would be.

"I'm just tired," she said. "I just woke up." She paused. "Be careful."

"I will. Got to go," he said, and she could hear his smile, even through the tinge of vertigo she still felt, the listless feel of her legs after two hours curled up on the floor.

She hung up, then went to the foot of the bed, crossed

the room to the bedroom window, and pulled up the wooden blinds.

Snow lay thick across the backyard, covered everything. The seats of the lawn chairs were packed with what looked like a foot of snow. Snow was banked halfway up the back fence. Snow had covered the seats on the swingset, so that she could see only the thin chains from the top crossbar, the chains leading straight down into snow, disappearing there. And snow still swirled down.

She stood there a moment, touched a finger to the cold glass of the window, the other hand still holding the drawstring on the blinds. She saw the condensation of heat from her finger on the glass, saw how the gray silhouette flared up around it.

She eased down the blinds, crossed back to the doorway and into the hall, black now with the coming night, and into Michael's room.

He was still asleep, his back to her, the dinosaur footprint sheet and blanket wrapped about his waist, one arm out before him, touching the wall.

She loved his room, loved the posters on the wall—one of a panda from the San Diego Zoo, where they'd gone when he was still in a stroller; another with the outlines and names of the tracks of all the animals one could find in the Rocky Mountains, sent by her brother; another one, on the closet door: *Jetsons: The Movie*—and she loved the way the room seemed littered with debris: Lego pieces, picture books, a single shoe. One of his chores was to keep his room picked up, but she didn't mind when it got this way. Her son lived in here. It was his room.

There was the smell, too, the hushed infant of it— sometimes she believed she could still take in the traces of baby powder—combined with the boisterous child, the grass stains ground into knees, the sweaty socks. This was his room.

She went to his window, pulled the drawstring on the blue miniblinds, blinds that matched his blue wooden toy box, his blue desk and chair next to the window, a desk always covered with whatever project he was working on, though he was only four and hadn't yet started school. But he was always working, doing things, and this late afternoon in December, the room with whatever small light the afternoon could bear, she saw on his desk the tray of watercolors, the two thin brushes, the pile of printout paper Hugh had brought home for Michael to use.

Outside was only snow. She looked to the left, away from the house toward the woods they had played in earlier. She could see nothing, no evidence of their ever having been outside. Only snow.

She pulled the drawstring to the right, and the shade stayed open. Then she looked at the painting on the desk: nothing she could make out. Only red, she believed—she couldn't say for the dark of the room—and maybe orange, the shape of a house, perhaps, or a strange mountain, and the fact she could not say what it was, the fact the woods bore no witness of them, seemed to make some perfect sense: She still carried with her the confused quality of sleep that started in daylight and ended near dark, the feel that nothing she would encounter the rest of her life would truly make sense, bear logic.

"Mommy," Michael said.

She took in a breath, startled. He was sitting on the edge of the bed, the sheet and blanket pushed away. His hair was wild on his head, sprung up on one side, pushed forward onto his forehead on top.

"You sleepy head," she said. She smiled and held herself.

"Time to go out and play," he said and hopped off the bed. He scratched at his head, yawned, his eyes on her.

She was quiet a moment, glanced beside her out the window. She said, "I think it's too late to go outside. It's almost dark."

She turned to him and smiled.

He came toward her, then stood at the window, both hands on the sill. "Look at all the snow out there!" he said and started bouncing on the balls of his feet. "Look at it!"

"It's almost dark," she said, and she touched his hair, tried to pat down the lock that was twisted up and away. "And we're having a blizzard. A bad snowstorm. So I guess we can't go outside." She paused, then said, "Daddy will be home soon," as though this might be reason enough for Michael not to go outside.

He stopped bouncing, turned, looked up at her.

"You promised," he said.

Most all light was gone now, the hollow of his eyes dark, his face, the side toward the window, washed in gray. She could see his mouth open, hair still just as wild, saw the one hand still on the sill.

He said, "You promised, and you cross your heart, hope to die." He paused, and she could see him swallow. For an instant she wondered if he had the same thick taste in his mouth she had. "That's what you promised," he said.

"That was before you slept so late," she said, tried to fend off his words, the truth of what she'd said.

"You promised," he said again, and now it seemed all light vanished, and she lost in his face what she'd seen earlier, her husband and herself, even that proof of their son disappearing with the light disappearing, until there stood before her only a dark figure, no more distinct than the hulk of her house through snow as she'd driven up this afternoon, no more definable than a watercolor shape on a piece of printout.

"Tomorrow," she said to the figure, this boy.

"You promised," he said again, and left her, disappeared into the dark depths of the room she loved so much.

This was what she tasted on each pill she took: her son's face, the touch of their own blood in his looks, his gestures, his words; that snow, gray light, her son's smell, the feel of his hair.

Her husband gone.

Each morning, when she looked into the mirror, swallowed down the secret and truth of the pill, she tasted again the bewilderment of an afternoon's sleep, a promise broken, a boy's eyes lost to her for the dark. She tasted again the sad fact that promises, like people, were broken more often than kept intact, forces we wish were in our control—snow, the length of a day, the smooth minute before a boy raced down a bus aisle—finally out of our hands.

Each morning she took the pill, swallowed, and tasted her son's life all over again.

☘ THE CAR WAS gone.

She stood on the front porch, before her the wooden walkway over the heaped dirt that lined the road back here. The sun had already cleared the line of trees a mile or so away across the marsh so that she'd had to hold a hand up to shield her eyes.

But the car was gone.

"Miss Walker?" came Roland Dorsett's voice, and Laura blinked, swallowed, quickly turned to it.

He stood at the van parked next door, in his arms a beat-up and oil-stained cardboard box, flaps torn and hanging down so that she couldn't see his arms.

He said, "You all right?"

She tried to smile and swallowed again. She still had a hand up to block the sun, in her other hand the sailboat mug. She looked at where the car had been, where she'd left it last night.

"The car," she said, and turned to him.

He didn't move. He wore glasses, had on the same baseball cap he'd had last night when they'd watched from the bedroom window. But the windbreaker was gone, and he had on a navy blue sport shirt, yellow words she couldn't make out above the shirt pocket. He had on old khaki pants, stains of different colors here and there, a tear at the knee, and wore black high-top tennis shoes.

He looked at her, then smiled a moment, let it go. He said, "Your husband drove it off. Six o'clock on the dot. Yours truly came out, said hello, and he was off." He smiled again, finally turned from the open side door of the van, and took the steps up his own walkway. "Denny's told me more than once your Hugh's a good worker. Good company man."

He was on the porch now, wiped his feet on the mat before the front door. He managed to get a free hand to the doorknob and pushed open the door.

"Oh," Laura said, and forced a laugh before this man would disappear into his house, his presence and his wife's, the woman with fire-engine red shorts and Black Azure hair, suddenly something more necessary than anything she could recall: The car was gone.

The car was gone.

But the laugh she'd forced came out hard and dry and too loud in this new morning air, beneath all this light. "Of course," she said, quieter. She shrugged, brought down her hand, held the mug with both hands. She smiled. "He went to work," she said, and she laughed again, careful with the sound.

He smiled, held the box with both hands again. He nodded at the box, looked back at her. "Breakfast's coming soon as I get this waffle iron geared up," he said and gave the box a quick shake. She heard metal things move. "Supposed to hit eighty today," he said.

Then he went inside, and from behind the house came the hard screech of the power saw: Winnie Dorsett already at work.

She turned to where the car had been, and suddenly the entire day stood before her, staggeringly huge, a giant stone settled at the base of the steps down from their cottage. She'd been the one to remind her husband of the fact he'd have to go back to work today. But how could she have forgotten?

The power saw whined, then stopped.

Simple: There'd been the work of remembering the list this morning, and the work of recalling her husband the night before, behind her and inside her, the two of them engaged in a rote task meant to reenact the conception of their son. And there'd been the work of placing the pill on her tongue.

Facts enough to consume her attention, she knew, while her husband drove north on the Garden State Parkway.

But there was another fact, one she kept low and hidden, let surface only when it seemed she needed to hold onto a moment that belonged to her, a moment so secret, so small and intimate, it would never know any spoken words, never be revealed: Hugh had told her the night she'd informed him she was pregnant that he knew when it had happened, knew it was up in that room at the Craignair in Clark Isle. He *knew* it, he'd said, and had taken her into his arms, danced slowly through the kitchen.

And she'd let him believe this, let him carry it inside him like a piece of good luck, his belief in his own ability to divine the point from which that life had begun, when in fact she'd known it was on another night, once they were back home from vacation, when she'd felt him move beside her in the middle of the night, and the two had made love nearly in their sleep, no words between them, no moment she could actually remake into a waking one, the two of them simply moving together in the dark, shadowed face to shadowed face, her legs around him, their two bodies the warmth of sleep as they moved together.

She hadn't gotten out of bed that night, hadn't gone to the bathroom, but instead had drifted back to sleep when he had finished, her husband slipping back into sleep just as easily.

This was the night, she knew, the two of them sleeping through conception their fourth month at trying; the next morning she'd awakened with the dream of their making love small and quiet in her head, her T-shirt still on, her underwear somewhere beneath the sheets at the foot of the bed. Once Hugh'd left for Hess, herself ready to walk out the door for work at Princeton Memorial, she'd looked at her Hallmark pocket calendar and counted the days since her last period had begun: fifteen.

She'd left for work then, the car almost driving itself along 522, trees beside the road the cool green of May, the farmland with new growth, only rows of green nothings she couldn't yet name, but growth all the same. And, once she'd gotten up to ICU, seen the new girl, Cyndie, off to sleep her day away, it'd seemed to Laura none of the patients on the ward would die, that each of them— Mr. Sunderland and his quadruple bypass; the teenager, new since yesterday, who'd lost an arm and leg in a motorcycle accident; even Mrs. Titiano, here for twenty-nine days, unconsciously awaiting her death at the hands of a cancer that'd been detected only two months before—would survive this, live to see light through trees on a winding country road, or wake in the middle of a night to the warmth of a husband or wife.

Then, thirteen days later, there had come no blood, nor on the fourteenth day, nor the fifteenth, and so on, until she came home from Dr. Bolchoz's office and waited in the kitchen for her husband to come home from his job. Then he had made his declaration: "You remember that night, the last night up in Maine?" he'd begun.

She'd smiled through his words, nodded through his

solid belief in himself, and kept all the while, even through his waking her the night after they'd buried their son to make love to her that way they had in Maine, her truth: They'd both slept through making their son.

So that, though her husband believed himself to be mourning their child, proclaimed himself to be "remembering" him, it was she—the child's mother, for God's sake—who knew the most intimate history of the boy, knew even the night upon which he'd been conceived, knew the nine months and six days she had carried him, could still feel where his feet had been beneath her sternum, knew where his elbows were when he'd jabbed her from the inside, this the most intimate a human could ever be with another, his growing inside her a conjunction of blood and bone that made mere sex and its proximities of flesh seem only emblem, nothing more than the brief agreement of two bodies to find a third.

The power saw screeched again. She turned back to the door, saw her hand move to the knob for no reason she knew: There was nothing inside there she needed or could use.

But the car was gone.

The power saw stopped, and she heard from the back of their house words shouted out to open sea air: "Goddammit, Roland!"

Her hand hesitated only a moment before it let go the knob. Then she turned, moved onto the walkway and down the steps to the empty place where the car had been, walked right through the huge stone there, headed for what might come on a day as sparkling and hollow as this.

For a moment, as she made her way along the porch toward where she heard the power saw start up again, she thought of their van, tried to picture these two allowing her to borrow it, letting her get away from here to the places on her list.

The van had a shiny metal ram's head as big as a fist for a hood ornament, and as she'd walked between the houses she'd seen it had Pennsylvania license plates, a license plate holder that read:

NO JOB—NO MONEY

I MUST BE RETIRED

She pictured herself rolling along the roads down here in a dark blue van, waffle irons and power saws and whatever else they kept in the back of the thing sliding back and forth with each turn she took, her presence made more anonymous because of the Pennsylvania plates: Nobody'd know then that she even lived in this state. She was just passing through, two hands on the wheel, clenched between the fingers of one a list of places she had to get to.

"Miss Walker," Roland Dorsett's voice came to her once again, this time from just beside her, and she turned, saw the man inside the open window next to her.

She smiled at him, and leaned to the screen. She could see him inside now, the bottom of the window even with the kitchen counter. He held a pair of tongs in one hand, had the baseball cap pushed back and high on his forehead. She smelled food. She smelled coffee.

She said, "I hope you don't mind my coming over."

"You don't know what a pleasure it is having company down here this time of the year," he said. He smiled, shook his head, and touched the bill of his cap. He left the counter before her then, turned to the stove to her left and a frying pan there. He touched at something in

90

it with the tongs. "But you come on in now. We're about to get this shindig going."

"Okay," she said, turned from the window and continued to the back.

There, at the far end of the back porch, stood Winnie Dorsett between two sawhorses, her back to Laura. Across the sawhorses was a length of white vinyl siding. Winnie turned on the power saw, its shrill whine even louder than Laura could have imagined, and cut through the siding, two pieces falling to the deck when she was finished.

Winnie turned around, the power saw still in her hands. She had on safety goggles and only glanced at Laura, then went around the sawhorse closest to the dock, placed the saw on a wooden table, nothing more than two-by-fours and a sheet of plywood pushed into the corner of the porch.

Winnie turned, started working off the leather gloves she wore. They were old and stained, but looked soft, and Laura wanted to feel them, wanted to know the jarring burst of a power saw in her hands.

Winnie was smiling, and as she came closer, Laura could see the flecks of white plastic that dusted her forearms and the red shorts.

"You're going to love this sausage we got for you," Winnie said. She had the gloves off, slapped them on the tops of her thighs, and brushed away the dust on her arms. "This siding," she said, not leaving room for Laura to speak, though Laura'd had no words lined up. "Cuts like a son of a bitch. Alcoa. Bear down on it a little too fast and the edge goes all raggedy on you. Shoots dust out on you like a ticker tape parade."

She looked up at Laura, smiled, and Laura knew it was her turn to speak.

"I love sausage," she said, and felt stupid for the words. She took in a small breath, managed a smile.

"Roland's specialty, one of a thousand specialties," Winnie said. She lifted up the bottom edge of her blouse, quickly tucked the gloves into the waistband of her shorts, then brought down the blouse again. She put her hands on her hips and looked at Laura. She tilted her head one way, then the other, sizing her up.

But Laura was still trying to put away in its proper place the ease with which this woman had tucked in those gloves, the natural quickness of the move, as though that place at her waist, snug against her tummy, were the only logical place on earth those gloves could go.

"It's just a pair of gloves, sugar," Winnie said. She shook her head, eyes still on Laura.

"Oh," Laura said, and felt herself blush. She smiled again. "I'm sorry. I—"

"Nothing to be sorry about," Winnie said, and then her hand was at Laura's shoulder, and she was turning her toward the house, ushering her toward the sliding glass door they had out onto the porch, the same sort of door the Halfords had. "You just haven't had any breakfast yet," Winnie said.

Laura felt herself nod. "That's it. That's all it is," she said, and hoped the words were true.

"Made these myself," Roland Dorsett said, and set the plate of sausages down in the middle of the table.

Laura'd already buttered her waffle and was pouring syrup on it when she saw them. They were huge, maybe a foot long apiece, and the plate was heaped with them.

"Put a couple more on than usual," Roland said, "seeing as how we got company this morning." Laura looked up at him, and he winked, smiled. He had a dish towel over one shoulder, and pulled it off, tossed it to the counter before he sat. *USS Yorktown CV 10* were the words on his shirt, the same words as on the baseball cap. "Got out the good china, too," he said.

Laura laughed, careful again not to make the sound seem forced: None of their plates matched, nor did any of the silverware or the juice glasses. The only things that matched on the table were their coffee mugs: thick white ceramic ones, plain and perfect.

Winnie reached to the plate and forked off two links. She said, "Roland's got a grinder and pump at home, left over from the old days. He makes this stuff rain or shine all year long. Surprised our hearts haven't burst for it yet."

Roland took three for himself. Winnie started cutting up one of the links, then stopped. She held a fork in one hand, a knife in the other, and looked at Laura.

Laura reached to the plate and pulled off a link for herself, tried to make room for it next to the waffle.

She cut off a piece of the sausage, brought it up. She smiled at them, then put it in her mouth.

The flavor blossomed on her tongue, and she chewed it slowly, carefully, tasted in it spices and herbs and sweet ground meat.

They were both looking at her, neither one eating.

She swallowed, said, "This is wonderful."

"Another satisfied customer," Roland said, and started in on his own.

They ate, neither Roland nor Winnie speaking much after that. Laura wondered at the two of them, wondered if this weren't how every meal this strange and perfect couple spent: quietly shoveling down sausages and waffles. Roland made another batch of waffles in the ancient stainless-steel iron that sat on the counter, then another. The waffle iron was round and scratched and shiny, and the steam up off it as new batter cooked inside, that smell and the smell of fresh sausage seemed the most lovely gift she could have received on a day that'd begun as it had. This day still sparkled, but the hollow feel of no car and no way to move from one real place to another had already begun to fall.

She knew she could have taken yet another walk along the beach up past the pylons or back along the road that fronted the cottages. But she'd done both already the first two days they had been down here, and had found on the beach nothing more than dozens of horseshoe crab skeletons, some as big as spare tires, littering the sand. She'd bent to one the first time she'd headed away from the house, late the afternoon she'd found the lighthouse and the first set of rows of flyers. She'd turned the thing over—it was the same color green as an army helmet, the size of a hubcap—with a stick, only to find the insides of the thing shriveled and brown, collapsed and decayed. She hadn't touched any others since then.

The afternoon of the second day she'd walked up the road from their dead end, passed house upon house that seemed no better than abandoned. There were house trailers here, and shacks, and what seemed broken-down houses ready to collapse in heaps where they stood. There were three or four places as nice as the Halfords', all of them on the water, and as she walked, she'd felt the water beside her the entire time, even when she couldn't see it for the houses, so that she'd been able to understand why people would want to come all the way down here to spend summers in shacks that might be only mounds of sticks when they came back the next year: It was that water, the light off it, the smell and taste of it, the sound of it everywhere you turned every moment.

But it had been that same quiet, the empty wash of it,

that had echoed in her too loudly; the road seemed a cavern to her, the houses sheer cliff walls, the water behind them some great and endless plain.

Hugh, of course, was back at the house.

She reached the end of the road at the opposite end of Reed's Beach only to find yet another empty house, this one with a No Trespassing sign nailed to the mailbox stand. A rusted chain hung from two short posts at either end of the mouth of the dirt driveway; beside the house was a pile of bald tires as high as the eaves.

There, tied off at the center of the chain, had been a torn and muddied strip of red cloth. It was nothing, really, only a small signal to whoever might not see the chain and was thinking of turning into the driveway of this broken-down beach cottage. The house was painted a dull red, more paint chipped away than still on the wood; a huge set of bleached antlers hung at the peak of the roof; a basketball hoop was nailed to a post across from the tires, no backboard, no net.

But there'd been something in how the beach wind that afternoon twisted at the piece of red cloth, made it dance in a way she hadn't imagined a piece of cloth could play, until she'd found herself staring at the cloth, and the chain.

She stared, and stared, afraid to let go of it with her eyes until, finally, she shuddered. It was only a piece of red cloth, but she'd turned from it, jammed her hands as deep as she could into the pockets of her jacket, and walked. She walked as quickly as she could, her head down. The wind was in her face as she walked, blew her hair back and away from her; her ears were cold and felt brittle. She only looked up once she'd made it to the little fork in the road, where Dorsett's Marlinspike General Store sat like a faded yellow box, square and impenetrable.

She'd stopped then, discovered she was out of breath, and found her face was wet from tears she hadn't known she'd given up. She brushed at her face, took in deep breaths to fill her lungs, and found it impossible, each breath minuscule.

She'd bent over, hands on her knees, taking in those useless breaths on the porch of the store. Then she'd stood, hands on hips, still trying for air that seemed not to be there, and she'd slowly gone to the only window on the front of the building, the old 7-Up sign still blinking on and off.

She looked in the window, the sound she made as she grabbed for air too loud, the sound of waves gone for her own shallow breaths in and out.

It was dark inside, but she'd thought she could make out a long deli case against the far wall, the glass of it, the white enamel paint, inside it empty metal shelves. To her left, by the front entrance, was a counter and register, above it, hanging from the low ceiling, racks for cigarettes. To the right, back in the dark of the building, she could see the ends of four grocery aisles going off into the black. As far as she could tell, the shelves there were empty, too.

Hung on the wall behind the deli case she thought she saw five or six of those sailor knot boards just like the one that hung in the front room of the Halfords', the varnished knots in rows, beneath them written in white paint those odd names. Sheep's Head, was one she remembered.

Finally she got her breath back, and turned, stepped off the porch, slowly started down the road toward the Halfords' place, heavy in her the emblem, for whatever it was worth, of a strip of red cloth on a rusted chain, beach wind twisting the scrap as it pleased. That, and rows of empty grocery shelves, a deli case standing empty, the silence of the tide.

All the more reason, she thought, to stick to her lists of places to visit, destinations she'd have to drive to in order to visit. Just not Reed's Beach.

And here she sat, in a kitchen not a stone's throw from the Halfords' place, a kitchen that suddenly seemed vaguely familiar somehow: There was the white stove and dishwasher, both new. There were the cupboards made from what looked like teak and the dark green Formica counters. The place seemed familiar, then she remembered having watched this same couple last night, moving in and out, in and out, her own silent and brooding husband standing still beside her.

Roland and Winnie Dorsett finished their meal at what seemed to Laura precisely the same moment: The two of them pulled napkins from their laps, wiped their mouths, and pushed their plates to the middle of the table.

Laura was working on her second link, her third waffle, and smiled at them, pulled up her own napkin, pushed away her own plate.

"Now don't go doing that," Roland said, and he shook his head, sighed. "We're just old people is all. We get so much in synch with each other we don't have to say more than twenty words in a day. We're done, but that don't mean you have to be."

"No," Laura said and smiled. "No. I usually only have toast and a cup of coffee. I've already made a pig of myself." She wadded the napkin and laid it beside her plate. But the truth was she would have wanted to finish the sausage, it was so wonderful.

"To work," Winnie said and stood. She dropped her napkin on her plate, then picked it up and took it to the sink. She ran water, started rinsing off the plate, and said over her shoulder, "Seeing's how your husband took off with the car, maybe you'd want to stay around, give us a hand with this job."

"Outside work," Roland said, and now he stood, took his plate to the sink, handed it to Winnie. He turned, leaned against the counter, then looked out the sliding glass door. "This weather's supposed to last until sometime tonight or so, and we've been cramped up in here doing the inside renovation since November. This is the first weekend since then we been able to get outside—"

"What do you mean 'we'?" Winnie said without looking at him.

He was quiet, still with his eyes out to the ocean beyond the porch and dock. He said, "But it's outside work, and we figured on getting the siding up on the back here, maybe even working off the old stuff on the front."

"In case you haven't noticed," Winnie said, and she turned, crossing her arms, the plates in the sink now. She looked at Roland. "It's me doing that outside work, not you. So don't be talking like you're the architect and carpenter both."

Roland looked at Laura and smiled. "She gets like this when I step on her turf. Feisty."

Laura stood then, came around the table toward the sink with her plate. Already she believed in the two of them, knew this banter was what went on whether some witness were here or not. They were real, as real as anything she might put on her list.

Laura smiled, said, "Now let me get this straight." Roland pushed himself along the counter toward Winnie, clearing the way to the sink. "You," she said, nodding at Winnie, who still stood with her arms crossed, "are the Armed Forces."

"You got it," Winnie said.

"Now come on," Roland said, and he uncrossed his

arms, pointed at the words on his shirt. "USS *Yorktown* CV 10," he said. "WW Two. Don't that count for something?"

"And you," Laura said. She pointed at Roland with her fork and set the plate in the sink. "You," she said, "are the USO."

Winnie laughed, pushed herself away from the counter. She turned and moved to the table, put a hand to the back of a chair, the other holding her side as she laughed. "The USO," she laughed.

Laura smiled at Roland, who shook his head. He pulled the cap down low on his face so that it touched the top of his glasses.

"Who invited you over here anyway?" he said.

"You did," Winnie said. She was still laughing, both hands to her side.

"Now if you'll excuse us to the trenches," Laura said, and the words from her, the sound of laughter in the room, the cool and brand-new air through open windows in the middle of February, all of it mixed together just then to make a moment she couldn't have believed might come when she'd stood outside the Halfords' place to find the car gone.

Laura smiled up at Roland Dorsett, who still shook his head. She stepped around him and headed toward Winnie, already turned herself, hands still at her side as the two of them made their way outside.

"Hey!" Roland hollered then, and Laura and Winnie turned.

He was quiet a moment, the smile gone. He reached to the counter, picked up the dish towel, and slapped it over his shoulder.

He smiled. "More coffee, sailors?" he said.

☘ **"HE WAS A COOKIE** on the *Yorktown*," Winnie said. She knelt to the long box of uncut vinyl pieces, each about twenty feet long. The cardboard box lay along the side porch that didn't face the Halfords', and hand over hand Winnie pulled out a piece from the open end. "He was there when it sunk at Midway," she said.

Laura hadn't asked anything, only reached down to pick up her end of the piece.

"No no, sugar," Winnie said, and Laura looked at her.

"You have to squat to lift. You can't bend over and lift, even if it weighs as little as this crap does," Winnie said, and Laura could see the concern on her face, how her eyebrows pinched together, her mouth pursed. "You have to lift with your legs, not your back. Believe me, I've been there and back again."

Laura nodded as though she'd never heard this news before, then squatted just as Winnie had and lifted her end of the vinyl. It weighed nothing.

They'd only worked halfway up the wall on the left side of the sliding window, Winnie measuring each piece with a tape measure she kept clipped to the waistband of her shorts when she wasn't using it. Before cutting a piece of siding, Winnie would lift up her blouse just as she had to put away the gloves, then take out the tape measure, hand it to Laura, who stood at the corner of the house. Winnie pulled the tape out until she touched the sliding window. "Seventy-eight and a quarter," she'd holler out each time, and Laura wondered why she had to measure every length if it was always the same. But she hadn't the courage to ask, figuring only that Winnie would let her know what she needed to know; questions seemed useless.

There was nothing about the work they were doing that Laura wanted to ask about, no questions she had the courage to pursue, afraid that, were she to seem too stupid, too tool illiterate, Winnie Dorsett and her hair might dismiss her, relegate her to the kitchen and her husband, in there washing dishes, straightening up, making more coffee right then. Or, worse yet, to the house next door, with its properly sequenced *National Geographics*.

Yet there were things she still wanted to know, so that when suddenly, Winnie kneeling at the box of uncut siding, there had come this bit of information—her husband had been a cook in the navy—she believed this to be her avenue in, her way of finding out what she needed to know, just as she'd found out what she'd needed to know at the bird sanctuary, at the lighthouse, and cruising up and down the streets of the Villas and Highlands Beach: those homes where the real people who lived down here year-round resided, small houses with Big Wheels and bicycles littered across gray lawns, some with Christmas lights still up, empty garbage cans at the curb, cracked concrete sidewalks.

They carried the siding piece to the sawhorses, then went through the ritual: Winnie reaching to her waist to reveal the tape measure, Laura's lifted hand to receive it, the two of them walking to their appointed places

101

alongside the house, Winnie's hollered words: "Seventy-eight and a quarter."

They returned to the sawhorse, Laura holding on to the end of the piece they would attach to the house.

Only after she'd been sprayed with dust yet again, the power saw off, did she ask, "What happened?"

Winnie stopped, looked at her. "To what?" she said. She went to the wooden table, put the power saw there.

"The *Yorktown*, I guess," she said, and shrugged. Already she was sorry for her words, that *I guess* certain sign of insecurity. "At Midway," she said, and smiled, tilted her head.

"God almighty," Roland said, and then he was sliding open the screen, was out on the porch.

"You asked for it," Winnie said.

She reached for the piece of siding in Laura's hands, and in Winnie's move Laura saw that in fact she had revealed herself to be an idiot, suddenly incapable, in Winnie Dorsett's eyes, of even snapping the siding to the house or of holding a tape measure.

Winnie took hold of it, but Laura held on, something rising in her just then, breaking surface with the pull of Winnie's hand.

"I can do it," Laura said, and though she tried hard to keep her smile, she felt it disappear, gone with the vague notion that this morning and whatever territory she'd hewed out here was about to disappear as well.

Suddenly she knew it was the Halfords' house next door, its immense emptiness, that was rising in her, the day still a huge stone but one settled now in her throat, constricting the muscles to her hands as she held tight to the piece of white siding Winnie'd cut only a moment before.

"You never heard of the *Yorktown?*" Roland said, and Laura looked at him an instant, his cap pushed back on his head again. The towel was gone from his shoulder, a thick wet stripe left where it had been. "You don't know about Midway?"

Laura's eyes went to Winnie, who glanced up at her yet again, then back to their hands, the two of them in a tug of war that lasted only a moment, only enough time for a man to walk out onto a porch, stand and inquire.

Winnie's eyes fixed on Laura's. She held Laura's eyes a moment too long, Laura knew, an instant too far, and Laura knew, too, that Winnie'd seen inside her eyes what Laura needed to keep hidden all this time, what she needed to hold onto harder and stronger than any piece of siding the two of them could ever cut.

Winnie let go.

"My," she whispered, and took a step back. She put her hands in front of her, laced the fingers together.

Laura took a breath and swallowed. "Let me," she whispered.

"I'm here to tell you what was the greatest battle in the history of warfare," Roland said. "Period."

"My, my," Winnie whispered again.

Her eyes were still on Laura, then she turned, quickly worked off the gloves as she headed toward Roland. But instead of tucking them into her shorts, she set them on the end of a sawhorse.

She stood before Roland, her face up to his. "We girls got to be heading out now," she said to him. "We need to head over to the Ace for some duct tape and whatnot."

Roland looked down at her, eyebrows up in surprise. He touched a hand to his shoulder, as though he'd expected to find the towel there. But it was gone. "We got duct tape in the Pine Sol box in the van," he said. "You know that."

"Then it's the whatnot we're after," she said.

She looked at Laura. She nodded and said, "Put that

piece down now, and we'll get on out of here. You and me got things to do."

She turned, headed around her husband and into the house.

Laura stood with the siding in her hand. She looked at Roland, then set the piece on the wooden table beside her.

Roland took off his baseball cap, revealed his shiny bald head, around it a silver fringe of hair. He slapped the hat at the tops of his legs, as though he were covered with dust from freshly cut siding.

But his pants were clean, as she knew his hands must have been, too, just having finished dishes she herself had dirtied.

She wanted to hear about the *Yorktown*, wanted to hear of the greatest battle in the history of warfare.

But there was a van out front, and she and Winnie had already sworn some secret pact she could not yet know. All she knew was that their eyes had met, and that Winnie'd let go. And she knew with no more than a single uttered word—*My*—that the death of her only child shone through her eyes no matter how hard she tried not to let it.

It hadn't been the Halfords' house, its emptiness, that had risen in her, she realized. The house, the kitchen table, the haunted attic, even the bed in which they had made love last night were all only symptoms. What had surfaced in her was her son's death once again.

Roland shrugged, put the cap back on. He said, "She's got a mind of her own, no doubt about it." He paused, crossed his arms, all serious, and said, "You know, Denny told us all about what you two been through."

"Rollie!" Winnie shouted from inside. "You just shut the hell up!"

"Oh," Laura said, his words no surprise at all. Nothing

was a surprise now. Surprise had ended with the immeasurable black surprise of Michael's death. Surprise no longer existed.

He cleared his throat and gave a glance over his shoulder at the house. He smiled, put the cap back on, then crossed his arms again, squared himself. He looked down at the deck, up at her again. "Whatever you need, you let us know," he said. "You count on us."

She stood before him, her chest tight, her breath gone shallow. Even though there'd been no surprise in his words, still his words had landed squarely beneath her sternum, that same place where her son had kicked from the inside so many years ago.

She attempted another smile, but found nothing. Then, because it seemed the only thing to do, she went to the sawhorse and picked up the gloves. They were as soft as velvet in her hands, and she looked at them, touched the stains across the palms and on the backs of the fingers.

She found a breath, swallowed. "A wonderful breakfast, outside work," she said, uncertain her words would mean anything.

She looked up at him. His hands were on his hips, his head down again, eyes locked on the wood a few feet before him, as though he'd been caught at something. "Thanks," he said and gave a quick nod without looking up.

"Couldn't have started any better than this," she said. She looked again at the gloves, worn and stained and purely necessary.

"Well," Winnie said, and Laura looked up, saw her just behind Roland, who turned to her, too, and took a step back.

She had lipstick on, a color as red as her shorts—Flame Red, Laura wondered, Classic Red?—and had penciled in her eyebrows a bit. Hung from the crook of her arm was a black patent leather purse the size of a boot box.

She cut her eyes at them both, first to Roland, then to Laura.

She said, "It's still only a pair of gloves, sugar. You want, we'll buy you a pair at the Ace." She paused, glanced at her husband again, then turned and headed around the side of the house. "We'll be back," she called out.

"Counting on it," Roland said.

Laura quickly put the gloves back on the sawhorse, felt her face go hot. For a moment she thought of heading over to the house next door for the list of places tucked inside the book of advertisements.

"Better get a move on," Roland said, and touched the bill of his cap, nodded. "She's not known for waiting around for things to happen."

"That's good," Laura said, and she started for the side porch, the list on the paper suddenly and miraculously clear in her.

She left him there, heard from out front the slam of a car door, the engine rev up.

But she stopped and turned back to Roland.

He stood facing her, the gloves in his hand.

He said, "She's had this pair for a good thirty years." He paused. "Takes a hell of a long time to get a pair into this kind of shape."

She said, "I've got time." She shrugged.

Winnie honked the horn, and she turned, ran for the van.

SHE WAS IN a van, and she was moving. That was what mattered.

"Where to?" Winnie said. They were at the end of Reed's Beach Road, before them Route 47, blacktop.

Laura turned to her, saw she had both hands on the steering wheel. She was looking at Laura, on her face no smile. She simply waited for an answer.

"What happened to the Ace?" Laura said. "That's the hardware store, right?"

"Nothing gets past you, does it?" Winnie said, then reached to the black knob on the gear shift between them and worked the metal rod with a grace Laura knew she'd never find.

From the rearview mirror hung a silver crucifix that swung with the right turn, toward the Villas and Cape May; wedged between the windshield and the blue metal dashboard was an array of receipts and fast-food wrappers, a flattened Burger King cup, the straw still poking out of it. The upper right corner of the windshield was cracked, a single line a few inches long that weaved through the dark blue tint across the top of the windshield. Loose at Laura's feet were a paint-stained screwdriver, a pair of pliers, and a small red fire extinguisher.

107

On the floorboard between them sat Winnie's purse and Laura's straw handbag; she'd retrieved it from the Halfords' bathroom while Winnie'd waited in the van. She'd touched nothing else, not even the list inside the advertisements on the kitchen table. Her maps and brochures were superfluous, she knew, as long as she had her handbag, and as long as she was with Winnie Dorsett.

Winnie had a thick pillow behind her so that she sat forward in her seat, and even then when she jammed in the clutch, she had to scoot to her left and lean forward.

She caught Laura watching her, said, "Don't you worry. I've put at least eighty of the hundred fifty-eight thousand we got on this mule." She scooted back.

"I'm not worried," she said and faced front. "Just looking forward to getting to the Ace."

Winnie was quiet a moment, then said, "We got to get things clear here and now." She pushed in the clutch, shifted again, settled back in her seat.

"Okay," Laura said, and tried to seem as if she did not know what was fast on its way. She turned in her seat, faced Winnie full on. She tilted her head and worked up a smile. She said, "You start."

Winnie kept her eyes on the road. "This may come out sounding like I'm an awful old bitch," she said.

She reached to the window handle beside her, quickly rolled it down, and put her elbow out the window. Immediately Laura's hair picked up on the wind inside the van, and she reached behind her, grabbed as much hair as she could, held it down. Still wisps of it flew, caught in her mouth and eyelashes.

Winnie's hair barely moved with the rush of air, sections of it only buffeted now and again. No single hairs.

"I guess," she started, and she moved in her seat, seemed to settle deeper in it. "I guess I want you to know I just don't have much interest in knowing anything in particular. About, you know." She brought her arm in from the window, gripped the wheel with both hands. "About what Dennis Halford let on had happened to you."

She looked at Laura, who still tilted her head, still held her hair.

"Fact is," Winnie said, "I don't know you nor your husband from Adam, and neither does Roland." She paused, touched a hand to her hair, though Laura hadn't seen it move. She put her elbow back out the window. "But here we are," she said. "And I'm here to tell you no pair of gloves is going to do for you what you need."

She took her eyes from Winnie and faced forward again. She swallowed. "I'm here and heading to the hardware store," she said above the sound of air in the window. She reached to her mouth, pulled a strand away. "That's all I know for certain."

Winnie downshifted, before them the stoplight for 658, the road that led back to Cape May Court House. This was the intersection she and Hugh had sat at that first morning, a morning only four days before but which seemed a year ago. It was at this intersection, she recalled, that she had had to awaken her husband from the waking stupor he seemed to have fallen in, him unable to make the turn toward Reed's Beach. *I don't know if this is a good idea*, he'd said, as though their driving all the way down here and the leave of absence he'd been granted and the loan of the cottage itself were all small errors in judgment, not what might save their lives.

She remembered her own words then, too: *This is the best idea.*

Winnie said, "I give this light another twenty seconds before it changes. Then we're going left to Court House, where the Ace is, for those all-important gloves you want." She paused, looked at Laura. "I've an idea, however, there may be other places we could go."

Laura looked at her. She said, "I don't know you from Adam either."

"Then we're even," Winnie said.

Laura quickly pumped the handle for the window, got it open. She put her elbow out, felt the sun through the sleeve of her sweatshirt.

She looked at Winnie, who sat with both hands still on the wheel, eyes forward, fixed on the light.

She took a breath, then faced forward again, said, "County Museum, Cape May Library, Higbee's Beach Wildlife Area, Cape May Diamonds, the *Atlantus*." The words came all at once, a single jumble of sounds.

"Quite a menu," Winnie said.

The light changed, and she gave it the gas, went straight instead of left.

"But you got it all bass-ackwards, sugar," she said above a wind even louder now, both windows down. "We'll get to the library first, farthest point south. Then we'll hit the diamonds and that godforsaken shipwreck." She shook her head, said, "Higbee's Beach won't be anything but sticks and mud this time of year. But I'll get you there. Then the museum, back up here at the court house." She paused and smiled. She glanced at Laura. "We can hit the Ace last off, get those gloves."

Laura let go her hair then, felt it whip around her, swirl of its own. Her hair danced at her lips and cheeks and ears, and she closed her eyes.

"You lead," she said. She was quiet a moment, the swirling touch of her hair on her face like some sort of mask hovering and touching, hovering and touching. But she did not pull the hair away, only let it fly.

"You lead," she said again, louder, the wind a music of its own in her ears. "But there's something I have to ask," she said, the words gone out of her before she could stop them.

"Ask away," Winnie called out.

"Two things," Laura said and heard her voice ring out above the wind. "First," she said, "are you the Dorsett of Dorsett's Marlinspike General Store?"

"One in the same," Winnie said. "Seventeen years of groceries. The only marlinspike deli on the eastern seaboard. Open every day, first of May through to the last of September." She was quiet, then added, "Small boat repairs and house renovations October to April."

Laura believed she could hear Winnie nodding through her answer, proud of herself and her husband both. Seventeen years, she thought, then took in the last of her answer: House renovations.

"You own the house you're in, right?" Laura said, and now her eyes shot open. She squinted a moment for the light that broke into her, then looked at Winnie.

"Is that question number two?" Winnie said. She had her hands on the wheel, was smiling. "This is a piece of cake."

"Follow-up to number one," Laura said. The spell was still here, she knew, even with her eyes open. There were more houses beside them now, she could see, and more of them closer together: This was the Villas, and she knew for no reason she could say that a pimple-faced boy with red hair in an odd cut lived in one of these small homes with front porches and rusted cars out front, the same old Big Wheels and garbage cans.

"'Nope, it's not ours," Winnie said. "Belongs to a couple by the name of Vigiano, up in Cherry Hill. We'll have the place done before we open up in May. We sign on one house at a time, one a winter, do things right." She glanced at Laura, back to the highway.

Then it came to her: the same sliding glass door as the

Halfords', the familiar feel of the Vigianos' kitchen, the new appliances, the teak cupboards. All of it, even the cool green Formica counters, were the same in the Halfords' kitchen.

Winnie downshifted again. They were nearing another light, this one at an intersection that held a Wawa, an Exxon station, a video store. Laura'd been here before, had driven this road each day she'd headed out on her excursions. Even last night she'd had to pass through here on the way home from the Acme.

Winnie stopped at the light, and now the place was different, the new and warmer air, the slant of the sun making it all over into something wholly new: Truth seemed to fall all around her, spill out the doors of the Wawa, flood the bays of the gas station garage. Hugh, in a fit of labored conversation once they had settled in that first day, had told her of how his boss, Mr. Dennis Halford—Denny to his friends the Dorsetts—had redone the place. Hugh had even pointed out the double-paned windows, the heat registers along the floorboards, the weather stripping in the doorjamb as all being the vice president's handiwork. He'd brought her upstairs and showed her the sheetrock ceiling up there, marveled at a recessed light above the desk: his boss, the carpenter.

She smiled, slowly shook her head. She didn't even have to ask whether or not the Dorsetts had renovated the Halfords' place, a truth given without inquiry, a gift.

"Now she's got the right idea," Winnie said, and Laura turned, saw Winnie nod at something out Laura's window. "That gal there."

Laura looked out her window and saw a girl in cutoff shorts, a tank T-shirt, and thongs climb into an old VW.

Winnie said, "You ought to think on retiring the Rutgers sweatshirt. Weather like this doesn't come through too often."

Laura raked her fingers through her hair, pulled it back and away from her face.

The light changed, and Winnie gave it the gas. The wind started up yet again, and Laura leaned forward in her seat, pulled the sweatshirt over her head. She had a light blue polo shirt on underneath, and immediately her arms covered over in gooseflesh, just as they had in the Halfords' bedroom each morning. She balled up the sweatshirt, stuffed it as best she could into her handbag on the floorboard, then held herself, ran her hands up and down her arms.

"It'll feel warmer in a minute," Winnie said. "You just put your arm out the window there. It'll come." She paused, and more of the same houses passed by. "Now, to your second question."

Laura didn't put her bare arm out the window, not yet convinced that would change things. Instead, she pulled her legs up onto the seat and hugged herself, her chin on her knees. The van banged over more bumps now and again, popped her around in her seat a little, but it was warmer this way, somehow more comfortable than with her feet on the floorboard, loose tools sliding into her feet.

"Your hair," Laura said. "What color is it?"

The question came too quickly, slipped from her without hesitation. But then the ease with which it had come made sense: Truth surrounded her, seemed to arrive just as easily from the Classic Red lips of this woman she did not know.

"Black," Winnie said. "What did you think?" She looked at Laura, her mouth open a bit, as though her question might be the stupidest thing she'd ever heard.

Laura turned, looked forward, found the crack in the windshield. She felt her face go hot, embarrassed for what she'd asked. "I mean what color," she said, "you know, on the box."

Winnie cleared her throat, said, "I'll admit to having my hair done once a week over in Malvern, PA, where we have our house. They lacquer me up so's I don't have to worry over it." She paused, and Laura stole a glance at her, saw she had the elbow out the window again, saw her smiling without opening her mouth, all as though Laura'd seen nothing.

"But the hair," Winnie said, and looked at Laura. Winnie smiled. "This hair is the real thing. I'll be damned if I'll ever let them dye a single hair on my head."

Laura looked at her full on, her hair and its color now something different altogether, a truth past believing.

"I'll take your staring at me as a compliment," Winnie said, and faced front. "But this hair's the real thing."

Laura said nothing, afraid any word might be the wrong one. She only looked at Winnie as though she had no choice, her only option the profile she and her motionless hair and Classic Red lips cut against the blur of South Jersey out her window, while Laura's own hair with its unidentifiable brown flew about her, more furious than ever. Points of it stung her face, struck at her cheeks and eyes and mouth.

Winnie glanced at her again. "Look at you," Winnie said and shook her head. She was still smiling, eyes back to the road. "Stunned by an honest answer and a beautiful head of natural black hair." She paused, then said, "It don't take much to knock a person down, does it?"

Laura held her knees even closer to her chest, let the wind work through her hair. "I guess not," she said.

Finally she turned from Winnie, faced front again, took in the crack in the glass and the trash on the dashboard and the houses they passed one more time, then closed her eyes.

"Doesn't take much at all," Laura said above the roar of the wind and the way it tore at her hair and played with it at once.

But there was one more question she wanted to ask, one that had been in her since she'd first seen Winnie outside her house, the power saw in hand.

Do you have any children? she wanted to ask, right here, right now. *Do you?* she wanted to ask, but the question stayed in her, unwilling to leave.

Three

☙ HUGH LEFT THE radio off. When he'd gone out to the car at six, there'd been in the east only the faintest idea of sunrise, the stars above him sharp and clean, and it'd seemed to him useless to break the quiet and the stars and the near light with whatever radio station he might be able to find down here.

He'd stood at the car, eyes to the gray sky above the jagged line the trees across the marsh made against the horizon, and felt the absence of cold, nowhere in the air the cut it had carried each day here so far, even to last night, only a few hours before, when he'd been out at this same car and digging up groceries.

He'd opened the car door, set his briefcase on the seat, then had taken off his parka, the gloves, tossed them on top of the briefcase. Only then was he cold, the air stiff through the material of his shirt, sharp on his just-shaved face, his tie already tied and tight at his throat.

It was what he wanted, this cold. It was what he needed, he felt, in order to maintain the sense of detail he took in, the importance of making all things he knew over into his son and his memory.

Cold air on his skin.

He took in a breath, but felt on the air in his lungs

119

that the depth of cold was only relative; inside him, the air didn't cut at all. The temperature—forty-five, he thought, maybe fifty—wouldn't last long, would shoot up as soon as the sun broke above those trees.

But for now it was cold.

"Just like I told you last night," Roland Dorsett said from behind him, and Hugh turned, saw the old man standing at the top of the steps to his porch. He was fully dressed, had the billed cap on, a blue short-sleeved shirt, khaki workpants. He held a white coffee mug with both hands.

"Excuse me?" Hugh said and glanced to the east again, then back to the man he'd watched playing Uno the night before. He wondered if the man's wife was up yet, the woman with the hair and the lips.

"Just like I told you last night," Roland Dorsett said. He looked up to the sky, nodded. "That wind up from the South. This is going to be one fine day. A day like this," he said, his eyes back to Hugh now, "you can't begin to figure how fine it's going to be."

"Well," Hugh said. He shrugged. The car door stood open, his parka and gloves on the seat, beneath them his briefcase, ready for a day at Hess, a day, he figured, that could be no better than any of the days he worked there. Only this day there was a two-and-a-half-hour drive tacked on to it.

"Well," he said again.

"That's a deep subject," Roland Dorsett said, and chuckled. He took a sip of the coffee.

Hugh had smiled, shaken his head at the man, and started to climb into the car, his moves calculated to show Roland Dorsett he was in on his small joke, bore him no ill will, but wanted away from him just the same.

But Roland Dorsett had only taken a step down from

120

the porch, then another, as though he were planning to follow Hugh all the way to Woodbridge.

"You had coffee yet?" Roland said and stopped on the last step before the road. He took a hand from the mug and pointed with his thumb behind him. "You won't believe the donuts I make. A fresh pot of coffee and a couple-three donuts'll make you a brand-new man."

"Rollie!" came the woman's voice from inside, disembodied: Hugh could see her nowhere. "Let the poor man get to work. He's got a hell of a drive in front of him."

"The wife," Roland said, both hands on the mug again. He shrugged.

Rollie, Hugh thought. And Denny, and Sal. And Winnie, he remembered: this man's wife. *Where did these names come from?*

"She's right," Hugh said. "Two-and-a-half hours from here." He paused, one foot already on the floorboard, his body halfway in. "I've already had a couple cups. But thanks."

Then he had climbed in, settled himself in the seat, pulled closed his door.

Roland had taken a step back up toward his porch, then turned as Hugh started the engine, gave it the gas. He turned the headlights on, the light slicing away the quiet gray of a morning before dawn, just as the old man's words had cut through the quiet cold he'd been holding onto for however small a time he had left.

That had been two hours ago, traffic on the Parkway churning up the closer he got to work. And he hadn't yet turned on the radio, the silence in the car even larger now, not even his wife here with him to help him find accommodation to the absence of sound. He pictured her back at the cottage, still sleeping after last night, he imagined, or maybe up and doing whatever it was she

121

would do without the car. He imagined her staying out on the porch all day, sipping coffee, or maybe off on one of her walks up or down the beach: the only options she would have until he came back.

He saw that in the silence of the car, and in the growing February light around him, his only option for the entire ride up, even until he arrived back at the Halfords' cottage and the room upstairs, was to remember his son and events and reminders and days. If he couldn't remember the anonymous days of his son's life, then his memory of his son was somehow worthless, hard and cold and dull at once.

The silence of this drive was what he wanted, just as he'd wanted the cold on his skin, just as he'd wanted only the moonlight through the octagonal window last night, and the feel of the sextant in his hands. There was a perfection he thought he might be able to find in remembering his son this trip, so that he measured miles through the brown and gray woods beside him with moments he could recall, offered up with each green mile marker, each toll booth, each highway sign.

Small things came to him: the brown of his son's irises, the way light came to them and shone there, the whites of his eyes a white so clear and perfect he knew there would never be anything any whiter, any clearer. There had come, too, the touch of the boy's hand, the way his son's hand in his own had changed from the tight clutch of a fist around the tip of his index finger in the hospital the morning he had been born, to a succession of hands all in a moment: next the hold so tight he thought his index fingers would turn blue as his son, before him with his arms up and holding to both of Hugh's hands, took first steps across the carpet in the apartment in Woodbridge; next, the feel of his son's fingers around his index and middle finger, then around three fingers, and four, then his son insisting he had to hold hands palm to palm, like grown-ups did, until, finally, Hugh was left with his hand empty, his son finding in his own time that he hadn't the need for his father's hand as they crossed parking lots, or as they walked through malls, or as they moved upstairs to bed each night. This succession of hands belonged to the same child, one who grew and grew along the Garden State Parkway, so that Hugh had found himself suddenly at the Toms River toll booth, his own empty hands holding tight to the steering wheel, one of them letting go of its own and fishing from his pocket a token, tossing it to a mesh basket that seemed a hundred yards away. The light turned green, a horn sounded behind him, and he gave it the gas, emerged from the booth into the same emptiness and silence he wanted with him, cars speeding around and away from him.

Even in the midst of more traffic the closer he came to work, the sun low above the trees that lined the highway on his right so that the visor did nothing to block it from his face, he saw his son in a thousand moments, the sheer volume of the images he had a joy to him and a weight. He'd found what he'd wanted, an unbroken, seemingly endless line of moments, only now to have them roam inside him at will, as though his having wept last night at the sight of a deck of cards and a couple playing away were some floodgate that had been opened. Here was Michael, the floor of his room carpeted with bits of Lego of all shapes and sizes, bursts of red and yellow and blue and white and black, in his son's hands an impossibly elaborate airplane he'd devised by himself: seven wheels, five wings, a cockpit at front and rear. Hugh remembered standing at the door into the boy's room, and watching, his son bent to the task of finding precisely the correct and necessary piece. "Flat black four by eight," he'd heard his son whisper, "flat black four by eight, flat black four by eight," his son on his knees, the model in one hand, the other sifting through the Lego pieces before him.

He saw his son in Laura's parents' backyard in Matawan, a yard in a hilly and fenceless neighborhood, one yard bleeding into another so that his son could climb the grassy slope behind her parents' house to the top of a rise three yards away, where he would lie on the grass, arms extended above his head and parallel to the ground, then roll down the hill for what must have seemed to Michael a mile. He never tired of it, Hugh remembered; his son smiling the entire time, that smile disappearing for an instant with each turn, then reappearing, disappearing again, Michael endlessly turning and turning in spring and summer grass, then through leaves in the fall. Only once there was snow on the ground would he surrender himself to the sled his grandfather kept in the rafters in the garage, the slope miraculously changed into a sledding run that ended at the base of the fireplace at the back of the house, so that on snowy Sunday afternoons Hugh and Laura and his in-laws spent reading or talking or playing cards in the living room, all they could hear from outside were the muffled thumps of the sled against brick all afternoon.

But it was his son rolling down the hill that came to him most vividly, his son's flickering smile unadorned and beautiful. The only embellishment he could recall of the clean and precise joy his son must have felt rolling down the hill, and the same joy Hugh himself felt watching him, was the memory of one evening in early summer when Hugh and his father-in-law were barbequeing hamburgers out on the brick patio. Laura had leaned out the sliding glass door onto the porch and hollered to Hugh, "Call Michael in. Time to clean up for dinner." Hugh had looked up to the hill then, spatula in hand, his father-in-law talking on about new rate hikes for his parking spot at the station, and Hugh had watched as his son rolled yet again downhill, a Mickey Mouse T-shirt on, blue shorts, barefoot.

Then had come the detail that only now seemed a miracle: At that instant the fireflies started in, dusk closing around them all, and suddenly his son seemed framed in fragile light, shooting stars come to earth to illuminate Michael in a way he could not have imagined possible. The fireflies and their immaculate and delicate light swirled and circled, flickered as did his son's own smile.

And there came to him again the picture of Michael and Laura playing Uno, his son's legs kicking endlessly beneath him, his son moving and moving, and already he was on the bridge over the Raritan, cars maneuvering around him for no apparent reason, it seemed, and suddenly he could not recall having stopped at the last two tolls, could not recall having opened his window and tossing into the mesh basket his tokens. He was only traveling in one of a half-dozen lanes of traffic, spread before him central Jersey, the Hess building already visible in the distance, the air crisp and clean and clear.

Yet even with his destination now in sight, there still swirled in him the triumph of this trip: a silence that had allowed the anonymous moments to surface unbidden: He saw his son and the boy next door, Gerry Rothberg, standing at the Staten Island Ferry terminal, the two boys in colorful parkas, Michael's a bright blue with neon green stripes across the shoulders, Gerry's black with neon pink stripes down the sleeves. Both boys had on orange wool caps and stood at one of the windows, their backs to Hugh, their hands pressed to the glass and making gray silhouettes, though the boys did not notice. They were waiting for the next ferry to the city, where

Hugh and Gerry's father, Ted, and the boys would spend the March day at South Street Seaport, maybe stop in at Ted's office on the fifty-first floor of the Trade Center to see what they could see. Boy's Day Out, they had all called it.

But Hugh, the bridge behind him, signs starting up that said he ought to be in the right lane in order to make the ramp for Woodbridge, remembered nothing past that image of two boys waiting, recalled nothing of the ferry ride, or of South Street Seaport, or whether they had even made it to Ted's office. Nor could he remember past climbing the stairs toward the top of Barnegat Light one nameless summer day; all he could recall was the movement up a steel spiral staircase, rough bricks surrounding himself and his wife and his son, Hugh bringing up the rear, above him Laura, then Michael, who had on a pair of swim trunks from the waterslide back at Beach Haven. Yet in the image he held as he took the ramp off the Parkway at Post, then went left onto Route 9 and under the Turnpike, each move he made with the steering wheel, with his feet as he worked the gas and the brake, as preordained and unacknowledged as tossing a token into a basket, he saw that each of these memories, each shard in him that he'd allowed to be placed there, spoke only of an eternal movement: He only saw his son moving up steel stairs, saw his white slip-on Van's, no socks, as his son took step on step on step up toward the light at the top, though neither he nor his wife nor his son ever reached that light and whatever view of Breach Inlet and Long Beach Island might present itself. He saw only two boys waiting, their hands giving off heat against cold glass to make silhouettes of their fingers for as long as Hugh let the image steep in him. He saw the privacy of a son's search for the right piece of Lego, *flat black four by eight* a chant Hugh could hear inside the car with him, his son's free hand never finding the piece he needed, his fingers forever raking through sharp and shiny bits of color. He saw his son's legs kicking beneath the chair, that image from last night the one to have started all this off, his drive from Reed's Beach to Wood-bridge now nearly complete, a monitor on a desk on the seventh floor waiting for him to flip on to let him help hold things together at Hess Inc.

There still remained in him all of these unfinished im-ages, until, finally, he saw his son rolling down a back-yard hill, ephemeral bursts of light curling and circling about him, High left only to watch and watch while his son rolled and waited and climbed stairs and searched. Michael would never find the Lego piece, he knew, would never reach the top of the lighthouse, never step foot on the ferry. He would roll downhill, arms out, eyes squinted shut, his smile there always.

This, too, he saw, this eternal motion, was what he wanted: so long as his son never emerged into a summer afternoon at the top of Barnegat Light, so long as the model airplane went unfinished, the ferry never came, his son would not finish out his days inside all else that had happened to him. The sequence of events, the small history his son had been allowed, could be held static, and Hugh could watch, and watch, the burden and joy of all these images enough for him.

Then came a knock at his car window, and he saw he was parked at the Hess station in front of the building.

He turned to the window and saw a young, clean-shaven boy in a green Hess baseball cap and white Hess uniform, above one shirt pocket *Ryan* stitched in forest green thread, tapping at his window.

He did not remember pulling in, only then glanced to the fuel gauge to see he was below empty.

"Mr. Walker," the boy was saying, and it seemed a

miracle of its own that the boy knew him. "You got to cut off the engine," he said.

Then Hugh took a breath, found himself smiling in the practiced way he had done since a day three months and eleven days before. He nodded, turned off the ignition, rolled down the window.

Warm air came in at him, and he saw this Ryan—he knew the boy, he realized, knew he'd been working here at the flagship station a month or so—had on his summer uniform with the short sleeves.

"Scared me there," Ryan said, and smiled back at Hugh. "Thought you'd gone to the Twilight Zone for a minute."

"Sort of," Hugh said, still smiling, though he wasn't looking at the boy. "Fill it with the regular," he said.

"Like always," Ryan said, then disappeared to the rear of the car. Hugh reached to the handle between the seat and door, pulled on it, and listened for the small *pop* the gas cover made when it opened. But he heard nothing, then glanced in the sideview mirror, saw that the cover was already opened. Ryan had already put in the pump, was circling back to pick up the squeegee to clean the windows.

He didn't remember opening the cover, either.

Ryan pulled the squeegee from the black plastic bucket on one of the posts that held up the awning, gave it a quick shake to get rid of the excess water. Then he went to Hugh's windshield, gently lifted up the wipers, scrubbed at the glass with the sponge side of the tool.

"This time yesterday we weren't even cleaning," Ryan said. "Even the wiper fluid we was using seemed like it was freezing up." He shrugged, flipped the tool over, and started wiping away the water in brisk, even strokes. "Then this," he said and nodded away from the car.

For a moment Hugh started to turn, to find what the

boy was talking about, then he knew: the day, the one that'd started for him two and a half hours ago with useless words from an old man in a baseball cap. The same day that'd given up enough pictures to keep him for as far as he could see.

"Geez," Ryan said, stood back from the car. His eyes were still to the day out past the gas station. "Then you get a day like this one, and you wonder what the hell happened to yesterday. A day as good as this one, you don't know what the hell's going to happen." He stopped, looked down at Hugh. He nodded. "I may even head to the beach today," he said. "Freeze my butt off if I hit the water. But it'll be enough just to go lay out down there."

He turned, headed for the rear window, and started in. "What a day," Hugh heard him say.

Then came the hard *click* of the gas pump.

Only then did Hugh lean forward, see before him out the windshield the huge white concrete building beside the gas station: Hess Inc.

He had his briefcase. He had on his tie. He believed himself, for a moment, ready.

Then, as suddenly as his arrival here, he saw his son reach the top step of the lighthouse and emerge into light, saw his son whisper *Aha!* and reach down, pull up a flat black four by eight, saw the orange ferry put in, *John F. Kennedy* in bold black letters across the bridge. He saw, with Ryan's outstretched hand waiting for the money Hugh saw himself retrieve from his own wallet, a wallet filled with school photos of a child irretrievably dead, his son reach the bottom of the hill, slowly come to a halt, then sit up, dazed, the smile even wider for how dizzy he felt, his eyes caught in their own planetary spin, darting back and forth and back and forth, trying to catch on to something that would stop moving.

"Michael," he saw himself call out to his child, "come

129

clean up for dinner!" and he watched Michael stand, wander sideways toward him and the house, smiling while fireflies glanced and darted around him, until Michael laughed, said, "Sparks! The world's on fire with these sparks!"

Hugh knew the story from there, knew how his son's days had proceeded from each of those end points to the largest end point of them all, and now he was suddenly awake this day, before him a day that had already shut itself down with the mere appearance of a concrete building, a day that had been assessed by both a gas station attendant and one Roland Dorsett as a day that had unlimited possibilities, a good and fine day.

He'd been the one, he saw, to call in his son.

A good day. A fine day.

❧ HE NEEDED TO speak to Mr. Halford.

The elevator doors opened, and he stepped onto the seventh floor, before him the glass cubicles and men and women he knew, most all of them holding coffee mugs and moving in slow motion. Light came in through the windows in a way that reminded him of midspring, a warm light, he could tell, just by looking at it and the way it shone on desks and monitors and terminals and everything else up here.

He nodded at co-workers, smiled at the secretary who'd leaned into his meeting with Ed Blankenship and the other payroll head, Marshall Skolnick, to tell him of a telephone call from a doctor. He said hello to others here, all of them cordial and easy with their own greetings and morning words: Oscar Neelon, Joan Waxman, Marcia Putnam, Anthony Ramirez.

But it was Mr. Halford he needed to see, to talk to. That was, after all, something of the point of coming in to work, though ostensibly it was to keep his job, to handle payroll software and all its glitches.

Then he was at the doorway into his own cubicle, briefcase in hand, the same as he had arrived here the morning he'd turned to the sound of his son calling out Uno

131

to his wife. This was his point of entry, a room with a desk stacked with printouts on either side of the blotter, stacks thicker, taller than any day he'd worked here before.

Now he wanted time with Mr. Halford to find out what the man knew of stars and nautical charts, of Sheep's Head and Bowline knots. He wanted to know how he'd weather-stripped the place, insulated it, put in those double-pane windows.

"Glad you decided to come back," Ed Blankenship said, and Hugh felt Ed's hand on his shoulder, turned to him.

Ed had been the one to hire Hugh out of programming down on fourth. He stood a little taller than Hugh and was bald with a fringe of thin black hair that grew to his collar in the back, covered his ears. He had a mustache and goatee and was shaped like a pear, his black pants belted too high up. He wasn't smiling at Hugh, but looked him in the eyes, gave his shoulder a gentle shake.

"How you doing?" he said, then squeezed his shoulder.

His face seemed too close, Hugh thought, the man's body too near him: He could smell his after-shave, an unidentifiable, metallic odor, could taste the coffee on his breath.

"Feeling good," Hugh lied, and shrugged beneath the weight of the man's hand on his shoulder. He let his eyes fall from Ed's a moment, then brought them back up. "Feeling pretty good."

Here was the first of the first to ask him, the other morning words and greetings he'd received merely the everyday words. Here was inquiry, and Hugh could not say whether Ed's question was genuine or not.

But in Ed's eyes, a blue-gray Hugh hadn't, as far as he knew, seen before, he thought he could see the same old weary concern, the obligatory call to question Hugh had

132

endured since the day he'd come back to work a week after the funeral.

Hugh blinked, and felt the weight of the briefcase still in his hand pull at his arm until it seemed it might separate from his shoulder.

Ed squeezed his shoulder again, said, "I'd be lying if I said we didn't miss you. That's the god-awful truth." He smiled. "I hope Laura's doing okay, too," Ed went on, and now his hand fell from Hugh's shoulder, buried itself in Ed's pocket, where he moved coins and keys around, and suddenly this might as well have been Roland Dorsett—Rollie to his wife—standing before him. The whole world was trying its damnedest to help heal him, when he knew what he'd known the morning he had pulled closed the door to his home, his wife waiting for him in their car, heater on high, Reed's Beach still waiting to be discovered: He didn't want to be healed.

Ed stopped smiling, looked behind Hugh. He nodded.

Hugh turned, looked at the desktop and the heaps of printouts.

"I don't mean to head right into business," Ed started in, his voice different now, "but about 5:30 last night Waxman pulled up with a SOC7 on the Rhode Island batch."

Hugh entered his office, finally, and now the walls seemed close, the thin glass that separated him from the rest of this world somehow tighter, clearer.

He set the briefcase down, though there came no relief with the release of its handle, its settling on the floor beside the terminal. He could no longer remember what it was he kept inside it that made the briefcase so precious, so necessary. He hadn't opened it the entire time he had been at the cottage, and did not know whether he would open it today or not.

Ed went to the front of the desk, still moved coins in

his pockets. He said, "God-awful serious, far as I can tell. She hung around here until ten o'clock, then packed it in, left the dirty work to the boss man."

Hugh sat in his desk chair. The arms seemed higher than what he was used to, the seatback out of place, pushed into the small of his back too hard.

He leaned forward, pulled the first stack from the left of the blotter.

There on the top sheet was the log-off time, 21:49, the letters *WAXM*, and *MSA:HRMS/2/22*, Waxman's ID and the call letters for the program followed by the date.

Three months and eleven days.

"She didn't quite make it to ten," Hugh said, though his eyes still hung on the date, and the way the numbers, three twos, seemed to reverberate against each other, fight for prominence, though they were only ink on paper. Nothing more.

Ed said, "Listen, you okay?"

Hugh looked up and saw Ed, still with his hands in his pockets.

The entire day lay before him. There was nowhere to go, even though the floor beneath him might fall away at any given moment, the briefcase beside him might fall open to reveal nothing more than blank sheets of computer printout.

Hugh swallowed. But then he smiled, eased back in the chair once more, the millionth time, it seemed, and put his hands behind his head.

He said, "You going to stand in here and play pocket pool all day long, or are you going to stand aside, let a professional get to work?" They were calculated words, words he'd weighed before giving them out, though he did his best to make them seem a joke. But there was no joke in them: He wanted Ed Blankenship, his first and best friend on the floor, out of here.

Ed smiled. He shook the coins and keys even more loudly now, leaned his head back, the fringe of hair down to his shoulders as he did so. "Oh baby," he moaned, "oh baby, oh baby," the muffled clatter of metal from inside his pockets growing more furious each moment. Then Ed let out three quick grunts in succession, the sound from his pockets in synch with the sound from his throat.

He sighed, let his shoulders drop. He smiled. "Finished," he said. "Got a cigarette?"

"Get the hell out of here," Hugh said, and shook his head, looked back at the printout.

Ed turned, started for the door. "You going to dine downstairs?" he said over his shoulder. "I'll sit with you, if you don't already have a date."

"Just make sure you change your pants," Hugh said, as though he'd eased right back into the banter of work here, and back into the seamless life filled with the everyday battles they all fought: where to eat lunch, what the expiration date on the milk carton was as he pulled a gallon from the shelf on his way home, whether or not the Wawa on Sunday mornings had any boxes of Entenmann's chocolate donuts left. The larger issues of the day.

"Always keep a second pair in my office," Ed said. He was at the doorway now, and stopped, turned. "I practice safe pocket pool."

"Shit," Hugh said and made to wave him away, his eyes back to the printout.

But there was one last thing Hugh wanted to say, one last move to make in this wordplay meant to bring him gently back into the reality of what it was they all did: sorting numbers and letters into and out of formulas day in and day out. Even after a child died, Hugh saw, there were still maverick computational phrases to find and conquer, SOC7s to ferret out and smash.

Ed turned to leave, but Hugh said, "Hold it." He lifted one page of the printout, then the next, and the next, then flipped back to the first.

He glanced up at Ed, Hugh's face all serious, no smile. He said, "I thought you said I was after a SOC7 on this one. So what's this SOC4 doing in here?" He pointed to a slip of letters halfway down the first page.

Ed took a step back into the room and looked toward where Hugh's hand lay on the paper. "What's a—" he started, but stopped.

"Gotcha," Hugh said, quickly leaned back in the chair again, his hands behind his head again. "What's a SOC4, you want to know?"

Ed's hands were to his face, his head down, though Hugh could see he was smiling. Slowly Ed shook his head, said into his hands, "I can't believe this. I can't believe this."

"Eddie Blankenship don't know what's a SOC4, everybody," Hugh hollered from his desk, and three or four people passing by outside his office stopped, grinned, shook their heads, then moved on. "I gotta tell Eddie Blankenship what's a SOC4, Amereda-Hess!" he hollered.

Ed brought one hand down and put it on his hip. The other pinched at the bridge of his nose, his eyes and mouth all squinted up. Still he shook his head. He said, "Oh, you asshole. I can't believe this."

"Edward Blankenship," Hugh said, and now he sat up, laced his fingers together, and set them neatly atop the printout. He was going to play this out as well as he possibly could, because he'd seen what he'd suspected, now knew certainly what he figured must have been on everyone's minds, no matter how generic the morning words they'd all given him, no matter how forsworn they had all seemed to the importance of their coffee cups. Ed Blankenship, for all his quick banter and easy jokes,

136

would never have fallen for this one, never, unless he'd been preoccupied with watching Hugh, wondering and wondering at what he would do next.

"Mr. Edward Blankenship," Hugh said, his face serious again, ready to deliver the oldest punchline in the building. "You would do well by this company to remember that, though a SOC7 is a matter of a numeric configuration slipping into a program where only letters exist, the answer to the question you were about to ask, 'What's a SOC4?' is: to keep your feet warm." He paused, then hollered out toward the doorway, "To keep your feet warm, Ed Blankenship," and yet another couple of people stopped, grinned, moved on.

"I taught you that one," Ed said, both hands at his hips now, the pear shape even more well defined. "I taught you, and you turn on me like this."

"Got to keep you on your toes," Hugh said, then waved him out again, picked up the printout, and started in. "Go get yourself some more coffee."

"Yes, sir," Ed said, and Hugh could see above the top of the printout in his hands Ed salute, heard him click his heels together, then turn, leave. "See you at lunch," he said.

Hugh said nothing, only pretended to pore over the sheets a minute or so longer, the letters there meaningless for as long as he let them remain meaningless, all of them nothing until he popped the program into the mainframe and searched for what fragment of numbers appeared among a host of letters.

But already this morning he'd found something more important than any SOC7: In Ed's forgetting the oldest computer joke any of them knew, he saw that they were all watching him, gauging their reactions and movements by his own. That was why, he knew, the glass walls now seemed so close, why so many people seemed to cruise past his office, why the smiles and morning words had been as precisely generic as they had been. He'd spent the last three days at a vice president's summer cottage, and now he was back, and they all wanted to watch, see how the wound might have begun to heal. Or to fester.

But the more private he kept it, he knew, the less likely it would be to heal: only he would be allowed access to the gash, only he himself allowed to touch on it, feel the shock of it through him when he saw the wrinkled bedspread back at home tonight, the way his son's blue bookbag hung on the chair in his bedroom. The wound belonged to him, and no one, not even a wife who would call it self-pity, not even a colleague's sincere hand on his shoulder, not even the proclamation that this would be a fine day with limitless opportunities, would disallow that wound.

Then he let go the printout and sat up in the chair, struck with what he'd left out of the words he'd traded with Ed Blankenship: Had he seen Mr. Halford yet? Was he in?

He pushed himself away from the desk, the wheels on the chair moving easily on the thick plastic carpet guard beneath him. He swallowed, caught a breath, put his hands out, and held on to the edge of the desktop.

The monitor beside him, the same one behind which Mr. Halford had first mentioned the cottage, was still off, a dull black eye staring at him.

He let go the desktop with one hand, touched at his forehead, then reached to the desk drawer, pulled it open.

There amidst pens, pencils, paperclips, rubber bands, the usual debris inside any desk drawer, lay a sheet of extension numbers, everyone in payroll who had a phone.

He pulled it out, the sheet creased in several places, doodles in the margins, everything from stick men to

138

cloudlike swirls to a small monitor, the word *SHIT* written across the screen. Some of the numbers were circled, some crossed out; others—Domino's Pizza, Laura's number from when she'd worked at the hospital—were added in at the bottom.

But one listing about a third of the way down the page had gone unscathed, the numbers sharp on the paper. He could not remember having called it, had never had occasion: "Dennis J. Halford, Vice President Finance" his entry read, and across from the column of names was his extension: 9500.

Everyone else, himself included, was listed only by last name, no title; each corresponding number, too, began with a seven, the number of their floor.

He picked up the phone, listened for the tone, and heard his own breathing over the line. His eyes took in the numbers one last moment, then he looked to the phone, reached his index finger to the bank of square lighted buttons, touched the only one of five not flashing.

He watched as his finger hovered over the number 9, uncertain why his palms were wet, why his hand wouldn't punch in the number it knew: He was living at the man's house for now, had tried yet again to conceive their next child in the man's own bed, had inhabited his things, his rooms, his life. It would be this man and the knowledge he carried, he knew, that would bring Hugh himself back into the old life, let him know what a life lived with children growing up around you and with you would be like.

His finger still would not move, though he willed it to.

Then he glanced past the phone and through the glass wall behind the monitor, saw two cubicles away Joan Waxman at her desk.

She was frozen a moment, her mouth open, eyes on

him. Then she waved, a quick and abrupt move: He'd caught her watching him.

Then she mouthed the words *How are you?* through the glass walls, shuffled the stack of paper in her hand, shuffled it again, and bounced the sheets into line on her own desktop. She adjusted her glasses, and he knew why she was watching him.

He punched in her number, knew it without having to look at the sheet still on his desktop. He watched her answer her phone.

"Hugh," she said, "how are you guys doing?" She glanced at him, then at her phone, and back to him.

"We're fine," he said and gave her the thumbs up sign. He eased back in the chair, his eyes solid on her, daring her to fiddle with a pen or bend a paperclip. "Doing fine," he said, the lie easy out of him.

"Listen," he said then and paused. He cleared his throat, and watched as two offices away she leaned toward him in her chair, waiting, he knew, for him to let slip some piece of information that might support the answer he had given her, or betray it.

"Listen," he said again, and she nodded, adjusted her glasses again. *What's a SOC4?* he wanted to say and knew she'd answer, *I don't know. What?*

But he said, "Have you seen Halford around yet?" With his free hand, he folded over the sheet, slipped it into the open desk drawer, and pushed it closed.

THEY HAD BEGUN watching him the moment he had run from the office three months and eleven days before, murmured words behind him as he slammed again and again at the button for the elevator down.

But their watching had found its most finite beginning point when, at the funeral three days later, he and his wife and all their blood accomplices seated in the screened family partition on the right side of the chapel, here had come Ed Blankenship and Joan Waxman and Marcia and Oscar and Pam and Greg and Tom and Anthony, all of them. Even Mr. Halford.

They watched, and even in the midst of a grief that had begun to destroy what he believed was a benevolent world, one in which children did not die, and in which their fathers grew old watching them grow up, he had seen the looks on their faces: the wide-eyed and startled; the bowed heads, averted eyes; the squeezed shut eyes thick with tears, though none of them had been the ones to have had their child die.

They watched him and his wife, and even without looking at them, he could feel their eyes boring into him while the pastor of the church Laura's parents attended spoke from a lectern at the front of a bright and shining

141

new chapel at Monmouth Memorial Gardens. Somehow things had been taken care of, decisions made, plot and casket and in-ground memorial plaque schemes settled upon, the three days since he had kissed his son's forehead an unraveling movement of darkness and foreign places, until, finally, they had settled here, a casket of glimmering mahogany and brass before them, heaped around and before it monumental sprays of flowers, while words tumbled down at him from a man he did not know about the nature of God and the grace of children.

They were watching. Not only his co-workers, but Laura's co-workers as well, other nurses, a few doctors. Laura's brother had come down from Michigan, Hugh's sister from Boston. She had sat on his left, Laura on his right, next to her, her parents, then her brother.

He had not seen his sister in over three years, and when she came to their house the day after Michael had been killed, he had not recognized her, had wondered who the woman was with brunette hair and a yellow blouse and eyes the same brown as his moving through the kitchen toward him. When she leaned into him and cried on his shoulder about how much she loved Michael, he had only held her out of some duty to grief, whoever the party, himself already becoming familiar with the unknowable territory. Only when she had pulled back from him, touched at her eyes, her mouth a cruel twist of lips as she cried, did he see his own mother in her, and how his mother had cried when his father died of a heart attack eleven years before, herself to follow him only a year and a half later with a cancer that consumed her body in forty-nine days. By the time he was twenty-three, this sister in his arms twenty-eight, they were both orphans of a sort, familiar, he believed, with grief and death and mourning.

But when he looked at his sister's face as she cried,

and recognized her, brought her back to his chest, and held her, nothing had happened: The belief that a prior touch on death, even the death of a mother and father, would serve as some kind of anchor in the gray fracture of the first day after his son had died proved itself to be only that: belief, and not truth.

So that the woman to his left at the funeral, the older sister who had been married twice and who had no children, became spectator as well, just as Laura's flock of relatives were spectators, just as the pastor, even her own mother and father and everyone else in the chapel. They were all spectators.

And there were moments he granted himself—dangerous moments, precarious and black—when he let play in his head the echo of Laura's moaned *No no no*, the idea in him that, with her denial, she had also become spectator.

But the blackest moments, those moments when he knew he stood on the edge of a chasm, a bottomless abyss into which he was not certain he had fallen yet or were about to, came to him in the midst of the ceremony, indicting moments when he knew himself to be the spectator: the moments when, in the hospital, everyone's moves, even his own, had seemed too large; the moments when he had seen himself staring at sheets of paper on the desk at the Memorial Gardens office, his signature somehow appearing at the bottom of eight or nine sheets of paper; and the moment when, in the middle of the eulogy, he had glanced away from the casket, looked down at his right hand, and found his fingers intertwined with his wife's, her sobs barely audible, the knuckles of both their hands white, bloodless. He, too, was a spectator, only holding on.

Yet when those black moments came over him there in the chapel—all the world filled with spectators at the death of his son—there suddenly broke in him a certain fragmented relief at the fact that they had chosen to leave the casket closed. If the world were watching, he knew, then they would have to watch him and his wife, and not the body of the child—the only true participant here—they had assembled to bury. Relief was what he felt. Only a shred of it, a splinter. But it was there.

They had made the choice to leave it closed the afternoon before, when they had brought down to the funeral home the clothing he would need, Hugh the one to enter their son's room for the search through his closet, Laura even then unwilling to enter the room. His wife stood just outside the room, mouth closed tight, eyes wide open and on him, while he had gone through his son's dresser, looked for a pair of socks, a pair of underwear, a belt. For an instant, the time it took to burrow for the right pair of socks in a drawer of clothing hopelessly strewn in the manner only a boy could bring off, he believed this might have been any other foray into his child's possessions.

Then it hit him, the fact of this mission, and he stood, socks and T-shirt and underwear in hand, and surveyed the room, decided then and there that he would survey this room each day from now on, the detail of it—the row of Hess firetrucks on the shelf above the toy box, the red-painted cigar box filled with rocks on the dresser, the books jammed into the shelves opposite the bed—the closest he could ever hope to bringing back his son.

He had chosen a pair of black corduroy pants, a blue oxford button down, a brown leather belt, black socks. He turned to the door, and there stood his wife. He stopped, looked at her.

Her eyes were on the clothing in his hands. She shook her head only once, a violent and purposeful gesture:

144

These were not the clothes he usually wore, not the boy he was.

"No," she said, that word out of her once again, hanging in the air, and he had looked down at the items in his hands, nodded.

"And no one will see him," she said.

He looked up, saw she'd backed away from the door and was leaning against the hallway wall.

Then Jack, her bearded and bald older brother down from Ann Arbor, stood next to her and took hold of her hand. Still her eyes were on what Hugh held.

"Laura," Jack said and glanced from her to Hugh and back.

"The casket," Laura said then, the word huge and awful and ugly, its presence in the room something Hugh wanted to fend off, destroy in the instant she had spoken it. "It will be closed," she said.

Hugh didn't look at her, nodded again.

"Laura," Jack said again, as though with the word he could heal her, the older brother's role never surrendered. "We can go down to the kitchen."

"No," Hugh heard, and this time it had come from him. He felt his hands holding tight the clothes in his hands, saw the two of them staring at him, brother and sister.

"No," he said again, quieter, and now sounds came up from the kitchen below them, sounds he knew had been there all along but hadn't heard for the lesson gathering the wrong clothes for his child had been. Voices rose and fell with words about everything and nothing at once: food preparations for tomorrow, flowers, early snow in Michigan.

Hugh believed he could distinguish all these pieces of conversation from below him in the moment he stood before his wife and brother-in-law, his mission not yet

145

complete, his choice of clothing a failure, his wife correct: The casket would be closed, and their child would wear what he would on any other day.

He turned, hung the shirt and pants back up in his closet, and pulled down a pair of blue jeans, the knees white, nearly worn through.

He stood with the jeans and looked at his wife, still backed up to the wall. It did not occur to him to ask her in; her eyes told him she would not.

Then he looked at Jack, said, "You can go on downstairs now," and nodded. He said, "You can drive us over there in a few minutes."

Jack had nodded, looked at his sister. He lifted her hand and kissed it. He patted it, then let go, disappeared down the hall.

Now his wife's eyes were closed, and he knew without words she would not open them until he had found the right clothing. He opened the dresser, replaced the black socks and the leather belt, brought out a blue canvas belt, a pair of white sweat socks, the soles permanently gray from play.

He closed the drawer and heard from below him no sounds now, conversation ceased, he knew, with Jack's return. He imagined his brother-in-law down there, standing in the kitchen, silent, the rest of them taking up that silence, talk on everything and nothing at once made clearly useless by the fact Hugh and Laura were up here, and were finding the right clothes in which to bury Michael.

He opened the next drawer down, the bottom drawer, and saw right there at the top, neatly folded and ready to wear, a red crewneck shirt, one corner of the breast pocket pulled away where, Hugh imagined, his son had torn at a pen there or had wrestled too hard with Gerry Rothberg in their backyard. The shirt was faded, too, and

Hugh thought of how comfortable it must have felt to wear.

He pulled it out and slipped closed the drawer.

He stood, turned to his wife.

"Here," he said, and held them up.

She opened her eyes, her mouth still the same thin line. She didn't nod, didn't blink, only looked: signal enough he'd made the right choice.

But a choice, he knew, that was no choice at all: These were items his son would have worn anyway.

"His tennis shoes," Hugh said. It was a question, but he'd given no intonation, no inquiry. He only spoke the words.

"In the bedroom," she whispered. "In the bag from the hospital."

Later, once they had driven to the funeral home to leave the clothing, Laura remaining in the car while Jack and Hugh went inside, and once they had had a dinner of a nameless soup and pale crackers, and once the house had settled down into an early evening in November, there had come a call from the home, the faceless director informing them their son was ready.

This drive they made alone, neither speaking. They held hands, Hugh maneuvering the car with one hand along the two-lane roads and out onto 33, finally delivering them to the home, their headlights cutting a swath of yellow light across the gray brick as they pulled in. Dim light shone through the leaded glass front door.

They didn't look at each other before they climbed out, simply let go hands and popped open their doors, closed them, then came around the hood, held hands again.

The director opened the door for them, ushered them in with a small sweep of his hand, and they followed him down the oak-paneled hallway. To their left was a doorway, and Hugh remembered that this was the door into the room in which a business transaction had occurred between himself and this man, and in which he and Jack had given the same man the clothing, informed him the casket would be closed the next day.

The director stopped at the double doors at the end of the hall, leaned toward them, and pushed them both open. The doors stayed in place, and he put his hands behind his back, disappeared.

It was his son, and the oak-paneled walls pressed at his shoulders, emptied his lungs.

When his father had died, and they had viewed him, he had not been Hugh's father at all, the blue of his face after the heart attack never really gone; instead, it had been a man, someone he had known once, but nothing beyond that. His mother, emaciated, had seemed an ancient woman, perhaps a distant and aged great-aunt, no matter how much rouge they had put on her, how nicely coiffed her hair.

But this was his son, and the belief he had known something of death before this was, finally and for all time, set aside: His son inside the casket looked like his son, wore his son's clothes, his hair combed as Michael combed it.

He reached in, touched at his son's forehead, felt the cool of it, tasted on his own lips yet again the cool of his son's skin when he had been inside the hospital room. Then he touched at the tear in the shirt where the pocket had pulled away.

This was Michael.

Then Laura reached in as well, and suddenly he saw that she had something in her hand, a cloth, and as it unfurled from her hand, draped itself across their son's chest, and as she tucked its edges into the satin crevasses on the far side of their son, he saw that it was Michael's old blanket, the one he'd had since he was in the bassinet in their bedroom in the apartment in Woodbridge: yellow with blue stripes, the satin edges of it long gone, holes worn through here and there. Michael had slept with it until after he had turned six, the blanket useless as blanket long before that. Hugh and Laura had finally retired it themselves when, after washing and drying it one Saturday afternoon, the two of them sorting and folding the clothes that lay warm and soft on the sofa, Laura had held it up, holes and all, and said, "What do you think?" "Gone," Hugh had said. Michael hadn't even missed it, though he'd slept with it every night of his life until then.

"Where was that?" he whispered to Laura, and reached his own hand, tucked the lower edges into the satin, the frayed bottom edge of the blanket reaching just below his son's waist.

She did not answer, and he was sorry he'd asked as soon as the words had left him: She had known where it was, had had presence of mind enough to find it, and had brought it here. That was all that mattered.

And his son was covered by the blanket.

It was a gesture, he knew, just as the blanket in the last days before they had hidden it away had been merely gesture for Michael, thin companion for sleep. But Michael had needed the blanket, had known until it had not reappeared after a washday that sleep would be impossible without its company; this gesture, the laying on of the blanket, was one they two needed, an instant they now owned, infused with value, because it was their own gesture, no one else's. Michael had worn the knees out on his jeans, had somehow torn the shirt; Laura had retrieved the blanket, smuggled it in unbeknownst to him, set about placing it with their child; Hugh had touched the boy's forehead. No one else on the face of the earth would ever be responsible for these facts. No one, save for a faceless funeral director, the one who would finally close the casket on their son, would ever know about this blanket, or the clothes their son wore.

Then, in a move even more astounding than a blanket appearing from nowhere, he watched as his wife reached above and across their son, touched the open half-lid, her fingers gripping tight the edge of glossy wood, and started the lid down.

Then his hands were with hers, and in a gesture larger and truer than any he would ever know, the two of them pulled down the lid, set it gently and easily into place.

They watched him and Laura through the ceremony, believing themselves, he knew, to be bearing witness of one couple's grief by amassing on a cold and bright November morning, and listening to the words of the pastor.

And even this God the pastor invoked, the God who had granted Hugh and Laura the grace of their child, even this God was only a spectator, Hugh knew. This same God had, it was widely held, watched as his own son, one Jesus Christ, had hung on a cross until he'd died, the world and its woes more important to the Father than the love and care of His only begotten son; the pastor's words, his calling down on them the grace, mercy, and peace of this same God Almighty, only revealed to Hugh even more clearly the distant and cold and untouchable face of God. For all the gentle words this pastor handed out, for all his sympathetic tone, his delivery of the old news that God worked in mysterious ways, there came no comfort. Only the revelation that this stone-hearted God, the one who'd let his son die while His face was turned, was only one more of the crowd of spectators everyone assembled here had become. God's only hand in this was to take away, then watch what would happen. If, Hugh thought, He existed at all.

They all watched as Hugh and Laura made their way from the chapel and into the waiting limousine for the quarter-mile ride to the plot, and watched them take their seats at the graveside. They watched as Laura, in yet another gesture, but one hollow and senseless, he believed, after what they had finished last night, dropped a single white rose onto the casket once it had been lowered into the ground, and they watched Hugh himself then drop a handful of dirt after her in yet another gesture. They watched all of this, and yet that secret, the clothes their son wore, the blanket over him, the pulling closed of the casket themselves, kept the proceedings as private as any act that could ever take place between husband and wife, as private as what they had done to conceive him.

They had all seen nothing, Hugh knew, only grief's gestures, sorrow's affectations: True grief, he saw with the last glimpse of his son in the oak-paneled room, was a secret that defied divulging. There was no way to know it unless it had been bestowed upon you, no way to pass it on once it had arrived.

Still they watched him, even to this day in an office in which warm light fell through the windows, believing themselves somehow partaking of his grief, and as he pored through screen after screen, through Management Science America's troubleshooting disks, through quotient derivation after quotient derivation deep inside the language of the program, he still held on, aware each second of the weight and claim of gesture.

🦚 "SO," ED BLANKENSHIP said, and peeled the cellophane from around the egg salad sandwich he'd bought. "What's the captain's summer palace like?" He balled up the cellophane and set it next to the cheese french fries on his tray.

This was lunch with Ed in the cafeteria, a huge room on the second floor with a dozen or so Formica-topped tables, eight seats to a table. Two walls of the room were windows, he and Ed at a table that looked out at the Turnpike, cars moving past, all of them on their way somewhere else.

Hugh wanted to be in any one of the cars moving south out there, wanted away from here. He still hadn't turned up the problem with the Rhode Island batch, had three calls, none of which had been returned, in to MSA for help.

Each time he'd popped through the program and its data this morning, the same report rolled onto the screen:

ABEND

He and Joan Waxman had worked through it again and again, always with the same result: an abnormal ending, the word big and forbidding on the screen. And, Hugh believed, speaking too easily to him, as though some unseen hand were signaling him through the network of yes or no delineations that an abnormal end was the only one he would encounter. The word had seized him, made the morning fly past him, the time filled with such program detail as to overwhelm him, while a parade of officemates leaned in and said something chummy or sympathetic: "Welcome back to hell," Oscar Neelon had said, him with his starched white button-down shirt, handpainted oranges on his tie; "Ed says his feet are cold," Pam Hart had said, then gave her small, cheerleader wave, fingers only right up next to her face, the dimpled smile; Anthony Ramirez had stopped in, looked over Hugh's shoulder at the ABEND on the screen, and suggested they run the VSAM CICS schematic.

"Only what we ran two hours ago, bright boy," Joan had said from where she sat in the corner, the reams of paper now in her hand.

"Still ticked over last night," Anthony had said to her, then to Hugh, "We're pleased you're back." Then he'd left.

"The corporate We," Joan said once he was gone, and Hugh'd looked up, saw her roll her eyes, rustle through more paper, all of it melodrama. "As if being office boy around here made him a vice president."

"So why'd you go out with him?" Hugh asked and grinned, though his eyes were back to that word on the screen.

"Don't start," she'd said.

No one had seen Mr. Halford yet today.

Hugh looked at his tray and saw he held it with both hands, though he'd been sitting across from Ed a minute or so. On the tray was the same lunch Hugh always bought here: ham and Swiss on a kaiser roll, a bag of Cheetos, a can of Diet Coke.

He drew his hands away from the tray and set them

in his lap a moment. "Hugh's Executive Plate," he said, and gave a small laugh, glanced at Ed. He brought his hands to the sandwich, started unwrapping.

"You're avoiding the question," Ed said. "What's the summer compound, the emperor's estate like?" He bit into his sandwich, chewed.

Hugh looked at him full on. "Some things are just too personal. I'd feel like I was divulging company secrets if I told you."

"Satin sheets?" Ed said, took another bite. "Red?" He smiled, swallowed, took a sip of his French Cherry Snapple.

"No comment," Hugh said.

Ed shook his head, took another bite. "Hess man through and through," he said.

He knew, too, he wouldn't tell him any of the contents of the house, nor its location, nor about the sextant, the charts, the books. Not from any sworn allegiance to Hess, Inc., but to some sort of private barrier, the same one that kept Ed's eyes on Hugh each minute, weighing and judging his progress toward some undetermined point of health, when the death of his son would have finally been healed over only into a scar, a reminder of what had once been.

So he lied to Ed, the man who had hired him onto the seventh floor, had brought him into the glass cubicle that now seemed no better than a coffin of his own, but which had, those years ago, seemed as big as his living room after the terminal, monitor, and one-drawer desk he'd been chained to on the fourth.

He lied, because it seemed to Hugh that the best way through this day and the one to follow, two days that separated him from a world he could then inhabit with no interference, would be to give them all what they wanted, the gesture of a smile, the hearty laugh, the healed heart.

He said, "All right, I surrender," and put up his hands, shook his head. "I'll tell all," he said, then picked up the sandwich and took the first bite. He chewed, swallowed, said, "Just don't accuse me of being a Hess man."

Now Joan showed up with her tray: a bacon double-cheeseburger and Mountain Dew. She took a seat across from him and next to Ed, the audience already forming up, Hugh thought.

"First thing," Hugh said, and took a sip of his soda. He'd been able to taste nothing of the sandwich, in his mouth only food. "First thing is, it's a strip of beach with these huge homes, all of them stucco. Pale pink, green, blue. All of it."

"What's this?" Joan said, looked at Ed, then Hugh.

"He's telling us how the other half lives. The man before us being the other half for right now." He nodded at Hugh, then pulled up a french fry dripping with the yellow sauce the cafeteria staff called cheese.

"I'm not part of the other half. I'm only a spectator," Hugh said, aware of the word in his mouth, the irony of it: They watched him, while he watched them. He said, "We can't even put our feet up in there, it's so nice. It's like a magazine, the place. Wicker and marble. Sunken tub."

"Wouldn't you know it," Joan said and opened her soda. "The rest of us live like dirt while the mucky-mucks drink champagne every night."

"It's got a circular drive, too. White gravel," Hugh went on as though Joan hadn't spoken. "They've got this huge picture window that looks out over the ocean. Vertical blinds twelve feet long," he said, and now he only held on to the sandwich, halfway between the table and his mouth.

Ed grinned. He leaned back in his seat then, took a

french fry, and brought it to his mouth. A drop of cheese fell from the fry, landed square on the middle of his tie.

The three looked at it there, watched as Ed, unperturbed, dabbed it up with his pinkie, put it to his mouth. He wadded up a thin napkin from the dispenser on the table and wiped at his mouth. He dipped up another french fry, didn't lose anything this time.

Hugh kept on with the story, as now Greg Lindeman showed up, asked if he could have a seat; then came Pam and Anthony together, Joan crossing her arms and half-turning in her seat across the table from them. Next came Oscar and Marcia, the whole payroll programming crowd, trays in hand, all of them at one table, while Hugh kept on, word after word leaving him with an earnestness and eye for detail—the giant clam shell sink in the master bath, the stained glass window in the foyer, the butcherblock island in the kitchen—that gave his audience, he knew, no choice but to believe.

They all watched Hugh, though Hugh made certain to meet Ed's eyes most often, let his words trail themselves toward the pear-shaped man with a goatee and no hair, a cheese stain on his tie. Ed, with his smile that seemed somehow to know more, a grin that held something Hugh could not name. And now Ed became his target, the end point of his foray north from Reed's Beach: He had persuaded them all, his officemates nodding, shaking their heads, tsking or whistling at each next detail he gave; all that remained was the conquering of Ed, and Hugh could go home tonight, sleep easy in the house in which their child had lived, secure in the fact there was only one more day here before he would be returned to the cottage, and secure in the knowledge he had fooled them all into the belief Hugh Walker was well on the road to being healed.

And still Ed grinned.

🪷 "MR. HALFORD," ED said, and entered Hugh's cubicle, "what brings you to the dungeon?"

Hugh had followed Ed out of the cafeteria and onto the elevator, his words all the while filling in yet more and greater lies. He was in midsentence, adding yet another detail to the catalog he'd divulged, this time the fact that the Halfords had not satin sheets, but some designer brand Laura'd seen in Spiegel for one hundred dollars a sheet.

But then Hugh heard Ed call out Halford's name, call it out, he heard, a little too loudly, cutting off Hugh's words, and Hugh saw Ed was with him, wanted to cover for him: This was the man down from the ninth floor, the man whose house he had filled all lunch hour with untold wealth, opulence none of them at the table would ever know. Their boss.

"Dungeon work, Blankenship," Mr. Halford said, and now Hugh and Ed were both in the office. Mr. Halford rose from the chair pushed against the glass wall, the same chair he'd risen from not a week before to hand Hugh a key and a hand-drawn map.

Ed put out a hand, shook with Mr. Halford, then Hugh put out his own. Their eyes met for only a moment as they shook. Mr. Halford nodded, said, "Walker."

Mr. Halford had on a forest green bow tie today, his skin, of course, as tan as always, and now Hugh knew how his skin could be that way, smooth and worn at once: the sea air, the wind down there, the sun out on the dock. The length of time they had looked at each other was no longer or shorter than any encounter in a hall or on the elevator, and Hugh knew in this fact that Mr. Halford had sent him a signal: They were accomplices, disguised here in front of the others.

"Didn't mean to interrupt," Mr. Halford said, and put his hands behind his back.

"Not at all," Ed said before Hugh could speak. Ed smiled and looked at Hugh, then to Mr. Halford. "Hugh here was just regaling us with the splendors of your mansion." He looked back at Hugh. "Sounds like a mansion at least."

Hugh felt his face go hot again. He had no idea what Ed would say and hoped he would say nothing.

Mr. Halford smiled, looked up at Ed. "Good God, Blankenship," he said. He'd started rocking forward and back on his heels, hands still behind him. "You know just as well as Walker my place is no mansion. A cottage, really. You've been there, Blankenship. You know the place."

Ed still looked at Hugh, still with that smile.

Hugh tried to swallow, found he could not. He tried to breathe, too, but could not do this either, and it seemed minutes before he drew in, gave a feeble smile in response, his eyes moving too quickly, he knew, to Ed and Mr. Halford and back again.

Ed had been there.

"Maybe he's elaborated just a little," Ed said and reached to Hugh, put a hand to his shoulder again, squeezed it just as he had this morning. Hugh could smell the after-shave again, the metal odor like a chisel into his head this time. "But it's apparent he's enjoying the place."

"I—" Hugh began, but Mr. Halford waved him off with one hand, eyes to the ground. He put the hand behind him again and cleared his throat.

"Rhode Island," he said, "is sweating. They smell what's going on up here. They're getting restless."

"Rhode Island," Ed said, "is, generally speaking, a sweaty state."

Mr. Halford cut his eyes at Ed. "I appreciate your attempt at easing a serious situation with a sense of humor, Blankenship," he said. He blinked, then looked at the floor again. "But this won't bring a resolution any quicker."

"Joan Waxman and I—" Hugh started, though he wasn't certain what other words might leave him. There had only seemed a crack in Mr. Halford's words, and it had seemed he ought to say something.

But nothing came, Ed and Mr. Halford looking at him a long moment.

"Dennis, you just tell Rhode Island," Ed finally said, his words hard and sharp and aimed at Mr. Halford, "we'll have resolution this afternoon. Six o'clock the latest."

He let go Hugh's shoulder and pointed at the air in front of Mr. Halford with that hand: "I've got Hugh and Joan on it nonstop."

He stopped, smiled again, put the hand to Hugh's shoulder again, his bones and muscles there on fire.

"So he elaborates," Ed said. He squeezed, harder this time. "He'll find that unseemly little blemish in the program, pop it like the ugly pimple it is." Ed gave his shoulder a small shake. "Right?"

Hugh tried the smile again and nodded, though he had

no idea, at least until a call came in from MSA, where to go next with the batch.

But the Rhode Island mess, Hugh knew, meant nothing beside the truth of what lay beneath this talk: Ed had sat through lunch and listened. He'd grinned, and had known all along of Hugh's lie.

Mr. Halford cleared his throat, glanced up at Ed. He said, "That will be enough, Mr. Blankenship," and nodded at him. He stopped rocking, said, "Now if you'll excuse us," and brought the hand from behind him again, gestured toward Hugh. "Private matters," he said.

"Six o'clock the latest," Ed said, and now his hands were back in his pockets. He nodded at Mr. Halford, at Hugh. "Too many elaborations spoil the stew," he said and then he was gone.

"Hugh," Mr. Halford said, and turned, sat in the chair once again. He motioned at Hugh's chair behind the desk, said, "Have a seat."

Still all the words and gestures, the signals that were there and were not, swirled around Hugh like a program of ghosts, one endless loop of apparitions that began nowhere and ended nowhere: Ed had been to Mr. Halford's house, that place he'd believed was his own. Ed knew of the upstairs room and the dock and the night, knew, perhaps, even that moon, what a sextant held up to it felt like. And Ed knew, too, that Hugh was only a liar, that in fact no healing had begun, the wound still fresh.

"Son," Mr. Halford said, "let's have a seat."

Hugh looked down, saw Mr. Halford still with his hand pointed at the desk chair. "Oh," he said, then, "sorry," and moved around the desk, sat down. He put both hands on the desktop, held on to the edge. He smiled.

Mr. Halford touched his bow tie and looked at Hugh. He said, "How are you and the missus doing down there?"

"Fine, fine," Hugh said. Ed's after-shave still seemed to hang in the air, and Hugh knew he'd answered too quickly. He paused a moment, said, "Beautiful down there. That view. Thank you for letting us have the place."

"Our pleasure." Mr. Halford sat up in the chair, put his hands on his knees: the same moves he'd made last week when they were in here together, and it seemed the long days in this man's rooms at Reed's Beach were a chapter out of a novel he'd never finished, a television program he'd changed the channel on.

He remembered then that this man held some secret for him, Hugh's way through what had been given him, so that the miracle of his next words as they left him seemed magnified in Hugh, too easy a blessing: "The wife and I want to have you over for dinner tonight," Mr. Halford said. He slapped his knees, then rubbed them. "We were thinking, since you were alone this evening, you'd appreciate some company. Keep us in touch with how the cottage was doing for you."

Hugh let go the desktop, let his hands fall to his lap. He smiled, nodded, and said, "Yes. Fine."

Mr. Halford shrugged. "The wife's idea, actually," he said. "I'm not the most adept at knowing the proper and polite thing to do. That's why she's around. Sally." He shrugged again, rubbed his hands together. "If she heard me say that was the only reason I kept her around, of course, she'd have my head on a platter."

Hugh laughed, found the sound from him easy and soft, true. He laughed.

Mr. Halford stood, hands on hips. He said, "We were hoping seven or so. But with the Rhode Island problem—"

"It will be fixed," Hugh cut in and somehow knew it would; Ed's promise a minute ago had been a stab at dead air, but was now a clean and shimmering prophesy: It would be fixed.

"Good to hear," Mr. Halford said, and Hugh stood, his hands on his hips, too. "Give Betty, my secretary, a call a little later, extension 9500, to get directions. It's down in Holmdel, not too hard to find."

"Ninety-five hundred," Hugh said, and nodded as though he were filing away the number he already knew by heart. He said, "No map this time?" and smiled.

"Excuse me?" Mr. Halford said, leaned his head one way, perplexed, Hugh saw.

"Nothing," Hugh said and shrugged himself. "It's just you gave us a map down to the cottage. I just—"

"Oh, that," Mr. Halford said. He crossed his arms, shook his head. He smiled. "That's the wife's handiwork, too. Me, I couldn't find my butt with both hands. It took me three years of weekends before I ever got the hang of finding the cottage. I couldn't begin to tell you how to get there unless Sally's drawn something up."

"I know what you mean," Hugh said and nodded, though the words were only words, meant nothing.

Laura, he remembered. His own wife. He thought of her inside this man's cottage, or spending the warm day out on his dock.

Mr. Halford turned and said, "Have to head out. Meetings to set up meetings." He paused, turned back to Hugh. "Rhode Island," he said, the smile gone.

"Done," Hugh said, and nodded.

Then he was out the door and on toward the elevators.

Hugh watched him move along the corridor, saw people nod at him, exchange quick pleasantries, Mr. Halford moving all the while, nodding himself.

Hugh sat down. He had until six, and turned his chair to the terminal.

ABEND was still up on the screen, just as he'd left it before lunch.

But now the word was different, held promise somehow. Now it wasn't as big and forbidding, but was only a bridge between this instant and the moment when he would be ushered into Mr. Halford's house in Holmdel.

Then the phone rang, and for a moment he believed it to be Betty with directions. Or perhaps Laura with news of how beautiful it was down there at Reed's Beach today.

He picked it up, said, "Hello?"

"A white gravel drive?" Ed said, and Hugh quickly turned in his chair, saw four cubicles down, over desktops and between terminals and through all these walls of glass, Ed leaned back in his chair, smiling, watching him.

Hugh was silent, not certain what to do, whether to speak or to listen.

"Your face is, to coin a cliché, stricken with fear," Ed said. "I don't know why it would be." He paused. "Be happy."

Hugh tried the smile, tried to shrug.

"Ease up," Ed said. "This isn't blackmail. This isn't anything." He paused, and Hugh saw him stop the smile, sit up in his chair. His eyes were on Hugh, and now Hugh knew that Ed had broken through, had changed from mere spectator to participant.

Ed said, "You have to do what gets you through." He paused. "Nobody here's out to get you. Understand that." He paused again. "It's important you get through this."

Hugh did nothing, the receiver to his ear, behind him and watching, he knew, like the spectators he'd gauged everyone here to be, the dull gray eye of the monitor, the word *ABEND* displayed there.

He looked at Ed, looked at him, the silence on the line between them a wash of white sound.

Hugh cleared his throat. He leaned back in his own chair now and put one hand behind his head in the old gesture, the ancient one: This is no problem.

Hugh said, "Where's Waxman? She's in on this too, you know." He paused, eyes on Ed. "Six o'clock is fast approaching," he said. He shook his head, chuckled himself, and said, "Rhode Island is sweaty."

"Hugh," Ed said, but Hugh turned back to the monitor, and to that word.

"Ed," Hugh said. "Let's just get Waxman in here and get on it."

"You know," Ed said, and it was strange now to have only his voice, no goatee and tie to look at, though they talked like this a dozen times a day, the two of them staring at their monitors. "I've been down there," Ed said. "I don't give a good goddamn about what you told everybody. But I've been down there." He paused, and Hugh heard him take in a heavy breath, let it out. "For my own reasons," he said, his voice now gone quiet. "So I know what it's like down there. And it's not like anyone's going to take it away from you. There's nobody up here going to—"

"Rhode Island," Hugh finally said, filled with enough words from Ed in his chair four coffins away.

"Rhode Island," he said again, and hung up.

He looked at the word on the monitor and put his fingers to the keyboard. He held them there, ready, poised for whatever he had to do.

Four

❀ THE LIBRARY SAT next to a gingerbread bed and breakfast with red clapboard siding, white trim, turrets and slate shingles.

This was Cape May proper, the tourist part of town, the houses with junked cars out front, sagging porches, garbage cans long gone. There were only gingerbread Victorians now, every other one a bed and breakfast.

But the library was a small, flat building, a concrete wheelchair ramp up to the metal door, stucco walls painted a dull yellow, a dirt and grass lawn. The place was no bigger than the downstairs of their house in Englishtown.

Winnie parked the van and cut off the engine. They hadn't spoken since Winnie's revelation of dumb truth: It took, in fact, very little to knock a person down. Even only an honest answer and a beautiful head of natural black hair.

Winnie said, "We have arrived," and climbed out, slammed shut the door. The sound of it, metal against metal, echoed inside the van, rang in Laura's ears.

Winnie went around the front of the van and stepped up onto the sidewalk. She took a few steps up the ramp, then stopped, looked at Laura. She nodded. Sunlight banged off the patent leather purse.

"Doctor's orders," she said. She smiled, her lips never parting. "The library in Cape May. Stop number one." She nodded toward the building, her eyes on Laura.

"Any time you're ready," she said.

Laura took her straw handbag from the floorboard, popped open the door, and slammed it shut. She moved up the ramp and past Winnie. She wouldn't look at her, wouldn't let their eyes meet.

Inside the front door was a small mudroom, three posters on the walls: a benefit by the Agape Clown Ministry, a concert by Ringers-on-the-Green, a lecture on vascular surgery at Shore Memorial Hospital. There were small holes in the walls, staples, too, where the walls had been crowded with announcements during the summer season. For a moment Laura let herself see what Cape May must be like then, how beautiful and fun and active all at once, people stopping in at the library mudroom just to get a look at colorful posters about all the goings-on.

But this was still only February, the warm air outside some strange dodge by winter, the walls of this room empty save for those three posters. She glanced at Winnie behind her, arms crossed, purse hanging down, her mouth in a frown: silent reprimand somehow for a morning Laura felt slipping from her, all control surrendered to Winnie and her purse, a van with a cracked windshield.

The library itself was only a large room, one wooden card catalog file, nine or ten rows of shelves, three round tables with chairs. A circulation desk crowded with books, magazines, piles of newspapers sat to the right of the room. A black woman with hair swept to one side so that it crested in a single wave above her left ear stood behind the desk, smiled as they came in.

"Hello," she said. She took a book from the top of a

168

pile, pulled out a card in the little sleeve inside the cover, stamped it. "How are you doing?"

"Fine," Laura said, and smiled, nodded.

"As well as can be expected," Winnie said.

"Glad to hear it," the woman said and stamped the next book.

Winnie went straight to the shelves, as though there was a book she'd wanted for weeks but'd had no chance to make it this far away from Reed's Beach. Laura watched her disappear into the stacks and found herself standing with her hands at her sides, a librarian stamping books her only company here.

She knew what she wanted: books about this place, about South Jersey and Cape May and the Villas and the Bird Sanctuary and all else she'd seen so far. She wanted books that would give her words to fill her, expand inside her so that what she knew had begun to break in her might already begin to mend or, at best, become clouded with the history of a place, with books about the thin surface of the earth she stood on right now. All this in the hopes, of course, she would not succumb as her husband had.

For a moment she thought of the bed this morning, the feel of its emptiness, Hugh already gone for Hess. She thought of the warmth of the room, the touch of new light in through windows. She thought of the company afforded her by a man named Roland Dorsett and that of his wife, a woman back in the stacks and searching for words to fill her own self, and Laura wondered exactly what Winnie's own story might be, knew somehow that she'd been broken, too: Wasn't that what she'd seen in her eyes back at Reed's Beach, in the way hers had lingered on Laura's, Winnie's single word *My* an agreement between them that they had both seen something and that Winnie had come through, was there to help marshall Laura on and through herself? Why else were they out here?

"Can I help you find anything?" the librarian said.

Laura looked at her, saw she'd lost the smile. Her eyebrows were up, the hand with the stamp poised over a book.

And Laura saw Winnie then, saw the black hair, her face as she peered at Laura from around the end of a row of shelves: just Winnie's head, looking at her, then disappearing.

"Miss?" the librarian said.

"Books on South Jersey," Laura said.

They were reference books, books the librarian—"It's just our policy," she had smiled, "like every library"— wouldn't let leave the building. There were only about a dozen of them, all on a low shelf on the wall beside the circulation desk: *Iron in the Pines, South Jersey Towns: History and Legend, Forgotten Towns of Southern New Jersey, More Forgotten Towns of Southern New Jersey*. There were others, all of them with variations on the same theme, all of them handled and beaten, spines broken, pages yellowed.

She'd wanted to bring them home, search them for clues, histories, anything she could take from them, but then had come the librarian's now familiar smile, the next book in her pile stamped as if to punctuate her words: "Those can't be checked out."

Winnie appeared again, this time from around the end of another row of books. She didn't look at Laura, there at the circulation desk with her own pile of books, but only came around the end of a row, her hand trailing along the spines, her purse dangling from her arm. Then she turned and disappeared down the next row.

Laura looked at the librarian again, tried her own

smile, and picked up the stack, went to the round table in the far corner of the room. She set down the books, pulled out a wooden chair, sat, and started in.

She read. She skimmed pages, looked at photos, some maps. They were all well-meaning books, all old, out of print, and seemed like fables to her, stories told around a fire at Girl Scout camp: chapters with titles such as "The Furnace in the Forest," "Shane's Castle," "End of the World: Cranberry Hall." The language in them was outdated and romantic and weighed down by the authors' dreams of grandeur and ruin, when she only wanted fact, unadorned image, sentences she could hold in her hand like a leaf or a rock or a feather.

"Much like time itself, however, the Atsayunk flows serenely on," she read in one of the books, "giving majesty to the great lake, spilling over the dam into foaming eddies, seeking its familiar course, as it has over the centuries—through the pinelands, into the Mullica, and on to the sea."

In another, she read, "One dark and chilly night, not long after Bill's death, Peggy's house, a ramshackle structure, burned to the ground, the old woman dying horribly in the flames. Though the ruins had revealed what had been her body, no trace was ever found of the hoarded money and it was generally conceded, for many years, that Peggy had been robbed, murdered, and burned to conceal the crime."

Then Winnie stood beside her at the table, and Laura jumped at the sudden flesh and blood right there, a living woman with three books in her arms, a woman with no smile and who held up her watch in a way that made certain Laura could see what time it was already, that sent her the signal without speaking a word: *Hurry up. We have places to go.*

Laura looked back at the page, at the story of a woman

171

incinerated to conceal another crime. She blinked, pictured her own house in Englishtown burned to the ground, only the brick foundation left. The image seemed easily conjured. No trick at all. Except that there was no charred body. Only smoke and ash.

"Look up Reed's Beach," Winnie said, and reached down with her free hand, pushed toward her one of the books, *South Jersey Towns: History and Legend*, from the scattered heap on the table.

"What?" Laura said and looked at the book. It had a blue and black cover, a pen and ink drawing of a huge house like some of the ones she'd seen when they'd reached Old Cape May.

"The index," Winnie said, and Laura looked at her, saw her nod at the book. "Look up Reed's Beach in the index, sugar." She paused. "You do know what an index is for, don't you?" She smiled. Only the corners of her lips moved up, her eyes on the book.

Laura said nothing, turned back to the book. She nodded and sighed loud enough to be heard: her own signal to a woman she wasn't certain of at all. The cover of one of the books Winnie held, she'd seen, had a picture of a bare-chested man holding close a woman in a flowing pink gown; the other book jacket had a picture of a winged creature, batlike with glowing red eyes. She didn't know this woman at all.

She opened the book, flipped to the back. There she found a listing for Reed's Beach—only one—and turned to the page.

"Read that," Winnie said.

Laura started at the top of the page, but then here was Winnie's hand on the page, an old woman's hand, she saw, wrinkled and worn and red at the knuckles, and Laura thought for an instant of soft leather gloves, of the protection they seemed to afford but which finally made

172

little difference: Hands grew old. This was an old woman's finger pointing to a paragraph halfway down the page, the fingernail short and trimmed and old, tapping at the page.

"Start here," Winnie said.

Laura read.

One of the contributions of the Quakers to the history of Cape May Country is the legend of the "Quaker guns." During the War of 1812, Reed's Beach on the Delaware River about three miles west of Cape May Court House was a spot favored by the British for filling water casks and restocking stores.

One night, according to the story, the Quakers who had long suffered British raids without protest gathered for a discussion of the situation. A day later the shoreline of Reed's Beach was bristling with cannons peeping out from the underbrush. The British discontinued their raids.

The "Quaker guns" were actually logs shaped and painted to resemble cannons, a trick credited to William Douglass, a ship's carpenter of nearby Sluice Creek. By this deception the Quakers were able to continue their creed of not taking up arms but saving their goods from those who did.

"That's all there is to know," Winnie said. "The astounding history of Reed's Beach. Logs and Quakers." She paused. "Pretty heady stuff."

Laura closed the book, then closed her eyes. She said, "There's plenty more I want to know. I want to know more than just about Reed's Beach. I want to know—"

"Maybe so," Winnie cut in, "but there aren't enough hours in the day. And you gave me to know you wanted to get to several important locations here on the Jersey

Cape. Perusing books for words about places you could stand at and see with your own eyes seems a waste to me."

"Books are not a waste," the librarian said from where she stood behind her desk, and both Winnie and Laura turned to her. "They are conveyors of history and thought," she said.

She wasn't smiling anymore, the stacks of books gone. Instead she held in one hand a long wooden spindle, with the other hand threaded a section of a newspaper onto it.

She said, "You ladies are welcome to talk in here so long as there are no other visitors. But this is a library. And as soon as someone else walks in that door, you will be quiet." She paused, glanced down at the spindle, and tugged the section into place. She looked back at them, her forehead furrowed. She said, "And as long as you keep bad-mouthing books, I'll have to ask you to silence yourselves."

"Listen, honey," Winnie said and started toward her, books in hand. "I'll just be checking these books out here, and we'll be on our way, and you can just settle your juices because we'll be out of your hair." She set the books on the desk.

Laura stood, amazed at what words came forth when she was around this woman, amazed at what passed before her eyes. Amazed there was nothing she could do besides be dragged by her for the rest of the day. Now they were as good as being kicked out of the Cape May Library, stop one on a day she'd seen already begin to break, a day that'd begun with an empty bed and that would end with one. A day, she saw, with too many hours in it. This day.

She leaned over, began gathering the books on the

table, and heard the librarian call out, "Just leave those. I'll reshelve those, thank you very much."

Laura turned to the woman, saw she looked at neither Winnie nor herself, her eyes on the three books before her, saw her stamp the cards she placed inside the little sleeves.

Then she looked up at Winnie. "Three weeks," she said. The wave perched above her ear seemed to shiver.

"Have faith," was all Winnie said.

Winnie handed the books to Laura, put the key into the ignition, and started up the van.

Laura held the books in her lap. She pushed aside the top two, the romance and the horror, saw the third one she'd checked out: *Slate Shingles: History and Restoration*.

Winnie said, "Never know when you'll run into a slate roof needs reshingling."

Laura looked out the windshield. The sun had already started in on the inside of the van, and she thought she could feel beads of sweat on her upper lip. She squinted at all the unwelcome light, at the red gingerbread bed and breakfast next door.

She said, "Guess so."

Then Winnie reached to the books, pulled from Laura's lap the top one, *The Thorny Rose of Love*. She flipped through, looked at a page here, a page there, her old woman's finger tracing its way down the words until she flipped to the next page.

She stopped, tapped the finger hard halfway down a page. "Here we go," she said. " 'There he stood, in all his naked manhood. She quivered at the sight of his bronzed, well-toned chest and his huge muscles. And she gasped when, finally, she let her eyes fall to his majestic virility, that glorious and powerful object of her desire, so large and thick she knew she could not deny herself of its pleasures.' "

175

She stopped and looked at Laura. "I've read this book nine times," Winnie said. She was smiling, shook her head. "I'll be damned if I've ever seen a majestic penis before. Every one I've ever seen has looked mighty sickly to me, like some pitiful blind hairless creature."

They both laughed, the sound a sudden and loud surprise in a world she'd figured contained no surprise. She couldn't remember the relief of laughter, couldn't recall when last she laughed or smiled at some strange and odd nothing, laughter for laughter's sake.

"Winnie!" Laura said, and felt herself gulp down air, felt tears in her eyes, tears that had nothing to do with what she kept at bay each moment she breathed. New tears, ones she let go.

Winnie closed the book and looked at the cover. She held it with both hands, still shook her head. "History and thought," she said, this time quieter. She let out a long, deep breath. "Bullshit," she said.

Laura laughed at this, too, the sound inside the van all sharp color and angles and new. The floorboard was still littered with fast-food trash and various tools, between them still a straw handbag and a patent leather purse. But now there was a new sound in and around them, and the sound itself worked to keep it at bay, she heard, worked to hold it off, though she hadn't designed it this way.

"Just pitiful creatures," Winnie said and looked at Laura, handed her the book. Laura'd finally stopped laughing, shook her head, wiped at her eyes with one hand, took the book with the other. She let out a small laugh and looked at Winnie.

Their eyes met again, and Laura saw in her that, yes, in fact, this woman had been broken in some way, and that even in the face of this fact Winnie's smile was genuine, as was the way she talked, the words she let out, the

176

way she carried herself and leaned her head and smiled without ever letting out the secret she held. Laura saw all this in only that look.

She wanted to know then, even more than any book on local legend and fact, even more than any touch of eyes or words passed or any laughter in daylight, what Winnie had gone through, as though she might find a common fact, a tie to Winnie that would make certain whatever lay ahead of them on this day would not be lost to her.

She brushed at the tears that fell from her eyes, felt the pain of laughter in her chest and side and in the constriction of her throat. She felt all of this.

Winnie put her hands to the wheel, still looking at Laura. She gunned the engine, a sound as surprising and joyful as their laughter, the empty street outside their open windows choked with all the gingerbread and Victorian charm anyone could ever want, settled there in its midst a stucco library and a scratched and dented van with 158,000 miles on it. That sound, a loud and ugly engine noise, made her laugh yet again, a short burst from her, and she settled the books in her lap, shook her head again.

"Looks like you're feeling no pain," Winnie said to her, smiling. She gunned the engine again.

"Oh, yes I am," Laura said, the truest words she had let out in as long as she could remember.

"Then good," Winnie said. "Pain's good for you. Sees you through." She nodded hard, reached to the black knob on the gear shift, and worked it until she found what she wanted, all without taking her eyes off Laura.

Laura nodded, and believed she had found something of what had broken Winnie, some glimpse into her own story: pain seeing you through. She straightened the books in her lap, nodded again, and held tight to the pain this laughter had given her.

"To the *Atlantus*," Winnie said then, and faced forward, eased out the clutch. They were moving again, new warm air slowly swirling into the van, making way for more new air as they moved.

She had no books to bring back to Reed's Beach, stop one on the day's agenda lost already. But it was surrender, she saw, that mattered. And she'd already surrendered this place, with its angered librarian and stamp pad and books to be reshelved, and she no longer envied that woman. There was a place they had to visit, somewhere to go.

"To the *Atlantus*," she said, her voice almost a whisper, lost to the strain of laughter and the sound of the engine and the crash of light through the windshield and the welcome and shining pain she held.

❀ WINNIE DROVE BACK along Sunset Boulevard, past a 7-Eleven at the intersection with Broadway, once more past all the old homes with porches, homes that had nothing to do with gingerbread or turrets or Cape Cod Red paint behind them in Old Cape May.

Then they were on a stretch of road with no homes, only tall gray and brown brush beside them, walls of brush, above them a sky too blue, Laura thought, a blue as painful and necessary as the surrender she saw coming.

Next they passed a few more homes, these on the left, gravel yards and fresh cedar siding and windows: Cape May Point, and here came the brown-and-white highway sign, CAPE MAY POINT STATE PARK AND BIRD SANC-TUARY, the arrow pointing to the left.

A few moments later Winnie slowed down, inside the van the sudden metal echo of rocks shot up from beneath the tires. The road ended here, spread before them out the cracked windshield an empty gravel lot. There were no homes here, no thick brush. Only a broad, empty parking area with two small buildings, old shacks, really: To the left sat a peach-colored shack with a porch, a tin roof, atop it a plywood sign, CAPE MAY DIAMONDS

179

AND SHELL SHACK in black hand-painted letters. Opposite that building, to her right across the gravel lot, sat another shack, this one white, atop its tin roof a plywood sign painted in the same hand: CAPE MAY POINT ICE CREAM AND DRINKS.

Out past the end of the lot was the water. The Delaware Bay, Laura knew from the maps she'd left at the Halfords' place. This was the Delaware Bay, the same body of water she and her husband had stood at last night, the two of them uttering their son's name almost simultaneously, though she hadn't said Michael's name because her husband had said it. It was just that the name was always there, like blood just beneath the skin: Only the smallest break, the slightest tear—a husband watching the moon as though it might speak to him of loss—let flow unspeakable volumes. Her son's name had slipped out just like that, like blood from a wound. Michael.

This, too, was the same body of water, the same cool blue she'd seen only this morning from the Halfords' kitchen, their dock poking out into the blue as if it had some right to be there, as if it might be able to hold up against whatever punishment that water and the wind and sky could give. And she knew what a hollow confidence that dock offered: They had only to look left down the beach to see the rows of broken pylons in a trail like black bones up from the earth.

They moved across the gravel, the rocks shooting and cracking beneath them, until Winnie turned to the left and parked before the shell shack. She cut off the engine, and dust swirled up around the van, the air no longer moving inside with them.

She said, "We have arrived," Laura vaguely aware of the words as being the same ones Winnie'd used when they'd pulled up to the stucco library in Cape May.

"Stops number two and three," Winnie was saying. "Cape May Diamonds and the *Atlantus*. We'll kill two of the birds on your menu with this one stone," Winnie said, and Laura heard from beside her the van door open once again, the same slam shut.

But her eyes were to the water out her window, that window rolled down, her arm out in the light, and for a moment she tasted the dust, tasted the earth itself in the roll of a cloud of dirt.

Her eyes were to the water, to that blue and what lay out there, something she could not quite yet make out but which, in some miracle and curse at once, she believed she recognized, believed she knew.

Winnie stood waiting at the front of the van yet again, this time Laura only aware of her presence; she saw in her peripheral vision an image of color and words and attitude, but it was the unidentified something out in the water she focused on, the something out there she knew and did not know.

"Sugar?" Winnie said, and Laura brought in her arm from outside, with the other hand reached beside her, found the straw bag on the floorboard between the seats. Always this straw bag, she thought. Always this straw bag, no matter where she went, as though there were no choice in the matter of its accompanying her.

She opened the van door and stepped out. She felt herself push closed the door, then start across the gravel, head toward the water.

"Well," Winnie was saying. She was behind Laura now, Laura on her own, moving toward something she believed she did not want to see but had already seen.

"Well, sugar," Winnie called. "I think I'm just going on over to the beach, rake up some of those precious diamonds. You feel like communicating, you let me know."

181

But there was something out in the water, she saw, that seemed to rise in her, black itself, and as she crossed the lot she saw that there was a rock jetty out past the beach, a jetty poking into the Delaware Bay, a jetty in which she could have all confidence: No squall or hurricane would move these stones, stones that reached out toward something in the water, a black hulking mass.

What she saw out there was what she had seen since the moment her doorbell rang on a November afternoon, her believing it for a moment to have been their son Michael joking around, him home from the bus at precisely this time each day, only to open it to Gerry Rothberg, face flushed with sweat and heavy breathing, his eyes stricken, she could see in an instant, as he tried for air, his hair sweaty and stringy as he looked up at her, then behind him, then at her again, his chest heaving, then the words uttered by him, only a little boy, the son of their next-door neighbors, words that would end the world and start a new and black one, as black as what lay out past the black stones of the jetty she was fast approaching now, her legs moving of their own, moving with no assistance whatsoever toward an unidentified structure that seemed to speak to her the same words Gerry had: "It's Michael," he had said. "It's Michael."

She had run after the boy, him already gone off her porch and looking at her over his shoulder, those eyes still stricken, shattered for what he knew, she'd seen, and for what he knew she herself would know soon enough, so that for a moment it seemed a kind of guessing game the boy next door had devised: *Chase me, chase me*, the game seemed to have gone, *and I will show you a truth you can never believe.*

Laura stopped a moment, saw a sign planted on the beach, black with white letters:

REED'S BEACH

S.S. ATLANTUS

REMAINS OF EXPERIMENTAL
CONCRETE SHIP, ONE OF TWELVE
BUILT DURING WORLD WAR I.
PROVEN IMPRACTICAL AFTER
SEVERAL TRANSATLANTIC TRIPS
BECAUSE OF WEIGHT. TOWED HERE
AND SUNK AS WHARF IN 1926.

She took the words in in an instant, then moved past the sign and closer to the jetty, the wreck of a concrete ship suddenly all she could know of a race from her house after the neighbor boy, the two of them cutting between houses, through yards and into woods in what she saw was these boys' secret path, nothing she'd known about before, and as she followed Gerry, she realized she had on only her socks, no shoes, and for a moment and for no reason she could name, she thought of poison ivy, and wondered at the miracle of how these boys had gotten home through this growth without ever emerging with reddened skin, scratches.

She moved onto the jetty now, and the black rocks she stepped on one to the next to the next seemed to give her some secret of their own; their sharp edges and slippery wet from small waves lapping combined with the fact they did not give, would not falter beneath her weight, seemed to speak in the same secret language of Gerry Rothberg's eyes: *Chase me, chase me,* they seemed to speak as she stepped and stepped, arms out for balance, in one hand the straw handbag, a weight that seemed as heavy as eight years' walking the face of the earth, eight years, and a weight that seemed nothing more than a shell, an antler, a feather.

183

Then they emerged from the woods, Gerry still in the lead. But now he stopped, before them both the bright and sparkling shine of a school bus across one lane of gray and tired asphalt, the bus's flashers going, the air around her filled with the peculiar dry black smell of exhaust and old tires and burnt oil.

They were on the driver's side, the red **STOP** sign sticking out from below the driver's window, and she saw that there were no children on board, no driver, and for an instant that seemed longer than she had known her son, had known her husband, had known her parents, even her own name, longer even than the sun had held its place in a suddenly thin and breakable sky that beat down on her and gave beautiful color to a yellow school bus, black jetty rocks; for just that instant she allowed herself the belief that everything was going to be all right, everything was going to be all right, and yet even inside that moment of belief the earth's gravity began in earnest its irreversible work on her, started to press down on her heart, take all air from her as she saw Gerry move around the front of the bus, slowly stepping backward, hands on hips, eyes on her—*a truth you will never believe* his eyes spoke—until she was near the end of the jetty, out past its end something black, and at the same moment moving across the asphalt, around the front of the bus, stepping on rocks and rocks in an effort to find what lay around the other side of the bus.

Children were crying as she neared the end of the jetty, children in quiet tears, silver sound like waves lapping, tide moving in or out, she could not say which as she saw the swarm of children, the bus driver nowhere, nowhere, Gerry Rothberg moving into the crowd of children crying on this side of the bus, children whose heads turned when they saw her. Here at the end of the jetty, Laura's eyes to the flat and sharp and cloudy rocks, were Melinda

184

D'Abo, Henry Joiner, Carl Hagerty, Martha Stonesifer, Jason Rutledge, all of them acquaintances of her son Michael, children with whom he had talked and fought and played, all of them turning and looking up at her on a beautiful and cloudless day here, in early February, warm air in off the water on a day that had seen her lose, finally, what she'd held onto: control over a loss she could not measure, that control given somehow to a woman with black hair, a house on Reed's Beach, a husband who sat in an upstairs room and worried over tide and time and the moon. She'd lost, she saw in the wreck of the *Atlantus* before her, her son.

The end of the jetty now only seven, six, five rocks before her, she began to see what lay at the center of the swarm of children only five, four, three children thick, the handbag now a weight past bearing, but a weight she could not lose, would never lose; the secret it bore as she stepped on the last rock of the jetty, looked up from the rocks to the wreck of the *Atlantus*, was the final piece of evidence of how much she loved the child she lost, how much she missed him, and proof, too, of what she wanted beneath her skin, kept like blood inside her, a part of her she would always need but did not want spilling from her for fear she might bleed to death.

It was her husband who was bleeding to death, she saw. Her husband. And she did not want to die that way. She wanted to die with her son pumping through her each moment, a beat in her heart every moment she breathed, a love and loss set so deep inside her she could not lay claim to any waking knowledge. Just the proof of his presence, what she tasted every morning in the pill she swallowed.

She reached the last rock of the jetty, and felt as though the jetty itself were some dagger into that heart.

Now her life spilled all around her, made the sea she stood before bleed red while children parted before her.

And the children parted.

And the children parted.

Gerry Rothberg stopped, stood aside, his eyes to what lay before them on the ground, and revealed to Laura the bus driver, a woman, kneeling before a boy. The woman was sobbing, a hand to her face, the other flat on the ground, and though Laura could not yet see the boy's face for the woman kneeling beside him, she saw a blue and green plaid flannel shirt, saw jeans and a yellow belt, saw he wore only one tennis shoe, the other foot in a white sock.

This was what she saw: the *Atlantus*. She held the handbag with both hands, squinted at the light up from the water.

It lay a couple hundred feet off the end of the jetty, and bore little resemblance to a ship. Three separate parts stood above water, two of them large and high, the third smaller, lower in the water. She saw what she believed to be portholes on the left side of the middle portion, the piece that seemed most like the side of a ship, flat and wide. She could see, too, that the entire thing was hollow: The wreck was settled at an angle to the right, so that she could see inside, as though it were a dollhouse cut open. But it was hollow.

And it wasn't black, she saw, but shades and hues and tints of black: brown-black, green-black, purple- and red- and blue-black. Rust-black and moss-black and weather-black and sorrow-black and grief-black, the God in heaven who'd given her this death letting fall into her lap this wreck of a ship.

The *Atlantus* wasn't black, nor was it a ship. It was, she knew, her own grief, the thing she could not touch but touched every moment, the black hulk in her she

knew and did not know. This was what she'd felt lodge
in her throat this morning at the Halfords', the car gone;
what had made her loosen his name from her mouth, set
it aloft on the cold wind on the dock last night.

This was the death of her son, she saw: concrete, ragged and broken and worn by the world, immovable and
beyond reach.

She could not touch it, though she could see and hear
and taste and smell its evidence every moment she lived,
and this fact, its residing just off shore, just past belief,
seemed the largest and coldest fact of all. The wreck was
out there, just as was the death of her son, the same blue
water lapping against them both as lapped beneath the
Halfords' place, as lapped at her own feet right now, the
same blue water as lapped at every shore on earth. This
was what she knew of death: a black of many colors just
beyond reach, black colors quivering in the tears she felt
falling now.

She sat down then, the cold of the stone beneath her
welcome and bitter. She held the handbag to her chest,
clutched it tight, as though it, too, might be picked up
on an errant wind, born aloft like the name of her child,
and lost.

She'd seen this before, and had never seen it.

She'd been here before, and had never been here
before.

The children parted, and never ceased parting.

"Take a look at these," Winnie said, and Laura saw
her hand, the old woman's hand, held there beneath her
eyes, too close.

She did not know how much time had passed, the sun
above her still slicing down in what seemed the same
angle, as though it had stopped altogether. She was still
crying, the shipwreck out there still quivering, the sound

of her sobbing not at all different from the silver quiet of the children who'd gathered around her here at the end of the jetty: Henry, Martha, Melinda. Gerry. All of them, except for Michael.

She looked at Winnie's hand, saw through her tears a different glistening, a shine and white glitter. Her throat seized up, her teeth clenched.

"Cape May Diamonds," Winnie said and moved her hand, made the shine move. Winnie stood beside Laura and a little behind her so that she could not see the woman's face or blouse or shorts or that purse. She saw only her hand, heard only her voice. "Find them all along the beach for free. Charge you a quarter a piece for some of these up in that shell shack."

There were small stones in Winnie's hand, clear and round, the largest no bigger than a pea, the smallest the size of a BB. Each one caught a piece of the sun stopped above them, carried that light inside it to make it glitter and shine, fractured light that danced in this woman's hand.

"Take a look at this one here," Winnie said, and now Laura was aware of Winnie kneeling beside her. Winnie pointed a finger from her other hand to the smallest stone. "Quartz's all it is," she said, "rubbed raw on the beach there until it shines up like this." She pinched the stone between two fingers and lifted it up.

It was perfectly clear, Laura saw, a fine piece of polished quartz. But then the stone and Winnie's fingers quivered yet again, gave over to the tears she let out, and the silver air in and out of her came again, children gathered around her once more.

Winnie whispered, "You want to tell me what's wrong?"

She knew, of course, no words to give to this stranger. There existed no words to pass on, existed nothing more than the truth of a shipwreck, a bus with its flashers going, the perfection in a piece of rock. Even her husband, once he had arrived at the hospital, stumbling toward her in the same sort of quiver the day shook in right now, had had no words for her, had had no comfort to give or understanding to offer or reason to follow. They two had simply stood in a hospital corridor, leaned against a white wall, and she had looked up at him, waiting for this man to hand to her words, the right words. But he had not spoken.

She did not answer Winnie, only folded her knees up closer into her chest and held the bag even tighter for the proof inside it, the tomb there.

Winnie placed an arm around Laura's shoulders and held her, the hand with the diamonds gone, before her once more only the wreck. She said, "Now girl, now baby," and held her.

They were words. But not the right ones. The right ones, she knew, needed to come from her husband, her partner in this, fellow passenger on the ship out past her reach.

But Winnie's small words had seemed to carry some weight, seemed somehow like the fractured and broken light that shot back from inside Cape May Diamonds, so that Laura let herself lean into the woman's arms. Then, as carefully as she had done anything before, as carefully, she believed, as she had closed the lid on her own son's coffin, she placed a hand inside the bag.

"You say to me what you want to say," Winnie whispered. "I'm only going to listen. That's all."

But Laura had no intention of speaking, knew the uselessness of air passed through the vocal cords, saw it only as the bodily function it was.

Her hand was inside the bag tucked in her lap, there between her stomach and her legs, her knees up to her chin. Still she leaned into Winnie, her hand moving deeper into the confines of the bag, and she felt different odd pieces of her life: Here were her car keys, her wallet, a brush, a packet of Kleenex.

She felt then the empty pillbox, the hard plastic case, and thought of Hugh, of his own heart bent toward the impossible task of impregnating his wife, and there tore in her chest a twisted pain made sharper by the presence of the empty box: She loved Hugh, but loved Michael.

For an instant she thought to bring out the box, reveal it to Winnie, seek from her counsel, as though this stranger might find a way through this matter, the matter of life or death it seemed having a second child would entail.

But she did not, simply let the box go. The packet was not what her hand was searching for. What she was after was buried even deeper, like her heart, far back and hidden. She hadn't touched what she knew was in her purse since before her son had died.

Before, she thought, and let her breath break her in two, her shoulders heaving.

Then she touched it, there at the bottom: a round cylinder. She touched it, let her fingers wrap around it, let her hand pull it from the depths of the bag, and she thought she might now know the pain of a heart ripped from within its work: Here it was.

She brought it out of the bag. It was nothing, only a black plastic film canister with a gray snap-on lid, the kind of canister that came with a new roll of 35-mm camera film.

She held it in light now, the first daylight it had known since before his death, when she used to add to its contents now and again, when there came from her son something she thought she needed to keep.

"Now what do you have there?" Winnie asked and

reached a hand to the canister, touched at it. This was the same hand that held the diamonds, Laura knew, inside her fist pieces of stone that swallowed and cherished light when held in the sun.

Laura said nothing. She took in a breath, took in another, and pulled back the lid, let fall its contents into her open hand.

Only a tightly wound roll of papers held with a red rubber band.

She held the roll in one hand, the canister and lid in the other. Then she placed the canister back inside the purse, its treasure revealed, the tomb empty.

"You don't have to show me anything you don't want to," Winnie said.

But Laura was already pulling at the rubber band, rolling it down the paper until it came off in her hand. Winnie'd asked the question— *You want to tell me what's wrong?*—and here came the answer.

Laura slipped the rubber band around her thumb, and now they were only pieces of paper, scraps and receipts and Post-it notes, and she took the roll of them in her hand, tried to smash them flat between her palms. It worked, to a degree: The pieces still wanted to curl into themselves, but now she could read them.

She let her legs go, felt her knees part so that she sat cross-legged on the rock now, Winnie still behind her to her left; still she could not see the woman but only heard her soft words in her ear.

There were about a dozen small slips, recorded on each a few words or numbers or information, even a drawing or two: the truths of her son's life, evidence he had breathed and walked and talked.

She looked at the first one, written on the back of a pink phone message memo from the hospital, and she remembered having run into work and written the words

191

down, words that had come to her from Michael in the back seat on the way to Kinder Kare. *Michael, May 6, 1988*, she had written. *Points to a car's license plate & says, "Look, M for Michael!"*

She held the paper in one hand, her fingers of the other closed over the rest of the pieces, protecting them from whatever wind might choose to visit them this moment, lift them out of her life and into the vast gulf of water between her and the wreck. She read it again and again, savored the words from the child seat behind her, the sound of his voice in her head, a sound that had started with his cries at birth, a new human given them, and a sound that had ceased on a road in Englishtown. That morning he'd recognized a letter from the alphabet.

And then she surrendered, passed the paper to Winnie.

She surrendered. She had come all the way here, had driven all over Cape May in search of what would fill her, only to end here, surrendering her child's life, something she'd carried with her every day she herself breathed, to a woman she did not know, a woman who, she felt certain, had her own story, her own sorrow to reveal, but who hadn't yet found it necessary to reveal: *Pain's good for you. Sees you through*, was all Winnie had surrendered.

Winnie took the piece of paper, moved from kneeling to sitting, and Laura could see her now, the woman's profile in sunlight. She held the piece of paper with both hands, her eyes poring over it. Their knees touched, the two of them perched on the last rock out.

Winnie looked to Laura. Their eyes met a long moment, longer than when they had been pulling against each other on the dock in Reed's Beach. They looked at each other, Laura's eyes warm with weeping, her breaths still shivering in and out.

Winnie smiled and nodded. Her lips did not part with

the smile, nor did she speak. She only smiled, held Laura's eyes.

Laura could not smile. But it seemed this woman's silence and her nod were gifts enough: No words, even Winnie knew, existed that could speak louder than her child's voice just then, his voice recorded on small scraps of paper.

Winnie gave her back the memo. Then she read the next one, this on a yellow Post-it note: *Michael insists on calling his slip-ons his coupons—8/1/87,* and she remembered the white slip-on sneakers she'd bought for him at K Mart, easy to put on and take off, him in and out of the house all day. She handed this, too, to Winnie, who took it, read it, and handed it back.

The next one was a happy face, drawn by Michael in pencil on a corner of yellow legal paper, the head bumpy and misshapen, the eyes big empty circles, the mouth a flat line with its ends pointing up. He'd been only three when he'd drawn this, she remembered, Michael getting into Hugh's briefcase one morning before either of them were up. He'd filled three or four sheets with the faces before they found him on the floor at the foot of their bed, and it had been this corner she tore off, secreted away to the film canister she'd already started by then.

Her eyes filled again, made the happy face waver, shake, and she held onto it longer than the others, held onto it with the belief that what she was surrendering was in fact too much, had gone past what the woman beside her ought to know. But still she handed it over, letting Winnie hold it, a piece of paper upon which her own son had drawn.

Winnie smiled. She handed Laura the drawing, and Laura looked at it yet again, her eyes brimming, and she placed it at the bottom of the small stack.

But then Laura looked at the next one, written on the

back of a deposit slip torn from the checkbook. She read it, and read it again, felt the world in its orbit, that same earth she had tasted in the dust of the gravel lot, spin beneath her: This note read, *"The moon is teasing the sun!" Michael, October 19, 91, on seeing the moon out in the morning.*

She saw Hugh at the end of the dock.

She saw her son, a first grader then, standing at the end of the drive, ready for the walk with Gerry Rothberg to the bus stop on Milk Farm Road, ready for the ride into school. Ready, pointing to the sky, to the moon there, a thin crescent teasing the sun coming up in the east. "The moon is teasing the sun!" he'd said, and she'd stepped out onto the front porch, looked to where he was pointing above the trees, leaves on fire with October red and orange and rust.

She saw a path through woods.

She saw her husband, worried over the moon.

She rolled the papers up, slipped the rubber band back over them. She reached into the handbag, brought back out the canister, put the roll in, and snapped closed the lid.

🌸 THE TAJ MAHAL.

Her eyes were hot, she knew, her face puffy. Laura knew this, and touched a Kleenex from the packet in her handbag first to one eye, then the other.

She had broken, finally, had given all she had away to Winnie, and now this was where they had ended up: Trump's Taj Mahal.

She had not known they were headed here, had only watched as Winnie'd driven: road after road, bridge after bridge, pine barrens and marsh for what seemed days.

They were in a long and wide hallway, had just gotten off the elevator from the parking garage, now moving with other people across the purple and orange and red and burgundy carpet, to their left a long row of windows. She could see through the windows the giant marquee on the building, the gold and red and iridescent plum spires and flourishes bright in the midday sun, TRUMP scrolled across the largest balloonlike tower, beneath it in blood red letters on a black background TAJ MAHAL, a circle of shimmering lights surrounding the whole thing.

She was at the Taj Mahal.

Everyone around them walked and talked and smiled

as though nothing in the world were any more important or less a loss than a day spent gambling. Women with hair swirled up even higher than Winnie's and with sequined sweatshirts painted with leopards or giant flowers walked beside them, accompanied by men with patent leather shoes and knit sportshirts too tight, swelled out over bellies.

At the end of the hallway lay a bank of glass doors through which people streamed, and as they neared the doors, Laura looked at Winnie, tried to smile, and saw that in fact Winnie fit the bill here entirely: red knit shorts, shoes with thick heels, floral print blouse. That hair.

But the woman beside her knew things.

Winnie smiled at her. Her huge purse, a purse that seemed to match these old men's shoes perfectly, was crooked in her arm, the other at her side, and Laura wondered if Winnie herself bore some secret inside it, some tomb of her own.

Then Winnie reached her free hand to Laura's shoulder and touched it. She said, "Just what the doctor ordered," her voice strong and clear even in the midst of the swarm of words and laughter and movement from all these day gamblers down from Passaic. "Me being the doctor this time," she said.

Laura tried to smile, touched the Kleenex to her eyes once again, though the tissue was wadded up to nothing, useless. She shrugged, not certain what her own gesture meant: only a response to this woman, a woman who knew more about her than even, Laura believed, her husband.

Hugh.

Even Hugh had no idea about the film canister, fragments of the son's life she carried with her each day. Nor did he know of the pills. He knew nothing of the pills, and knew nothing of the deceit in his wife, a deceit designed, she knew, to keep herself from the truth, always imminent, that their child was dead, the pill each morning a way to stave off death, a way to remember his life, to taste it, to feel it.

Now the question she still needed to ask Winnie seemed even farther away, even more remote with their presence in this crowded hallway: *Do you have any children?* she wanted to ask. But all words had left her, gone with the unfurling of the evidence of Michael's life.

They were at the doors now, one of the older men in patent leather shoes and knit pants—red and blue plaid—holding open the door for the two of them.

Winnie, hands clasped at her chest, smiled, said, "A gentleman in New Jersey," and nodded, moved past him. "And handsome to boot. What'll God give us next?" she said over her shoulder, still smiling.

He smiled, nodded at her, then at Laura, who glanced at him as she moved past him and through the door. His hair was white, done up in a big pompadour above his forehead, his face flushed with broken blood vessels.

Just inside stood a woman waiting, Laura figured, for the man who'd held open the door. Her blue-white hair was teased and stacked, and she had on eyeliner as thick as black worms, pancake makeup that hid nothing. On her ring finger was a diamond two or three times as large as the one on Laura's engagement ring.

Laura could see the woman was staring at Winnie and had both hands tight on her bag. Her lips were pursed, the lipstick, what seemed the same shade of iridescent plum as the flourishes on the building, wrinkling up into thin canyons of an old woman's skin.

"Quite a catch you got there," Winnie said to her and nodded at the man. He still held open the door, people filing in as though he worked here. Then another older man took his place, patted him on the back, let him move inside.

The woman only let out a breath through her nose, a short exhaust of sound, said, "I know your type." She turned and smiled at her husband coming toward them.

"Only too well," Winnie said to her, then, to the man, "Thanks, honey, for the courtesy." She winked at him.

"My pleasure, pretty lady," he said and nodded at her. Finally, he looked down at his wife. She wasn't smiling, was already pulling him away. He lost the smile, cleared his throat.

All of this in a few second's time, Winnie's life, it seemed, played out before her: a confidence of movement and words beyond belief, the ability to size up and tear down at a moment's notice.

What, Laura believed, may have already been done to her: She'd opened the tomb, let fly her son's life. And Winnie hadn't spoken the entire drive here.

But now they were inside Trump's Taj Mahal; now they were in a different world. Not that the world of South Jersey so far this warm February day was the same old world; not, too, that the world she'd entered a day in November of last year was anything she'd ever become accustomed to.

But this was the Taj Mahal, and she stopped, looked at it all just inside the lobby: the brilliant rich colors, the shop windows loaded with booty, the gold and burgundy and red and orange and glass, the chrome and shine and bitter glistening of all these colors and lights. And the people, the people, all of them swarming, filling the lobby, jammed onto the escalator, swinging from the chandeliers.

All these people. Even Winnie, witness to all Laura herself had surrendered when they'd been out at the *Atlantus* and Laura had broken, spilled her life and the contents

198

of her purse for Winnie to see; even Winnie. She was one of them, and Laura wondered again what it was Winnie had to spill of her life, what secret this smiling woman held.

Winnie's question, the one that'd unraveled and revealed Laura: *You want to tell me what's wrong?*

As small and killing and right a question as that.

Cross my heart and hope to die.

You remember that night, the last night up in Maine?

The moon is teasing the sun!

Here they were, Winnie standing before her, a hand out to her. Laura saw Winnie and the colors and the shine and the people, all these people, shimmer in her eyes for the tears she knew might crest any second now. She had more Kleenex in the packet in her bag, a packet she'd put in months ago but had never used. But she didn't dare open the bag for what she knew might spring forth full-blown again, what she carried with her too much to look at again, to read.

She was aware of movement around her, saw now in the ugly clarity of all this light and in the shimmer of her eyes that she was simply one of them. She was one of the swarm of people in this palace, a trip to the Taj Mahal a hopeful pilgrimage, intended happy ending to the gray world left up in Passaic. Or Englishtown.

This place, she saw, was the opposite of where she'd wanted to go, the least real place in all South Jersey, maybe the world. One needed only to look at the color and light in here, Laura thought, to see how false was this world.

Winnie's hand was still held out to her. She heard Winnie's words: "Just what the doctor ordered," she said again. Then, quieter, so that the words seemed only smoke high and above all this movement: "Trust me," and suddenly it seemed perhaps this was the place she

199

had needed to go all along: She'd sought the real, but perhaps needed to find what was not. She knew real, had seen it at the end of a jetty, had seen it on the other side of an empty bus. She'd seen it in her husband's eyes.

"Trust me," Winnie said again, and held out her hand in the lobby of the Taj Mahal, movement and light and color slicing through Laura like knives and sunlight, gold and royal blue and plum and turquoise and gold all swirling around her.

She knew nothing of this woman, she saw. Only that her husband had been a cook on an aircraft carrier, and she could fix things. Only that.

But she reached for Winnie's hand anyway and took it, because Winnie knew things about her now, and because she knew no other way out than the hand of the woman who had brought her here.

Five

He WAS LATE.

He'd told Mr. Halford he would be there by seven, and now it was seven thirty-five, and here he stood, his car door still open, the house before him—white columns, twelve-pane windows, black shutters—lit in a way that made him feel that perhaps he would be better off just not entering. The white gravel driveway, linked to the street by knee-high lights of its own, curved up the huge front lawn, paralleled the porch, turned, and disappeared behind the house. There was too much light, and there were too many windows, too many columns across the front of the place, the oak front door too big and heavy even to open.

But he needed inside. He needed to speak to this man, though he could still plan no certain thing he wanted to say. He knew there were words that needed to pass between them, words about raising three boys now grown and gone, words about the care and use of a sextant, about how to weather-strip and install forced heat and read nautical charts and measure the moon and account for tides.

All this, he knew, in order to let that wound lay open for as long as he could. He needed information, words

that would form a thin veneer over his genuine life, the
one filled with the death of his son, so that he might
savor alone what everyone in the office—even his wife,
the women who would not enter their child's bedroom—
watched from a distance.

He'd finally nailed the SOC7 at six-forty, Waxman having given up at five-thirty. Ed Blankenship, his day filled,
Hugh knew, with work of his own—he had the base pro-
grams for the entire production and storage facilities—
had leaned in one last time at six-thirty and said, "We
promised resolution by six."

"I'll take this one in," Hugh'd said, though he saw no
clear end before him, no resolution. He hadn't looked up
from the screen. "No guts, no glory," he'd said. He was
quiet a moment, then smiled to himself. "No pain, no
gain," he said.

"Just let me get MSA on the horn one more time. It's
their goddamn program," Ed had said, and Hugh saw
out the corner of his eye Ed take a step into the cubicle,
a hand out for the phone on the corner of Hugh's desk.

"See you tomorrow, Ed," Hugh said, his eyes still to
the screen. "I'm landing this one all by my lonesome."
He shrugged.

He hadn't been able to see Ed's face, his reaction,
hadn't gauged any look from the man. But he had heard
the silence, the absence of words from a man usually
handing them out whether they were wanted or not.

By that time the sun had gone, the only light through
the windows of the far wall a dull gray-orange, a color
he could not recognize for a moment, a color he believed
he had not seen before: gray and orange.

He'd looked back at the screen, wouldn't allow himself
to see the light outside the window, that strange and
vague and hollow marriage of color through glass.

Now he was alone, and there were no longer any spectators. Only the mission of completing the batch, getting Rhode Island to stop sweating.

He'd looked at the screen, at the mass of equations and quotient derivations, the language that spoke only in 1s and 0s, a world so simple and logical and devoid of all grief that he wanted to sink into it, be swallowed by so many *Yes* and *No* and *No* and *Yes* qualifiers.

He stared at the screen and suddenly glimpsed the world he wanted to inhabit, the one in which only those Yes and No questions could be asked, and he saw for an instant the giant arcs of loss and love, the two of them intertwined across the expanse of time—he had only the rest of his life to live, only that—those arcs stretching all the way back to one single, quiet question: *Do you love your son?*

The floor was silent save for the high-pitched hiss, barely audible, of the screen before him, the computer itself.

Yes, he typed in.

He looked at the word there, saw how incongruous it was against the mass of numbers and letters, punctuation marks and slashes and spaces. This was the real world, he thought, the one in which he actually existed: random numbers, random letters, inexplicable symbols.

He deleted the word *Yes*, but placed inside himself the knowledge the answer still existed. He hadn't typed over the word, hadn't put in *No*. He'd only deleted, and it had seemed, too, this parallel to the exact truth of accident—his child had been deleted, not negated, not denied—was some sort of dark miracle. His son no longer existed, but did. He'd lived, breathed, spoken. This was fact.

And then he saw the SOC7, the data exception.

Like all exceptions, it lay in plain sight, easy once one had found the source:

205

{I/771:R91}I⁻}

It was there just four lines below where he had typed in
the word *Yes;* he would not have seen it, he believed,
were he not alone on the floor, were he not here to hear
only the hiss of electricity through circuits.

He deleted the line, given the access code by the MSA
trade rep earlier that afternoon, when they'd chosen to
return his call from that morning. Then he entered the
correct equation:

{771:R91}⁻

It had been only a misplaced end bracket, right there
after the second numeral 1, a bracket placed too early in
the derivation, but one that shut off the line before it
was completed.

A typo.

An accident.

He pushed himself away from the screen, heard the
wheels of the chair across the hard plastic carpet guard
beneath him. He stared at the screen, his hands in his
lap.

Only an accident, an end bracket placed too soon, cutting off the equation to let the whole of the program
ground to its own ABEND, every equation after the one
cut short therefore nonsense, worthless.

He closed his eyes.

An accident.

"A SOC4 is to keep your feet warm, partner," Ed said,
and Hugh shot open his eyes, turned to the sudden sound.

There stood Ed in the doorway. He wasn't leaning
against the jamb, didn't have his hands in his pockets.

He didn't have his coat. He only stood there, filled the doorway, no smile on his face.

Beyond him, out the windows on the far wall, the sky had gone black, night now settling in.

Hugh sat there, hands still in his lap. He blinked at the night, the orange-gray already gone.

He looked at the man in the doorway again and thought for a moment what he knew of him: No children was the first thing that came to him; divorced a year or so ago came next. Overweight, funny. Laura liked him, he remembered, had told Hugh so after a party Ed'd given a while back, a party at which Ed had danced the Hustle for the crowd, then had pulled in his wife, Charlotte, to do it with him, then the whole of the party had taken it up. A living room full of Hess people doing the Hustle when, as far as Hugh could recall, he hadn't seen it danced in a good twelve or thirteen years, back when he and Laura were in college and used to go out to Lily Langtry's on Route 9.

Hugh had danced the Hustle there in Ed's place. He'd remembered the dance, and he and Laura had joined in with the crowd, all of them sweating and laughing, half-drunk in a house in Colts Neck.

Hugh had danced.

He looked down from Ed and turned back to the screen, the now-revised SOC7. There were backtracks he had to take, exit channels through the language. There was distance to put between himself and this cancer he had cut out of the program before he could run it.

"Thought you'd left already," Hugh said and logged in the next exit code, the one that would make his correction stick for all time and eternity. "Found the problem."

"Bully for you," Ed said. Hugh again saw him enter the room from the corner of his eye, saw him sit in the chair backed up to the glass wall. "Will wonders ever cease," Ed said. He paused. "This is what you were hired to do, by the way, so don't expect any fanfares from this quadrant."

Hugh said nothing, logged in the next phrase, and fell farther from the typo, the grand accident.

"Money well spent," Hugh said. "Your having hired me, that is. Not necessarily on this program. Nothing but a goddamned typo in there."

"Hired to snag typos," Ed said, and Hugh heard him let out a breath, heard him give a small laugh. "Money well spent."

Hugh logged in yet another exit phrase and saw the derivation he'd repaired disappearing fast before him, buried already.

"I was down there after Charlotte and I broke up," Ed said.

"Bully for you," Hugh said.

"Bully for me," Ed said.

"Listen," Hugh said. He turned the chair to the desk, pushed aside piles of printouts on the desktop, made just enough room to put his own hands flat on the blotter. "Listen," he said again. He glanced at Ed, then at the night outside the window. For a moment he thought of last night's moon, the weight of the sextant.

Hugh was quiet, only looked at Ed, there in the chair against the glass wall. Then Hugh said, "Why?"

Hugh looked down at the desktop, at the papers, at his hands. They looked like someone else's hands.

"Why what?" Ed said and shrugged.

"Why did you let me go on about Halford's place?" Hugh said. He was still looking at his hands.

"Is that what you really want to know?" Ed said. His voice was quiet now, smaller. "Because if it is, I'll tell you the reason right now: I let you go on about the place because I figured it was what you wanted to say at the time. What you needed to say."

Hugh looked up at him.

Ed shifted in the chair. His hands were still together in his lap, but he lost the smile. He said, "But I don't believe that's what you want to know. I think you believe somehow I'm going to rob you, that I'm here to take something from you." He paused. "Or maybe you think I'm going to go toe-to-toe with you and what happened to you. Swap sorrow for sorrow." He shrugged and looked at the floor. "Wrong," he said, this time even quieter, almost in a whisper. "I'm not going to."

He looked up at Hugh. He shrugged, but didn't smile, only let his eyes hang on Hugh's.

"This is no contest. Never was. All I figure is this: Maybe there's something you can tell me." He paused, seemed to think on what he'd said. Hugh believed he could still hear the hiss of electricity all around them. "Or," Ed said, "maybe there's something I can tell you." He paused. "But I'm never going to know, *we're* never going to know, until somebody talks."

Hugh didn't look away, simply stared back at him, suddenly aware that there was some new language Ed had offered up, not the twisted and convoluted one he himself had become fluent in all those days back at work. Not the language of distance and reserve, of fear and hiding.

Because, Hugh saw and had always known, this was what he had done: been afraid, and had hidden.

But Ed was offering up a new language: the truth.

Ed let out a breath, said, "Charlotte and I broke up. That's all." He paused. "But I guess that's plenty enough. And I needed time to be somewhere else." He stopped and took in a breath. He looked at his hands again. "And if you need to talk—"

Hugh closed his eyes. He could either surrender to his

own language, a language that was no language but one
that would keep them talking in the endless loop they'd
started with, or he could surrender to what Ed seemed
to want to speak, this language of truth.

He swallowed. He opened his eyes and found he'd
moved his hands on the blotter, the palms now up.

He looked out past Ed, out to the night. There, low in
the sky, he saw what he believed must have been the first
star out, a fixed pinpoint of white in the black.

He saw his son rolling down a hill in a backyard in
Matawan, saw the lights of fireflies like splintered life
from as small a star as the one in this February night
sky.

He saw his son, and knew he could not give him up,
could not let him and what he knew of him be diluted
by speaking to this stranger, this man named Ed.

He looked at his hands. He said, "I've got two more
exits to make off the Rhode Island batch, then I'm
headed out." He paused and wheeled the chair back to
the terminal. "Supposed to be at Mr. Halford's in twenty-
five minutes, all the way down to Holmdel." He made a
show then of looking at his watch, put out his arm so
the cuff pulled back, then brought it close to his face.
"No way in hell I'll be able to make it by then." He shook
his head. "But at least I got the SOC7 smashed."

"Bully for you," Ed said. He was already back in the
loop.

Ed stood, said nothing. Then he was gone.

Now here was the house: more light than he could take
in, a stunned white and pure light.

And this, he knew only then, was the language he
wanted to speak. Not the language of affluence, of a huge
house in Holmdel, the accompanying cottage on Cape
May.

Rather, it was this language of light, the way it shone and gave shadow and illumination at once. This light, he knew, even the small light cast by those lights along the drive, spoke its own words, words he wanted to know. He wanted the truth it gave, but wanted to hide in the shadow it gave as well.

He wanted, he finally saw, to see, but not be seen.

The front door opened. There stood Mr. Halford, behind him a perfect and gleaming kind of light, soft and warm and shining: a chandelier, Hugh could see, hung in the foyer of the house.

"Come on in," Mr. Halford called out. "We've been waiting for you!"

Hugh held his breath a moment, then closed his car door hard, almost slammed it to see whether what lay before him, this perfect language, might shatter and disappear.

But nothing happened. There had been only the sound of a car door closing, then Mr. Halford's upraised hand, beckoning him in.

"We heard you coming!" Mr. Halford called out, and opened wide the door.

He STARTED TOWARD Mr. Halford, toward what he could see of that chandelier and warm light and whatever unknown words were going to fill this evening until he would have to leave this place, head back to the empty house in Englishtown.

Then he was at the huge oak door, a door with a polished brass kickplate and polished brass knocker in the shape of a lion's head. Mr. Halford stood just inside, backed up a step as Hugh came in.

"Hugh, my boy," Mr. Halford said and held out a hand for Hugh to shake. He had on a tweed jacket, a gray turtleneck, navy slacks.

No bow tie, Hugh thought, and felt suddenly out of place in his own tie, the same tie he'd worn all day, the same shirt, the same pants. All of it clothes he'd put on in the dark of this man's cottage at Reed's Beach what seemed a month ago.

"Mr. Halford," Hugh said, and took the man's hand, squeezed and shook hard, felt himself smile. He saw in Mr. Halford's eyes the shine of a man's old age, a man with a perfect tan and weather-caressed skin, a man who lived in a palace and had been blessed with three lives and so much light. "Sorry I'm so late," Hugh said. He

212

looked down at his tie, at the pen in his shirt pocket. "Didn't even have time to get home and freshen up before coming over."

"No apologies, Hugh," Mr. Halford said. "You don't think I've ever stayed late at the office?" He let go of Hugh's hand and pushed closed the door behind him. "But I'm anxious to find out about the Rhode Island problem."

Hugh glanced up, saw above them the whole of the chandelier, luminous slips of crystal amidst thin gold branches, three tiers of lights suspended from a high ceiling.

Here was light, enough light for Hugh to hide in and to allow him to search through this man for the knowledge he wanted. He looked back to Mr. Halford.

"Nailed that bad boy, Mr. Halford," Hugh said. "Nailed it to the ground," he said, and it seemed somehow that the words were the first he had spoken of this new language.

"Good to hear," Mr. Halford said, "good to hear." He clapped a hand to Hugh's shoulder and ushered him farther in to the foyer. "Once and for all," he said, "the name's Dennis."

"Dennis," Hugh said. Still he smiled. "Of course."

Mr. Halford's hand was heavy on his shoulder. The light banged down on them.

"I guess Rhode Island can go ahead and quit sweating, head for the showers now," Hugh said. He put his hands in his pockets, forced a laugh.

Mr. Halford leaned his head back and gave out a hearty laugh, one that seemed to ring through the foyer, twist up and through the chandelier, fill the air. "Hugh," he laughed, "I've smelled Rhode Island all afternoon. Let's hope those bastards up there wash with Comet."

Hugh laughed, crossed his arms, and almost believed

in the feel of the words he'd given, the feel of the laughter in his chest.

"Boy talk?" Hugh heard. He and Mr. Halford both turned.

At the far end of the room was a staircase that swept up in a smooth curve from the hardwood floor, above the staircase a tall window with too many panes to count.

Hugh saw first her hand on the banister, saw the simple glistening of a ring, a shine and movement even from this far away as she moved down the staircase.

Then he saw Mrs. Halford. She was smiling, and had salt-and-pepper hair parted in the middle and flipped up on the sides, the curls there just above her shoulders. Even from this far he could see her beauty, the same sort of beauty he might assign to Mr. Halford: sunlight, skin worn but not tired. She had on a bright yellow turtleneck, green flannel slacks.

She made it to the bottom of the staircase and moved toward Hugh, both hands out to him.

"I don't mean to cut in on all this boy talk, but I'm Sal," she said, and Hugh had no choice but to put out both his hands, take hers in his.

"No boy talk," Mr. Halford said. He was smiling at her. "Just the Rhode Island problem."

Mrs. Halford's hands were warm, and Hugh thought he could feel callouses on them. Not what he'd expected.

She said, "Whatever happened, I don't want anymore talk about work in here. This is dinner, a nice evening. So no more." Smiling, she glanced at her husband, then at Hugh. "We hope the cottage wasn't too much of a mess when you got in," she said.

He felt himself still smiling, the strange force of it.

"Not at all," Hugh said. "It wasn't a mess at all." He held her hands, her fingers in his, then let go. She held his hands a moment longer, and for an instant he was

214

embarrassed he'd let go first. There'd been something good about her hands, about the warmth of them, the tough feel of them.

He glanced to Mr. Halford, then to her. He looked down, saw the shine of the chandelier on the hardwood. "You've been more than generous," he said. "Too generous."

"Our pleasure," Mrs. Halford said, and laced her hands in front of her. There was the ring, Hugh saw. It wasn't huge, as he'd imagined it would be. It was only her engagement ring, a solitaire about the same size as the one he'd bought for Laura when they'd gotten engaged, nestled next to it the thin silver wedding band.

She looked at her husband, said, "Of course this old codger's no help when it comes to cleaning up the place." She paused, moved to Mr. Halford, and looped her arm through his. "There's this duck boot out on the dock that's been there for three years, ever since we had the thing rebuilt." She looked at Hugh. "Have you seen it?"

"Actually, yes," Hugh said, those two small words even as they left his mouth heavy and fake. *Actually* he had said. *Actually.* "It's still out there," he said.

"Of course it is!" she said and laughed, the sound filling the air just as Mr. Halford's had. She pulled at her husband's arm, held him closer to her.

Mr. Halford gave a small grin, rocked back on his heels, then forward.

She looked at him. "I've pestered Denny to pick that thing up forever," she said, "but he just never gets around to it, and now I believe it's become a part of the natural landscape down there." She turned, looked at Hugh. "And I'll be damned if I'm ever going to pick it up. It's Denny's boot. Not mine."

Denny, Hugh thought, then remembered: *Sal.*

"It's become a point of honor," Mr. Halford said. "I'll

be damned if *I'm* ever going to pick it up." He smiled, shook his head.

Hugh gave a small chuckle, shook his head, too. "Well," he said, and laced his own hands together in front of him. He was quiet a moment, then said, "Then I'll be damned if *I'm* ever going to pick it up either."

They all laughed, and Hugh believed he'd spoken more of this language. He felt pleased somehow, felt his chest ease even more.

She turned, her arm still looped in her husband's, and led them toward white double doors to their right. With her free hand, she touched one of the doors, barely pushed it, and sent the door sliding back into the wall. Then she pushed the other, and the door disappeared without sound into the wall.

It was a room Hugh might have found in a magazine: walls paneled in dark oak, an oriental rug that stretched from one end of the room to the other, a red velvet couch, two overstuffed brocade chairs. Against the left wall was a wet bar recessed into the wall, all light and mirrors, above the sink a row of crystal decanters filled with amber and red and brown and clear liquids. Rich blue swags framed the windows to the right; between them sat a small high table, on it white roses in a crystal vase.

Against the far wall was a stone fireplace, flat stones one atop another from floor to ceiling. Inside the fireplace itself was a fire already burned down; small flames moved along the charred logs.

And above the mantle—a thick beam of a dark wood set into the stones of the fireplace—hung a painting of a huge sailboat on a gray-green sea, the boat heeled over, sails nearly touching water, scattered across the deck men in striped shirts, white caps. A single recessed light on the ceiling was aimed at the painting, lit it so that Hugh's eyes had nowhere to go but there.

Mrs. Halford let go her husband's arm, said, "We actually sit in this room, believe it or not." She laughed. "Even though it looks like a museum. But it's nice to read in at night, nice to sit with a fire and read."

"A Mulhern," Mr. Halford said, and moved to the fireplace. His arms were crossed, his eyes on the painting. He nodded. "The original. That's the *Indigo Princess.* Made the purchase one summer at Camden." He leaned his head one way and the other, sizing up the painting as though he'd never seen it before. He looked to Hugh, winked. "Camden, Maine, that is." He smiled. "Not New Jersey."

Hugh felt himself give a small laugh. He moved through the room, stood a few feet from Mr. Halford. He crossed his arms, too.

He looked at the painting. The men on deck were all holding tight to lines or to available hardware: a cleat, a wench, a mast. They were each minuscule in size but drawn in such detail he could see faces on them, moustaches and beards, the wind in the hair of a sailor whose cap was gone.

And there was the color of the water, the green and gray of it, and Hugh could only think of the orange and gray of the dying light back at Hess, could only think of Ed and his words, that old language of prying, of trying to steal the truth of Hugh's history from him.

"Drinks, boys?" Mrs. Halford said from behind them, and Hugh turned, saw her at the wet bar. She held a square decanter of clear liquid in one hand, its cap in the other.

"Tanqueray and tonic," Mr. Halford called out. He hadn't turned from the painting. "Nectar of the gods," he said. He glanced at Hugh again, winked again.

Hugh looked to Mrs. Halford, smiled. "The same," he said.

He turned back to the painting, arms still crossed.

He said, "Nectar of the gods," just loud enough for Mr. Halford to hear, then smiled, shook his head: more words in the new language.

Mr. Halford's eyes were still to the painting. "Look at the lines on that ship," he said.

Hugh looked at the painting, traced the way the full mainsail billowed out, its arc smooth and sharp against the blue sky behind it, as smooth and sharp as the moon he'd measured only the night before.

And here came the image, like a dream, of a curtain cutting a line through a window one midnight in Maine, a line as smooth and sharp, he knew, as the line of his son's jaw, the curve and touch of it just that smooth, just that sharp.

He closed his eyes.

"Beautiful lines," Mr. Halford said and slowly let out a breath, the sound a low whistle.

Hugh opened his eyes. He breathed in, put his hands behind his back, held them.

He looked at the men on deck, at the way each man clung to what he could, the gray-green water only a few feet away as they hung on.

He waited for a word to come to him, some response to this man beside him. He waited, expected just the right one to emerge from somewhere inside his heart and head, some new piece of the vocabulary of light he wanted to know.

But nothing came to him.

"Your drinks," Mrs. Halford said from behind them, and shook the glasses, the sound of ice and liquid and crystal filling him.

❧ THOUGH HE DID not want them, pictures of his son started coming to him now, even there in the living room of the Halfords' home, a gin and tonic in his hand and small talk coming at him, none of it the talk he wanted, none of it words that would pierce who these people were and what they could tell him.

He wanted to know where Mr. Halford had gotten the nautical chart thumbtacked beneath the octagonal window upstairs, wanted to know the history of the sextant, when he had gotten it and where, and how precisely to use the thing. He wanted to know what storms Mr. Halford had weathered down at Reed's Beach, if he'd been through hurricanes there, if flood tides ever threatened the place.

And there were things he wanted to know of Mrs. Halford as well: her hands and the way she seemed able with only a touch and word to disarm this vice president. He wanted to ask her how much gin she'd put in his drink, the thing almost too strong to swallow. He wanted to know about her hands.

He wanted to know about their sons, wanted to know how they had turned out, what they did for livings, what it had been like to see them come home from school unharmed each day, see them graduate, see them date and fall in love and marry. He wanted to know what it was like to see them alive.

All this.

But what surfaced was small talk, talk of the weather and how warm it had been today, talk of the bulbs Mrs. Halford had planted last fall and her hopes they wouldn't think it spring already, come right on up, and die once the cold came back. There was talk, too, of work, quiet questions by Mr. Halford, Hugh's obligatory answers: how Oscar Neelon was working out, why Waxman had quit early, if Ed had finished up with the St. Thomas facility program. Mrs. Halford *tsked* each time she overheard them, threatened to take back their drinks and not serve them the steaks she'd had marinating all afternoon, called, "Now stop that" when Mr. Halford went on with it in spite of her.

Yet here were the images of his son, and not the old ones, not those he had unleashed this morning in the silence of the ride up from Reed's Beach. These, for no reason he could name, were images he had not thought about, he believed, since he had seen them take place. Only now they surfaced, here, in a place laced with the booby traps of a new language: He knew no ways to introduce the topics he had imagined taking place here in this palace, saw no avenues in to the new language he could use to hide inside.

So he nodded at Mr. Halford's assessment of Joan Waxman and how she seemed worthy of the company but hadn't yet proved herself, hadn't yet shown the "testicular fortitude"—Mr. Halford whispered the words, glanced behind him at his wife to make sure she hadn't heard, then smiled at Hugh—executives at Hess needed to move forward.

And while Hugh nodded, he saw Michael at the breakfast table, saw Laura with multiplication flashcards. Michael had a pencil in his hand, was bent over a piece of notebook paper on his planets of the solar system placemat. They were in the middle of a quiz, he knew, Michael glancing up to the next card Laura held, writing down a number, glancing up again, writing again.

Then he saw Michael stop, eyes to the white rectangular card before him, and heard his son whisper through clenched teeth *Eight times seven is, eight times seven is, eight times seven is.* He saw his son's eyes open wide, glaring at the numbers on the flashcard as though they were betraying him somehow, holding back a secret he needed in order to get on with his life.

Fifty-six! Hugh heard himself yell inside this memory. There he stood at the front door, his briefcase in hand. *Fifty-six! It's always fifty-six. It'll never change. Seven times eight is fifty-six!*

He'd yelled these words at his son, and as he nodded yet again at Mr. Halford's words about how the stones in the fireplace had been quarried at some town in New Hampshire and hauled all the way down here especially for their fireplace, Hugh remembered then the scores his son had made on his math tests: 56, 61, 49, 52.

They drilled each night, Hugh and Laura trading off quiz for quiz, their son never seeming to get it, to let it settle in his head that these were simply a series of numbers that always gave up the same answers. *It's just like memorizing the telephone number,* Hugh had tried to explain one night, *or like your address. Do you know your telephone number?*

Yes, Michael had whispered. They were at the kitchen table, dinner dishes cleared, Laura at the sink and rinsing, slipping wet plates and utensils into the dishwasher. Hugh was in his seat, Michael at his. Between them on the table lay a half-finished pile of flashcards, in Hugh's hand the equation 4 x 9 = ____.

Do you know your address? Hugh said. *Do you?*

Yes, Michael whispered even more quietly, the word small and hushed beneath the rush of water, the clatter of silverware.

Same thing, Hugh had said. *Same thing! Four times nine is thirty six. Say it.*

Michael's mouth moved, his eyes to his hands in his lap.

Say it, Hugh had yelled. *Louder!*

Hugh, Laura said, and he'd looked up to her at the sink. She stood frozen there, yellow dishwashing gloves on, a shiny wet plate in her hand.

Then Michael had cried, his mouth gone to a jagged line, eyes closed tight. He made no sound, only leaned forward until his forehead touched the table.

Mr. Halford laughed at what his wife had said from the couch and Hugh nodded, smiled.

He did not know why this had come to him, knew no order of events in the evening thus far that would hand to him what he did not care to see: himself yelling at his son, yelling and leaving for the office, yelling until his son cried there at their own kitchen table.

He had come here to learn something, believed only a few minutes ago that he had begun to partake of their language, had begun to believe he could indeed hide and be seen at once.

Mr. Halford shrugged and turned to Mrs. Halford on the sofa. He shook his empty glass, held it out to her, and now Hugh saw himself pushing the lawnmower one May Saturday. Michael, maybe three years old, came out of the garage then, a can of red spray paint in his hand, something Hugh'd left in the garage after he'd repainted the wheelbarrow. Then the boy sat cross-legged on the driveway next to the left rear wheel of Hugh's car and sprayed the tire, made circles and circles while Hugh watched.

Hugh let go the mower handle, the engine cutting off. He saw himself take long strides across the yard, the lawn cut in neat strips, the smell of mown grass sharp and sour in his nose.

Then he was at the driveway, saw himself reach down, yank the boy up by one arm, lift him off the ground.

You know better than that, Hugh'd yelled, and he recalled that, even in the moment he had said those words, he wasn't certain they were true. What could this boy know?

But he took the spray can from the boy's hand anyway, tossed it into the garage, and slapped the boy's hand.

Michael yelped, then wailed.

Mrs. Halford said, "How was the drive up from the cottage this morning?" and Hugh spoke, said words that seemed somehow to please her. He saw her smile, nod.

But even in the midst of her smile, whatever mother's secret she held in the warm callouses of her hands, still he felt his chest tighten once again, felt the sense he'd had outside: that if he were to slam the car door too loudly, all he saw would shatter around him, along with it all hope of knowing what raising children on past eight years old was about.

He felt his smile grow hard, chiseled into his face. He felt his tie too tight at his throat.

He saw his son bent over before him, hands on his knees, saw the wooden spoon in his own hand. They were in Michael's bedroom, the room with the blue desk and chair, the bed that had gone untouched for three months and eleven days now.

But on this day the bedroom window was broken, hot July air pouring into the room, glass shards like flat daggers strewn through the flowerbeds outside the window: He and Gerry Rothberg had been playing baseball *inside* the house.

His son had on blue shorts, a yellow Six Flags–Great Adventure T-shirt. He wore white sweatsocks and high-top tennis shoes.

And Hugh, listening to Mrs. Halford with all he could give, every last shard of attention he could muster for her, saw his own hand speeding down, felt the jolt of the spoon on his son's buttocks.

He could not stop it. There was nothing he could do to stop it, neither this memory nor his own hand inside the memory.

His own hand.

Michael shivered at the force of the spoon and broke out in a sob.

And Hugh said to the room, "Where are your sons?"

The words had come out too loud, he knew. His words echoed in here, tumbled across and around the opulent furniture and cold drinks and soft light.

Mrs. Halford, at the wet bar with the square decanter in hand, turned to him, blinked, smiled, and he realized only then she had been in the middle of a sentence.

He looked at Mr. Halford, who stood silent at the fireplace.

He thought it was the tightness in his chest and at his throat, believed it to be the gin, perhaps, or the nature of these hollow words they had passed between them.

But still he could not say why these things had come to him. They were moments he did not want invading his grief, the perfect memories he had accrued all this while, such as the moment just after birth when he had held him and spoken his name for the first time: *Michael*, he'd whispered, then looked to Laura, smiling and pale and trembling in the birthing chair, her arms out to take him, their baby at once pink and blue and wet with the blood of his mother; the two of them one Saturday afternoon hammering together a fort built of plywood and two-by-fours leftover from when Hugh had put in the workbench in the garage; the first goal Michael ever scored in Pee-Wee League soccer, his son simply kicking the ball from midfield, the ball slipping through the swirling mass of four-year-olds, only to roll slowly into the goal, all momentum gone, until the ball stopped without even touching the back of the net.

These were what he wanted carried with him.

He was in a mansion, a palace, and had almost found refuge.

Then he had spoken the truth of his mission—*Where are your sons?*—and the palace had shattered, crumbled into shards of its own: Mr. Halford, still silent, looked to his wife, who stood with the decanter still in hand, still with her eyes on Hugh.

Hugh tried to find the smile it'd seemed might never leave his face only moments before. But he found nothing, only put his drink to his lips, took a long sip at the gin.

It was Mrs. Halford who moved first. She put the cap back on the decanter, and Hugh saw that she hadn't poured any gin in Mr. Halford's drink, the glass still empty save for the ice.

She looked at the bar, then the mirrored shelf. She settled the decanter on the shelf, touched it one last time, as though there were some perfect place for the bottle, some exact angle it needed to find there on the glass.

She set the glass on the bar and turned. She wasn't smiling, only laced her hands together again, just as she had in the foyer. But now the diamond, that ring on her hand, didn't shine, didn't move with the light. It was only a ring.

She said, "Well," and glanced at her husband again. "Truth be known," she said and took a deep breath. A piece of a smile played across her face, disappeared. "Truth be known," she said again, "we weren't certain you'd want to talk about anything like that." She paused, seemed to tighten her fingers around one another. "We weren't sure we could say—"

"The boys, the boys," Mr. Halford let out, and he quickly crossed the room to the wet bar, picked up his drink. "The boys are doing well, quite well." Mr. Halford's back was to Hugh now, but Hugh could see his face in the mirror behind the shelves. He reached up to the gin, took it down, his eyes focused on filling up his glass.

Hugh could tell there was something wrong and believed it to be his words, the blunt and ugly edge of them, the prying into a language it was perhaps possible to know only within the lives and confines of this house, of the histories of these two people and the histories of their sons. And he saw then he hadn't ever partaken of their language, their way of walking through these fine rooms and wrapped within this warm light.

"The boys are doing very well, given the circumstances," Mr. Halford said. He replaced the decanter and pushed it into place on the shelf, the bottle askew, ugly for this new angle. Hugh wanted Mrs. Halford—*Sal*, he thought, *Sal*—to touch it again, set it right.

"Given that the youngest will be doing community service in Neptune for the next six months," Mr. Halford said, and he turned, now all smiles. "Only on probation for the next two years."

"Denny," Mrs. Halford said. She reached a hand to him, touched his elbow as if, Hugh saw, she might be able to set him back in line, just as she had the bottle.

But Mr. Halford didn't look at her. He hadn't looked

at Hugh either, his eyes instead to the painting above the fireplace. His glass was full; Hugh hadn't seen him put in any tonic. This was only gin.

He held up the glass in a small toast, smiling. "Given that my youngest has been convicted—" He stopped, the glass in midair. Still he only smiled at the picture. "Given that, my boys are fine. All's right with the world."

"I apologize for my husband," Mrs. Halford said. "We've had a rough day of it." The same piece of a smile moved across her face, but this time it seemed to catch, hold on. She put her hands together again and glanced at Hugh. "We've had to find—"

"I apologize for myself," Mr. Halford said. He was looking at Hugh now, the glass down. "I apologize," he said, and Hugh saw then, in this soft light, and in these dark oak walls that suddenly seemed to push in on him, that before him was only a man, one who had aged in a moment: He saw his skin for what it was, beaten, burned by the sun too many times. And he saw the shine in the eyes of the man as fear, the truth of fear dug into them.

"I have no room in this world to bemoan the fate of my children," he said, eyes straight on Hugh, whose tie seemed even tighter now, his chest crushing him. Hugh lifted his glass, took in the last numb trickle of gin and tonic.

"Denny," she said again, and now she looped her arm in his, pulled him close to her again.

"But when you raise them up—" he started, then stopped. He blinked, and Hugh heard something catch in his throat, a raw breath like some kind of cry.

"I have to leave," Hugh said.

"Please don't," Mrs. Halford said. "Our youngest was in court today. He was—"

"I have to leave," Hugh said again, then said, "I'm sorry. I've interrupted." He paused, the empty drink in

227

his hand. He looked around for something to set the glass on, a coaster, a magazine, anything. But there was nothing.

He turned, looked at Mrs. Halford, Mr. Halford.

He was the spectator now, he saw, the same kind he'd seen watching himself all day long at the office. There were things this couple knew that he would never know, histories he could never touch.

Just as beneath him was his own history, the thin ice through which he had no choice but to fall, always and only that beneath him: his son, these memories, both the joyous and horrible, both the wanted and rejected, all of them burning in him just as hotly as the words *accident* and *son* and *Michael* had seared the palms of his hands as he'd made his way into the hospital only to have his wife fall into his arms, her hollow *No no no* perhaps the only true language he had ever heard spoken.

Laura.

He thought of Laura.

"Please," Mrs. Halford said, and now she was moving toward him, her hands out again. "Please," she said. "We have dinner all ready."

He put out his hands again for what he knew would be the last time. He put out his hands, took hers, felt the callouses.

He'd already shattered it all, broken every window in the place.

And so he turned her hands up in his, looked at her palms.

There were her hands, pink and clean, but across the tops of her palms and at the fingertips the skin was thick and beaten, hard and red. And there were the two small slivers of silver, the backs of her rings.

She pulled her hands away, squeezed them shut. She gave a small laugh, her eyes on his chest. She said, "I'm out in the garden all year round, unless the ground's frozen solid." She laughed again. "In the garden, or the greenhouse." She put her hands together at her chest, as though in a prayer. She met his eyes, then half-turned, with her thumb pointed behind her. "We have a greenhouse out the back, on through the kitchen," she said, still smiling. "Would you like to see?"

"Sally," Mr. Halford said. "Dear," he said.

Hugh looked at him. He wasn't smiling, held the glass at his side, his arm down.

"Sal," Mr. Halford said. He leaned over, set his glass on the coffee table, then moved to her and touched her elbow with his free hand. "Sal," he said, quieter, almost a whisper.

Her eyes hung on Hugh's a moment longer, her thumb still hooked back toward whatever cavernous greenhouse must have been attached to this mansion. She smiled at him a moment longer, too, then closed her eyes, squeezed them shut.

She turned to her husband, leaned into him, and Hugh watched as his boss put his arms around her, gently patted her.

Hugh took a step back, felt his legs touch the chair behind him. He said, "I'm sorry," and Mr. Halford looked at him, smiled. He nodded, the move barely a move, so small Hugh might have imagined it.

But the smile was a genuine one, Hugh could see. This much was true: An old man with a son in trouble, never mind what had happened to the other two, had smiled at him. An old man with a wife it seemed might be shattering even as he watched had smiled at him.

"There'll be another night," Mr. Halford said and nodded again. "We'll have the both of you over."

"Yes," Hugh said, the word quick from him. "Certainly," he said.

* * *

229

His headlights bit into the black spread before him, cut across the lawn, stabbed into the trees a hundred yards away.

The air out here was colder now, much colder than he would have thought, given the way this day and its sunlight and blue had played itself out.

But now it was cold, and without thinking, he leaned to the dash, switched the heater to high, and felt the shot of cold air at his ankles.

Laura's move: Start the heater first rather than let the thing warm up.

He thought of Laura, and looked out the passenger window, saw the house in all its glorious light.

There were rooms in that house, rooms, he knew, inhabited by their own ghosts, ghosts unknowable, invisible, but there all the same. Were he to come back here on another night, as Mr. Halford had said, it would only be another night, beneath all they said and did, beneath their gestures and words and smiles always and only their own private language, nothing he would ever learn to speak.

He saw, too, in the empty windows, in the clean and gleaming light, that he knew Mr. Halford better than he'd imagined he could ever know him. Mr. Halford was himself, he saw: Hugh, a man, only that, hiding.

He placed his arm on top of the seat and looked out the back window to the long gravel driveway behind him. Too far to back down, he knew, and so he put the car in gear, started forward toward, he hoped, some widening, a way to turn around, a way to head home.

The gravel screamed beneath him as he followed the drive, his headlights moving, sifting through the woods at the far end of the lawn, landing and moving again on bare trees.

REED'S BEACH

Then there was a building before him, white brick, three black garage doors, all of them shut.

And here was the greenhouse, some twenty yards off to his right, poking out from the back of the house.

It was a miracle of light and glass and emerald green parked here in a February night, jammed onto the back of a big white house. It was a greenhouse, barracks-shaped, glass and glass, every pane frosted over with the growing cold out here, the warmth in there. Rows of white lights inside made the smudged shapes of green all the more violent, all the more terrible and unexpected and beautiful, and he took in a breath, stopped the car just to look at it.

Then he saw movement inside, saw at the farthest end of the greenhouse, where it seemed there might be some table pushed up to the glass, a person.

Mrs. Halford, her yellow turtleneck behind the frosted glass only an idea of yellow, her arms only the hints of arms, her head only a round smudge.

She was working something with her hands, he believed he could see, something before her on the table, and he imagined her belief that a plant needed repotting on this night and this night only. It could always and only be this night.

He knew this belief, this feeling, the ache in the bones, the pull of muscle on that bone, the night outside and the world in your hands, waiting to be dealt with. He knew this feeling, the feeling of utter helplessness, though it seemed something as small as repotting a plant—something as small as stopping in at a boy's bedroom that hadn't been touched—would provide enough air to let one through whatever next moment might arrive, and whatever piece of grief that moment might carry with it.

He knew this feeling, and watched as her hands worked and worked.

231

She stopped, leaned forward over the table, and rubbed at the glass. She put her hands to the glass, peered out.

All this in a moment, her moves so quick he did not realize she was looking at him out here, and before he could move, turn the wheel, and disappear, he thought he knew what she saw: Only a man on his way home to an empty house, a man whose son had died, a man, he believed, she did not and could not know.

But then she waved, her yellow arm above her head like one of the huge leaves of green through frosted glass, but moving, signaling him, signaling him: *I know you*, she signaled him. *I know you*.

He looked at her, watched her arm moving. Then his own hand was up, and he gave the smallest of waves back to her.

He knew she could not see him. But still he waved, his hand just moving, fingers together.

She stopped waving, her hands at the table again, working clean soil, he knew, working and working.

He turned the wheel, his headlights shifting yet again, giving him more empty trees, more vast lawn, and he was gone, moving down the drive, Mr. Halford already inside as he passed the house and all its abrupt light and on down the gravel lit with knee-high lamps.

Then he was at the street, the only light his own headlights, around him this dark. He knew the way home from here, knew which streets to take which way in order to arrive at that empty house.

But the street before him, the dull black asphalt, seemed some line he could not decipher, another language he could not understand.

The warm air from the heater moved into his legs now, carried that warmth in and through him, and he thought yet again of Laura, thought of her eyes, the way she'd looked at him in the hospital, waiting for words from

232

him, and the way she had looked at him only last night in the kitchen of the Halfords' cottage, the way she'd been waiting for him there as well. He thought of her eyes and of their own language, the language of truth her eyes demanded of him.

Then, through the woods across the street, those bare gray branches into which his headlights made vague stabs of light, there came to him what seemed yet another dark miracle: The same moon he'd watched last night started its rise, a moon splintered and broken as it made its way slowly up through branches like bones, a moon of small shards of white and perfect light.

It was a light like none he had seen before, splintered and broken and rising still, until, in only the few moments he sat at the foot of the Halfords' drive, this moon rose and broke free of the branches, knit itself up, finally, into one whole and perfect light.

A full moon. The same moon he had watched last night at the end of the dock, its right edge sanded away and soft only hours ago. But now it was whole.

And it was in this light, this whole moon brighter and fuller than any moon he had ever seen before, that he suddenly saw he and Laura already owned their own language, one untouchable by anyone else, just as whatever language the Halfords spoke in the false light of the mansion behind him was a language he could not touch.

There existed already their own language, one that need only be spoken to begin, he believed, its own grammar and syntax and vocabulary waiting only to be uttered.

This, he believed, was what she had waited for him to speak: the language of grief between them.

Michael, she had whispered only an instant after he himself had spoken their child's name.

He watched the moon, watched it rise until he had to lean forward to see it out his windshield.

🌸 **BEFORE HIM WAS** his own house, the snow that had been banked along the foundation Saturday morning gone, melted. He was in his own driveway now, the gray house lit only with his headlights.

He turned off the lights, cut the engine. The house disappeared into the immediate black. He sat there, heard the engine start its ticking. He felt the cold already seeping back into the car, into his ankles.

This was where he would spend the night, himself alone in the house, alone with the room in which his son had slept, alone in the room in which he and his wife made love. Alone with the black of all the rooms in the house.

Then the moonlight started in, his eyes slowly adjusting to this dark.

Here came his house, the outline of windows, the lines of the clapboard. He could see the front door, the row of low scotch heather he and Michael had planted two summers ago along the front of the house, those thin sticks now given some definition, some shape and figure by the moon above.

Then came the silver branches of trees beside him, the silver cast to the lawn, the shadows of trees across dead grass. Detail moved around him, as if these shadows and light were some dance he'd interrupted with his driving here, something he'd shut down with the cut of his lights through the dark, the sound of his engine.

He believed he could see in the dark a rolled up newspaper on the front porch, the darkened carriage lamps on either side of the door. He believed he could make out the reflection, perhaps, of the trees in the glass of the storm door, and the lace designs of the curtains in the front room windows.

He leaned forward and looked out the windshield to the second story, the window on the right. Michael's window.

He thought he could see the blue miniblinds half-opened in the window, miniblinds his son had twisted open a day three months and eleven days before.

And he remembered this window broken, felt in his hand the smooth wood of the spoon, the sharp shock of it against his son.

He felt the ugly rise in his throat, a rise and hard knot that seemed would never leave him.

He blinked, and knew then the way tears worked against seeing things clearly, the way tears worked only to scatter details one wanted assembled and full in one's eyes: The blinds his son had opened wavered and disappeared into the black of their child's window, left him with only the belief he had seen evidence of his son's hand.

Because, he knew, he hadn't been able to discern, truly, blue miniblinds in a black window. He'd only imagined it, that window up there black, above the roofline stars like the same fireflies, always those fireflies, that had danced around his son.

But he could not see inside the window. He'd given himself this detail, as though he had earned it somehow,

235

when all he had earned this day was the discovery of an end bracket placed too soon and the cold and sobering fact that Mr. Halford had no words to help him along.

He believed he loved his son, believed that he had been in some ways a good father, though still here with him was his own hand striking Michael, and his hand at the doorknob each morning, himself headed for work.

But belief was all he owned, and somehow in the light of a moon he knew he could not move, that belief seemed enough, but only enough to last him until he could speak of it with Laura, speak of the huge and unwanted thing residing in him as real and untouchable as the knot inside his heart, a thing so huge and alien he knew of no analogies.

He would speak of it with his wife. They would speak, and he would tell her of holding their child moments after his birth, speaking his name, giving out for the first time to the air around him, to the entire universe above him, to all these stars and this tired moon that word *Michael;* he would tell her of the way Michael had hammered plywood onto two-by-fours when they had built the fort, him holding the hammer with two hands and missing three times out of four, finally bending the nails on purpose so that they went down faster; and he would tell her of missing Lego pieces, of moving up the stairs behind him at Barnegat Light, and he would tell her, too, of a wooden spoon, of the way it felt in his memory and the way it felt now, here in his hands and heart, because he could not understand why this memory could come to him.

And he would tell her of the fireflies, their son rolling down the hill, Laura's father talking on about work while he himself had seen the twirl and twist of their son inside fragmented light.

He looked at the house.

It was an empty house, and for a moment he thought he might know why Laura would not enter their child's room, thought he could feel her own pain: Though it was an empty room, it was a room too full, the objects in the room and the room itself simply too real to take in. Their son had lived there, a fact that would never disappear.

He rubbed his eyes, wiped away the wet, and looked again at Michael's window.

He saw the window clearly, saw the black of the glass. This time he imagined no detail about it, saw nothing that was not there.

He felt for the keys in the dark, turned on the engine, his eyes to the empty window, a window that seemed somehow to carry with it the first truth he needed to speak, the place to begin with Laura: He had come all the way home but found he could not enter their house without her.

He looked down to the dashboard, saw in the green digital clock on the radio the time: *8:42.* He could make it back to Reed's Beach by eleven if he moved.

He reached for the headlights, but before he could find the knob in the dark, he saw out his window movement in the trees across the yard.

He swallowed, thought to turn on the lights, maybe flush whatever ghost this might be from its hiding place.

But it wasn't hiding, he saw as it moved, moved, then broke from the bare trees into the yard, and he saw it was a man, a man walking across his yard toward him.

The man raised an arm to him, and he thought he could see the arm moving, just as he'd seen Mrs. Halford's arm signaling him. And this shadow seemed to signal the same thing to him: *I know you.*

It was Ted Rothberg, he saw. Gerry Rothberg's father.

He left off the lights, rolled down his window. This was Ted Rothberg, father of the boy who'd lost a race with his own son, father of the boy who had retrieved Laura from this house before him.

He'd come through the trees from his house next door, his place situated such that Hugh could not see it from here, even through the bare trees.

The air from outside came in on him, and he could feel the two—warmth at his ankles now that the engine was on, and this cold on his face—fight against one another. Even above the soft tremor of the engine he could hear now Ted's steps across the grass, the dry crush of his shoes on the dead and silver grass.

"Hugh," Ted called, raised his arm again, and waved.

"Ted," Hugh said, his voice loud and lost across the dark lawn.

Ted said nothing more until he made it to the car. Still Hugh could make out no face, even in the moonlight. He wore a parka, the hood back and on his shoulders, his hands in the jacket pockets.

He stopped at the edge of the concrete drive, two or three feet from Hugh. There were stars above him, Hugh could see from where he sat, on either side of Ted's shoulders the line of trees he'd come through, and the trees and those stars seemed blessings on this man, a gift from that God who'd taken Michael and had spared this man's son.

If Gerry had won the race, he thought, he might be the one crossing Ted's yard right now, the one whose feet crushed dead grass with each step, his own hands jammed into his parka. For a moment he pictured what Ted might be looking at right now, just as he'd pictured what Mrs. Halford might have seen from inside a glass greenhouse: only a man—Hugh was his name—sitting in a car, headlights off, engine running in the driveway of his empty home.

But this time things were different, he saw. When he'd

been at the Halfords' he had no idea what he would do once he got home, how he would fill his evening and night.

Now he knew: He was on his way to Laura, on his way to Reed's Beach, to try out this new language he'd been given through no choice of his own.

"How you doing?" Ted said.

Hugh looked at the line of trees to Ted's right, those trees beyond which sat this man's own house, where Gerry watched TV, perhaps, or read a book or finished homework at this exact moment.

Hugh said, "As best as can be expected, I guess," and he tried to give a smile.

They were quiet a few moments, the only sounds the engine and the heater running.

Ted said, "Where you guys been?" He paused, shrugged. "We didn't know you guys were going anywhere." He turned and nodded at the house. "We've been picking up the mail and the paper for you. We've been keeping an eye out for you, and when I see you pulling in the drive, I figure I better come over here, see what's up." He turned back to Hugh, shrugged again, looked down.

"I thought Laura would have told you," Hugh said. He shifted in the seat, looked out the windshield. He felt the cold winning the fight against the heater. He said, "We're down at this cottage my boss loaned us. A place called Reed's Beach. Almost to Cape May." He paused. "He— my boss—is letting us use it. For the time being."

He thought to go on, wanted for an instant to spell out other things to him: the leave of absence with pay, his needing to show up two or three days a week. He thought to tell him of the water down there, the way it lapped under the house at high tide, and he wanted to tell him of the strip of land, Delaware, you could see across the bay.

He thought of telling him about only last night and the touch and taste of Michael's name just before he'd spoken it, the value it'd held just before he'd let it go, and then the immediate distance the word had found once he'd spoken it.

Hugh looked at him and knew how little his own words had given Ted: a place called Reed's Beach was all he'd said. But it was more than that.

It was where his wife was right now.

He took in a breath, felt words coming to him, and did not know if the ones headed toward him right now were ones that would put him back in the same old loop of hiding, the same loop he'd left his friend—*his friend*—Ed Blankenship in only a couple of hours before this moment. He did not know if he were about to utter words that would dump himself back into that gray-green sea of no hope, or if there might come to him some new and tentative words, the same words he'd known Ed had been offering him: the truth.

He looked at Ted, could not see his face, yet saw in him any one of a thousand anonymous days of fatherhood, the same days he himself had lived through, days of calling home to see if Michael's fever had broken, evenings with soccer practice and homework started too late, bedtimes with only one story, just one, then Michael's smile and pout so that Hugh read yet another, and another.

Mornings with flashcards, Saturdays with broken windows.

He'd lived through that. He'd lived through all of it.

Hugh swallowed. He looked out the windshield again, then back to Ted.

He said, "Do you remember when we took the Staten

Island Ferry over?" He paused. "We four. You, me, Gerry and Michael."

He'd said his son's name, let it out in conversation, as slight and unmeasured as any other word that existed.

Ted looked up, silent, and Hugh believed he had broken this moment, too, just as he had shattered the evening with the Halfords, blurted out words of inquiry about their sons.

But then Ted seemed to smile, somehow the moon giving in this moment just enough light to illuminate the lines of his face, his mouth moving into a smile.

"We froze our butts off," Ted said, and Hugh saw him slowly shake his head. "And the boys—" He stopped, looked at Hugh.

He said, "Go on."

Ted looked down again, moved a foot, and kicked at the grass beneath him. "The boys were fighting the whole time we were on the ferry." He paused, looked up at Hugh. "You remember that?"

"No," Hugh said, the answer true. He said, "All I remember is waiting at the terminal. On Staten Island." He paused, turned again to the windshield, the gray house. "And I remember the boys standing at the glass." He paused again, the words coming from him alien and old at once.

But here they were, coming up, coming up, and he heard himself speak the picture that had come to him on the drive this morning, back when he had been on the Parkway up from a place called Reed's Beach.

"They were standing at the glass," he heard himself say, "and they had on these bright parkas. They had their hands up on the glass, their hands on the glass"—and now he saw his own hands in front of him, fingers spread as though he himself were touching the same glass his son had touched, his son and this man's son both—"and

241

you could see the condensation around their hands. The glass was fogging up around their hands."

Still his hands were out in front of him. He couldn't see Ted, couldn't tell what effect, if any, this strange movement of hands and his halting words had on the man.

But it didn't matter. He'd heard his own words, had seen in them the wisps of condensation on glass. He'd heard the truth of what he knew.

He took his hands down, put them in his lap.

This was all he could remember, as far his words would carry him, and he turned, looked at Ted.

He said, "What were they fighting about?"

"Nothing," Ted said right away. He was still smiling and shrugged. "Something about hot chocolate, I think. But nothing." He paused. "Kids," he said.

Hugh smiled. He said, "Kids."

"But we froze, all of us," Ted went on, and now his words, Hugh could hear, were speaking their own truth, speaking what he saw: "We froze our butts off walking around South Street Seaport, and then we went over to that Chinese place at Pier 17." He stopped again, and the quiet that came after the warmth of his words seemed too heavy, the silence a weight on them both.

"You don't remember this?" Ted said. "I feel like I'm blabbing."

"You're not," Hugh said and looked at him. "You're not talking too much at all." He paused. He saw them now on the boardwalk at South Street, saw them now hunched in the cold wind, saw the boys bumping into each other on purpose as they walked. They weren't fighting now, he saw, but were just kids, freezing cold on a big adventure. And he saw them, too, at the Chinese place, the four of them sitting at a table near the window, so that they were still cold, and he saw, too, deep bowls of hot and sour soup brought to them, smelled the fragrant steam up off the soup, saw the four of them eating with wide white plastic spoons. All four of them—Michael one of them, Michael alive and breathing and perhaps kicking Gerry's legs beneath the table, Gerry kicking right back, two boys with conspiritorial grins on their faces as they lifted spoon after spoon of soup to their lips, and ate.

But that was as far as he could go, ushered here by Ted's words. He'd been there, could now recall this all, but needed Ted to lead him through this story, through this memory.

He said, "I remember some of it." He smiled. "I remember we sat next to the window, and we were still freezing."

"That's right," Ted said. "I remember that."

They were quiet a moment, still the only sound the engine, until Ted said, "So, you staying here the night, or are you headed back down there?"

"Headed back," Hugh said and for a moment regretted this, regretted he'd already decided to go. He wanted to stay here, wanted to talk, hear more of what he'd lost to memory.

But Laura was down there, Laura and everything she had to say to him.

He looked at Ted again, said, "I guess I wanted to know one thing. About that day."

"Go ahead," Ted said.

He swallowed. He said, "Did we make it to your office? I mean, did we get up to the Trade Center?"

"Oh, did we," Ted said, and here he was, slowly shaking his head again in the moonlight. "We could see everything, it was so clear. Perfect day, cold and clear. It was like we could just bend down and touch the Statue of Liberty, it was so clear." He stopped, let out a low whistle, astonished, Hugh could see, at what he himself could remember. "Brooklyn, Staten Island. We could see Sandy Hook out past the Verrazano." He paused and gave a small laugh, a sound sharp and foreign and good in the dark. "I think we could see all the way to Asbury Park that day."

Hugh saw it, saw the blue-green water, the deep blue sky and sunlight, the Statue of Liberty close enough to touch. He saw red brick buildings in Brooklyn Heights, saw Fort Jay out on Governor's Island, saw the expanse of steel of the Verrazano Narrows. He saw Jersey, too, the spit of land curling up that was Sandy Hook.

And he saw himself kneeling beside his son, saw himself pointing out each landmark he knew and naming it for the boy, his son smiling and pointing to one landmark after another and asking for more names, Hugh sometimes shrugging, sometimes knowing, Michael nodding and pointing and asking yet again.

He saw his son's eyes taking in the world, saw the way sunlight played into his brown irises to make them glisten like polished stones, and the way sunlight made the whites of his eyes so white there was no word to capture that color.

"I remember," Hugh said.

Ted was quiet, took his hands from his pockets, crossed his arms. He said, "That's good. Because it was a good day."

Then Hugh turned to him, this new memory in him crisp and clear. He would tell Laura of this, too.

He said, "How's Gerry doing?"

Ted took in a breath and seemed to hold it. He said, "Pretty good." He paused. "He has dreams sometimes."

Hugh said, "I'm sorry."

"Don't be," Ted said. "Don't worry about us at all."

Then they were silent, as though they had completed

what they had set out to do: pass sentences between them, give each other words that carried weight, made memories breathe inside them.

Hugh touched the gas and heard the engine pick up. He placed his foot on the brake, put the car in reverse. Still he hadn't turned on the headlights.

He looked at Ted, and now he could see his face, though there was no more light out here than before. But he saw his face, the face of a friend and next-door neighbor, the father of his son's best friend. He knew this man.

He was smiling and put out a hand to Hugh.

Hugh took it, and they shook.

"You be careful driving down there," Ted said. His hand was warm in Hugh's. "Don't worry about anything, the mail or anything. We'll be here, so don't worry."

They let go at the same moment, and Ted crossed his arms, took a step back from the car. He turned, nodded at the porch. "I'll even read your newspaper for you," he said, and Hugh could see the smile.

"You do that," Hugh said. His foot was still on the brake, still holding his car from moving out of the driveway, from leaving this place and the words he knew they could exchange all night long.

He said, "We'll give you a call," then remembered work the next day, remembered all that had been left undone with his being consumed by the Rhode Island batch. He said, "Or maybe I'll just stop in tomorrow night. After work." He eased up on the brake, felt the car inch back on the driveway.

"That'd be fine," Ted said, and now he took another step back. He seemed to nod, the dark and distance between them carrying off the detail he'd seen only moments before until, once Hugh had reached the foot of the drive, it might as well have been himself standing in his own front yard, and another man backing out of the drive, his headlights off on a full-moon night.

Ted waved, that arm above his head, and Hugh reached an arm out his window, waved back.

Then Ted turned and went to the front porch. He bent down, picked up the newspaper, then moved across the front of his house, disappeared back into the trees.

Hugh looked at the house again, at the storm door, the lace curtains in the front windows. He looked at Michael's window, let off on the brake, and saw the house slowly recede from before him.

Then he turned on the headlights, the house and yard and driveway, the windows and bushes and trees all lit with a single set of headlights, a pale, white light cast across what he owned, where he lived.

But it was enough to let him see it all. Enough, too, to let him see even from out here that, in fact, the blinds in his son's window were still half-opened.

Six

❀ LIGHTS FLASHED, AND three purple *Trump Taj Mahal* logos rolled into place before her. Quarters spilled into the tray at the bottom of the slot machine, an outpouring of money that seemed too loud, the rhythmic clatter of coins only drawing attention to her: People up and down the row of slot machines stopped momentarily and looked at her, at the money. But then they went right back to business, fed coins into their own machines, pulled the arms, waited.

Winnie, two machines away to Laura's left, was the only one who stopped altogether, came over, and stood beside her as the money clicked out.

"Crimony!" Winnie said, and put a hand to Laura's back, patted her there.

Laura hadn't yet looked at her, only saw the lights, the line of logos, the coins still coming.

"Twenty-five dollars," Winnie said. "Not a bad return on a quarter, now is it?"

Winnie reached down, raked her fingers through the coins, fished up a handful, then let them slip through her fingers back into the trough, as though she were a pirate stooped at a chest of gold.

Around them was movement, movement, people pulling and pulling, some silent, others jabbering at the machines as though they might talk back. The woman at the machine next to Laura's had on a pale blue pantsuit, white hair twisted into a bun atop her head, and was mumbling something no one, Laura knew, could hear, the only evidence she was speaking the way the cigarette perched on her lip bobbed up and down; another woman, this one in a red jacket and skirt and with black hair cut in a shag—she seemed more a secretary on her lunch hour than anything else—squinted with each pull, her lips stretched wide to show her clenched teeth. She didn't wait for the slot machine to stop rolling before her hand was to the slot, quarter at the ready. Laura turned then to take in even more of these people, saw at the slot machine directly across from her a man in bib overalls and a yellow T-shirt, a few single strands of gray hair plastered down to the top of his head. Though she couldn't see his face, she saw the way he stamped his left foot each time the slot machine came up with an empty array of symbols.

They'd been down here for over an hour, walking around, neither of them saying much. At first Winnie'd led her by the hand, until, after a few minutes standing at a craps table deep in the casino, Winnie'd let go, and Laura'd had to stand there and watch dice roll across green felt, watch people nod or holler or twitch as those red plastic cubes rolled down the length of the table, her own hand strangely empty.

They'd walked and walked, Winnie always the one to take the first small move away from whatever table they were at, always the one to lead her to the next station, swirling around them men and women with determined looks, eyes focused on whatever game of chance their world centered on at that particular moment.

Always around them, too, was this fake and sharp light given off by the chandeliers and recessed lights, around them the false light off glistening brass fixtures and glass and colorful mixed drinks carried on trays held high up and above it all by waitresses, even their uniforms detailed in glittery light.

From a distance, when she was first down here and'd seen these waitresses, they seemed to Laura all glamour and color and sex in the midst of so many old people throwing away money, and the glitter off their uniforms had seemed somehow generous, good in a way: The waitresses made the gamblers and the tables and the cards and all this light seem sharper, more adult and festive and fun. Each wore a short ruffled skirt and dark stockings, lavender high heels, a hat with a single purple feather poking two feet straight up into the air.

But then, when she and Winnie'd been standing at a roulette wheel and watching the ball skitter against the circling numbers, one of the waitresses had suddenly appeared next to her, delivered a Bloody Mary to a man in a denim shirt and gray workpants seated at the table. Laura saw her close up, saw acne-scarred skin beneath the makeup, the makeup itself barely able to hide the thin wrinkles beside her eyes; saw purple eye shadow as thick as paint all the way to her eyebrows; saw her hair, blond except for the roots, where it changed to a bright red.

She watched the women more closely then as they walked around, served drinks, took orders and tips. They were all women with too much makeup, she saw, lips even more stark and red than Winnie's, all of them marching up and around the tables with their trays, and Laura tried to picture who these women might be, where they lived, what they did when they weren't inside this false palace. She tried to picture what they did when they were outside, surrounded by South Jersey and warm air and real light in February.

She'd seen these women at the dry cleaners, she knew, and at the Friendly's, having lunch and a Fribble, and she saw them with children on their hips, husbands to feed, garbage cans out front of their houses, some of those houses with Christmas lights still up.

And she saw the woman with red roots coming home to a house in the Villas, though she knew how far away that was from here, all the way down to Cape May and to the Delaware side. But jobs were few down here, she believed, and she saw her, the acne-scarred woman with eye shadow it probably took a half-pound of cold cream to take off, coming home to a teenage son, a red-headed kid who worked at the Acme as a bag boy, one who tossed people's food into plastic sacks with no rhyme or reason. Laura saw the two of them in a kitchen, the boy eating an afterschool snack of microwave chili he'd lifted from the store, the mother asking him how his day at school went as she lit up a cigarette and leaned against the kitchen counter. She had on a sweatshirt and red sweatpants and heavy socks.

It was a Rutgers sweatshirt, Laura saw, and her own red sweatpants, her own heavy socks she'd given the woman in her imagination.

Then Winnie had started away from the roulette wheel, turned, and looked to Laura, who came up from the life of the waitress, came back into her own life, the one shifting beneath her as she walked toward Winnie, followed her still.

She led them back to the banks of slot machines, this place the greatest source of commotion and frenzy of all, people lined up and feeding, pulling, waiting. They had passed through this area when they'd first come down into the casino itself, back when Laura's eyes had been

filled with the heat and clouds of the moment at the end
of the jetty, back when her face had been hot and her
breaths hard to take in.

But she'd also been able to take from there the vision
of Cape May Diamonds, those pieces of small stone that
took in sunlight and gave it back even brighter, even
more glorious and redemptive than the real thing, it
seemed, even when held up by the aged fingers of the old
woman leading her around just then.

At the slots Laura'd followed Winnie to a raised
glassed-in booth, seated inside it a huge black man with
a white tuxedo shirt, purple bow tie, and cummerbund.
Winnie reached up to the small round window on the
booth and handed the man a twenty. Laura hadn't seen
her dig in her purse, hadn't seen the money come from
anywhere. "Quarters," was all Winnie said.

The man nodded, took the money, and set two rolls of
quarters in clear plastic wrappers on the counter, pushed
them through the slot beneath the glass.

Winnie nodded, took the rolls, turned to Laura. She
held one out to her.

"Oh," Laura'd said. "I can't—"

"This is also what the doctor ordered," Winnie'd said,
her hand still out with the roll. "Take one of these and
call me in the morning."

"Really, I wouldn't want—" Laura'd said.

"You have no choice," Winnie'd said. She reached to
Laura's hand at her side, the hand that didn't have hold
of the straw bag, and took it, placed the roll in her palm.
Winnie smiled again, curled Laura's fingers over the
coins. The roll was heavy in her hand, strong somehow,
as though simple possession of a roll of quarters made
the movement beneath her feet easier to take, though
there had still swelled in her the feel of the jetty, the

black grief she'd seen in a sunken ship, water lapping at rocks.

"We got work to do," Winnie'd said.

"I said, 'Not a bad return on a quarter, now is it?'" Winnie said. She paused and crossed her arms. "Hello?" she said.

She looked at Winnie, at her black hair, at her arms crossed in some sort of defiance, some fierce will, this woman waiting for response from Laura.

Museums, buildings, shipwrecks, Hugh had said only last night. *If that's what you think is important, then you're free to have it.*

And something in the light around them and in the movement and in the sounds, something even in the list she had memorized and since abandoned to the will of this woman—even in the image of a waitress wearing the same clothes she herself had worn the afternoon she'd seen children parting before her to reveal to her the truth of the rest of her life—all of it moved in her, ushered her forward into fake light and movement, so that she had no choice now but to look into Winnie's eyes, had no choice but to feel form in her mouth and throat and heart the words she knew she needed to ask this woman.

Winnie wanted surrender, Laura saw, surrender to the absurdity of jamming money into loud machines in the hopes those machines would pay you back troughs full of cash, and surrender to the notion that pain could, perhaps, see you through. Ignoring pain, she knew only then, never let it find its release, never let it grow away. Only after surrendering to the pain you held could you find your way through, hope to emerge on the other side of it.

Pain's good for you, this woman had said. *Sees you through.*

She looked one last time at the people attending the slots, then to Winnie, still with her arms crossed.

She felt the weight of the straw handbag on her arm, a weight that seemed the only thing she could bring with her into this surrender.

She took in a breath. She said, "Do you have any children?"

The words left her in almost a whisper, a sound so quiet she wasn't sure she'd even spoken them. "Do you have any children?" she said again, this time louder.

No one at any of the machines stopped moving, stopped inserting and pulling and waiting. If they'd heard her, heard Winnie, heard any of this exchange between two women from Reed's Beach, they weren't showing it. They only fed the machines.

And then came the next question, one she hadn't planned at all, but a question that seemed the only next one to ask, chained inextricably to the first.

"What do you fear?" she heard herself say, the words clear and distinct and simple, as easy to hear as Winnie's own.

Winnie smiled. Slowly she nodded.

She said, "Now that's a question." She paused. "Now we're getting somewhere," she said.

Laura said, "What do you fear?" The words still came from her easily, still sounded real, even here.

"Soon enough," Winnie said. "Soon enough." She reached to Laura and took her hand, the one not holding the half-roll of coins, in her own.

"Let's go," she said and nodded again. "We're done now."

Laura blinked. "What?"

"We're done. Finished in here." She paused. "The work's done in here."

255

Laura looked at the trough, at the coins there. She turned back to Winnie.

"But—" she started.

"No buts," Winnie cut in, and held up a hand as though to stop any more words. Laura could see, held there in Winnie's palm, her own half-roll of coins, the clear plastic wrap.

"Blood money is all it is," Winnie said. "We came here, we played. You won. Now we leave." She gave a quick, sharp nod, and turned, started off down the row of slots, Laura's hand still in hers.

Laura looked back at the slot machine as they moved away, saw the woman in the blue pantsuit turn from her own slot and look at her. She stopped her mumbling, the cigarette still at her lips. Her eyes cut from Laura to the trough and to Laura again. Then, even before Laura'd rounded the end of the aisle, the woman bent to the trough, started grabbing up handfuls of the coins, dumping each into a large plastic cup decorated with the purple Taj Mahal logo.

"It's only blood money," Winnie said, and Laura looked at her, saw Winnie's eyes were fixed on the carpeted steps up and out of the casino pit, around them only the same gaudy light, the same movement and noise and all this ugly light.

"I don't keep winnings because making money isn't why I come here and do this," Winnie said.

They were at the street now, the inside of the van cold from the dark of the parking garage. The sun still hadn't broken the line of sight out the windshield, still hung just high enough in the sky.

This was the moment in the day that seemed most broad and empty, the time of day, she could see by the cut of the light, when her son used to come home, used to arrive at their door alive and intact from a day at school, whether with a knee torn out of his jeans or with a recess's worth of grime under his nails, a sad or a happy face stamp on the back of his left hand.

Winnie pulled out of the parking garage and into thin midafternoon traffic, the brick buildings and asphalt streets of Atlantic City nearly deserted, beer cans and bottles and sheets of newspaper scattered in the streets, the papers pushed along with the wind that had begun to pick up out here, the air grown colder since they had been at the shipwreck.

The happy stamps, Laura remembered, would have been when he was in kindergarten, when the value of a day had been measured solely, it seemed, on a smudge of green ink on the back of his right hand, the smile or frown indication of whether or not he had followed class rules: *Hands are for helping. Inside voices inside, outside voices outside. Follow directions. Don't run in class. Keep hands to yourself.* Rules simple enough and meaningful enough, but rules it had taken Michael a full three months to get hold of, to decide to follow, until, finally, the week before Christmas, he had come home with a happy stamp five days in a row. As a reward they had taken him to the Friendly's at Freehold Raceway Mall and let him order whatever he wanted. He'd gone for the Reese's Pieces Sundae, had picked off each single Reese's Piece with his spoon and sucked on it until the sugar coating had worn off, their son poking out his tongue to show them each time the little nugget of peanut butter on the tip, then swallowing it down. Only then did he start in on the ice cream, most of it melted by then, his face a wet mess of cream and chocolate by the time he was finished. Then he'd made a big production of licking as much as he could from his lips, his pink tongue nearly sweeping clean the mess, and Laura and Hugh had laughed.

It was this moment, this angle of light and cut of sun in the afternoon, when he would come home. It was this moment.

It was this moment, too, that had dragged long and hollow the days and weeks after the funeral, after she'd quit at the hospital, afternoons filled with sleep and sheets wrapped around her like ropes pinning her to the bed, and she recalled the light in through their bedroom window, November light, sharp and clear, each time she opened her eyes the light through the trees outside the window changing, changing, the sky moving from blue to white to orange and then red, the single moment of Gerry Rothberg's knock at her door, the single instant of his eyes meeting hers lasting as long as these afternoons pulled at her, as long as her life thus far, as long as she would live.

Michael was gone. Michael would not be back.

"It's not the money," Winnie said, and Laura saw they were already out of Atlantic City, were on a highway bridge, out her window a marsh, gray and flat, then water, small islands, all of it just like Reed's Beach Road after the low-lying scrub pines, this highway no different than the thin road that crossed the marsh, crossed it to the homes where Quakers had lived hundreds of years before and where wooden guns had staved off the British, and it seemed for a moment that she saw her own truth in painted tree trunks made to look like they could kill: She was in fact only filling her days, only filling them, and the words and brochures and maps she'd garnered thus far down here were, in fact, just as hollow as this moment each afternoon, just as harmless as painted trees. The hard facts she'd gathered would not keep the sun from meeting this moment, would not erase the afternoons she'd spent in bed watching the trees out her window, would not make the sun stop moving, would not stop time.

"It's because of the stupidity of it I go in there," Winnie said, and Laura turned, looked at her. There was only flat marsh out her window, too, the sun any moment now about to fall into sight, and with its proximity of brilliant light, a light already so bright she had to squint to look out Winnie's window, there came a relief somehow, a rising of the pressure on her chest, the weight on her heart. And there were her words.

"The stupidity of anybody heading into a building designed to strip me naked and make me think I had a good time at it to boot." Her window was down a few inches, and wind whipped in, made a sound just loud enough to make Winnie believe, Laura could tell, she had to speak louder than she would otherwise. The words were hard and sharp in here, and Laura thought to tell her she could hear her just fine. But she did not. She wanted to hold each word, wanted to see each one of them and carry it a moment before she fed it to her brain, let it do its deeper work of deciphering.

She needed this woman's story. She needed her answers, answers to both Laura's questions.

Winnie said, "Of course there's no way to beat the place over there. No way." She paused and let that hand fall back to her lap, the other hand now at the top of the wheel. She let out a breath.

She said, "But if I can walk away, I've won." She stopped again, let out another breath. "If I can walk in the door of something so ugly as that place and if I can see the emptiness of what goes on in a place as big and reckless as the Taj Mahal and come out alive, then I've won."

She turned, looked at Laura. She said, "And none of

this has a goddamned thing to do with gambling either, sweetheart."

"I know," Laura said, her words out of her quick and clean. And the truth. "But I'm still waiting for an answer. For your answers."

Winnie smiled, looked at her a long moment before turning back to the road. "Sweetheart," she said, "this is part of it." She paused. "If you're listening, then you'll hear that this is part of it all. I already told you." She paused again, looked back to the road. "There's no way to beat that place," she said, her words quiet now, "but if you can come out alive, you've won."

Laura looked at Winnie and squinted for the late afternoon light. She looked at her, saw her hair was still firmly in place, saw the collars of her blouse lift and dance and settle and lift again on the wind in from the window.

"You hungry yet?" Winnie said without turning to Laura, her profile still sharp and unmoving, the pitch of her voice back to normal, as though this question were the only logical thing to say.

Laura turned, looked out her window. She saw a white state highway sign, *30*, then, a few yards past it, a green and white road sign: *Absecon 1*. She shrugged.

"I got just the place," Winnie said, and nodded.

🐚 THEY WERE IN the pine barrens now, behind them the Garden State Parkway, before them only a thin strip of highway two lanes wide, the shoulders only sand.

Absecon, Conoverton, Seaview Park, Oceanville; they'd already passed through them all, small towns each, if they could even be called towns: a bank with a single lane drive-thru, a four-stall strip mall, a WaWa or 7-Eleven or Shell Minimart. Then, once past the hub, usually a single stoplight, there had come the antique stores, old white clapboard houses with hand-painted signs on the lawns out front: *Antique Outpost, 1819 House Antiques, Unique Antique.* Usually next to the sign was parked something meant to show how authentic each store's stock might be: an old wrought-iron and wood school desk at one, a white rocking chair at another, an ancient and rusted-over tractor at yet another.

There had been no cars at any of them this Tuesday afternoon, no one stopping to peruse someone else's historical artifacts and putting a price on them, as though history might be something anyone could just sell off to the highest bidder.

It was nothing like that, Laura knew. History came hard to you, stayed with you, big and ugly and reckless, a fountain of blood.

261

Here were the pines, scraggly and thin, but so many of them she couldn't see back more than a few feet. This was the pine barrens, the area of the state everybody'd heard stories about. Pineys were what the people who lived back in here were called, people with broad foreheads and eyes set too close together, people who'd sooner shoot at you than give you directions if you were lost; and there were the stories of those people who *had* gotten lost back in here, the highways indistinguishable one from the next, just roads people stumbled over and took, until they were simply circling and circling back in here, lost forever.

And there was the Jersey Devil, too, this place his known residence for the last couple of hundred years. Laura'd heard all the stories around campfires when she was at Girl Scout camp, how the thing was the child of a witch and Satan, born back in the Colonial days, and how the thing was still sighted now and again back in here, how its cloven hoof tracks were sometimes seen in the sand along the shoulders of these highways, how its howl was heard late at night by those stupid people who'd gotten lost back here, only to end up with a flat tire or overheated engine in the middle of the night.

Stories. Nothing more, none of them holding any more truth than the next. They passed an occasional house along the road, rusted tin roof, asphalt shingles for siding, bald-tire planters strewn across the sandy yards, bare sticks poking up from them. It was easy to see, Laura thought, how you could get the idea these people were backward and lost themselves and wouldn't want you in here.

But in one yard sat a satellite dish, in another a brand-new Jeep pickup, the cardboard license plate advertising the dealership still in place. In yet another yard was a sleek, flat speedboat, metallic blue and silver, along with another satellite dish, and Laura imagined everyone in each of these homes perched at a television set and watching MTV or CNN or The Nashville Network. The girls in these shacks, she knew, wore their hair replete with stacked bangs that towered over their foreheads, the boys with black T-shirts torn in strategic places, across their chests names like Poison and Whitesnake and Guns 'n' Roses and, of course, The Grateful Dead displayed like flags taken in battle. Their mothers worried over grades and how to stretch dinner with only a box of macaroni and a can of Spam; their fathers came in from work bushed and hungry.

No different than any families anywhere.

But there still remained in Laura, as Winnie turned and turned again, drove deeper into the barrens, the pines seeming to lean closer in on them the lower the sun fell, the longer the shadows crept across the asphalt, the feel those stories had given her when she was a child, the shiver down the length of her spine, the cold breath at the top of her neck, and she wondered at all one kept from childhood, what memories.

And she wondered then what history of himself had Michael carried, what her own child had known.

She looked out her window, saw within the pines dead growth, wiry vines and shrubs that had lost their leaves to the winter, thick dry foliage that gave a gray depth to the pines crowding in on themselves and the highway, and remembered from her own childhood a brother, older than her, who built balsa wood airplanes out in the storeroom on the back of the house in Matawan, remembered how he let her watch him place the thin sheets of tissue paper over bare struts of wings, remembered the clear dope painted over the material and the supercharged stink of it, and how it dried until the wings were taut as drumheads.

She remembered all this as though it were somebody else's history, a diorama in a museum, her peering in from darkness at flat and frozen scenes, peering and moving, peering and moving.

What would Michael have known? she wondered. What would be his memories? What would he recall, what would he believe about his life?

He had a mother who loved him, she hoped he would have known, a mother who'd given him up from inside her, a mother who'd bore him into the world through a pain so cavernous and sharp she could not recall its feel or tear, only its notion: *pain*.

But it had been a pain nowhere near the one she carried with her each moment she was alive now, a pain so acute that even to glance at it, even to catch a glimpse brought her close to her own death, and there had been many moments when, just after he was gone, those days when she had lain in bed and watched the sky change color, that this pain had clamored inside her such that her own death would have been welcome, the sun through the trees as she'd slept and not slept beckoning her, willing to take her in its arms.

These were the pine barrens, though there seemed nothing barren about them at all: Still the trees crowded the road, still they drove, still Winnie turned onto yet another road with sand shoulders and gnarled, thin pines thick beside them. The sun came and went from the windshield now, came and went, just touched the tree-tops flickering before it in a way that made her think of a silent movie, the images thin and shaky and too fast, too fast, until, suddenly and without warning, the sun blasted in with no interruption from trees.

She blinked and squinted at the burst of light, then looked off to Winnie's side, saw blossom from nowhere an entire tract of homes, a subdivision of houses with pastel siding and wide green lawns and new trees in front yards.

"Goddamn developers," Winnie said, her elbow still out in the air. She slowed down and looked out her window. "Wasn't but five years ago and there wasn't a soul out here but people who wanted to get lost and *stay* that way." She shook her head, stopped the van altogether. "Look at that," she said and shook her head again. "They even got goddamned sidewalks. Curbs even."

But before Laura could say anything about what she saw—clean, crisp houses, glistening cars, lush green winter grass—Winnie gave it the gas and turned right, directly opposite the street into the tract. Then they were on a sandy road, and homes appeared within the trees, smaller, old homes with screened porches and brick planters, carports that housed boats and gas grills and neat, plastic garbage cans.

The road twisted inside these woods, and here were more houses, summer places, she could see, set up for play.

"Where are we?" she said.

"A minute more and our destination will be revealed," Winnie said. She smiled and glanced at Laura, then back to the road. "And this is my treat, too. Lunch."

She saw more water now, flat and wholly undisturbed water, water that didn't bleed off into its own horizon, as did the water at Reed's Beach. This water held its own borders: She could see the other side of it now, caught small glimpses of homes like the ones before her nestled in the trees over there, on the water the reflections of trees, and of the white sky, the sun going lower each second they breathed.

The road widened and turned to the left, and they were in a sand parking lot.

"The Sweetwater Casino," Winnie said and pulled in.

At the far end and to the left of the lot was a wooden

265

building with a low roof and big windows; past the building was a long brown lawn that sloped down to the water. The water was just as still now, the reflection from across the lake even clearer, a mirror, perfect and clean, held to the homes and woods over there.

Winnie opened up her door, climbed out, and Laura climbed out as well, their movements in tandem, as though this were all decided beforehand. The two of them met at the front of the van, started toward the flagstone path at the end of the lot.

They moved down the path side by side, but when it veered to the left and toward the restaurant, Laura stepped off into the brown grass. She didn't look behind her but knew Winnie was right there, following her down toward the water.

"The Mullica River," Winnie said from behind her. "Iron's why it's red," she said, and now they were both stooped to the river, Winnie reaching out to the water and touching it, pulling up a cupped hand full of red water. "The Mullica River. Filled with iron. All this part of the state's nothing but iron bogs. Rusts up the water real pretty."

It was red, Laura saw, the water red as blood. Red water, and Laura thought of the fountain of blood back at Atlantic City, that hollow palace filled with lost people, people just as lost as both Winnie and herself. Just as lost, she saw, as anyone walking the face of the earth.

Just as lost as Hugh, trying to make sense of his days in his own way: living in his memory of their child while trying to make another child with Laura, never knowing the latter would not occur so long as she tasted the life of her son each morning.

She looked at the water, at the red of it, and saw the sky above reflected there, a sky still blue even on the surface of red water, and this fact seemed amazing some-

how, seemed, too, a betrayal, as though the color of this
water should have tinted the reflection, or the sky itself
should have given away its blue to the water.

But it was only water, only sky, and for a moment she
thought again of her brother's airplanes, the taut paper
wings, the balsa wood struts, the tender and delicate care
he bestowed on the toys, and she thought, too, of her own
chasing of the airplanes once her brother finished them,
Laura given the job of retrieving each one from the other
end of the lawn, a joyful chore, one she loved for the
sunlight in her eyes as she ran beneath it, the sky above
her, suspended in it a creation defying gravity, if for only
a few moments. Then came the touch of it in her hands,
as though she were carrying air itself, or the brittle skele-
ton of some small and wonderful bird.

It was a memory from her own childhood, she saw,
true and simple and sharp, that had come to her just
now on the banks of the Mullica, and suddenly, in the
blood-red water and the cut of light and this woman beside her, there came a certain relief, a rough-hewn and
quiet comfort: Their son had lived a life, too, had had
his own memories to hold, perhaps of a huge sundae at
a Friendly's in Freehold, perhaps of a morning when
he'd seen the moon teasing the sun. Or perhaps, she
hoped, even the memory of the troll in a snow-filled forest, of snow angels flying together through woods beside
their home in Englishtown, their wings touching, flying
together.

He had his own memories, his own life, and as she, too,
reached now to the river, placed her hand into the cold
water and brought up her own handful of red, she saw
what she had not allowed herself to see: There in the
shade of red in her hand was her son's room, a room
cluttered with life. The red-painted cigar box on the
dresser was in there, inside it his collection of loose

rocks, everything from the Peacock Ore Michael had bought on a field trip to the Franklin Institute to the piece of brick he and Gerry Rothberg dug up in the woods one day and had brought home, convinced it was something of value. There was even a chunk of concrete as big as his fist in there, and it occurred to her only now that she did not know where it had come from, had never asked her son. And on the dresser was the small copper-painted Statue of Liberty, a rubber band ball as big as a grapefruit, the Manalapan Soccer Association patch she'd not yet sewn to his athletic bag.

She saw herself then with her son's blanket, saw her hand in the box in her own attic the afternoon they were to bring down their son's clothes to allow someone to dress him. She saw the yellow and blue and green blanket with the frayed ends there in the box of baby clothes, saw her hands take it out from where she'd intended it to stay until her son had children of his own, and saw herself hide it away in the straw handbag, inside it even then the canister and its contents, and she saw her hand reach in and give it back to her son there at the funeral home, saw herself surrender this supreme symbol, the one that had seen her child from his first day on earth to then, that moment when they closed the casket lid, their hands together and pulling it down, sealing him away forever, and as she let the red water trickle through her fingers, let the cold water go away, her heart seemed to split itself in two with the thought she would never touch that symbol again, never feel against her cheek the soft warmth her son had fallen asleep with most all his nights. She would never know that touch again, yet in the same moment it seemed her heart had been rendered whole, had come together in some miraculous moment of healing, because she knew the blanket was with her son, would always be with him.

She'd surrendered it.

But his room was still here, and there were still things she could touch, hold in her hand, feel. There was even, she knew, some half-finished symbol in there, the scraps of construction paper across the top of the blue desk.

Perhaps they could figure out what he'd started, Laura thought. Perhaps, if Hugh called tonight, she could ask him what he thought might have been in their son's mind when he'd cut up all those pieces.

Surrender, she thought.

She stood, Winnie rising beside her. Laura put out her wet hand then, looked at Winnie, and the woman took it, their eyes meeting only a moment, each woman with a handbag to carry, each with whatever story her life had to surrender to the other, and in the giving, Laura saw, each would somehow give back to herself her own life. That was how people lived, she saw: They told each other stories of their lives, gave to each other their histories, surrendered them, no matter how hard and reckless it had come to you, no matter how high the fountain of blood. You surrendered history.

Laura felt Winnie squeeze her hand, felt the warmth of her fingers against her own.

"I never had any children," Winnie said, her words quiet. "We tried. But we never could."

Laura turned to her, saw her mouth drawn tight into a thin, straight line of red, her eyes to the river.

"That's something I missed in my life," Winnie whispered.

Laura looked back to the water, to the reflection of trees and summer cabins and blue sky. She thought again of her son's life, of a cigar box and a brick and a yellow and blue and green blanket.

It's something to miss, she wanted to say. But the silence between them seemed to speak well enough, Winnie's words, her eyes to the river all the answer she needed.

They stood at the river a few moments longer, then, as though this moment were itself fixed in their lives like a star in the sky, they turned, started back up the lawn.

❀ "YOU WANT TO know what I'm afraid of, too," Winnie said. She touched the water glass, moved it an inch or so to reveal the sweat ring on the tablecloth. Her eyes were on the glass, then on Laura.

Laura didn't look away.

The restaurant was empty, around them empty tables with crisp white tablecloths, empty glasses, silverware wrapped in white napkins. Rough clapboard walls were hung with framed photographs from the early days in South Jersey, women in full-dress swimsuits, men with handlebar moustaches, all of them posed on dunes somewhere.

Winnie and Laura were seated next to a bank of windows that looked out on the river, flat and shining with that reflection of sky and trees.

"You want to know what I'm afraid of," Winnie said again, "and it's Rollie I'm afraid of. It's him."

She looked up at Laura again, smiled a moment. "Not what you thought, eh?" She paused. "Not what you thought I was going to say, I know. You thought I was going to come in here and tell you I was afraid of death or taxes or some such thing. I know it. So I hope I'm not disappointing you." She stopped, seemed to sit up

271

straight in her chair. Though they'd already ordered—
the waitress, a woman perhaps as old as Winnie, hennaed
hair in a curl just above her shoulders, a flip sprayed
into place, had drawn from her hair a pencil, scribbled
and nodded as Winnie'd ordered the crab salad sandwich
and a bowl of clam chowder, Laura, a dinner salad and
the fried shrimp plate—Winnie still held her purse in her
lap, and Laura wondered at what black treasures she
herself might have secreted away inside.

"And don't go to thinking," Winnie said, "there's any
horror stories of how Rollie beats me every night or some
such garbage. There's nothing like that to tell."

She sat up even straighter and gripped the strap on
the patent leather purse with both hands. She took in a
deep breath, closed her eyes a long moment.

When she opened them, she was looking at Laura, and
took from her lap the purse, settled it on the floor beside
her, then leaned forward, put both arms on the table.
This was the woman who'd brought her to the jetty, the
woman who'd taken her into the depths of the Taj Mahal
and brought her out, alive and intact. This was the
woman to whom she'd surrendered the contents of the
canister, shown pure and perfect moments of her child's
life.

Winnie looked at her, leaned closer. "I'm not going
to give you one of these I-cried-because-I-had-no-shoes-
and-then-I-saw-a-man-who-had-no-feet-stories," she said.
"Shoot me if I do. I'm not trying to get you to feel sorry
for me. You wanted to know. I'm telling you."

Still Laura said nothing, still she would not look away.
It was this woman's history she was after. Her story.

But Roland, her husband. Roland, the maker of waffles
and sausage. This same man was what Winnie feared.

"I lost a lung and a lobe," Winnie said, her voice quieter now, made over into the same pitch and timbre she'd

given the single word she'd uttered this morning, the one that had started them on this trek through the depths of South Jersey and into whatever truth of love and living they would find: *My* was all she'd said this morning, and now here they were.

"A lung and a lobe," she said again, still just as quiet, and she nodded once to herself and those words, as though speaking them were some seal, a promise kept. "Nineteen seventy-five. I was a three-pack-a-day girl for thirty-three years. Of course there's no way for me even to tell you this without sounding like a walking ad for the lung cancer people. But there's no joke in this. There's no way around it. That's what I did for thirty-three years, and I lost a lung and a lobe for it."

Laura thought to say something to her, speak *I'm sorry* or another few words that might or might not accomplish anything. But she said nothing, only watched the woman.

"Rollie was there with me, too," she said. "Rollie was there with me the whole time, every minute of everything, from sitting in the dark in an X-ray screening room and looking at those spots on my lungs up until sitting in the chair next to me in the doctor's office when he told me it was all gone, that they'd got it all." She lifted her index fingers, touched the tips together, and made a sort of steeple out of them. She smiled, and shook her head just the smallest way. "That was in '75, eighteen years ago. We'd already been married twenty-nine years by then." She shook her head again, and here came the waitress with water. She topped off first Winnie's glass, then Laura's, said, "Your order'll be up in a flash, girls." She turned and weaved her way back through the empty tables.

"My kind of gal," Winnie said, and nodded at her back.

273

"But that hair," she said. "Box red." She smiled, then went silent.

Laura looked at her own glass, at the sweat trickling down the side and stem. She said, "Why are you afraid of him then?" She paused and touched at a bead of water about to slip down the glass. She said, "If he stayed with you, why would you be afraid of him?"

"Because," Winnie said right out, and her voice was back where it had been, soft and quiet, almost, Laura thought, afraid of itself. "Because I'd been married to him twenty-nine years by then. By '75. By then I thought I knew a thing or two about who he was. I knew what he did when he went to bed at night—brushed his teeth, Q-Tipped his ears, then read a chapter of Mickey Spillane—and I knew what he'd say when he woke up: 'Another day, another nickel.' I knew he still took navy showers, just like he did in the service. Let the water run just long enough to get wet all over, then turn it off, lather up, rinse off again. I knew he never left the seat up on the toilet, too, never once in twenty-nine years did he do that. He answers the phone by saying 'Yellow.' A little joke of his. He counts to three after a light turns green before he'll go on through. Reads the newspaper last page to first. Shaves pastrami so thin you can read through it."

She stopped, picked up her glass, took a sip, set it back on the sweat ring. "But it wasn't until then I found out what I really knew about him. About my husband, this Rollie character." Her eyes were to the glass, staring at it as though there were some memory of her own playing inside the water, some scene from her life dancing inside the shards of ice.

She was quiet a few moments, then said, "I already told you he was a cookie on the *Yorktown*, and no doubt when we get home he's going to figure some way to work into the evening his big story of being at the Midway. Of him being on the *Yorktown* when she sank."

She turned in her seat, looked out onto the water. Laura saw her swallow, saw her take up a breath. She saw the fear this woman was trying to reveal and, for a moment, thought to tell her not to go on.

But Laura only picked up her own glass, took a sip of clear, cold water. She set the glass down, careful to do as Winnie had, precisely centering the glass on the wet ring left on the tablecloth.

Winnie said, "That story was one of the first things he ever told me. Told me over beers at the Shell Pile all the way back in 1946, back when everybody on earth who'd had anything to do with the war was out of work." She stopped, turned back to Laura. "You don't know about the Shell Pile, do you?"

"Not a clue," Laura said, and smiled.

"We'll have to get you over to the Shell Pile." She looked up and behind Laura, smiled, and here was the waitress with Laura's salad and Winnie's chowder. The woman set the food before them, nodded, said, "If I can get you girls anything at all, you just let me know."

Winnie nodded, still smiled. "This is just fine," she said.

The waitress turned and was gone. Winnie picked up her soup spoon, dipped it into the bowl.

She stopped, put the spoon down, and pushed the bowl away. She put her hands in her lap, looked at the bowl. "Can't hold a candle to Rollie's. Best to not even start, I'm so damned spoiled." She glanced up at Laura and smiled.

Laura held her fork above the salad, then stopped, settled it on the edge of the plate.

She looked at Winnie, shrugged. It was the story she wanted.

She blinked, looked back to the table, her water glass. "I met him at the Shell Pile," she said. "Over there with a couple girlfriends, us up from Norfolk for a big time in Atlantic City, back when it was Atlantic City and not this den of fools it is today. Back when it meant you were headed for a big and glamorous time when you said you were going there. But of course it didn't take long before we girls got bored even with that, and we ran into some boys out on the Boardwalk who told us about a place called the Shell Pile. A club, they called it." She paused, seemed to lean back a little in the chair, another smile playing across her face. "I can't remember any of them's names to this day. None of those boys. The girls, those two girls I can only remember the first names, Babs and Saralee." She stopped again and crossed her arms, lost in her own memory.

Laura said, "Norfolk. What did you do there?"

"Oh, Norfolk," Winnie said, and she gave a laugh, shook her head. "Norfolk, Norfolk. I was one of those girls worked in the shipyard. You heard of Rosie the Riveter? That was me, bib overalls and all, working on hull inner lining installation. As was Babs and Saralee. That's where I picked up smoking, too, started up at a pack a day, the break room at the shipyard so thick with smoke you had to dig your way through with a shovel." She paused. "Norfolk," she said and laughed again.

"And then we pull up in front of the Shell Pile in these three boys' car. The Pile was a dump even back then, not any sharper than it is right now, and we girls are all starting to wonder what was up, us out there on the beach at what looked like no better than a barn." She shrugged and put a hand to her glass again.

The sun fell lower all in a moment, Laura saw, and the water out through the windows and the trees and the lawn and the homes across the river all started just then to lose their edges, seemed to dissolve in the smallest way. The color had begun to disappear along with those edges, so that the brown lawn shifted to a shade of gray. The blue in the sky and on the water seemed washed out, moved toward white, and Laura felt now an urgency, an even stronger need for this story, as though there would be no day past this one in which she would share someone else's fear.

"But we gals were strong," Winnie said, and now she had an arm up like a weightlifter. With her other hand she poked at the flesh there, the soft, pale skin. "We were strong, and we weren't afraid of these clowns. We'd worked at the shipyard for two or three years by that time, and we could've duked it out with any one of them and won." She brought her arm down, put her hands in her lap. "We were invincible," she said and shrugged. "Or so I thought. Then they brought us inside the place, said since we were girls we wouldn't have to pay the one-time initiation fee of a dollar. And here's this club, the place just jumping. 'Pennsylvania 6-5000' was on the juke box in the back corner of the place, that I remember. And tables all set up with red-and-white-checkered table-cloths, and there's people galore in there, jamming in at the bar off to the left when you came in, and some of them dancing over to the right, on the other side of the tables. And I look up, and there's these socks hanging from the ceiling, just rows and rows of socks, sweat socks, argyles, black, yellow, red, checkered, you name it, just hanging there from the ceiling. And smoke, smoke thicker than the break room, and it was right then I knew this was my place."

"Where is it?" Laura said and leaned forward, her arms crossed and on the table. "The Shell Pile."

"There at Reed's Beach," Winnie said, the look on her face one of surprise, as though Laura—everyone—already

277

knew where the Shell Pile was. "Didn't I say that?" Winnie said. "Didn't I tell you that?"

"No," Laura said and shrugged. She smiled.

The waitress was back again, stood with her hands on her hips. "Now ladies," she said. "This is good food." She shook her head, smiling. "You haven't even touched this. What am I going to do with you?"

"Listen," Winnie said and looked up at the woman. She was smiling, too. "Truth is, sweetheart, seems we just needed to come in here and have a good gab session." She looked at Laura, said, "You still feeling hungry?"

Laura blinked, looked at Winnie, the waitress, then Winnie again. "No," she said. "No, not really," she said, and it was as if the words Winnie'd given this far, these small images she'd placed in Laura's head, had been nourishment enough: Her appetite was gone, though she hadn't eaten since this morning.

The waitress was silent a moment, just looking at the table, the food. Then she looked from Winnie to Laura. She smiled again, shook her head. "Order canceled," she said and picked up the salad and soup. "I know a good gab session when I see one," she said. Still she smiled, turned with the food, then stopped. "How about some coffee? Got some fresh-brewed."

"Terrific," Winnie said.

"Sounds fine," Laura said.

"It's called that because of the pile of shells out behind the place," Winnie started up once the waitress was gone. She let out a slow breath, smiled. "There's this pile of oyster and clam shells out back, must be twenty feet high, that's been growing since they opened the place back in the twenties. Back during Prohibition. That's when they started the place, sort of a speakeasy, only with none of that secret stuff, like you see in Hollywood movies. The police and all just let the place run, never bothered them." She paused, looked at Laura. "I thought I told you it was there at Reed's Beach. I could have sworn. It's all the way at the far end, the opposite end of the beach from the Halfords'. It's this broken-down barnlike thing on the inland side. There's this chain across the front of the driveway, got a little red scrap rag tied to it. Can't miss the place. Looks like a pineys' refugee camp outside. Bald tires heaped up, a basketball hoop with no backboard."

Laura already knew the place, had seen it the second day she was down there and'd walked the length of Reed's Beach. She thought of the red piece of cloth on the rusted chain, of the way beach wind whipped at it, thought of the cold wind and how that cloth had danced, something in its movement making her turn and head for the Halfords' until her chest heaved and she'd begun crying without knowing it, a red rag on a chain enough to knock her down.

"That's how this place got started, too," Winnie said and looked around the restaurant. "This used to be a casino of the first order, a true speakeasy with gangsters and rumrunners coming in along the Mullica from Cuba, putting in here. Cigarette girls and gamblers. None of this industrial gambling like over in Atlantic City. Just craps and roulette and blackjack. The Sweetwater Casino." She looked out the window again, then back at the walls, the tables, and slowly shook her head. "But there's something sad about this old place. I haven't been here in twenty years or so, and it hasn't changed much at all. It's like the place died when they turned it into a restaurant, left the club and casino business behind. Back in the thirties you couldn't find this place if you had a map. Now they got subdivisions at the foot of the drive." She paused, lost the smile. "Give me the Shell Pile any day.

You still got to pay a dollar to join, and every man who enters there has to give up his left sock the first time in."

Laura laughed then, the sound a surprise. "Why?"

Winnie shrugged, and the waitress appeared with two steaming cups of coffee in thick white mugs. "Here you go," she said, and she was gone.

The light was disappearing now, the objects outside losing even more distinction the later the afternoon grew. Now the trees across the lake were only black shapes, the houses over there just squares of brown. The water, though still, was a deep purple, the lawn gone to ash.

"Just an initiation. Something funny to do. Men. What they think of to entertain themselves." She stopped, picked up the coffee, winced at it just as she had at the soup. She set it down. "But there at the far end of the bar was my Roland. This thick black hair and broad shoulders, big hands and this easy smile. Me and Babs and Saralee all spotted him right off, just kind of shrugged away those nameless boys who'd brought us in. But it was me to get him, and why I can't say. Maybe it was my own smile. Maybe it was the way I held my cigarette. Maybe it was my own head of black hair. I can't say. Who can say about love and how it starts up? Just that the next day we were down to Maryland and getting married."

"What?" Laura said. "You got married that fast?"

"Why not?" Winnie said, and shrugged. She sat up and smiled. "We didn't have any reason not to. I was out of work in Norfolk, he was out of the navy. He had a car and some crazy scheme to start up a donut shop in Philadelphia. Seems the navy was crazy about donuts, and he was famous on the *Yorktown* for his donuts." She paused. "My mother and daddy were dead, dead in a car wreck when I was seventeen, and I had an older brother somewhere out in San Diego." She stopped, let the words hang there before them, as if, Laura thought, this piece of information might in itself be enough reason to marry a man with a car and drive off to Maryland.

"But we were in love," Winnie said, and her voice had gone quiet once again, had taken on the darkness, too, of the late afternoon outside, so that Laura could see, with the loss of detail to the world outside and the hue Winnie's voice had taken on, the way love could take over, let you lose your life for the specter of the one that lay ahead. No mother or father, a brother three thousand miles away. What else could you do if you stumbled into a handsome man with a car and prospects for the future?

"That was the first time I heard the story. The story of Roland Dorsett, Ship's Cook Third Class, and how he'd gone back aboard the *Yorktown* after she'd been abandoned, how he'd volunteered to go back aboard and keep the salvage operators fed for as long as possible from whatever stores were on board." She paused, let out a breath, on her face, Laura could see, pure love, enchantment with this man. She loved him, loved him still. "It's a story, one for the ages. The way he told it, too, right there at the bar, all hell breaking loose around us, people jitterbugging and carrying on, and it was like none of that even existed. All I heard was this story about how he'd gone into the depths of the ship, no power on so all he had was a flashlight, going down all the way to the third deck to find whatever food he could for the boys." She paused. "No use for me to even try and tell you what it was like, he told it so good. And he told it like he wasn't a hero, told it so's I could hear what had happened on board the *Yorktown*."

She paused, slowly tilted her head the other way, the late afternoon light through the windows falling about her shoulders, Laura thought, like the thinnest of cloaks, sheltering her. "It was history he was telling me, the

281

truth of it. A man who'd lived through it, come out the other side." She paused again, reached to the glass, but didn't lift it. "And then the story was over: a blast and rocking of the ship, him down there in the mess, and then all of them abandoning ship for the last time, the *Yorktown* gone after that. Just sunk, right there in open sea, Rollie on board the *Balch* and just watching her go down. When he was done with the story, his eyes were looking off past me. I remember looking at him, at his eyes and all he'd seen, and the way he'd told this story not to pick up on some black-haired beauty on a barstool next to him, but because it needed to be told, and I thought, I'll marry this boy. This is the one."

A few moments later she picked up the white mug and sipped at it. But she didn't put it back on the table, instead held it with both hands, as though the room had gone cold, though Laura could feel no difference in the air. Winnie held the mug close to her chest.

Her face lost expression then, her mouth no longer in a smile, and Laura knew what was next, knew without word or gesture that true fear was on its way.

"A lung and a lobe," Winnie nearly whispered, her voice as thin as the darkness descending outside. "He was with me all the way through that. And I thought I knew him. I thought I did." She paused, brought the cup to her lips with both hands, and here came the cold breath at the back of Laura's neck, the shiver down her spine that signaled her she'd been given entry somehow to this woman's own black treasure.

"He knew how much I liked that story. He knew how much it meant to me, how much I loved hearing him tell it. Which had to be why he told it to me there in the recovery room, there in a white room in a hospital in Philadelphia. I was in and out, but I don't think he knew that. I think he thought I was going to die on him, thought I was maybe already there for the way he told that story. But I wasn't dead. I wasn't asleep even. I was in that weird place when you come up from sleep and the world seems not the place you left it. Everything was white, and here was my husband's voice beside me, telling me of the *Yorktown*, and it was a peace I was feeling because of that story, because of how much I loved the way the man I'd been married to for twenty-nine years told it to me and to whoever would listen to him."

She paused, took up another sip of coffee, still held the cup close. Laura picked up her cup, too, took a swallow. It was already tepid, and now she, too, believed she felt whatever cold it was Winnie had already taken in. Maybe it was the early February evening outside the windows and making its way in, she thought. Or maybe it was this new story, Winnie's words.

"But when he came to the last part, the part about how there'd come this direct hit on the ship, him down on the third deck and scraping up canned jam and two-day-old bread for food, he stopped the story. He stopped it, and for a moment it was me who thought maybe I was dead, there in all that white. I figured maybe I had gone on and died, my husband left behind." She paused, sipped the coffee. "So I opened my eyes to see what'd happened, see if I was on my way who knows where. Heaven, I was hoping." She stopped, swallowed, her eyes still on the table, that glass. "There was my Rollie, right there next to me in a white recovery room, and I had no feeling at all in me. I knew I was alive, knew there was an oxygen mask strapped to my face. And I knew that somewhere right then somebody was dealing with my left lung and a lobe off the right, poking it maybe and looking at that cancer. But what I didn't know was my husband. What I didn't know—"

Winnie stopped and looked out her window. "Is it me, or is it getting dark in here?" she said.

"It's getting dark," Laura said. She smiled. "Still February, believe it or not, after the weather today. Still gets dark pretty early."

"Too early," Winnie said. "There's too much to do in a day."

Laura nodded and sipped the hot coffee. She wanted to say *Go on*, wanted to prod this woman into speaking the fear so imminent. But she knew Winnie would finish. This was her own story, the story of herself and her husband, of their love.

Winnie still held the mug, brought it to her chest again. "There was my Rollie," she said, her voice back to the intimate one it had been before. "There was my Rollie, and he was crying. From where I lay in bed I could see he had his Orioles cap on, could see his head was down and his shoulders moving, shaking, and he was crying." She paused and swallowed again. "I couldn't talk," Winnie said. "I couldn't move. I was just there in bed, watching him cry. I'd never seen him do that. I never saw him cry. And I wanted to touch him so bad, wanted to get my hand out from under all the hardware they had strapped to me so's I could just touch him, tell him I was here, I was okay. But then he cleared his throat, started on to the story again. His head was still down so he couldn't see me watching him. He started up on the story again, and I can remember trying to remember how to smile because I couldn't move at all. I wanted to smile because here he was, still getting on with the story."

Laura heard a catch in Winnie's throat, heard a woman trying not to cry herself. Laura placed her hand on the tablecloth, set it palm up, and Winnie reached, took it, held it tight.

She squeezed it once, then let it go, brought her hand back to the coffee cup.

Winnie'd surrendered. Laura knew it in only that touch, the single squeeze. She'd surrendered, had needed that moment of help in her hand, and she heard Winnie take in a breath, clear her throat.

"But this time it was different," she said. "Here he was, making his way down the deck, all hell breaking loose, him with just a flashlight down under all that steel, down there just trying to find food for men who were trying to save the whole ship. But he was stammering his way through it this time, stumbling, catching sometimes on the words he'd always used to tell the story, then just piecing it together. And then."

She stopped, turned to the water out there again, and here was her profile once more. But now it was a silhouette in the amber sky to the west, the sky behind her out the window.

"Then," she whispered, "then he put in something he'd left out every time he ever told that story before, and the way he stumbled through it gave me to know this was the truth." She sat up straight again, though she still held the cup close, still seemed to want to let the warmth of it seep into her. "The ship's listing way to port, and he's making his way with the flashlight along the deck, one hand to the starboard wall, touching it. But this time his foot steps on something, something that gives as he steps on it. This time he steps down into something that gives underfoot, and he slides the flashlight down to the deck floor, and there's a man there. There's a dead man there, a sailor. And Rollie bends over and shines the light closer, and he sees in all the listing and the groans of this ship on its way down that it's a bunkmate of his, another Ship's Cook Third Class by the name of Kaminski. Butch Kaminski. Flour Boy was this kid's nickname—all the cookies had nicknames, except my Rollie because of those damned donuts and how good he could turn them out. But this Flour Boy, Rollie is telling me, he's just dead there on the third deck floor, and Rollie, Rollie, he bends down and tries to bring him with him. He tries to carry him, tries to carry him out of there because Rollie wants his family to get him back from all of this. This is what Rollie's thinking while he's trying to lug this dead friend up a ladder. And then the ship starts to go, starts listing even farther, and there's these sharp cuts of sound down in there, and Rollie can hear this water somewhere, rising up on him from down deep. And he sees he has to let this man, this friend, this kid he's only known four months, he has to let him go. And he lets him go. Lets him go, there on the third deck, and all he has time to do is what they taught him in basic training, the purpose of dog tags. How you take them off the dead sailor, take one of them with you. And you put the other one sideways between the front teeth of the dead sailor and kick the jaw up, make sure and drive that tag up into the sailor's teeth so's it won't be coming out, and so if the body ever shows up, we'll all know whose it is."

She paused, and Laura wrapped her own hands around her cup, tried to let its warmth into her, too. She held onto the cup.

"And that's what Rollie did. That's what my Roland did. He kicked home that dog tag, and he left him there, because he couldn't get him up the ladder, and because the ship itself was on its way down."

Slowly she shook her head, her silhouette still to Laura. "Rollie's telling me all this in the white of a hospital room, telling me this true story of his he's carried around with him forever. He's telling me this story while I can't move, can't talk, can't even let him know I hear

286

him, that I love him and want to comfort him and touch him and hold him. There's not a damned thing I can do while he hands me some piece of his life he'd never let out before. And it comes to me, it comes to me there on the bed, a lung and a lobe gone; comes to me after twenty-nine years of being married to this man, that I didn't know him. I could never know him. I'd heard the story a thousand times, never once heard a hitch in his voice, never saw him bat an eye when it came to him hearing water around him, him moving along in the dark back up the ladder. I didn't know the man there next to me, and from that day to this I can't say as I know him, can't say as I know why he thinks it funny to answer the phone with 'Yellow,' nor why he reads the newspaper first page to last. He's told that story a thousand times since, and he's never once said a thing about that dead sailor again, never once said what he had to do." She paused. "And I never once let on what I knew. Never will."

She stopped, turned to Laura. Winnie's face was lost to her, the amber sky behind her now gone to purple. She set the coffee cup down on the table, put her hands in her lap.

And now the lights in the restaurant came on, shoved out whatever last sliver of light might have been making its way in from the windows. Slowly the lights above them, those small chandeliers, rose and gave out light, and here was Winnie, a woman in a rayon blouse, black hair still perfect. Her lipstick was worn down, her eyes red. She blinked and tried at a smile. She took in a breath, shrugged.

Laura looked down at her cup, saw she'd only taken a few sips, the cup half empty. Of course she could only think of Hugh, of what she knew of her own husband, of him in their son's bedroom, and she wondered what of his secret life in that room she would ever know.

And of course she thought of her son, of his words on scraps of paper, his fist raised with a green happy stamp, and she wondered what secrets of his own he'd carried, where he'd found that piece of concrete, what secret treasure he and Gerry Rothberg had believed they'd unearthed when they found the chunk of brick. What great forests they imagined they'd pioneered with their path between houses to the bus stop, that path she'd trod in her socks one afternoon in November.

Who can we know? she thought.

"I don't know him," Winnie said, "and so that's the reason I head out to the Taj Mahal every time it seems I might be thinking I *do* know him, every time I get to believing he's just saying Yellow to be funny. It's like I told you, I go in there and I touch on what it is everyone there believes might happen to them: that they'll strike it rich, that the woes and strife that brought them over there in the first place might disappear forever if they could just get their hands on a pile of cash." She paused and looked at her hands. "I go in there, that place waiting to eat me alive. But I walk away. I walk out alive, and I know that the painful things don't disappear. And I see the pain's good for you, makes you see that much more clearly what it is you have. I walk out of there and all I know is that I love Rollie and that I still don't know him. And maybe that's the best anybody could ever get out of her days: someone to love and a fear inside that love that makes you want to care for that someone. Just that."

Laura felt her own eyes go warm now, saw the woman, now lit with soft restaurant light, shimmer in her eyes. She loved Hugh. She loved Michael. She thought she knew some things about both, and now one was gone.

Now Winnie's hand was on the table, there in this light

for anyone to see. There was her hand, palm up, just as Laura's had been for Winnie a while before.

"There's your answer," she whispered now. "I fear Rollie. I love him, but I don't know him."

Laura reached for her, took her hand, squeezed it. She held it, held it longer than Winnie had her own. She held it.

She said, "I have this dream some nights. It's—"

"Sugar, you don't have to say a word," Winnie said, and Laura worked up a smile, felt her chin quiver with it. She could see Winnie slowly shaking her head. "Sugar, I'm the one you asked. And I'm the one wanted to tell you. You don't have to say a word."

But Laura swallowed, felt the hard fist in her throat. She said, "There's this dream I have," and she looked as best as she could at Winnie, tried to focus through her tears on her. "Once every few nights I dream I'm at a kitchen table in a house I've never been in before," she said, amazed at the sound of her words, at how they were coming to her. At the jetty there'd been no words, only the evidence of her son. But now there were words, all of them lined up in her. She wanted to speak them, wanted to get them right, because it seemed she would never have this chance again, never be allowed to speak again.

She said, "And the table is spread with photographs of Michael. With pictures of my son. The tablecloth is white, and the pictures are all black-and-whites. He's got on a sweater and a white shirt and a bow tie, and in some of them he's smiling, in some he's not. Some of them has him sitting in a chair, or holding a toy, all like a Sears portrait, all of them posed." Laura paused, closed her eyes, and conjured the dream, the one she feared she might have each night.

"It's Hugh and me at the table, and we're looking at

289

these pictures, and we both know that he's dead. We both know we're looking at the last photographs of our son, and they're all posed. He's happy, Michael is, but he's posed, and there's this feel in me that this is all we have left. That he lived his whole life, and this is all we have left of him, photographs spread out on a white tablecloth."

She stopped, opened her eyes, and saw Winnie even more broken now, even more shattered by the tears in her eyes. She swallowed hard again, tried to get past the fist in her throat.

"And then I wake up," Laura heard herself say. "I wake up," she said, her voice wavering, moving away from her like rings across water, "and for an instant I know it's only a dream. For an instant I think, 'It's only a dream. This is just a dream.'" She stopped, creased closed her eyes. "But in the next instant I remember what it is I'm waking up into. What's there in the room, what's really happened, and that it's not going to change."

She felt herself crying now, felt her chest heave, and now Winnie was beside her, an arm around her and patting her for the second time today, and she remembered being out at the end of the jetty, Winnie's words when Laura'd cried back then: *You just say to me what you want to say.*

"It's that moment when it's only a dream," she heard, and believed it was herself speaking. "It's that second when I think it didn't happen. That's what I'm afraid of." She breathed in, heard the whisper of air into her throat, felt Winnie's hand on her back. "Because every time I have that second, I'm back there. I'm back when he was alive, and I can save him. I can pick him up from school, I can teach him not to run on the bus, I can make him stay home or take him to Friendly's or hold him. It's that second I'm afraid of, because then it's over, every possibility in the world to save him is gone, and it's only a dark bedroom. It's only a bedroom, and it happened, and there's nothing I can do, and I didn't save him."

She broke then, sobbed. She was aware only vaguely of Winnie's hand on her, aware of the lights in the restaurant and of Winnie speaking words to the waitress.

She didn't move, but stayed there at the table, her hand still in Winnie's, still holding tight. She'd spoken her fear, just as Winnie had. She'd spoken it, had touched with both hands that pain Winnie'd said was what got you through. She'd bathed her hands in the fountain of blood, she knew. Now all she had left to do was find her way through this pain Winnie spoke so highly of, and hope she would emerge alive.

Laura held tight to Winnie's hand, leaned into her.

It was only a dark bedroom she awoke to each night she had the dream. Only a bedroom, one empty of possibility.

But it was Hugh there beside her, she saw. It was Hugh, a man she might not know, just as Winnie did not know her own Rollie.

But it was Hugh there in the dark with her.

Seven

🦠 HE SAW THEM in his headlights, three people walking the dirt road that was Reed's Beach: Laura and the two from next door. Roland Dorsett and his wife.

The moon had led him here; he hadn't lost sight of it since climbing on the Garden State Parkway, had even seen it from the pay phone at the Toms River toll, then again from the pay phone just past the toll at Great Egg Harbor. Laura hadn't answered the phone either time, and while he'd driven, he'd worried something might have happened to her. But he could not picture what.

And still there had been the moon, beside him across the tops of trees beside the highway, directly before him as he'd crossed the cape toward Reed's Beach. It seemed, too, that the moon out there had been close enough to touch. If he were to roll down his window, he believed, let a sharp blast of cold air in, he could put his hand right out there and bring it back.

Now here was Laura walking alongside two strangers, and now the moon suddenly seemed too high, too far away.

He slowed down and saw how the three of them quickly looked up, startled at the light. They were to his left, walking on the inland side of the road and away from the Halfords'. He wondered what they could be doing outside—he glanced at the green numbers on the digital clock—at 10:51 at night.

Laura, arms crossed, her straw handbag hung at the crook of her elbow, stood on the inside, against the heaped dirt; next to her walked the woman—he couldn't remember her name, only that her hair was impossibly black; next to her, on the outside and farthest into the road, walked Roland Dorsett. As he'd looked up, the headlights reflected across Roland's glasses, sent tiny sparks of light back at Hugh.

Roland had on the same windbreaker he'd worn last night, the same *Yorktown* ball cap as this morning. The woman had on red shorts, Hugh could see, and a green zippered sweatshirt, a yellow scarf over her hair. And Laura had on her sweatpants and parka.

They were all looking at him. He could see his wife's hair moving in the wind out there, saw, too, their skin washed white in his headlights, as though they were frightened, eyes squinted against whatever intruder might be headed their way.

He pulled up even with them, and they passed from white and bloodless into gray, the three of them barely lit in the backwash of light the headlights gave off. He rolled down his window.

"Just like I told you, it's the man of the house," Roland said. He leaned toward the window, hands on his knees, and said, "Howdy, pardner."

"Hugh?" Laura said. She squinted harder, tried to adjust her eyes to this darkness after the flare of headlights as they had come toward her. She couldn't see him, the man behind the wheel of this car only a black figure. But she moved toward him, leaned down.

"Hello," Hugh said, and here was his wife, moving

toward him, her eyebrows knotted, hands jammed deep into her parka pockets.

"What are you doing here?" she said. Even as she gave out the words she heard how they sounded: an accusation, his presence an interruption.

Which was not how she'd intended to speak to him the next time she saw him. He was supposed to be here tomorrow night, and she'd already decided to tell him what she'd found about their son's room, wanted to tell him of how she wanted—at some point soon—to hold a red cigar box and examine its treasures; wanted to hold a plaster Statue of Liberty; wanted to touch with her own hands the scattered pieces of construction paper atop his blue desk.

Yet there were her words, the ugly sound of them. Still she could not recognize Hugh for the dark, and both these facts seemed to bear the perfect truth she'd come to at the restaurant: She did not know herself, and she did not know her husband.

Winnie and Laura had gotten home well past dark, dinner prepared and ready for them: stuffed crab for the appetizer, fresh mushroom soup, beef Wellington and escalloped apples for the entrée, chocolate–pecan pie for dessert. The meal had taken almost two hours to finish, what with the talk, Roland running on and on about how worried he'd been over them all day, Winnie talking about the siding they'd failed to get up that day and about how far that put them behind. Laura'd only listened, smiled, spoke now and again. And ate.

And there came from Roland only one question as to where they had been all day: "Did you win?" he asked once he'd served up the soup. He wouldn't let his eyes meet Winnie's, nor would he look at Laura. He sat, brought a spoonful of soup to his lips, and tasted it.

"Nope," Winnie said, her eyes on Laura. "But Laura here did all right." Winnie smiled. "She did just fine."

"Glad to hear it," was all he'd said.

They'd decided to go to the Shell Pile only after Winnie mentioned to Laura, once Roland'd served the pie and coffee, that she'd met him there in 1946. Winnie offered up the information simply, easily, as though it were a brand-new piece of dinner conversation, something Laura'd never heard before.

But the words were a test, Laura'd known, to see how Roland would react, what he'd do.

Of course, once Winnie'd mentioned the Shell Pile, he snapped his finger, said, "I got just the idea. Let's us go on down there, show this girl here a thing or two about the word *fun*." He slapped a hand to the tabletop. "Damn fine idea. The Shell Pile," he said, and forked up a bite of chocolate–pecan pie.

He took a sip of coffee, said, "That's the best place in the world I can think of to hear about the *Yorktown*, too." He smiled at Laura.

Winnie'd smiled at Laura then and nodded: Let the man believe it was all his idea.

Laura wanted to tell Hugh all this, of Roland's food and the Sweetwater Casino, of afternoon light and the way it cut through the trees there. She wanted to tell him of the shipwreck and the jetty, of Quaker guns and the Taj Mahal and the fountain of blood she'd touched. And she wanted to tell him, finally, of her dream of the photos, and her desire now to go into Michael's room, touch his things there.

But she'd given him the words she had, knew he'd feel the abruptness of them, might drop even farther into the world he roamed when he was inside their son's room.

So that all she believed she could do to let him know

298

she wanted him with her, wanted him to see she loved him, was to kiss him.

She took her hands from her pockets, placed them on the door where the window had been rolled down, then leaned in.

Her eyes still hadn't adjusted, and she looked closely at him.

Hugh saw her eyes taking him in. She was searching yet again, he knew, looking for some truth from him, and he wanted right then to partake of their own language, that language of grief only he and Laura knew.

He wanted to begin their new language with the surprise of his arrival, his showing up the first move toward the common ground of grief.

But not like this. Not with two strangers, onlookers and no more. He wanted no witnesses, no spectators.

Her eyebrows still knotted, her eyes still working to find him in the dark, she moved even closer to him. Then her lips were against his, and Hugh felt the warmth of her lips despite the cold out here, and she kissed him.

He'd thought Laura was mad at him, given her words, the quickness of them, as though he'd interrupted something he was not intended to see, and so the touch of her lips was a surprise. Then she was gone, her face away from his. He hadn't been able to kiss her back. He believed he'd smelled chocolate on her breath. Chocolate, and coffee.

"Hi," she said. She stood and put her hands back in her pockets. She was right: He'd fallen deeper into the hole he'd dug. He hadn't even kissed her back.

"Hi," Hugh said. She could see him now, believed he might have given a smile, though she could not be sure. "Surprise," he said.

"Surprise," Laura said. "I thought you were coming

back tomorrow night." She paused, tried hard to know what she would say to this man she did not know.

"Change of plans," he said and shrugged. He glanced out the windshield. He hadn't wanted it to start this way.

"Listen," Roland Dorsett said, "you two lovebirds are holding up the whole show. We're out here freezing to death, and you two want to smooch."

"Rollie," his wife said, and Hugh saw in the gray light Laura turn to her, saw her smile at this woman.

Laura turned back to Hugh. Here came his face, the startled look surfacing as her eyes finally adjusted. He was looking at her, then at Winnie, then at her again.

Roland Dorsett said, "We're headed down to the Shell Pile, get a little something to warm us up. You go park this rig back at camp and we'll all go on over there, okay?" Roland's hands were in his windbreaker pockets. He looked behind the car in the direction Hugh had come, then nodded back toward the Halfords' place. "Otherwise, our feet are going to freeze right into this dirt, and we'll never get there."

"Shell Pile?" Hugh said.

"A little hole-in-the-wall dive," Roland Dorsett's wife said.

Laura said, "Winnie and Roland were going to show me the place. Now you're here, we can all go." She smiled and looked at Winnie. In the gray, she believed she could see Winnie glance at her, then at Hugh.

She turned to Hugh. "But if you want to go back and rest," she said. "I imagine you've had a long day, and—"

"No chance," Roland Dorsett cut in. "This is a Shell Pile expedition, and we're all going. Once he gets this rig parked—"

"Rollie, now settle down," Winnie Dorsett said. "If he wants to get some rest, let the poor man."

Winnie, Hugh remembered. *Rollie, Dennie, Sal.* All these names.

Laura, he thought, then, *Michael.*

Hugh saw the way Laura looked at this Winnie, already knew why Laura hadn't been able to answer the phone: She'd been at the Dorsetts'. The two of them knew something, he saw in their smile, something that had to do with himself, and with this Roland.

He hadn't wanted to start it this way.

"Why don't I just drive?" Hugh said, his own words a surprise. He nodded at Winnie. "I mean, I can just drive us. I got the heater going."

"Nope, no sir," Winnie said and shook her head. She hugged herself. "Walking's fine. We been tooling around in the van all day long. I don't want to climb back in another vehicle for awhile, thank you very much."

"Wait," Laura said, his decision to accompany them a surprise, after the kiss he had not given her, after the words she'd started this out with, and she reached to the car, touched the cold metal of the door. "I'll ride back with you," she said, then trotted around the back of the car and to the passenger door, popped it open.

But before she climbed in, she looked across the roof to Winnie and smiled.

Winnie smiled. She nodded, then seemed to shiver, hunched her shoulders against the cold out here.

Hugh turned, saw Laura sitting down beside him, saw her place the straw handbag on the floorboard. He looked at her a long moment, then turned and looked out the windshield, and she wondered if he hadn't dug himself a hole so deep this day he'd buried himself alive.

He looked out the windshield. The headlights cut through the black down here, sliced a sharp wedge that illuminated the dirt road and the ramshackle houses, somewhere ahead of him and to the right, on the bay side of the road, his boss's cottage. Inside that cottage, he knew, was an empty upstairs room filled with the toys of a man whose life was empty on its own.

And if Hugh himself, as he'd seen in the last moments outside Mr. Halford's palace, were only Mr. Halford hiding down here at Reed's Beach, then this woman beside him had to be Mrs. Halford—*Sal*—a woman inside a greenhouse furiously repotting a plant in the belief she could give order to a life that had lost all order. This was his wife, hiding inside her maps and brochures, her excursions around Cape May, even he himself and his presence an interruption of her exploration of everything but the death of their son.

But Mrs. Halford had waved to him, had sent him a signal: *I know you. I know you.*

He knew Laura. He knew his wife, knew they had been given the most terrible moment any parent could ever be given. And here they were, the two of them alive, their lives left to live.

"Let's get going," Winnie said from outside Hugh's rolled-down window, and started away, arms still tight around her.

Roland turned, followed her. "Duty calls," he said over his shoulder. "See you at the store," he called out, and they were gone.

Then Hugh and Laura were alone.

Laura swallowed. "Surprise," she said.

She looked at him and swallowed again. She did not know him. But she needed to know him.

He hadn't wanted it to begin this way.

"Surprise," he said, the only word that came to him.

He turned back to the windshield, put the car in gear.

302

🌸 THEY MADE IT to Dorsett's Marlinspike General Store, said nothing to each other on the walk there except for comments on the warmth of the day, on the brightness of the full moon, on the return of the cold.

Hugh and Laura stepped onto the porch of the clapboard building, Roland and Winnie already there, waiting, the four of them, and the building, the road, the marsh that spread out before them, all silver for the moon.

"Fancy bumping into you here," Roland said and laughed. He pulled something from his windbreaker pocket, lifted it, and pointed it at the store window. Then came a beam of light that cut through the glass into the black depths of the store: a flashlight.

"Here she is," he said, and leaned toward the glass, looked in. Laura leaned to the glass, too, cupped her hands around her eyes. Then Hugh did the same.

They stood at the glass, peered in past the blinking 7-Up sign to the empty shelves, the empty deli case, empty cigarette racks. The beam slowly swirled through the room, moving, moving, roaming the empty store.

"Here she is," Roland said again, this time his voice almost a whisper, as though he might wake ghosts. "The

303

grindstone, 6 A.M. to 6 P.M. all summer long." He paused. "Some retirement, huh?"

The beam grazed the row of shellacked knotboards hanging on the far wall, back behind the deli case, the same boards as the one hanging in the Halfords' reading room.

"Where'd you get those knot things?" Hugh said, his hands still to the glass. "Those boards with the knots on them."

Roland stopped the beam on one of the boards, and Hugh could see the white lettering beneath each knot: Fisherman's Bend, Sheep's Head, Chinese Bowline.

"I made them," Winnie said, the only one of them not at the glass.

Hugh turned, saw her looking back toward the road. She held her elbows against the cold, the tails of the scarf fluttering beneath her chin.

Hugh turned back to the window. He said, "Mr. Halford's got one just like it."

"I made that one, too," she said.

Hugh was quiet a moment. "I thought he'd made it himself."

"He'll have you believing he's sailed to Bermuda, too," Roland chuckled, "what with all the saily crap he's got in his place. But the truth is the old fart doesn't have a clue."

Roland switched off the flashlight, and the three pulled away from the glass. He said, "I'll bet he's got you thinking he did all the work on his house, too. Put in the heating and insulation, what-have-you. Am I right?"

Hugh felt himself smile. He already knew this about his boss, already knew from the evening's proceedings at the mansion that, in fact, Mr. Halford didn't have a clue.

"Right as rain," Hugh said.

304

"We did it all," Winnie said. "Everything, right on down to weather-stripping the front door."

"I believe it," Hugh said.

Laura'd already heard the facts about Mr. Halford's house, only watched and listened while Roland and Winnie played out the scenes they needed: They were on their own down here, head honchos. They took shit from no one, not even a vice president at Hess.

"To the Shell Pile," Roland said.

She could see Winnie and Roland up ahead, walking in the moonlit dark. They looked strange there, two old people, Roland with his hands in his back pockets, Winnie still hunched, legs close together as she walked in this cold.

Hugh let out a breath. Still he wanted to begin with her, longed for the right words. He looked up to the moon, higher now, smaller over the bay beyond the houses. He could hear the water, the lapping of waves on the beach.

What words were there to give her? What ones would surrender up the clear image in his mind of a misplaced end bracket, one inserted too soon, or of Ed Blankenship with his back to a glass wall, waiting to tell Hugh of his own sorrow, his dead marriage? What phrases could give her his moments looking at a painting of a ship, the men on deck all pieces of himself, holding on hard for some way through whatever wind ripped at them? What words could he grab from thin air that would give Laura the look in Mr. Halford's eyes as he'd held his wife and nodded at Hugh on his way out of the palace, or what words could give Mrs. Halford there in the greenhouse or could even give the greenhouse itself, an emerald miracle at the back end of a mansion in Holmdel?

And what words could he speak that would show her

the memory he'd been given by Ted Rothberg, the clean shine in his son's brown eyes as they'd stood in the World Trade Center and looked down at a Statue of Liberty close enough to touch, Sandy Hook itself right there for the taking?

What could he say that could catch his son's eyes, the touch of Hugh's hand on his back, the solid knowledge of his existence?

He said, "I found a SOC7 nobody else could today. Made sure everyone in Rhode Island got paid this week."

"Good for you," Laura said. "People will eat this week because of you."

She was only talking, she knew. Only filling empty space between his words and the work of walking alone with him, here in bright moonlight, the shacks casting shadows across the silver road.

"Winnie and I spent the day together," she said. "I got up this morning and had my day all planned out, then came outside. I forgot all about you taking the car."

Hugh's eyes were to the ground in front of him again. He said, "So that's what Winnie was talking about. When she said she'd been tooling around in the van all day long."

"Yep," Laura said.

"So where'd you go?"

"Around." Her eyes were still on the Dorsetts, the two of them, however old they seemed to her, moving fast; she had to take long steps to keep up. She said, "The library in Cape May. Then on over to a shipwreck." She paused and swallowed hard. "It's called the *Atlantus*. It was an experimental ship, made out of concrete." She paused again. "After that," she said, and she could feel the rise in her throat, "after that, we just drove around."

Hugh said, "I read about that. The shipwreck. In one of your flyers." He thought of the blue flyer he'd picked

up and read last night while she'd lectured him on how
he was himself dying.

Just then a gust buffeted the two of them, cold wind
that seemed almost to tear through their coats, and
Laura moved closer beside him, leaned in to him in the
smallest way as they walked.

Hugh felt her against him, and brought a hand from
deep inside the warmth of his parka pocket, put his arm
around her. The cold cut into his hand, and still he
looked at the silver dirt before them, still he heard the
lapping of waves.

Roland and Winnie were stopped up ahead. Roland's
flashlight was on, pointed at the ground, a halo of light
around his and Winnie's feet. "Pick it up!" he shouted.
"This ain't no funeral march!"

"Rollie, goddammit!" Winnie shouted in a whisper so
loud Hugh and Laura heard her from this far away.

Roland turned to her and said nothing, only looked at
her.

"Oh," he said after a few moments, then, louder, "Oh."

He turned to Hugh and Laura. They were almost there
now, the circle of light on the ground growing the closer
they moved until, just then, they were there with Rollie
and Winnie, inside the circle, the four of them encompassed by artificial light.

"I'm sorry, you two," he said, his voice the same low
whisper it'd been when they'd looked inside the deli.
"I'm sorry. I didn't mean to—"

"Let's go," Winnie said, and now Roland's flashlight
waved through the silver night, brushed across the road
and back, then at their feet, finally landing on a chain
across what looked to Hugh like the entrance to a drive.
At the center of the chain was a piece of red cloth tied
off, twisting in the wind out here.

Hugh felt Laura go stiff beside him and stand up

straight, no longer interested in his arm around her, he believed. He brought his arm down, put his hand in the parka.

"Now watch you don't trip over our elaborate security system here," Roland said. He stepped over the chain, careful to hold the light on it, then took Winnie's hand, helped her over.

Laura saw the rag, saw how it twisted, just as it had the other day when she'd walked down here alone, a day that seemed months ago now. But even with Winnie here, even with Hugh beside her, there still seemed in the way the rag danced something frightening, some language of its own, the same dance that had made her leave this place and head for the hollow comfort of the Halfords'.

She looked at Hugh. He stepped over the chain, then put out his hand to her.

Here was her husband's face, pale in the moonlight, but him. Hugh.

Here was his face, and she could see in his eyes, and in his hair and mouth and smile, in all of this she could see Michael. She saw Michael.

She tasted the pill in this same moment, saw snow angels, woods. All this in an instant.

The straw bag in one hand, she reached to him with the other, and took his hand.

"Our multimillion-dollar recreational facility," Roland said and swung the flashlight beam to the right, landing on a post with a basketball hoop nailed to it, no backboard.

Hugh felt a laugh rise in him, felt himself give it away. He and Laura still held hands, walked up the dirt driveway behind Roland and Winnie. Once the laugh left him, he thought he heard her give a quiet chuckle.

He could not remember when he had last laughed this

way, a laugh that was not hiding anything. He had laughed at work, certainly, but he knew it to have been, of course, only gesture.

But he had laughed just now for no good reason but to laugh.

The beam swung to the left, shone on a heap of bald tires as tall as the shack at the end of the drive.

"Our recycling center," Roland said, and Laura heard Hugh laugh again. She gave up her own laugh, too.

Then they were at the house.

Roland shone the light on the door: only a wide red door, paint chipped and bubbled everywhere. The door was held closed by a deadbolt and a combination lock.

"Ooops," Roland said and took a step back from the door. "Almost forgot," he said, and the flashlight beam went to the peak of the roof above them, shone on a set of antlers nailed up there.

"The Shell Pile Museum of Natural History," he said.

Hugh and Laura laughed again, but Winnie said, "Let's cut the comedy and get inside. I'm freezing my butt off out here." Hugh looked at her, saw her shake her head in the moonlight. He'd heard on her words no anger, no malice. Only statement of fact.

"Say, little lady," Rollie said, and now the flashlight was on Winnie. "Buy a sailor a drink?"

Now Winnie smiled, a smile, Hugh could see, simple and plain, given out of love for this man fiddling now with a combination lock to a shack, and suddenly he believed he'd known this woman for years, believed, too, he'd known this man for just as long. He knew these people.

The lock opened, and Roland pulled it off, slapped back the bolt. He turned and shone the light in Hugh's eyes, the light flaring into his pupils a moment. Then the circle of light was back on the ground, the four of them standing inside it again.

"Now," Roland said. "As to the initiation rights." He cleared his throat.

"Initiation rights?" Hugh said. He looked up at Roland, saw him smiling.

Laura squeezed his hand. He turned and saw her smiling, too, looking to him. She nodded, looked to Roland.

"This here is a private club, youngster. You want to belong to the Shell Pile, you have to go through the initiation rights." He paused, clicked off the flashlight, and the world became silver again. "Ladies, of course, are automatic members. So don't worry about the welfare of your wife. She already belongs." Roland crossed his arms, tilted his head one way, and started rocking back and forth heel to toe, heel to toe. "And there's the little matter of club fees, too," he said, his voice flat, hard.

"Once you've finished with all these shenanigans," Winnie said, "I'd be glad to get on inside."

Hugh saw her in the moonlight, wondered why she didn't just go on in. But then he saw her smiling, saw it even in the moonlight.

"How much?" Hugh said and let go Laura's hand. He reached to his back pocket and pulled out his wallet. He did not know how much he had on him, maybe twenty dollars at the most. He opened the wallet up, held it close to his face, tried to make out the denominations there in the dark.

"A dollar," Roland said, his voice still tough, cold.

Hugh looked up at him. Laura laughed quietly beside him.

He would play this game, play it simply because he wanted to and because there was some joy in this, some easing of pressure on his chest, that laughter still hanging inside him, and he wondered what all had passed between these two women, and between all three of them this day.

"Damned steep," Hugh said, and sighed, pulled out a soft dollar bill, handed it to Roland.

"That's because we got standards to uphold here," he said. He took the bill and held it close to his face. Then he folded it in half, put it in his windbreaker pocket.

"Now," he said. "Take off your left shoe."

"What?" Hugh said. He didn't move for a moment, but here was Winnie's smile again, and then quickly, easily, he put the heel of his left foot to the toe of his right, kicked off the shoe.

The ground was cold, colder than he'd thought it would be, and he remembered in that instant Roland's words about this day, his prophecy of light and warm air: *A day like this,* he'd said in the predawn light before Hugh had left for work, *you can't begin to figure how fine it's going to be.*

And he saw only then that it hadn't been a prophecy of weather, no prediction about temperature or humidity or wind speed or precipitation.

Roland'd spoken of this day, its time on the face of the earth, the shard of history that had been about to occur. The same day Hugh'd walked through, and all that had come to him, that sequence of events in his own history that'd made him come here, seek out his wife with the plan to speak to her in their own private language. That was what Roland had spoken of, that next history we are each of us given with our waking up and rising from bed, with our standing up and moving.

He'd driven here, to her, instead of staying home.

"Take off your sock," Roland said, his voice still the same flat tone.

Hugh said nothing, only bent down and pulled off the sock. He glanced at Winnie across from him, then at

311

Laura, saw the two of them looking at each other, Winnie shaking her head, Laura smiling.

Hugh stood up, his foot even colder now. He felt gravel dig into the sole.

"Now give it to me," Roland said and held out a hand.

The sock was warm in Hugh's hand. He lifted it, let it hang in the wind out here. The sock moved in the wind, twisted a moment, as had the rag on the chain. Hugh handed it to Roland.

Roland held it with his thumb and index finger at arm's length as though the thing were rancid. He pulled out the flashlight, turned it on, shone it on the sock.

"A blue and gray argyle," Roland said and turned it this way, then that. "Pedestrian at best," Roland said. "Muted. Quiet." He brought it closer to his face and gave a small sniff. "A mild bouquet," he said, and both Hugh and Laura laughed. "Slightly tannic, but with a nutty glow about it."

Roland stopped, clicked off the light. "It'll do," he said. He put the flashlight back in the pocket and brought down his hand with the sock so that in the darkness he was only a man with a rag in his hand, that hand at his side.

"Finally, the secret handshake," Roland said and put out his hand.

Hugh looked at Laura again, and at Winnie, the two of them watching him now. Slowly he put his hand out toward Roland. It seemed to last minutes, this lifting of his hand to take another, Hugh uncertain of what to expect, what might happen next.

But Roland only grasped Hugh's hand, held it hard, and shook. He smiled.

"Glad you're here," was all he said.

❀ THEY MOVED PAST the doorway and into the black. Winnie went first, followed by Laura, then Hugh, and Rollie, who pulled the door closed behind him, slammed it hard.

The air inside was warm, smelled to Hugh of ancient cigarette smoke, to Laura, the faint musty odor of time, the room terribly black, utterly black to them both.

Then the lights came on, the place bursting with light, and there stood Winnie to the right, her hand on a large breaker switch on the wood wall.

Hugh squinted, as did Winnie, and Laura, and Rollie.

The place was just as Laura had imagined it, and nothing like Hugh would have imagined at all: one large room scattered with a dozen or so tables, all with crisp red-and-white checkered tablecloths, at every table four wooden chairs; against the left wall was a polished and shining dark wood bar, before it a row of black padded stools all pushed up and touching the wood; on the wall behind the bar were long wooden shelves crammed with commemorative soda cans and bottles, baseball caps, plaster statues of famous ballplayers; against the far wall sat a jukebox, all glistening chrome and glass. And everywhere, everywhere above them, hanging from the ceiling

313

so thick they could not see the ceiling itself, were rows upon rows of socks.

There were sweat socks up there, and wool socks and dress socks and yellow socks and blue and green and red socks and argyles and stripes and checks and plaids. There were long socks and thin socks and holey socks and frayed socks. Each was hung by its top edge, so that the toes pointed down, hundreds of empty socks.

Hugh said, "I thought this was an exclusive club."

"You got that right," Roland said, and now he was weaving his way around tables and toward the bar. "Not everybody gets in this classy of a joint. No sir. Why, we had to turn a guy back just last summer. New guy on the block. Owns some paint store chain over in Philly."

"Why's that?" Hugh said and looked at the socks again. "Why wouldn't you let him in?" He reached up, touched at the toe of a thick green sock, set it swinging back and forth. He could see up between the socks to the ceiling: pine boards, every sock thumbtacked into place.

"The guy had the audacity to show up over here with a pair of flip-flops on." He was behind the bar now, smiling, his eyes on whatever lay beneath the shining wood. "Like I say, we got standards to uphold around here." He bent down and disappeared behind the bar. "No way in hell we going to let just anybody in here." He reappeared, had four Rolling Rocks in his hands. He set them on the bar, then stood back, hands on hips.

"Your integrity is unparalleled," Hugh said. He smiled, and now he and Laura both took off their parkas. Hugh draped his over the back of the chair closest him, Laura set hers on top of his.

Roland laughed and shook his head. He pulled from his windbreaker pocket a bottle opener, popped the beers quickly, all four before Hugh'd even made it past the first table.

Then Roland stopped, both hands to the edge of the bar. He was looking behind Hugh, smiling. He said, "What's the matter with you?"

Hugh and Laura both turned, and saw behind them Winnie still standing at the switch. She still had the yellow scarf on, the green sweatshirt still zipped all the way up. Her arms were crossed, her eyes on Roland.

"You little conniver," she said.

Hugh turned to Roland, saw him grin.

"Hugh, let me tell you something," Roland said and nodded at Hugh, then the beers. "I came over earlier today and turned on the heat. Put out the tablecloths, dusted down the bar. Stocked the fridge, too." He picked up one of the beers and took a sip.

Hugh made it to the bar, placed his hands on the bartop, felt the cool and glistening wood. "Now granted, I didn't know you'd be showing up," Roland went on and handed a beer to Hugh, "but the wife over there thinks it was all her idea to get us over here to the Shell Pile. Thinks because she's the one who just happens to let slip over chocolate–pecan pie the fact she and I met in this nutty place and then leaves it that way, she thinks she's put one over on me. She thinks she's pulled a fast one on me, making me feel like coming on down here was my idea, when she believes it was her idea all along." He took another sip and swallowed. "And I know it bugs hell out of her I'd already set everything up, already got the heat going, got the beers iced down." He paused, took another sip. His eyes were on Winnie now, and he smiled, said, "I still got a few surprises up my sleeve. We men aren't as all stupid as you make us out to be."

"You conniver," Winnie said again, and Laura saw the smile as she moved from the wall toward the bar, slowly unzipped the sweatshirt, and untied the scarf. "You little schemer," Winnie said. She pulled out the stool next to where Hugh stood, settled herself atop it, the sweatshirt coming off and tossed a few feet down the bartop.

Hugh looked at the blouse, the gaudy floral print on silky material, and at the red cuffed shorts and at the klunky heels on her white shoes. He looked at her hair, that black he knew had to come from a box. And he looked at her face, and the way the woman was smiling at the man behind the bar, inside that smile what he knew was love. She loved him.

"So my words to you, Mr. Hugh," Roland said, though his eyes were on Winnie, "regards women. Always let them think they're in charge, even when they want *you* to think *you're* in charge." Hugh looked at him, saw the way he, too, looked at her, saw love in his eyes as well. It was nothing more than a shine, a stare, a grin. But it was love, and he'd seen it.

"Now then," Roland said, and here was Laura taking up the stool on the other side of Hugh, settling her handbag on the bartop. He saw he had no choice but to sit at the stool before him.

Roland lifted the beer up in a toast, and the other three lifted theirs. "To the Shell Pile," he said, and they touched bottles, a sharp sound in the empty room.

They took sips, Hugh's eyes to Roland and what he might choose to say next, Laura's eyes on Hugh, his profile, the shape of his jaw and nose and forehead and hair. Michael.

Roland brought the bottle down, set it on the bartop. "Almost forgot," he said and pulled from his back pocket Hugh's sock. The sock was brighter in here, Laura saw, seemed to allow more color, the blue richer, the gray full and soft.

"I got just the place to hang this one here," Roland said, and now he was moving off to the far end of the bar and toward the jukebox. "Follow me," Roland said.

Hugh stepped from the stool, beer in hand, and moved toward him.

Roland stopped a few feet out from the jukebox and looked up at the ceiling. "Take a look here at this one. This is the best place for your sock to end up. Right next to this one."

Hugh stood beside him, reached up with his free hand. He touched the sock there, a thin silk one, brown.

Roland pulled it to one side, said, "Can you see that up there? Can you see what's up there at the top of this sock?"

Hugh squinted, saw up where the sock had been tacked to the ceiling a couple of thin black straps attached to each other: a garter.

Laura watched from the bar, tasted the bitter beer on her tongue. Two men, one old, one her husband, stood across the room, peering up into socks hanging from the ceiling.

"That old fart," Winnie said beside her, and Laura turned, saw Winnie shaking her head, watching the two men. "That old fart. Sometimes he up and surprises me like that, him warming up the place, setting it up nice like this." She shook her head more slowly, and Laura lost what it was Roland was saying now, lost it in the look in Winnie's eyes, the way she barely touched her beer to her lips. Winnie held the beer there a moment, as though she thought to take a sip, but then brought it down. "But it's the surprise that counts. It's the not knowing what he'll do next. That's what counts. That's what to keep."

Winnie looked at Laura then, nodded, brought the beer up, and took the sip. She swallowed, winced just as she had at the coffee they'd been brought at a restaurant that now seemed in a foreign country, seemed a dozen years ago. "Just like what your hubby did here this evening.

His showing up down here," Winnie said. She looked at Hugh and nodded again. "I'll bet there's only one reason he came down here. It's you," she said. "And it's the surprise you keep."

"One guess who this sock belongs to," Roland said.

Already Hugh was smiling. "A garter," he said. "Silk. Brown." He paused, said, "Denny Halford himself."

"Bull's eye," Roland said and clapped a hand to Hugh's shoulder, let it hang there a moment. "I figure this ought to be the best place for you to hang your hat, so to speak. Right here next to the boss man," he said. He pulled a chair from a table, climbed onto it, one hand on the chairback, the other lifting Hugh's sock. Then he stood, reached into his windbreaker pocket, and brought out a thumbtack. Hugh saw the small glint of steel in Roland's hand and wondered in that moment if perhaps Roland had in fact known all along Hugh would be here, had stashed the tack in his windbreaker when he'd come down here earlier this day and turned on the heat, brought in the beers.

This man knew things, seemed to own something Hugh himself could not yet lay claim to, something he believed, too, he had lost forever in a brilliant and cutting moment that had happened three months and eleven days before, that moment when his wife had looked into his eyes in a hospital corridor and Hugh had come up empty, been able to give her nothing.

This man owned something, and Hugh believed suddenly that it was the truth he owned, the air around him emboldened by it, the angle of the hat—bill up—on his head inevitable and full of truth, the miraculous ease with which he produced magic items from his *Yorktown* windbreaker: a flashlight, a bottle opener, a thumbtack.

This all spoke to him a truth beyond which he believed he could touch.

But there were things Hugh owned, he knew, newly discovered but old in him already; pictures he would never lose: a son framed in fireflies, the glisten of winter light in his son's eyes, a boy and his mother playing Uno on an anonymous morning.

"Wait," Hugh said then, and Roland stopped, looked down at him, both hands up and lost inside the rows of socks.

He glanced back at Laura, saw her and Winnie watching him, though they were leaning toward each other, his word an interruption yet again.

Hugh turned back to Roland, saw he had his hands down now, still held the sock and thumbtack.

Hugh tried a smile. He said, "I don't think that's where I want mine," and tried the smile again. He shrugged. "My sock," he said. "I think I want it somewhere else."

"Can do," Roland said, and already he was climbing off the chair, pushing it back in to the table, settling it there neatly against the clean tablecloth. "I take requests. I can tell you where any one sock is in this entire joint. I can tell you a story about any damned one of these socks, give you a ballpark figure on when it was put up, tell you who it was." Roland paused, looked at Hugh. "So, where to?"

Hugh looked at his beer, swirled it a moment. He glanced back at Laura, saw she and Winnie both were watching him, their beers on the bartop, hands folded in their laps.

He looked at Roland. He said, "Where's yours?" He smiled, put the beer to his lips, swallowed down the last of it.

"I'm flattered," Roland said. He looked at Hugh, their eyes locked together a moment. Then Roland grinned.

"Follow me," he said, and passed by Hugh, moved back toward the door they'd come in.

"Watch out you don't keel over from the smell of that old man's sock," Winnie called out, and she and Laura turned to the bar, picked up their beers as if on cue. Winnie held hers out to Laura, and they touched bottles in their own toast. Winnie grinned, winked. She took a small sip, still had a little more than half left in her bottle. She swallowed, said just loud enough for Laura to hear, "He's gearing up now. He's warming up for his story now." She paused, put a hand to the bartop, and touched at the circle of sweat the bottle'd left there. "It'll be only a minute or two now, count on it."

She'd lost the smile suddenly, her eyes to the circle of wet, just as she'd stared at the circle left by the water glass on the tablecloth at the Sweetwater Casino.

"So what's wrong?" Laura asked, and as she'd spoken the words, she saw that this was her own foray into different terrain, that of Winnie's heart. It'd been Winnie to try and make clear Laura's life all day long, Winnie trying to give Laura precisely where she ought to look to find the piece of history she needed to see in herself. Not in a library, not at a county museum, not at any nature preserve.

No: It'd been at the *Atlantus*, and the Taj Mahal, the Sweetwater Casino. And now here, the Shell Pile.

"Winnie, what's wrong?" she said, and reached to her, placed her hand on Winnie's arm, let it rest there.

Winnie shrugged and still looked at the bartop. "It's the story," she whispered, and Laura could see Winnie's chin quiver, saw her blink. She glanced up at Laura, pieced together a smile that crumbled before she'd even finished it. She drew a circle in the wet, drew it again. She whispered, "I know the truth of it. That's all. And it hurts." She paused. "That's all. Just that pain of what I

320

know he's gone through, and him still keeping it at arm's length like he does every time he tells it."

Laura let her hand move up and down Winnie's arm now, tried to soothe her if only through this touch.

Hugh turned to follow Roland, saw the two of them whispering. Women.

"Hung mine up in 1945, September twenty-sixth to be exact," Roland said, and stopped a few feet from the door they'd come in, pulled another chair from the nearest table. He climbed up on it, reached to a white-gone-yellow sweat sock, the color of it, Hugh knew, proof enough of the dead cigarette smell that still swam in his head, and he imagined the place in summers filled with old people all smoking, imagined the blue haze of it all, the jukebox blasting some Perry Como tune. He smiled.

"Forty-eight years hanging up in this fine establishment," Roland said, louder now, his words aimed, Hugh could tell, at the woman behind him, though his eyes were on Hugh, "and nobody yet's complained about the smell."

Hugh glanced behind him, saw Winnie. Her eyes were to the bartop, a hand holding her beer. Laura had a hand to her arm, stroked her there. He couldn't tell if she'd even heard Roland.

"Say," Roland said then, and Hugh turned, looked up to see Roland with his hand on a bright green sock. The sock looked new, nowhere near as stained and old as the rest.

"You know this fellow here?" Roland said and shook the sock. "This one here's a request, too."

"Who's that?" Hugh said, and thought maybe this was one of Mr. Halford's sons, maybe even the mystery son, the one of unidentified trouble.

"Big boy name of Eddie Blankenship," Roland said,

and now he was tacking up Hugh's sock, hung it right there between Roland's and Ed's.

"Couldn't be a better place for mine," Hugh heard himself say, heard on his voice the certain edge of laughter: He would tell this to Ed, would talk to him, too, let him speak of his own sorrow.

Eddie Blankenship, Hugh thought, and shook his head.

Roland climbed down from the chair and slapped his hands together to dust them off. "Another one of you Hess boys. Denny sent him down here, too, though all that big boy was suffering from was a lousy marriage." He paused. "Not, you know, what you two been through."

"Rollie," Winnie said, though there'd been no attitude in the word. Only his name, and Hugh looked at her, saw she was still turned to the bar, Laura's hand still on her arm.

Hugh looked back to Roland. "No harm, no foul," Hugh said.

Roland smiled, then pushed in the chair. They stood back, looked up at the sock: only a blue and gray argyle, pedestrian at best, nothing among all these socks. He could turn around twice and never find it again.

But he knew it was there beside Roland Dorsett's and beside Ed Blankenship's.

It was enough, he knew.

"Now let's get on with our reason for being here tonight," Roland said and made his way around behind the bar. He nodded at Hugh, at his empty bottle. "Have another one, sailor?" he said, and Hugh smiled, nodded.

"Have to get in the right frame of mind for this," Roland said. "Otherwise this will come off as nothing but a string of words, no more than a river of words with no place to cross."

"He got that one out of the *Reader's Digest*," Winnie

said, and now she was smiling, sat with her beer in her lap, the bottle laced in both hands. "He got that out of that Toward More Picturesque Speech section you see in there."

"Damn it to hell, sister," Roland said to Winnie, and slapped the bar top again. "Will you just let me tell these people what they need to hear? Will you?"

She shrugged, and Hugh sat on his stool between Laura and Winnie, right back where he had started.

Roland brought up two more Rolling Rocks, popped them with the opener from the windbreaker.

Hugh took his, sipped it, and felt the cold.

"Now," Roland said, and his eyes went to Hugh's, seemed to measure him in some way he would never know.

Then he stepped back from the bar, crossed his arms.

He took in a breath, said, "All this happened."

🦪 THEY WALKED HOME, the wind bitter cold now. Hugh held Laura tight to him, Laura as far into his shoulder as she could get.

They said nothing, only walked, the two of them lost in the story they had heard. Roland and Winnie were behind them, and Hugh believed he could hear them talking, thought he heard quiet laughter back there. But he could not be certain.

The only thing he was certain of was that he had heard a true story. He knew the man who'd shone a flashlight inside an empty deli was the same man who'd shone a flashlight into the black of a sinking ship in an effort to feed the men salvaging what could be salvaged. He was only a cookie aboard the *Yorktown*, only made food for men whose lives were much more important, from the flyboys on down to the machinist's mates. He was only a cookie, but he'd done what he could do, had used the blessing of his hands to try and save a dying ship.

Now he knew Roland Dorsett's story, and thought of this time at Reed's Beach, thought of what the story of this time here might end up being. He thought of Ed Blankenship and of Rhode Island and of Lego pieces and the Halfords' palace and groceries in a car trunk. He thought of all of this, and he thought of Michael, thought of him framed in fireflies, miraculous bursts of light.

But he could not yet tell this story, could not yet see it as he'd seen the smoke and sweat and blue sea in Roland's story, and he wondered if indeed the language of grief in him were ready to be spoken, ready to be given freely.

Laura felt the warmth of Hugh's arm around her. She'd watched Roland tell his story, just as Hugh and Winnie had: eyes open wide, mouths shut tight except to take sips of beer. Roland had stood behind the bar, eyes to the ceiling, hands in the pockets of his windbreaker. He hadn't looked down the entire story, had only fixed on something up there.

She'd watched him, too, when he came to the moment late in the story when the ship was about to sink the final time, the moment Winnie'd told her of when he found the dead sailor. She'd watched for a blink, a hitch in his throat, a stumble of words somehow as he told of climbing up ladders in the dark, the slow, cold groan of the ship as it listed deeper and deeper to port.

But Roland didn't lose anything, did not betray fact inside the true story he was telling: His words only came, the images they formed in her head startling and true and terrifying. He hadn't even blinked, only told the story of how he made his way in the last terrible moments of the *Yorktown* to the hangar deck, then abandoned ship, jumped into the sea.

Laura'd glanced at Winnie then, just when it seemed Roland might reveal the presence of the dead sailor. She wanted to see how Winnie held herself when her husband chose not to reveal himself completely to any of them, chose to keep inside him his own secret of the job he had to do, the secret of the dog tags.

Winnie's eyes were right on Roland's, and Laura saw her swallow, saw her blink twice. That was all.

But it didn't matter. Roland had given her a story that she could keep, one that shadowed somehow her own discoveries this day, the ones that had started with the shipwreck of her own, the *Atlantus*, and the secrets she herself owned: the canister, the dream.

And the pills, the empty prescription that called out to her its need to be filled. She owned these, for better or for worse, just as Roland Dorsett owned the galley of a ship sunk at Midway, and she saw again the upturned loaves of bread he'd spoken of, the spilled cans.

She saw photos of her child spread across a white tablecloth.

They walked, said nothing, moved past the deli with its blinking 7-Up light, past shanties it seemed this cold wind might blow away, past the heaped dirt and porches and along the rutted road.

And then they were almost home, moving past the van, the Dorsetts' house lit from front to back. It seemed to Hugh that in the darkness of the house next door, the Halfords' place, what was left of his and Laura's lives now loomed too close. He knew that with entry into the house they would have to face each other and each other only, and they would have no choice but to speak the language given them.

Because on this day he had been given back his son, had found Michael in the anonymous days he'd seen and the hollow life his boss hid inside. And he'd been given his son in Roland's own history, the truth that matters out of our hands came to us, made things happen we could not keep from happening.

"Wait up," Winnie called from behind them, and they turned, stood beside the front of the van, the wind now in their faces as these two old people approached. Laura saw that Roland's arm was around Winnie, just as Hugh's was around her own, and she smiled.

"Hold on, sugar," Winnie said, then ducked from beneath Roland's arm and disappeared behind the van.

Roland stopped, put his hands in his back pockets. He hadn't turned the flashlight on yet, the moon so bright. Even the chain across the drive had been easy to see on the way back, the red cloth black in the dark, harmless, Laura had seen, after what she'd found this day: her son in Hugh's face.

Laura and Hugh heard the metal scrape of the rear door open, heard boxes pushed back and forth, tools shoved one against another. Then the door slammed shut, and here was Winnie coming toward them, something in her hand, Laura could see in the moonlight.

"Guess I forgot to tell you I had an extra pair out here," Winnie said. "Wasn't too certain, either, you were going to earn these today." She held it out to Laura. She shrugged.

Hugh could not tell what it was, thought perhaps it was a dishcloth.

Laura took it, held it to her face.

Gloves, she could see. Brand-new leather work gloves, stiff and scratchy, still stapled together.

She looked at Winnie, tried to see her eyes. She breathed in the rich leather smell.

Then she went to Winnie, held her tight, and felt once again Winnie's hands on her back.

Laura held her a moment longer, then let go, stood back. Winnie was smiling, and nodded. "You did," Winnie said. "You earned them fair and square."

Laura wanted to speak, wanted to say something, but no words came to her.

"What is it?" Hugh said, and reached to Laura, touched at the gloves.

"A gift," Winnie said before Laura could answer. "She's my apprentice now, and she's got to have the right equipment."

"Gloves," Laura said, and turned, looked at her husband. "Work gloves," she said, "for tomorrow." She looked at him, and wondered how their own history might change once they'd gone back into the Halfords' house, once they were back alone together. How would their history change?

Hugh felt the rough leather. He wondered what this was about, the gloves, this apprenticeship, the fact Roland stood with his hands in his back pockets and smiled at the women, some kind of secret between them all again.

But it did not matter. They could have this between them. It took nothing from him.

Yet he wanted to speak with this man, wanted to hear more from him. This was the man who'd let him hang his sock beside his. This was the man who'd fed all those men, who'd stared at stars and the sea, who'd been inside history and had come back to tell all of it.

He knew this man.

"Rollie?" Hugh said, and they all three turned to him, as startled, he believed, as when his headlights had first cut into them.

The wind blew colder, and the tide moving in seemed to sweep harder against the shore beneath both their houses, the Dorsetts' filled with light, the Halfords', empty and dark, filled with someone else's lives.

"Yessir?" Roland said.

Hugh paused and looked at the Dorsetts' house, at the lights, the clean lines. He looked back to Roland.

He said, "If I came over tomorrow morning before I headed up to Hess, would you make a few donuts?"

"Son of a bitch," Roland laughed, and the sound

boomed out over the marsh, broke through the wind, smoothed over the silver push of the waves. The man laughed, a sound like its own kind of thunder here at Reed's Beach, welcome thunder, summer thunder here in February. "Son of a bitch," he laughed, "I'd be glad to."

"He makes the best sausage you ever tasted, too," Laura said, and now she was leaning into Hugh again. He looked down at her, saw she was smiling up at him. He put his arm around her again, held her close.

They would speak the language.

He knew he would do it.

He thought of Roland again, of bracing oneself against the tremble and groan of a ship sinking.

He had listened.

He looked at Roland. He said, "You never even told me why the hell they call that place the Shell Pile."

Roland paused, let the laughter go a moment. He said, "Didn't I tell you?"

"Nope," Hugh said.

"It's the biggest pile of shells you've ever seen out back of the place," Winnie said, and nodded at Hugh, smiled.

"You show us tomorrow night," Laura said and looked back at Winnie. "We'll go back there tomorrow night." She turned, looked up at Hugh again. "Okay?"

"That's a deal," Roland said. "Tomorrow night," and he nodded at this agreement between them all.

"Tomorrow," Hugh said.

"LEAVE THE LIGHTS off," Laura said, Hugh behind her. She set the handbag on the table, careful not to look at the maps and brochures there.

She heard the door gently close behind her, heard Hugh take a couple of steps toward her.

She imagined then his hands around her waist from behind, the cold of his face on her neck.

But he stopped, stood somewhere behind her.

She moved along the front hallway, took off her parka as she walked, and hung it on the back of a chair at the table. She moved straight to the sliding glass door, put her palms to the glass, saw out there the dock, a silver arm out over black water.

Hugh had stood out there only last night with the sextant. He might as well have been on the moon himself, Laura thought, for the way he talked to her, for the way he fiddled with the sextant and the way he'd swaddled it, put it away. Just last night it had taken him almost an hour to get the groceries in.

But now.

Now they were here, and he seemed different. He *was* different, she knew, just as she knew herself to be different, knew she'd surrendered today to her own history, given herself to it. Now, in this very moment, inside this very instant, she saw that they both stood on the absolute edge of their own history. They could make of what their lives had left some new story, a story that would not leave behind Michael, but which would take him up, let him live with them and in them and yet let them move on toward some next history.

It would start here, now, in this house owned by strangers, and would begin with words from one or the other of them in this dark room.

And she could see no reason in this moment why it could not be her to begin.

She looked out at the silver dock, the black water. She said, "How do you start?"

Hugh saw her silhouette against the sliding glass door. He could see her hands against the glass, hands just like their son's hands when he and Gerry had stood at the Staten Island Ferry terminal that morning, waiting for the *John F. Kennedy* to put in.

He could see, too, the dock, the moonlight banging off it out there.

He loved her, and he loved his son, and he felt in these moments that somehow he was being asked to give up one or the other. Whatever answer he gave to the question she'd asked would force him to align himself with either his son or his wife, the other forsaken.

He knew his son's name, and knew his wife's name, knew her eyes in the hospital, searching him for some answer. He finally saw in his memory of Laura the only truth: He would have no answer for her, ever, about the death of their son. Events out of our hands came to us. No consolation, no accommodation. No room for understanding. Their son was gone.

But there was his name, and he heard again the way they had both spoken his name only last night, Michael

331

coming to them separately but almost in the same moment, uttered like an echo.

He started toward her, took the first tentative steps through the hall. Then he stopped at the doorway into the bedroom, took off his own parka, tossed it onto the bed in there.

That was when he saw the lights from the Dorsetts' next door, artificial light through the Halfords' curtains, and it came to him: how to begin.

Where to start.

He went to her, took one of her hands from the glass. His presence startled her, though she believed she'd heard his footsteps across the floor, heard him moving toward her from behind. But then had come his hand on hers, pulling it from the glass, his hand warm, swallowing hers. She saw him in the dark and light, saw him looking at her, felt herself being pulled away, pulled away.

He led her through the kitchen, then into the reading room, past black shelves of books put into proper order, and he thought again of the order the Halfords wanted in this world, order that would never exist in his and Laura's life.

He moved up the stairs, and she decided that, certainly, she *did* know him: Here he was headed back up to Mr. Halford's room, and that sextant, the charts and books and tools. Here he was, headed for what he had put away so neatly just last night, and she knew he hadn't changed at all. Only now he wanted her with him.

But he hadn't touched the switchplate at the bottom of the stairs, that gold angelfish switchplate. And now, as they mounted the steps, she thought she saw the faintest smile on his face, just the smallest thin line of it.

Then he turned, looked back up the stairs to the darkness, and he led her, his hand still warm.

REED'S BEACH

When they reached the top, he paused a moment, looked out the small octagonal window there, and saw the rows of broken pylons trailing up the beach. They, too, were still there, just as in this moment there still existed in him the pictures of his son, the glisten in his eye as he surveyed New York Harbor, his son moving up the steps before him to the top of Barnegat Light, his son's chant *Flat black four by eight, flat black four by eight,* the succession of hands in his, from the blue-pink of the infant to the last hand letting go.

These would not leave him, and now the story of Reed's Beach began taking shape in him, suddenly and without warning, a story that would encompass time and love and water and land and light, all of it, and that would end only when they left here, headed for home, back in Englishtown, headed toward the rest of their lives.

Laura, too, paused at the top, looked out the window. She saw the broken pylons, remembered having walked down there alone, and remembered, too, the book at the library, the story of Reed's Beach and the Quaker guns, the grand disguise meant to show strength and invincibility when, in fact, there was nothing behind it, only painted wood, and she pictured rows of painted logs down there, saw British ships just offshore, wondering what to make of this show of force, deciding, finally, to surrender the idea of raiding this hamlet, moving on.

And now she saw she'd surrendered to Hugh and his design for this moment, their entry into their own next history sealed, her question gone unanswered: *How do you start?* This room seemed no start at all, only retreat into their history, even with the lights off up here.

Still he pulled her, felt in the way she moved she wanted no part of this, wanted nothing of this room and what it stood for: an old man's retreat into himself. He could not blame her. She knew the truth of this room, its safe haven from the black sea of being a parent: Hold the sextant to the moon, chart a course across the sea, pretend you knew what to do even when you had no idea how to take the next breath.

His own story. Hugh.

He looked across the room, saw the way light, just like last night, made its way up from next door and formed another octagon, this one collapsed and tilted, on the slanted ceiling.

He pulled her, pulled her, and she wondered what he might do next, the dormer filled with the desk and all the equipment behind her now, he still leading her across the room.

Then he was at the window, and she saw him look down, saw light from out there shine in his face, give to her her son and her husband at once, him bathed in gray, his features squared and perfect and bright.

She reached her free hand to his face, touched her fingertips to his cheek. Here he was.

Hugh turned to her, and she saw that, yes, he was smiling.

But it was not a smile she recognized, was not a smile she knew in him. She thought she could see, too, a glisten in his eyes, a startled shine even with this smile, and she touched her fingers higher on his cheek, higher, until she touched just below these eyes, and felt the warmth of tears on her fingertips.

"Look," he whispered, and felt his life and all he had hidden from his wife these three months and eleven days, felt all the gestures of grief he'd made all this while, felt all of this give way, fall from beneath him. He knew what the world felt like when one jumped from a ship, trusted the sea below to swallow you, yes, but to buoy you up once it had. He felt the air in him leave, and felt his son's name in his throat again.

She huddled closer to him, moved to the window, and looked.

She saw the Dorsetts down there, seated at the same table at which she'd had breakfast, the same table she'd eaten dinner at as well.

They sat across from each other, Roland with his back to them, his windbreaker still on, *USS Yorktown* in those huge yellow letters across the back. Winnie still had on the green sweatshirt, the scarf off now, her hair still the same perfect shape it had carried all day long.

They were playing a game that involved colorful cards, Roland laying down a card on what seemed a discard pile, then Winnie doing the same, then Roland. But this time Winnie did not lay down any cards, instead had to draw off two cards from a stack beside the discard pile.

They were talking to each other, too, and for a moment she wondered both why her husband was weeping and what these two spoke about, whether it involved the Taj Mahal or a sailor named Flour Boy. She wondered what it was they spoke of in their lives, what other truths they kept from each other, what other secrets they shared.

Then she took in a sharp breath, felt it cut into her in an instant, like the cut of a million stars above an ancient sea, a million cutting angels slicing into her with what her husband had brought her to see.

They were playing Uno.

Hugh saw her face in the light from below, saw her surprise and sorrow and, he believed, joy, and he swallowed, sorry for even the one day he had kept this from her, even that one day. He should have awakened her last night, brought her here, given this to her to show her he loved their son and that he loved her and that even when he was leaving for Hess, had the briefcase in

335

hand and was making his way out of their lives for each day's brief shard of their history together, he loved them. He loved them both.

Tears filled her eyes, and she felt the air still leaving her with this vision, a vision shattering in her eyes, and she rubbed at her eyes, wanted kept clear this picture of the Dorsetts playing Uno, the game she'd played with Michael each morning, a game she had not played since a day that involved a path through woods, a bus on the roadside, her husband coming to her in the white hallway of a hospital. She had not played this game since then, and believed she would never play it again.

But here it was, and she watched as Roland put down a card, then Winnie, then Roland again. And now Winnie placed her last card down, placed a hand, palm up, on the tabletop, and she watched as Roland reached to her, took that hand, and held it.

She saw Winnie smile.

Then Roland let go, gathered the cards, straightened them, shuffled them, passed them out, and Hugh could feel Laura leaning into him now, felt the warmth of her face on his chest, felt her tears through his shirt as he watched them down there, and while she wept.

Pain's good for you, Winnie's words came to her. *Sees you through*, and here was the truth: Here was pain, and here it was, seeing her through.

He wept as well, his eyes closed, his son there in each breath he remembered to take and in a game of Uno and in the sorrow he knew would never leave, the sorrow he would only have to build room for, he and his wife both, a sorrow that would never leave either of them.

And he didn't want it to, because in that sorrow he found its twin, the same joy he believed he'd seen on Laura's face the moment she recognized the game, and the same joy this game gave to her and to himself: the joy of their son.

But now he felt Laura pull away from him, saw her look up at him. She touched at her eyes as she backed away, swallowed into the dark of the room. He watched as this shadow made its way to the stairs, glanced back at him again and again as it moved down the stairs, and then she was gone.

She moved through the reading room, knew what it was she wanted to show to Hugh, and when she made it to the table, she took up the straw handbag, thrust her hand deep into it, pulled out in one move the canister.

She moved to set the handbag back on the table but stopped, remembered the beige plastic box of pills. She reached into the bag again, found the cold, hard box, brought it out.

She looked at it, the box a secret, each cold and empty day since an afternoon in November, she saw, a necessary secret.

But she no longer needed the pills, just as she no longer needed the brochures and guides strewn across the table beside her. What her husband had just shown her, and what Winnie had taken her through, had brought her life back to her. She needed no maps, no pills.

She placed the box back into the handbag, set the bag on the table.

Her cycle had ended, and she would not renew the pills.

Nor would she tell him the secret, but would keep it, hold it tight, just as she would hold tight her memory of the taste of each pill and how on that taste she saw her son's face, the touch of their own blood in his looks, his gestures, his words. With her surrender to the next child they would find, she would make new room in her heart to hold close two snow angels, wings touching, flying together, and to hold close the troll of the forest, and to hold close her son's figure receding into snow-filled woods, herself following him, calling his name, calling him.

She loved Michael, and loved Hugh. Loved even herself, she allowed, the pills dark evidence of how close she held him in her heart, the canister and what it contained her own room with a blue desk, words Michael had spoken and pictures he'd drawn enough to carry her and, she hoped, Hugh until they were safely home.

Home, she thought, and felt a smile rise in her, even through her trembling.

Hugh heard her before he could see her, and then here was her shadow again, moving toward him this time, and here came her face, her smile even inside the sorrow he saw.

She stood close to him, held something in her fist.

"Listen," she whispered, and she opened her hand. He saw in the dark the round black thing there, and then she popped off the lid. It was a canister, he saw, and he watched as she pulled from it a roll of paper wrapped in a rubber band.

She twisted off the rubber band, let it fall.

They were scraps of paper, he saw. Small scraps of paper. She unrolled them, held them tight together with both hands. She looked up at him.

She said, "He said these things."

And even before she spoke he saw they were already fluent in the language, that no matter what she said now, they were speaking the same tongue.

She turned around then, leaned her back against him. She held the papers up to catch the light from below, and said, "Michael, May sixth, 1988. Points to a car's license plate and says, 'Look, M for Michael.' "

He could read the words, even in this light, artificial

light from the place next door, and this fact seemed a miracle to him.

She looked up at him over her shoulder, saw his face in the light from below, then glanced from him to the Dorsetts, still playing Uno.

He smiled, felt himself tremble.

She moved that first piece to the bottom of the pile, read the next: "Michael insists on calling his slip-ons his coupons. August first, 1987."

She stopped, looked at him again. She said, "Do you remember those?"

"White," Hugh whispered, given another singular memory, just as he'd been given by Ted Rothberg. "You bought them for him at the K Mart on 33."

She nodded, amazed at what he remembered, but then not amazed at all.

He was Michael's father.

Slowly she moved the paper to the bottom, and now before them was the deposit slip she'd not let Winnie see at the end of the jetty.

She held it and said nothing, only looked at it.

Then came her husband's whispered voice: " 'The moon is teasing the sun,' Michael, October nineteenth, 1991, on seeing the moon out in the morning."

He'd never seen any of these, never heard her speak of these moments at all. He knew what it was to hold his own secrets: the fireflies, his son rolling down the hill. And the dark feel of the wooden spoon in his hand, the nonsense of punishment that seemed perfect logic.

Perhaps one day he would give her their son rolling down the hill behind her parents' house, Michael's dazed stagger and smile as he rose in twilight from the grass, hollered, *Sparks! The world's on fire with these sparks!*

And perhaps one day he would ask for her help in deciphering why he could still feel the sting of the spoon in

339

his hand, still saw shattered glass and his son bent to
the pain he would give.

But in this moment there seemed room only for these
scraps of paper, the history each revealed, and he was
glad for them, and glad for the warmth of her against
him.

Now Laura moved on to the next one, moved away the
deposit slip to reveal a happy face on the corner of a
piece of legal paper, the figure barely visible in the light.

Again Laura said nothing, only held it up, the head
still bumpy and misshapen, the eyes still big empty circles, the mouth still a flat line with the ends turned up.

It would never change, she saw, would always and only
be this, their son's rendering of a happy face. Only this.

Then she saw Hugh's hand reach up, saw his index
finger gently touch the face, saw him slowly trace its
outline. He touched each eye, too, then, with two fingers,
carefully touched the lips of this smiling child, and in
this instant they both knew he was touching their son's
lips, touching him for the first time in this new history
they'd begun here at Reed's Beach.

This was their son's mouth, his eyes, the smooth curve
and soft feel of his face, his neck, his hair, and now Laura's hand was on Hugh's, moving with his across this
drawing their son had made, a drawing of himself, they
both knew only now.

He felt her hand on his, felt the warmth. She felt the
cool back of his hand, felt how steady it was as he traced
the picture yet again, their hands becoming a part of this
drawing, until they had both touched him, touched him
in touching this face, their hands together.

They touched him.

Epilogue

⬙ LATER, THERE CAME into the bedroom light from the moon, soft and silver light that seemed to slip through their dreams, rouse them with its perfect and dark light so that neither knew who had awakened first. But there was moonlight, they both were certain, slicing its arc across the bed and through them. Only this light and, beneath them, like a quiet silver dream of its own, the tide working its will, moving water, moving water.

He reached a hand to her, moved a lock of hair from her neck, placed his lips against her white skin.

She moved almost imperceptibly, her face turning from him but in a way that gave to him even more of her neck, and he kissed her there again, slowly, and again, until she moved onto her side, faced away from him. Then she reached to her hair, with one hand pulled all of it away from the back of her neck. Gently she pushed herself into him, and he kissed her neck, and the top of her back.

And, just as each time since their child had died, she moved to her knees, and he moved into her, the smooth white length of her back before him, his hands tracing slowly across her and up and beneath to her breasts and back to her hips, him holding on and moving into her as

341

she moved against him, all the moves together a seamless design of joy and sorrow.

But in the moonlight of this night, there arose in her a single word, one married somehow to this light, and the way it moved through the room as slowly and quickly as time, as slowly and quickly as history itself: *No*, she whispered.

He stopped, and felt her move away, saw the white of her back twist and disappear, and then she was beneath him, looking up at him, her husband, the father of whatever child they would be given next.

Like this, she said now, and reached to him, put her arms around his neck and pulled him close to her, and as he moved into her, he knew the need for this different way, and he saw in how this full moon cut through them both the need for his surrender to her, the giving up of his promise to the way they had made their first child. He had to surrender to the way she wanted to find the next one; only then would this next child be born into their world truly new.

The moon cast shadows across them as they made love, fell through its arc away from them, and when they finished, this same moon and the same tide beneath them led them toward sleep, the rich and dreaming sleep of the living, a sleep in which dwelt their son's name, spoken and unspoken in each dark breath in, each sweet breath out.

Michael, they breathed.

Michael.